THE POWER

BERKELEY BLACKFRIARS • BOOK TWO

J. R. MABRY

Apocryphile Press

1700 Shattuck Ave #81

Berkeley, CA 94709

www.apocryphilepress.com

ISBN 978-1-947826-00-7

Cover graphics by Milo at www.derangeddoctordesign.com

CLAIM YOUR FREE BOOK

To find out more about the Berkeley Blackfriar's universe, download your free copy of *The Berkeley Blackfriar's Companion*. Includes short stories set in the Blackfriars' universe, photos of main characters, a complete glossary, a walking tour of the Blackfriars' Berkeley, recipes from Brian's kitchen, a short history of Old Catholicism, a Q & A session with author J.R. Mabry, links to music and videos associated with the books and more!

Click on BookHip.com/DXDCAS to get your free copy!

REVIEWS

If you enjoy the Blackfriars books, please help other people find them by leaving an honest review on amazon or kobo or wherever you buy books. Thank you!

OTHER BOOKS BY J.R. MABRY

The Berkeley Blackfriars Series:
The Kingdom
The Power
The Glory

The Christmas at Bremmer's Series:
What Child is This?

The Temple of All Worlds Series:
The Worship of Mystery

DEDICATION

This book is dedicated to three friends who have gone before us into perpetual light, each of whom inspired a portion of this story:

PAT CROSSMAN
RICHARD STEVENS
J. W.

Et lux perpetua luceat ei...

ACKNOWLEDGEMENTS & CAVEATS

Grateful thanks to all of my friends who encouraged me in the writing of this novel, especially my wife, Lisa Fullam, who heard every chapter as it emerged and offered invaluable encouragement and feedback. Special thanks are due to those who read the first draft carefully and made invaluable suggestions, especially: Lola McCrary, Liza Lee Miller, B.J. West, and Kate Gladstone. Thanks also to my editor, Jason Whited, for making the second edition sparkle.

Special thanks to Josephine McCarthy, whose fine *The Exorcist's Handbook* provided wonderful inspiration. It was she who introduced me to the Sandalphon (and I hope you will thank her for it, too).

Liturgical rites are adapted from the *Roman Catholic Ritual for Exorcism*, the 1979 Episcopal *Book of Common Prayer*, and the United Church of Christ *Book of Worship*. To shield myself from possible litigation, I have changed the names of some institutions, especially in the Gourmet Ghetto neighborhood of Berkeley in which the friars live and work. Those familiar with the area will no doubt sort out, fairly easily, what is what.

Love is the opposite of power.
That's why we fear it so much.
—Gregory David Roberts, *Shantaram*

And our faith is a power
which comes from our natural substance
into our sensual soul by the Holy Spirit,
in which power all our powers come to us,
for without that no one can receive power,
for it is nothing else than right understanding
with true belief and certain trust in our being,
that we are in God and he in us,
which we do not see.
—Julian of Norwich, *Revelations of
Divine Love*, 54th chapter

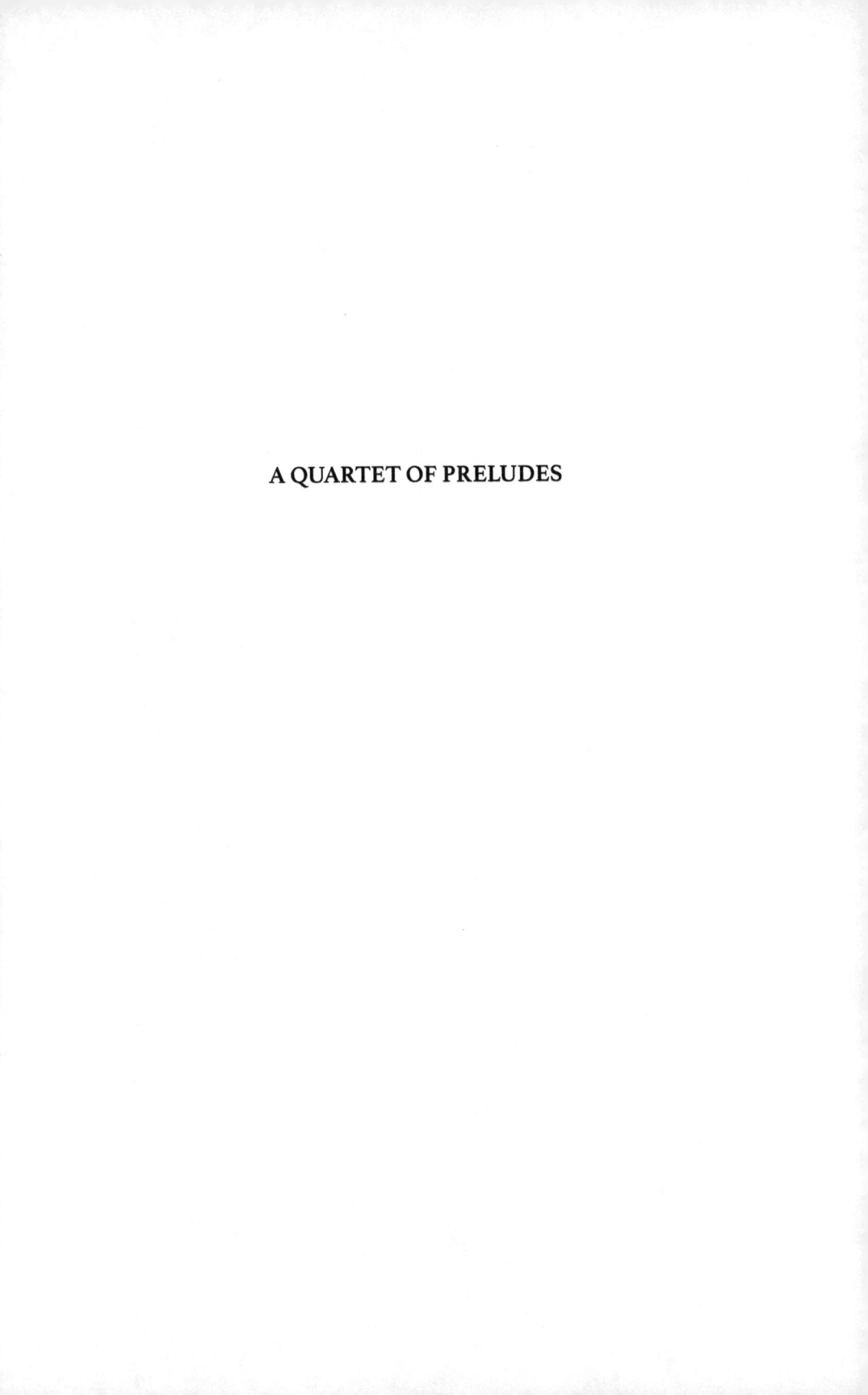

A QUARTET OF PRELUDES

PRELUDE 1

THE FIFTH CRUSADE AGAINST THE MUSLIMS

AMID THE SHRIEKING of the dying and the stench of the dead, the Ong Khan Toghrul crested the hill and reined back his mount. His eyes burned from the smoke. He squinted, trying to assess the scene. Behind him were five hundred men, all of them Mongol warriors, faithful Nestorian Christians ready to lay down their lives in the cause of the Savior.

His nostrils twitched at the stink, and his horse shied with impatience. "My Khan," said his lieutenant from behind him. "What are your orders?" But he was not ready to answer. His eyes flicked to the city walls, which were still holding against the Crusader army. *Although this is hardly an army*, he thought, taking stock of the wasted might of Europe before him. Most had been slaughtered. Here and there, living soldiers were clustered—no, *huddled*—apparently without leaders.

His lieutenant moved parallel to him, and touched his elbow with a mail-gloved hand. "Jahn?" he said. "Jahn, the men need direction. This is a killing ground..."

Toghrul nodded his assent. "Yes, but it will not be ours." He turned to face his lieutenant. "Tsogt, send messengers to these soldiers of Europe—those that are left. They can die or fight under our banner. It is their choice." Tsogt nodded briskly and began barking orders.

Toghrul watched as horsemen sped off toward small pockets of soldiers spread out across the battleground. With a grand gesture, he signaled an advance. He watched the Christians of Europe gawk with wonder at the great Christian army of Mongolia speeding over the hill to save them.

Within the hour, the Christians of Europe had either been assimilated into his ranks or dispatched by the sword. Fortunately, only a few had objected, and they were those who pretended to leadership. Jahn Toghrul spat. *Leaders in name, perhaps*, he thought bitterly.

Only one of their so-called leaders had joined them. The khan summoned him, and when the man appeared before him, he sank to his knees instantly, though it was obvious he was a noble. *Here is a man who knows the intrinsic hierarchy of warriors*, Jahn thought, and dismounted to speak to the man without shouting. "I am the Ong Khan Toghrul, king of the Kerait Mongols, called Jahn at my baptism. You are?"

"Sir Philip of Longacre, of England, sire." The man's tunic was torn, his hair matted with filth. He kept his eyes on the dirt.

Wise man, Jahn thought. "I have heard that you who follow the Bishop of Rome consider us heretics," Jahn said, a testy edge to his voice. "Is this so, Sir Philip?"

"I...I know nothing of this, my lord." The man looked quickly from side to side, but he did not look up. Jahn fingered the Talisman of Amitiel, which hung on a cord from his neck. It grew cold. "You lie."

The man looked down at his knees, and his face turned beet red. He nodded furiously. "That is what they say, my lord." He held his breath, but then blurted out, "But it is not...my own opinion, sire."

Jahn's eyebrows raised. A bemused smile crossed his lips. "Really,

Sir Philip, and are you in the habit of questioning the teaching of your bishops?"

Sir Philip's face was so red that it seemed ready to burst. "Um...no..."

There was no way out of this, Jahn knew. He did not suffer fools, but he was not entirely without mercy. "Tell me what has happened here."

The man nodded, visibly grateful for the change in subject. "Two weeks ago, we laid siege to the city. Twenty thousand of us."

Jahn scowled. "Twenty thousand?"

"Yes, my lord. The Egyptians fought well."

"I see that they have." There were scarcely four hundred men left. Together with his own horsemen, they would hardly make a thousand. "How did they accomplish this?"

"They...they are charmed bowmen," Philip said, spluttering for an explanation. "They have demons shooting at us. And then, there are the raiders."

"Tell me about the raiders."

"They attack us at night. They attack when we are besieging the city—when our backs are to the hills. They are led by a sultan, Al-Kamil, they call him. He is like a ghost."

The khan grunted and stepped away, surveying the sandy hills. "Sir Philip," he said, "you will not be false with me again. Tell me, will your men follow you?"

───────────────

The siege was hard, and doubly so since half of his men were wasted guarding the army's rear flank from a Saracen army that might or might not appear. They did not, and by midday, the tower door folded in on itself with a booming crack that the khan heard from half a mile away. The European Christians swarmed into the tower. The slaughter was quick.

Tsogt rode to him, fierce and breathless. Blood stained much of his mail, the Khan noticed, but was relieved to discover that it was

Saracen blood, not his lieutenant's. "We have the tower, my khan." Jahn nodded curtly. "Many of the Saracens laid down their arms," Tsogt continued. "I thought...you might want to talk with them."

Jahn smiled grimly. "You know me well, Lieutenant. Lead the way." Within minutes, the khan was striding through the tower door, which was splintered beyond repair. Before him, Saracen soldiers knelt as he passed, averting their dark eyes. His own men stood behind them, swords at the ready, drunk on the victory of the day.

But the khan knew better. *A tower is not a keep*, he thought to himself. *We still have much to do.* When he came to the end of the corridor, he stopped and turned regally. He looked down on the Saracen before him. "Tsogt," he asked, "how many are they that live?"

"Exactly a hundred men, my khan." Tsogt answered quickly and with confidence.

Jahn drew his sword and with one swift motion, severed the Saracen's head from his body. "There!" he shouted at the men on their knees. "Now there are ninety-nine, one for each of the ninety-nine names of your heathen god." The Saracens quaked, but they dared not raise their eyes to the Mongol king. Some of them mumbled prayers in Arabic.

Jahn stepped over the body, its blood spilling over the stones of the floor, creating a slick crimson pool. He faced the next Saracen, who was visibly shaking. Jahn clutched at the Talisman of Amitiel and spoke, a note of kindness entering his voice. "You, Egyptian, what are you called?"

"Mohammad, Sire." A spreading stain on his breeches betrayed that the man had just wet himself.

Jahn sniffed. "I dare not say the name of your heathen prophet, for it is offensive to the Lord of Heaven. Tell me, Egyptian, where is Al-Kamil?"

The man's eyes grew wide, but he said nothing. The khan placed the flat of his broadsword at the man's neck and slowly turned it so that its razor-sharp edge came to bear. "You will answer," Jahn said quietly.

"I...I do not know."

The talisman grew cold in Jahn's hand. "That is a lie," he said over his shoulder to Tsogt. "Egyptian dog, called by the name of the blasphemer prophet, you are lying, and the cost for lying to the Lord Khan is death. But I am a merciful king, and I will give you one more chance to live before you see Hell. Where is Al-Kamil?"

In answer, the man squeezed his eyes tight and shook his head. With a flourish, Jahn cut his throat, the blood of his neck creating an arc in the air as the sword flashed past. "How many are left, Tsogt?"

"Ninety-eight, my khan."

Jahn looked out the window and measured the sun. "Good thing the day is still young." He stepped to the next man, huddled on the floor, and placed the flat of the blade against the quaking man's temple. Jahn looked up at his lieutenant, and smiled. "Hell will feast well today."

PRELUDE 2

HOLY APOCRYPHA FRIARY, PRESENT DAY

A HALF HOUR BEFORE anyone would stir in the old farmhouse that served as the friary of the Old Catholic Order of Saint Raphael, there was a rustle of wings in the yard. The cherub touched one foot to the earth, then the other, and paused to gain his balance. When he straightened himself, he stood nearly nine feet. His hair was white like bleached wool, and his eyes shone with fire.

Beneath his arm was a package wrapped in cloth that glowed in the dim light of dawn. The angel knelt and unwrapped it, unfolding the cloth with care and laying it aside. He had uncovered a mirror framed with rough wood. He propped it against the house near the back door and turned to go.

"Hey!" a tiny voice shouted. "Where the fuck do you think you're going? Where am I? Are you just going to leave me here?"

The angel turned back, lowered his face to the mirror, and placed a raised index finger to his lips. "Shhhhhh," the angel whispered. Even so, his voice rolled like thunder.

Looking around to be sure that no one had been disturbed, the angel waited. He heard no shouts, detected no movement—only the twitter of birds and the distant honking of early morning traffic. Satisfied, the angel turned to go. He made to launch himself, but just short of flight, he clutched at his chest, stumbled, and fell to the grass. A low moan shook the earth.

A short time later, a muffled barking pierced the air, followed by the slam of a screen door. A large yellow Lab bounded out onto the lawn, barked once, froze, and sniffed at the air. He dropped his nose to the ground and began to follow the scent.

In a moment, he was hovering over the angel, drooling onto the divine countenance. The angel opened one eye and saw an enormous black membrane, slick with mucus, whiffling and snuffling with curious abandon. The angel reached up to touch the nose, choosing it as his point of entry.

PRELUDE 3

LODGE OF THE HAWK AND SERPENT, SAN FRANCISCO

STANIS LARCH LIT THE censer and then stood back in a posture of prayer as the smoke, fragrant with frankincense and myrrh, filled the temple. Once the air was thick with haze, he approached his Enochian table and sat on a high stool. The table was covered with symbols and signs carved precisely according to the instructions of John Dee, the court astrologer of Queen Elizabeth I.

Reverently, Larch removed a red velvet cloth from its place in the center of the table, revealing a shiny black stone about seven inches across and two inches thick. Larch breathed deeply and uttered an angelic invocation in the Enochian language. Closing his eyelids halfway, his focus became soft, and he rested his gaze upon the stone.

He concentrated on his breathing—even and deep coming in, long and slow going out—freeing his mind of concepts, and likewise freeing his eyes to see whatever the spirits chose to reveal.

At first, he only saw wisps of nondescript images flashing here and there in the stone. A gauzy flash of white, the momentary appearance of a horse's head neighing, the spinning of a distant crown. A pickpocket looked over his shoulder, caught in the act. Larch watched him cringe in shame, and then run away out of the range of the stone's vision.

The picture blurred again but resolved into a vision of white lace. A young woman stepped out of shadow into full view and faced him directly. She was so beautiful that Larch caught his breath—he had to concentrate to get his meditative rhythm back. Like the surface of a pond, the disturbance in his meditation made the vision blur and fade. But as he unfocused his eyes and settled back down into a contemplative state, the young woman appeared to become more solid.

He became aroused just looking at her. She appeared to be about twenty, and her lithe form was barely hidden by the wispy gauze that covered her. Long, light-colored hair hung nearly to her waist, and her nose turned up in a fetching, sprightly way. He could see the points of her apple-size breasts clearly, and they moved from side to side as she swayed back and forth. It made him crazy. There appeared to be a slit in the gauze that hung to her ankles, revealing a leg that seemed just a little too long, yet ended just a little too soon. Larch ducked to see if a change in perspective would afford him a glimpse just an inch higher beyond where that slit ended, to where legs joined together maddeningly just out of sight, but to no avail.

"What vision do I behold?" he spoke out loud.

"What vision are you looking for?" the young woman answered playfully.

"I seek Wisdom," Larch said.

"Oh, you'll have to go a very long way up the food chain to find *her*." The young woman shook her head. Golden bangs fell over her eyes in a way that Larch found absolutely irresistible. If this were a human woman flirting with him as openly as this ghostly vision seemed to be doing, Larch knew he would already be out of his clothes.

"Who are you, then?" Larch asked. "By what name may I call you, and what are your powers?"

"Call me Pim," the woman said, twirling her hair fetchingly and raising one leg as if ready to begin a dance. She didn't dance, though. She seemed merely to be playing with him. "And as for powers, I don't have many. But what I do have, I use pretty well." She *was* flirting with him; Larch was sure of it.

"I am a man with many questions," Larch said carefully.

"I'm not what you'd call a very *smart* spirit," Pim answered, a little apologetically. "So, I don't really know if I can help you."

"I want knowledge," Larch said.

"Oh, poop on *knowledge*," Pim said, with a little wiggle. The urgency in Larch's groin leaped as he saw her breasts bounce. Did she notice? Of course she noticed. It was all on purpose. "But I *can* give you something much, much better."

"And what is that?" Larch asked.

"I can give you *power*," she said, sucking on her index finger.

PRELUDE 4

SAINT JAMES' EPISCOPAL CHURCH, THE BERKELEY HILLS

REVEREND FELICIA DUNNE closed the door to the sacristy and turned the key in the lock. She spun around, placed her hands to her cheeks, and squealed. Her girlfriend, Jan, mirrored her perfectly, and they shrieked at each other in glee for several seconds before proceeding to hop up and down.

"Oh my God, Baby," Jan said, placing her arms around her partner's shoulders, "You did so good today."

"I did, didn't I?" Felicia nodded, almost in tears. "Oh my God, I think I did!"

"They are going to *love* you!" Jan said, adding in a singsong voice. "But not as much as I do." She drew her partner in for a kiss, which was long, luscious, and slow.

Felicia held her partner's head lovingly as they kissed, Jan's dreadlocks feeling rough on the reverend's fingers, her perfume intoxicating to her, inflammatory. When their kiss broke, Jan said, "As sexy as the...what do you call this, Honey?"

"A chasuble," said Felicia.

"Right. Sexy as that thing is, I can't wait to get it off you."

"I don't see anyone," Felicia giggled.

"You know the Altar Guild is going to be pounding on that door any minute," Jan warned.

"I think we have time for another kiss." Felicia put her nose on Jan's and stared deep into her brown eyes. "Do you think the sermon was too harsh?"

"Honey, you got to tell these white people like it is," Jan playfully switched her accent, sounding an awful lot like Felicia's father. "'Cause if you don't, they ain't gonna respect you for a moment. You know that's true."

Felicia felt her partner's thumb trace her cheekbone, and she smiled. "I know that's true. It felt right when I wrote it. It felt right when I preached it, too."

"It *was* right, Baby," Jan said, switching back to her own voice. "These folks are going to stand behind you." She raised herself up on tiptoe, pressing her lips against Felicia's again. The priest squeezed Jan's ample body against her own, and breathed in her scent, her head swimming with desire.

Just then a flash filled the room. Felicia drew back and looked around, alarm spreading across the features of her face. She heard the sound of a chair scooting back, and the figure of a man stood up, blocking the light of the tiny stained glass window that supplied the sacristy with natural light.

"My wife told me that these things were easy to use." The man's voice was deep and sonorous, possessed of an educated Louisiana drawl. He held up his hand, and Felicia saw the outline of a smartphone. "I don't like modern things, generally, but she insisted. I've never used the camera before, but I couldn't let such evidence just... well, evidence is ephemeral, isn't it?" The man stepped closer and smiled. After a few uncomprehending moments, Felicia recognized him.

"Oh, it's you, Bishop." She relaxed, but not much. Bishop Preston was new to the Episcopal Diocese of California, serving as an interim suffragan for Bishop McClary. It was he who had installed her today as the rector of Saint James's. "I didn't realize you were here."

"Obviously." His voice was grave. He placed the smartphone in his pocket. He looked at Jan with disdain and made a dismissive *scoot* motion with his hand. Felicia exchanged a worried look with her partner. "You should go," she whispered. Jan shot Bishop Preston a poisoned look but stepped quickly to the door, turned the key, and let herself out.

"It was a beautiful service today," Bishop Preston said gravely. "I'm just sorry there was so much wasted effort."

"What do you mean?" Felicia felt her panic level spike.

"Well, I understand that the good people of Saint James's spent years looking for just the right rector. And now they are going to have to start all over." He had begun pacing, his hands behind his back. "Pity, really. Very sad. God's people deserve better." He cocked his head at her, and she heard his unspoken words loud and clear: *they deserve better than you.*

Felicia realized that she was sweating now. "I...I don't understand."

"Oh, but I think you do. You've been hired under false pretenses. You lied to these people."

"I did *not* lie to them!" She allowed a flash of fury to erupt in her voice.

"Oh, but my dear little pickaninny pervert, you did." He stopped pacing for a moment and smiled. It was an ugly smile. "You see, Sweet Pea, a sin of omission is just as wrong as a sin of commission. I know you didn't tell these people you were heterosexual—you wouldn't *lie*, after all. But you didn't tell them you *weren't* a pervert, either, did you?"

Felicia said nothing. She realized that her hands were balled up into fists. She willed them to open and felt the coolness of the sacristy's air on her palms. "Bishop Preston, I know you are new to this diocese," she began, her voice betraying her fear. She plunged ahead, "And so maybe you don't understand the kind of place it is."

"Do you think I'm an idiot, Sweet Pea?" the bishop snarled. "Do you really think I did not know the kind of sin-sick cesspool I was stepping into when I came to this place? Do you think our church raises fools to the episcopacy as a matter of course?" He waited a beat but did not let her respond. "My wife and I came here because our daughter is sick. You knew that, right? She's still sick, so we're still here. I volunteered to help because, well, I'm retired and I like to be useful." He smiled the kind of smile that an alligator might display just before eating a wounded rodent. "This is not the kind of place I would *choose* to live. It's a diocese populated by hippies, activists, and perverts of the most unrepentant variety—such as yourself. Hell, you may be all three."

Felicia kept her mouth shut. He had her on two out of three as she'd always been more preppy than hippie.

"But from what I've seen, there's a big difference between this diocese and this parish." He gestured toward the grand, wood-framed, gothic-arched architecture of the sacristy, and, she imagined, beyond it, to the rest of the building. "The homos might run this diocese, Sweet Pea, but they do *not* run this congregation. This is an affluent congregation, a *Republican* congregation. They are not fond of perverts."

He gestured to the smartphone in his pocket and began to walk toward her. She felt his menace increase with every step. "I wonder what your vestry will make of your sacristy shenanigans? And on your very first day as rector? What other indecencies await them? Their imaginations will simply *reel*." He stopped with his face mere inches from her own. "They deserve better. I will see a letter of resignation on my desk by tomorrow. Am. I. Clear?"

Felicia saw her future crumbling. Her heart nearly beat through her chest. The chasuble felt like a sheet of lead hanging from her shoulders. She felt faint, and stumbled to a chair by the door.

"Here, let me help you," the bishop said, taking her hand in an icy grip until she had settled into the chair.

"A letter" she repeated, staring straight ahead at nothing. "A letter!" she jerked upright. A flash of insight stabbed at her brain, and a bolt of hope struck at her heart. "Wait here, please," she said and rushed from the room. Without pausing to consider whether it was right, whether it was prudent, she rushed to her office—the office that had been given to her just this day—jerked open the top drawer, and snatched up an envelope. She turned on her heel and marched back to the sacristy.

The bishop was pacing again, a look of bemused triumph playing on his face as she opened the door. Felicia clutched at the envelope and spoke without rehearsing her words. "Okay, you asked for a letter. I'll make you a deal."

"A deal? How quaint. This sounds like one of those 'stages of grief,' or some such nonsense that we're always hearing about from the liberals."

"A letter for a letter. I'll give you this one instead of my resignation. I'll give you this letter, and you destroy that picture. You let me keep my job."

"That must be *some* letter, Sweet Pea." A note of pity entered his drawl.

"The last rector wrote it for his successor, whoever that might be. I found it in the drawer. It was sealed. It was obviously meant for me, so I opened it. You leave me alone, and it's yours."

"Well, I suppose you'll have to let me see it. For all I know, it says, 'Welcome to Saint James's, you poor, sorry bastard.'"

"It doesn't," she said defiantly. "You'll see."

He snatched the envelope from her trembling fingers and pulled the letter inside free. He unfolded it and turned his back to the window to catch the best light.

As he read, Felicia watched his face carefully. She saw his eyebrows shoot up. She saw a range of emotions pass over his aging features: amusement, shock, lust...triumph. He looked to the ceiling, obviously enraptured, fantasizing, intoxicated by the possibilities the letter portended.

Eventually, he looked down at her with the curious expression of a man who has decided to have mercy on an insect. "Yes," he said. "This letter will...satisfy me." He began to walk from the room but at the last minute turned back to her. "I'll keep that photo as our little secret—but I'm going to keep it, just the same." He nodded, obviously approving of the prudence of this course of action. "The perverts need to be kept in line in this diocese. This way, I'll know that at least one of them will keep to the straight and narrow." He opened the door to the sacristy. "Good day, Rector," he said and was gone.

FRIDAY

1

THE CROWD ROARED. Terry stood up and whistled.

"Ow!" Kat howled, dropping her newspaper and slapping him on the shoulder. "That hurt! Knock it off!" She picked at her ear for some remaining hearing.

Terry ignored her, jumping up and down and whistling more insistently. His small frame barely registered on the metal bleachers as he hopped. His features—half-Japanese, half-European—screwed up into a howl, followed by another shrill whistle.

"Arggggh!" Kat growled, snatching a Kleenex from her bag and stuffing it into her left ear. She could almost have been Terry's twin as they were nearly the same size and their hair was the same jet-black shade of midnight. She lacked his Asian heritage, however, as well as his whistling skills.

As the roaring of the crowd subsided, Terry took his seat again, punching at the air. He wore a bright yellow T-shirt that said Jesus Wants Me for a Sunbeam.

Kat cocked an eyebrow. "No cassock today, Terry?"

"Do I look like I'm at work?" Terry asked. "A girl gets to break out and show a little style sometimes, doesn't she?" Then he whistled again. "Besides, all my cassocks are in the wash."

Kat leaned over and yelled so Susan could hear her over the din. "I never would have taken Terry for a sports fan."

"He's not, generally," she said, her plump face a mixture of amusement and compassion. She ran her fingers through her blonde perm. "Notice that I artfully sat with a person between Terry and myself?"

"Oh thanks a lot!" Kat yelled back. She glanced at the tournament floor where two contestants bowed to one another and faced off for another bout. One lunged at the other, who bounced back out of reach. The attacker kept coming. He threw a punch, but the other grabbed his wrist and twisted it away.

Kat held her newspaper in front of her face to block her view. "Remind me why we're here!" she yelled in Susan's direction. Out of the corner of her eye she saw Dylan seated on Susan's other side, digging into a bag of peanuts.

"Will you stop being silly?"

"This is violent. There's no difference between this and...and those gladiator fights in ancient Rome."

"Except that none of those people are slaves?"

"Some of them are Christians."

"None of them are here against their will. Also, have you seen any blood yet?"

"I'm not watching, remember?"

"I haven't seen any blood, and I've been to plenty of these." Susan was beginning to sound exasperated.

"Someone is *going* to get hurt; it's fucking karate."

"Ah hate when you get them shriveled black peanuts!" Dylan shouted his complaint. "There should be a 'bad-peanut-exchange' booth."

"It's *not* karate," Terry corrected her. "It's aikido."

"Same diff," Kat said dismissively, turning the page.

"Different diff," Terry insisted, but then he was on his feet again, whistling and shouting as the crowd stirred to life.

"Oh God, you could have warned me." Kat punched Susan's arm.

"That right there," Susan said, rubbing her arm, "*that's* violence."

"This man is crazy," Kat breathed, barely audible beneath the shouting of the crowd.

"What man?" Susan asked.

Kat pointed at her newspaper. "This governor, Ivory. Did you see this? From Michigan. He's talking about bombing Dearborn."

"Whaaaaat?" Susan said, looking over at the paper. Kat held the paper so she could see the headline: Governor Vows to Obliterate Michigan City. "What's *that* about?"

"It's an anti-Muslim thing," Kat said, turning the page to skim the rest of the article. "You know, Dearborn has the highest concentration of Muslims in the country."

"Yeah, so?" Susan looked worried.

"So, he's talking about...here, listen: 'You've got to eliminate the rot at the root,' he says."

"That's folksy," Susan called. "He's not serious, though. He can't actually be talking about bombing an American city. It's a stunt."

"It's gotta be," Kat agreed. "But there's a lot of people taking him seriously. Here's a Catholic archbishop who's ripping him a new one, and the senior rabbi of Temple Shek...I can't pronounce it. Anyway, some high Jewish muckety-muck letting him have it. *They're* not saying it's a stunt."

"It's a stunt," Susan pronounced. The crowd roared. "Did you see that?" Susan slapped at Kat's shoulder.

"I'm reading," Kat said loudly in an annoyed tone.

Terry turned on her, "Look, Miss Faints-at-the-Sight-of-Blood, your boyfriend is up next, and we're here to support him. You can't do that hiding behind your newspaper."

"He's going to get hurt," Kat complained, turning another page.

"We've been here two and a half hours, and no one's gotten hurt yet!" Terry yelled over the crowd. "That's the whole idea of aikido!"

Kat rolled her eyes. "I thought it was karate."

"In karate, the goal is to hurt your opponent," Terry corrected her, his voice containing an edge of exasperation. "In aikido, the goal is to keep *anyone* from getting hurt at all."

"What kind of martial art is *that*?" Kat asked, her face bunching up in incomprehension.

"The kind that doesn't like violence and tries to prevent it," Terry said. "Something that you should approve of."

"Wait, how does that even work?" Kat asked.

"Okay, see that guy in the far corner?" Terry pointed.

"The fat one, old guy?"

"Yeah, him. He's the attacker; he's called the *uke*."

"As in ukulele?" Kat asked, raising one eyebrow.

Terry ignored her. "It's his job to try to hurt the other guy, the girl, there. She's called the *tori*."

"Oh my God!" Kat squealed. "That is a girl! She's small. She's going to get creamed!"

"Just *watch*," Terry said. "It's her job to take the energy of her opponent and deflect it so that it doesn't do any damage to anyone. Aikido is the art of compassion for your attacker. You don't hurt him, but you don't let him hurt you, either."

"So, how do you win?" Kat asked.

"Well, you win here by scoring points. But in a street fight, you win the fight when your attacker gets tired and gives up."

Kat sat up straighter on the bleachers. "That's kind of fucking brilliant."

"That's what we're trying to tell you."

"And Mikael is good at this?" she asked, a newfound awe coming into her voice.

"He's a black belt," Susan affirmed.

"Why don't I know all of this?"

"I don't know!" Terry shouted back. "Maybe because you put your fingers in your ears, shouting 'la-la-la-la' every time the subject comes up."

"Do not."

"Do so."

"Pig."

"Jackass."

"Weasel."

"Capybara."

"Oh, good one," Kat said, grinning. "You win."

"Hey, hey, hey, guys, hold up," Susan said. "There's Mikael."

Dylan and Terry both leaped to their feet and started screaming and whistling as Mikael entered the floor. His shock of unruly black hair made a dramatic contrast against his white, pajama-like *gi*.

"I'm afraid to look," Kat said, burying her face in her paper.

Terry snatched the paper from her and threw it under the bleachers.

"Hey!" Kat protested.

"Oh, grow a pair of fucking ovaries!" Terry shouted. "This is your *boyfriend*. You can stand to watch for the next five minutes."

Kat slunk down and crossed her arms, pouting. But she watched. The crowd eventually settled down and took their seats again. Kat felt a rising anxiety as she saw Mikael approach his opponent. Then another person stepped out onto the floor. And another.

"Wait!" Kat shouted, "that's three against one!"

"Yes," Terry answered. "It's called *randori*, multiple attackers. It's the category Mikael is competing in today."

"Oh shit. I remember him using that word, but I didn't know what it meant," she said into Susan's shoulder. "This is fucked up."

"He'll do fine," said Susan, patting her shoulder. "I hope."

"Oh thanks," Kat said. "Oh my God, look! They've got sticks!"

"Yeah!" shouted Terry. "Aikido was designed originally to defend against sword attacks with one's bare hands. The sticks are vestigial of that."

"TMI," Kat said, batting Terry away. She held her breath.

Mikael bowed to his opponents and then stepped back. Like lightning, however, he lunged toward the first attacker, who threw a punch at Mikael's face. Mikael dodged to the left, met the man's fist in the air with his open hand, and guided it past his body, throwing the man off balance. The uke rolled away and got to his feet again.

By that time, Mikael had turned toward another uke, a woman about twice his weight. She punched at his chest, but his hand was quick, deflecting the blow up, her hand shooting over his head instead. At the same time, his elbow caught her on her collarbone. Mikael yanked at the deflected hand, still held firmly at the wrist, twisting her counterclockwise as she fell.

"Oh my God!" Kat shrieked. "He's really good!"

"That's what we're telling you!" Terry called back, not taking his eyes off the tournament floor.

Kat could scarcely look away, but out of the corner of her eye she saw Dylan wrestling to fish his cell phone out of his pocket. She looked over as he put it to his ear and saw his mouth form the word, "Hello?"

She looked back to see Mikael throwing another opponent end over end. He landed with the sound of root vegetables hitting a kitchen counter. Dylan stood up in his seat, but he was the only one. Kat looked over and saw the look of alarm on his face.

"What is it?" she called.

"Gotta go," he said, pocketing the phone and starting to climb down from the bleachers. "It's Dicky."

2

BRIAN SLID a tray containing a freshly thawed turkey in the oven for a long, slow bake. He closed the door and straightened up—as straight as his hunched back would allow—and breathed deep in satisfaction. He knew his housemates would return from the tournament excited and famished, and Mikael would be ready to eat half the turkey by himself.

Tobias scratched at the door and barked.

"Stay out there!" Brian called. "You'll just be bored silly if I let you in." A few dishes were scattered across the table, left over from breakfast. He smiled the weary smile of a man whose work is never done, and placed his earbuds in his ears, starting up this week's *Kabbalah Today* podcast. He carried the dishes to the sink for a quick rinse before placing them in the dishwasher. As he ran a glass under the water, he caught a yellow flash out of the corner of his eye.

"Hey, what are you doing in here?" he said to Tobias, his hands on his hips. Tobias wagged his tail and barked once, loudly. As the rabbi on the podcast began to chant his ritual opening, Brian wrinkled his brow and went to investigate the screen door. The latch worked fine. He looked at Tobias. He looked at the latch. He looked at Tobias.

Tobias barked. "How did you...?" he said, but then he waved it away. "Probably didn't latch right when we came in this morning," he said out loud, as much to himself as to the yellow dog.

Tobias barked again and stood at the door.

"Crazy dog, you just wanted in!" Brian complained.

Tobias looked at Brian, and then at the door. He barked.

"No," Brian said and leaned against the counter with his arms crossed.

Tobias barked, more insistently.

"No," Brian said again, more calmly. Then he cocked his head as he watched Tobias approach the screen door, rear back on his hind legs and, fumbling at the handle with both paws, scratch down the screen as he fell forward.

"Hey, don't damage the screen!" Brian shouted at him.

Tobias reared up and once again fumbled at the handle with his paws. This time, however, he triggered the button, and the door swung open with force as he fell against it.

"Well, I'll be damned..." Brian said, incredulous. He followed Tobias into the backyard. Tobias led him to a spot near the back fence and barked, nudging at something with his nose. Brian saw nothing but matted grass.

"What? What are you barking at?"

Tobias looked back and forth, and barked with what seemed to Brian was frustration. The dog tried another tack—he ran over to where a large, framed mirror was propped against the house, near the back door.

"What's this?" Brian said, picking it up. The rabbi in his earbuds was explicating the gifts of Binah, so he did not hear the tiny voice calling for his attention. "I must have missed this coming in this morning," he said, looking from the in-law cottage he shared with his partner, Terry, to the back door of the old farm house the order called home. "Pre-coffee, don't you know?" he said to Tobias. Tobias barked once, and apparently satisfied, he stood by the door, wagging his tail, waiting to be let in.

"Um, I've got my hands full," Brian said to the big yellow dog. He held up the picture frame. He waited to see what Tobias would do. To his amazement, the dog reared up, felt at the handle, and swung the door open. Then he wedged his body in the crack and stepped sideways to open the way for Brian to go in.

"Fuck me," said Brian, stepping up into the house.

3

WHEN DYLAN ARRIVED at the Oakland boarding house where Richard was staying, he found a gaggle of people standing out on the lawn. Some of them looked panicked, some of them frightened, some merely concerned. When their eyes lit upon Dylan's robust form, the double breast of his black cassock flapping in the breeze and sweat streaming from his brow, some of them glared as if he were somehow to blame. *Who knows?* he thought. *Maybe I am.*

"Ah'm Father Dylan, Richard's order mate. Ah got a call. Can someone tell me what's wrong with him?" he asked breathlessly. He wiped at the sweat on his forehead with a handkerchief. No one said anything to him, but one woman pointed up at the steps of the slightly dilapidated Victorian.

"Uh...okay, thanks," Dylan said, and made for the steps. Huffing and puffing, he made the landing. The door was wide open, so he knocked to be polite, paused a few seconds, but then went on inside.

Around a corner he caught sight of three people standing outside a door, stock still. "Hah, Ah'm Father Dylan Melanchthon, Richard's number one. Is somethin' wrong with Dicky? Ah'm a little—"

A man about ten years younger than Dylan put a finger to his lips, cutting him off. A young woman of about twenty, slim with red hair, stood with her ear to the door, her eyes wide. The other woman was closer to Dylan's own age and degree of plumpness. She looked scared.

Dylan froze and listened. A loud "thump" sound came from the room. "What was that?" Dylan asked, concerned.

"We don't know," the older woman replied. "But whatever it is, it's hitting the ceiling. The neighbors are out on the lawn, fit to be tied. It's been going on for an hour and a half now."

"How long between bumps?"

"It's not regular," the younger woman said, her ear still plastered to the door. "But every couple of minutes. Sometimes less. Sometimes more."

Dylan looked at the young man and pursed his lips. "Is this Richard's room?" he asked. The man nodded. "Do you have a key?" Dylan asked. The man shook his head. "He padlocked it from the inside."

"Shit," Dylan said. "Waal, with yore permission, Ah'm just gonna break the door down. Is that all right?"

The young man exchanged looks with the two women, and they reluctantly agreed. "You his roommates, then?" Dylan asked. They nodded.

"All right. Well, stand back—this may take a few tries."

Dylan backed up as far as he could to get a running start. He pushed off the far wall and aimed his shoulder at the far right edge of the door. He heard a crack and felt a stabbing pain in his shoulder.

"Was that you or the door?" the man asked, wincing.

"Ah'm hopin' it was the door," said Dylan, rubbing at his shoulder. For once, he gave thanks for his ample weight—it seemed to cushion him from the worst of the impact.

Dylan backed up and took another running start. He hit with even greater force, and a visible crack appeared in the door.

"Ahhh!" Dylan shouted, and shook out his arm. "Motherfucker, that hurt!"

"Are you supposed to swear?" the younger woman asked, eyeing his cassock with suspicion.

"Don't Richard swear?"

"Yeah, like all the time," she said, her eyes shifting from side to side. "That's weird, too."

"Nah, we're in the same order. Cussing is part of our charism," Dylan said. He backed up again for another run.

"What's a...*charism*?" the young woman asked.

"It's a gift," Dylan said, concentrating on the door.

"Cussing is a gift?" she looked confused.

"Some people got it, and some people don't," Dylan said and launched himself toward the door.

The door swung open and cracked against the far wall as it hit. Dylan danced around, yelling, "Shit motherfucking passion of Christ!" He rolled his arm around in its socket but soon turned his attention to the room. It appeared to be empty. Dylan looked around, confused. The shades were drawn, and water damage streaked the plaster walls. A mattress lay on the floor, covered only in a fitted maroon sheet. He looked back at the door where the three room-mates stood peering in. They were looking up, their mouths gaping open. The younger woman looked down at Dylan and pointed up, above his head.

Dylan looked up, and there was Richard, floating in the air near the ceiling. A blanket hung off his body, and a bicycle helmet was firmly strapped to his head. Dylan watched as the body lowered slightly but then floated upward rather quickly, Richard's helmet colliding with the ceiling with a loud, ominous "thud."

"Aw, shit, not again," Dylan said, his hands on his hips.

The older woman stepped into the room, cautiously approaching Dylan. "How?...What?" She looked down at him. "What are we seeing?"

"Uh...yer seein' a guy, like, a floating guy"—Dylan looked from side to side like a trapped rodent—"with a fine grasp of helmet safety."

"How is he...How does he *do* that?"

"Waal, *he* isn't, actually." Dylan turned to the young man. "You'n gotta broom around here?"

The man peeled his eyes away from Richard and in a few moments threw a broom from the doorway at Dylan. Dylan missed it but picked it up from the floor. He held the broom over his head and guided Richard until he was floating just over the mattress.

"Uh...okay, Duunel. Enough's enough," Dylan spoke to the demon sharing Richard's body. Richard had been hosting Duunel for nearly six months now, ever since they had foiled the plans of a local tycoon to eliminate all children, dogs, and avocados from the face of the Earth. The demon had taken up residence in an innocent little girl, and Richard had persuaded it to inhabit him instead.

"You let him down, right now," Dylan continued, "or you're gonna be one sorry-assed hellspawn, and I ain't lyin'. Richard has a deal with you, but I sure as fuck don't. Drop him. Now."

Like a sack of bruised plums, Richard fell onto the bed. His mouth was open, and a snore emitted from it like only those with sleep apnea can manage.

"Now you let him wake up, you shit-for-brains snake!"

Richard's eyes snapped open. "Dylan," he said, looking around, getting his bearings.

"Dude."

Richard sat up and unsnapped his helmet. "You broke my door."

"You got the whole neighborhood out on the lawn talkin' 'bout poltergeists."

"*That's* not good." Richard rubbed at his eyes. "Coffee?" he asked.

"Yer damn tootin'," Dylan agreed. "And a doobie for mah nerves is what Ah'm thinkin'."

4

Brian heard a rustle at the front door, and then a roar as his housemates blew into the foyer like a summer storm. They laughed and hooted, and it was clear to him that their degree of merriment was high. Tobias barked and zoomed past him on his way to the front door, his ample yellow behind wagging profusely.

Brian leaned against the doorway and folded his arms, looking for all the world like a lean, satisfied, Semitic question mark. "I'm guessing the tournament went well?" he said. He knew it had, of course. Terry had texted the results hours ago.

"Mikael rocked the fuckin' house!" Kat announced, hanging her coat on a hook by the door and grabbing Mikael around the waist to give him a proud squeeze.

Mikael was in the middle of taking off his own coat, so the hug was awkward, but he paused and soaked it in. He looked over at Brian and nodded.

"It was cool." Kat let go of him and straightened his gi. "And you can wear those jammies to bed anytime you like, tiger."

Mikael's eyebrows perked up. "That sounds like an invitation."

"Invitation, hell," Kat said, making for the kitchen. "That's an appointment." She paused to kiss Brian on the cheek. "Hi there, Sweetie. I'm sad you couldn't join us."

"I've been to my share," he said without a note of resentment. "It's been a busy day around here, too."

"Hey, Baby Doll," Terry said, reaching up for a big wet kiss from his hubby. Brian bent down and gladly acquiesced, tasting toffee and mint and...cardamom? He drew his head up from the kiss. "Fuck! Did you guys eat?"

Terry slunk and tried to slip into the kitchen. Brian grabbed the back of his shirt and turned to Susan, the one person from whom he knew he could get a straight answer. "Well?"

Susan looked at Mikael, then at Kat, then at Terry, and finally back at Brian. "Well, um..."

"You did know that I've been cooking all day for you ungrateful turds, right?"

"Brian, relax," Susan cooed. "We're famished. We were all the way in San Jose, and we were sinking into hypoglycemic shock. We grabbed a couple of samosas from the sidewalk vendor outside the arena, just to hold us over. We all split one—except for Mikael, who could have eaten the whole cart if we let him." She gave Brian a reassuring hug as he let go of Terry's shirt. "We did *not* let him."

She touched Brian's beaked nose with her finger. "Now, what's for dinner?" She winked at Terry, who breathed a sigh of relief and successfully completed his entry into the kitchen.

"Turkey," Brian announced, pouting and barely mollified. "With bacon-apple stuffing."

"Because you can never have enough turkey," said Terry.

"And squash with chipotle applesauce," Brian concluded.

"Wow. That's autumnal," Kat noted. "Not that I'm complaining."

"I collected a lot of recipes this winter, and I thought I'd give some of them a try," Brian explained.

Just then the door opened again, and Dylan stepped in. "Hah, gang," he announced. He removed his coat and turned to Mikael. "Ah expect you kicked some butt."

"I was successful in making sure no butts were kicked at all."

"So, you won, is what yer sayin'."

"I am."

"Good job!" Dylan rubbed his hands together. "Someone please tell me dinner is close to bein' ready."

"One half hour," Brian said, looking at his watch. "Just enough time for you all to say Evening Prayer."

"Thet sounds like a plan," Dylan agreed and led the way to the chapel.

5

DUUNEL ALWAYS FELT SLIGHTLY uncomfortable when he slipped in between. He couldn't go far, or he would lose his host—sorry host that he was—but infernal discipline demanded that he check in regularly to update his master and receive orders.

Duunel mused on just how far askew the human perception of demons was. Humans assumed that order was good and chaos was evil, and so it must follow that demons were an anarchic lot. *But nothing could be further from the truth*, Duunel said to himself as he waited for his lord to appear. In fact, demons were strictly regimented. It was the Enemy that trusted his minions and allowed so much disorganized squalor. By comparison, Hell ran like a Swiss watch—with every demon knowing his place, every order obeyed without question, every command carried out with speed and efficiency.

Demons that failed their superiors were not coddled. They were not given second chances, training, or therapy. Usually, they were simply relegated to lunch.

In a few moments, a haze appeared to form in the in-between, and Duunel stood at attention before it. When it resolved, a great dragon with the head of an eagle appeared, glowering at Duunel with one great, glowing red eye. This was the great demon prince Maaluchre, whom Duunel had been privileged to serve since the time of the Great Deluge.

"My master," Duunel said, prostrating himself.

"Rise and report," said the prince.

Duunel rose, standing once again at attention. "The human sleeps," Duunel said. "Or, more accurately, he's passed out drunk."

"You had a hand in this, I suppose?" The prince did not look displeased.

"Sadly, no. He does this to himself, quite willingly. But I've certainly been working on vice amplification in other areas."

"I can tell you are amused," the prince said. "And yet *your* entertainment does not advance *our* liberation."

"My lord, the members of his order have been our only real predators in this part of the world for years. And among them, he is the most potent and effective. As long as I inhabit him, he is out of commission."

"And our Father is well served," the prince nodded. "And yet the others are not *ineffective*."

"Alas, no, my lord. They are quite competent. Just last week they crippled poor Alak."

"What horde is he in?" The demon prince looked up, trying to remember.

"Cthollud's, seventh plight."

"That *is* tragic," Maaluchre scowled, his red eye glowing hotter. "We cannot afford to be losing such powerful allies at such a crucial time. Not when our Father is on the move."

"That is precisely what I'm saying," Duunel agreed. "But I have my hands full keeping this one busy. I can't stray from him, or my hold will be lost."

"Quite right, quite right," the demon prince agreed. "Well, we must think of a way to take out the rest of them at a single stroke."

"I have an idea," Duunel said. "After all, I have access to the human's thoughts and memories. I know what frightens him most. Killing the members of his order would be a huge endeavor, and in my opinion, our efforts could evoke...resistance. Better to keep a low profile so as not to upset the plans that are already underway."

"What do you suggest?" The red eye opened wide like the blooming of a crimson flower.

"I believe we can...relieve them of their power—quickly, easily, and at a single stroke."

Eagles should never grin, Duunel decided, as he saw the skin around his master's beak stretch back.

"I'm listening."

6

RICHARD CLOSED his eyes against one blinding ray of the setting sun. His brain was pounding, and he felt nauseated. He considered throwing up but decided to wait until the room stopped spinning.

That will teach you to drink too much, said the voice in his head.

"I drank just enough, thank you," Richard said out loud. His own voice sounded thin and distant in his nearly empty bedroom.

You're not the only one suffering now, you know, the voice complained.

"Oh well..." Richard wiped the back of his hand across his eyes. "I'm drinking for two, now."

I thought you Christians were supposed to be compassionate?

"I thought demons were driven by self-interest."

That is a curious observation, the demon in his head noted. *On the one hand, I love to egg you on because I enjoy seeing you damage yourself and suffer. It's one of the few great pleasures left to my kind—*

"Your kind..." Richard repeated.

On the other hand, in my current position, I can't do that without feeling the effects of it myself. It's different when I'm in complete control, then I'm not so eager to push you into...enjoyable situations.

"Always good to know you're lookin' out for me, Duunel," Richard said without a shred of conviction.

You know what would really help right now? the demon offered.

"I'm sure you're going to tell me."

You need some Vicodin—it will really help with that headache.

"Huh...do you think?"

Oh yes. Very much. Good stuff. I'd chew it if I were you. Take two, they're only five hundred milligrams, so you need more of them.

"Duunel?"

Yes?

"Go fuck yourself."

Richard heard a knock, but he ignored it.

I love the fact that we can cohabit so congenially.

The knock came again, louder. The door swung inward. "Richard?" called a male voice. Richard squinted without moving his head and saw one of his roommates come into view. "Hey, Doug," Richard said, not bothering to move.

"Um...can I talk to you?"

He's here to throw you out on your ass, you know, said Duunel.

"It's your ass, too, fuckwad," Richard mumbled.

"What was that?" Doug said, not understanding.

"No...nothing. Sorry. I'm a little...tipsy."

"Uh, I'd say you're falling down drunk, man."

"Tomato—toMAHto..." Richard said. He grimaced as he pulled himself into a sitting position. He felt his brains sloshing to the bottom of his skull, grating as they went. The Vicodin sounded better and better. He looked around for his shoulder bag.

Doug continued. "I've been talking to Molly and Sue, and we've come to a decision, and it's a hard one."

Richard leaned over and found his bag. He reached into the inner sleeve and found a couple of Vicodin left over from a root canal last year.

Two, said the demon. *Make sure to take two.*

Richard took one. "You want me out," he said to Doug.

"Um...I wasn't going to put it like that."

He hates you, said Duunel in his head. *Everyone does, really. They pretend that they like you, but they don't, not—*

"Okay," Richard said. "Tonight, I guess."

"Yeah. We can't have another...another night like last night."

"See what you've done?" Richard said to Duunel.

"Uh...how is this *my* fault?" asked Doug defensively. "I wasn't bumping against the neighbors' ceiling at 4 a.m. this morning."

"No, I wasn't talking to...never mind. I'm drunk, remember?" Richard chewed the Vicodin.

Take two, said the voice in his head.

"Shove it."

"Okay, no need to get nasty," Doug said, backing out of the room.

"Not talking to you, Doug!" Richard called as he fell back onto the bed. "I'll have all my stuff out in an hour. Is that okay?"

"That's...fine. Let me know if you want some help."

"That's very kind of you," Richard lay motionless on the messed-up bed.

Where are we going? asked Duunel.

"You figure it out. It's your fault we're moving."

We could pick up some chick at a bar and sleep at her house.

"Does that *ever* really work?" Richard asked. "Really?"

Not for people dressed like monks, admitted Duunel.

"Friars," Richard corrected him.

Assholes, conceded Duunel.

7

As the last chant hung in the air, Brian placed a giant platter containing the turkey and stuffing on the lazy Susan. For good measure, he lit a couple of candles and noted the encroaching twilight with satisfaction. He loved this feeling—of warmth and food and family. Tobias licked at his hand. He stooped and patted the big dog's side. "Right, let's get you some dinner, too."

Brian had just scooped a cup and a half of dog food into Tobias's bowl when the others started filing into the kitchen.

Kat sat in her usual place and reflected. "You know, I never really prayed before I came here. It's always calming, but there was something special in the air tonight. I felt...I don't know what it was. It was grace-full."

Susan nodded and sat herself. "I know just what you mean. Liturgy gives me that feeling all the time. I sink into it, and peace just flows into me like a stream of water."

Dylan sat next to his wife, saying, "Or like light through a winder when there's lots of dust particles floatin' in the air...like in an old house or a barn or...Wait, thet didn't come out quite as nice as Ah hoped it would."

"Nice try, though, dear." Susan patted his leg then gave it a squeeze. "Why don't you say grace, O Interim Grand Poobah?" she said, referring to his status as head of the order while Richard was demonically indisposed.

They all bowed their heads except for Dylan, who raised his hands in the *orans* position. "Good evenin', God. It's been a heck of a day, and we are all tired and hungry and grateful and glad. We give thanks for Mikael's victory. And Ah'm personally grateful that Dicky's okay. Please bless this food so that we can be blessings in turn. And since Ah sure love me that Jesus feller, Ah'm gonna pray in his name and his Spirit—amen."

Amens went up around the table, and suddenly there was a flurry of shaking napkins, pouring iced tea, and passing plates. "So, Mikael," Susan said, "since you're already on top of the world, I saw an ordination date scrawled on the calendar."

Mikael beamed. "That will be *Reverend* Mikael soon," he nodded, spooning some curried potatoes onto his plate.

Kat leaned over and planted a kiss on his cheek. "Do you feel *reverential*?" she asked.

"I don't feel holy, if that's what you mean," Mikael said.

"Ain't none of us feel like that," Dylan shook his head, taking a dinner roll. "Most a' the time we just feel like fakes."

"Is that true?" Kat asked.

Dylan met Terry's eyes. Terry nodded, "Yeah, pretty much. But you have to recognize that as a temptation."

"What do you mean, 'a temptation'?" Kat asked.

"I mean that the holiness isn't ours; it's God's," Terry said.

"We're not *good*, just stupid enough to say yes!" Dylan added.

"Exactly," Terry said. "But as you know, we are surrounded by enemies—demonic forces who would like nothing better than to stop us by whatever means they can."

"An' discouragement is a pretty effective means," Dylan said with his mouth full.

"Speaking of demons," Mikael said, "what's up with Richard?"

"Yeah, Honey," Susan said. "You raced out of the Coliseum, and we haven't heard a peep from you since. Is everything okay?"

"Ah woulda called if there was anythin' hairy. Ah just didn't want to alarm anyone. Everythin' is under control." He heaped a pile of green beans next to his stuffing. "After Ah got the call, Ah grabbed the bus—it was quicker'n you'd expect. Ah went to Richard's place—the boarding house near Piedmont." They nodded, as they were all familiar with the trendy Piedmont shopping district in Oakland. Everyone had been to Richard's new place at least a couple of times.

"It makes me sad just thinking of that place," Kat said, looking at her yams. "I mean, it's as nice a place as plenty I've roomed in, but... it's not *here*, you know?"

"Ah know it, and unless Ah miss my guess, Richard is gonna be out on his ass pretty quick 'cause Ah don't think there's any way his roommates are gonna let him stay."

"What happened?" asked Terry, tearing into his turkey with gusto.

"Um...let's just say there was a sleep-disorder incident."

"Uh-uh," Susan said, not looking at her husband. "We're not going to 'just say' anything. You're going to tell us the whole story in gory detail."

Dylan deflated for a moment but then took a deep breath and told them what he found.

"Thank God for the helmet, I say," Brian noted.

"And we went for coffee. Ah got a good liter of the stuff in 'im—Peet's Coffee, too, so you know it was powerful. We smoked a doobie—"

"*You* smoked a doobie," Susan corrected.

Dylan ignored her. "He was his usual cheery self by then. Ah don't think it's hit him how powerfully his roommates are shook up by this. Ah told him, they're probably gonna ask him to leave."

"And he said?" asked Kat.

"Ah think he's in denial," Dylan said, a little sadly. "You know, he's a good guy—a conflicted guy—but a good guy. And, okay, he's got a demon inside him, sure. Ah think he's just tryin' to look on the bright side and make the best of things."

"I bet he cries himself to sleep every night," Susan said.

"What makes you think that?" Dylan asked.

"Because I would," Susan said. "The people at this table are the only people Richard has in his life who really get him—"

"Uh...he's been playin' chess with Larch now and then, over at the Hawk and Serpent Lodge in the city," Dylan said hopefully.

"Like I said, *we* are the only people who really understand Dicky, and he can't be here," Susan continued. "Since the house is warded against demons, Richard can't come home so long as he's playing hotel to one of them. My guess is that he's so lonely it's tearing him apart."

"Seemed okay to me," Dylan said.

"You're such a man," Susan said dismissively.

Dylan looked at Terry. "You gonna stand for that?"

"You're such a *straight* man," Terry agreed.

Dylan opened his mouth and looked at Mikael for help. Mikael held up his hands. "I'm an insensitive boor and have the membership card to prove it, so don't look at me."

Dylan looked back at his plate. "Ah am *seriously* pussy whipped."

"Eat your dinner," Susan told him.

Just then, there was a knock at the door. Brian scowled at the wall clock. "Who could *that* be?" He sprang up and ran to the foyer, hoping to send whoever it was packing quickly. Opening the door, he saw the friendly and wizened face of Reverend Oberlin, the pastor of the United Church of Christ congregation two blocks away at Cedar and Walnut.

"Good evening, Pastor," Brian said, swinging the door wide. "How nice to see you! Come in; let me take your coat."

"Oh, Brian, is it? Good to see you, mate," the pastor said in his cheerful British accent as he stepped in. "Is your better half around? I'd like a word with him if I may."

Terry appeared at the door. "Pastor, would you like a bite to eat?"

The pastor's face fell. "Oh, I've disturbed your dinner! Damn. I'm so sorry," he smiled apologetically.

"No trouble," Terry assured him. "I was just finishing up. Why don't you take a seat in the office, and I'll meet you there in a minute?"

"Of course," the pastor said. "Please take your time."

The older man walked quickly away, a slight limp visible in his step. Terry sidled up to his partner. "Sorry, Baby."

"No, it's fine. Let me get a plate of cookies ready."

"You're the tastiest." Terry planted a kiss on his cheek.

A few minutes later, Terry trotted off to the office, balancing a tray bearing tea for two and a plate of snickerdoodles. Brian sat back down at the table, noting that most everyone was just finishing up and looking very satisfied indeed.

For a few moments, no one said anything, and as if a chill wind had blown through the room, the mood turned sad. Finally, Kat said, "So what about Richard?"

"It was a brave thing Dicky done, and no mistake." Dylan wiped his mouth with a calico napkin. "Ah wouldn'a dunnit."

"It's not okay, not having him home," Susan said. "He's like a little lost puppy most of the time, and I feel like if he's not surrounded by people who care about him and...well, quite frankly, keep an eye on him, he'll get hurt."

"He's already plenty hurt, Honey," Dylan said, not disagreeing with her.

"So, what are you going to do?" Kat asked Dylan pointedly.

Dylan looked behind himself, to be sure she was talking to him. "Uh...whaddaya mean, what am Ah gonna do?" He gestured at his ample belly. "Ah think Ah'm gonna eat me some pie." He looked at Brian with a fleeting look of panic. "There *is* pie, ain't there?"

"You'll have to settle for cobbler," Brian said.

"Peach cobbler?" Dylan asked hopefully.

"Quince."

Dylan's face bunched up in a skeptical knot. "Waal, the proof is in the...cobbler, Ah suppose. Bring it on, dude."

Brian cleared some dishes from the table first, glad to have something to do. They all felt helpless about Richard. And they all missed him. Brian knew Dylan, as Richard's best friend, missed him most of all.

"Frankly," Dylan began, "Ah'm amazed we haven't heard from him yet. Ah saw them roommates o' his. Ain't no way they're letting him sleep there tonight—or any night, for that matter."

Just then, Dylan felt his pocket vibrate. "Speak o' the devil," he said and fished around for his cell phone. "It's Dicky, all right," he said, looking at the screen. "He's at the Gallic Hotel tonight. Gonna start lookin' for a new place tomorrow."

Kat's face looked pained, and she reached over and squeezed Mikael's hand. He gave her a reassuring look. "It's going to be okay, Baby," he told her. "It always is. We're really a very blessed community."

"Blessed but sorely tried," Dylan said, typing furiously but awkwardly with his enormous thumbs.

"Can't we just un-ward the house tempor—" Kat cut off midsentence as everyone in the room glared at her. "Okay, okay, it was just an idea."

"Wait," Brian said, leaning back against the counter. "What if Terry and I moved into the main house and we unwarded the cottage?"

All eyes turned to Dylan. "What are you all lookin' at me fer?" He recoiled as he spoke.

"Because you are now our fearless leader, and this requires bold leadership!" Mikael announced.

"Ah am never fearless," Dylan complained, "and Ah ain't no leader, neither."

"Nonsense; you have been for months, now," said Susan. "You're just lucky things have been relatively quiet."

"Can we take a vote on this?" Dylan asked.

"Dylan, you are sub-prior," Brian said resolutely. "The order already did vote on it, when they elected you."

"Yeah, but Ah never expected to ever have to actually..." He looked at the table.

Susan reached over and squeezed his hand. "You aren't leading alone, Baby," she said softly. "The only people here are those that love you."

Dylan sighed but perked up when Brian set a steaming cobbler under his nose.

"Quince, you say?" Dylan said, sniffing.

The sound of the door closing in the distance brought everyone's heads up. Terry appeared at the door. "Smells like quince," he said, sniffing at the air.

"How the hell do you know what quince smells like?" asked Mikael.

"I was Quince Queen of Fresno County in 1995," Terry said defiantly. He placed his hands on his hips and turned up his nose. "I know my quince."

Kat looked over at Brian standing just out of Terry's sight, shaking his head, mouthing the words, "No, he was not."

"So, what did the pastor want, Terry?" Susan asked.

"An emergency," Terry said, taking his seat at the table and basking in the quincian odor. "Very sad, really. His mother-in-law took a nasty fall, and they're jetting to the UK on a red-eye tonight so they can go care for her."

"Oh, that *is* sad," said Susan with real compassion in her voice.

"So, he needs me to fill in for a few weeks," Terry said. "Services are covered—they just need help with visitation."

"A paid gig, I hope?" Susan probed.

"Thanks be to God," Terry said, nodding.

"Thanks be to God," they all said, more or less in unison.

"Hey, has anyone noticed Tobias acting strangely?" Brian asked. But before anyone could say anything, a phone rang in the office. Dylan sat bolt upright. "That's not good," he said.

"You mean, so much for nookie night?" laughed Kat.

"Saddle up, boys and girls," Dylan said, wiping quince from his beard. "We gots us a demon."

"I'll get the mice," said Terry.

8

TONY MORRELLO WAS ALMOST ASLEEP when the phone rang. He fumbled at the handset and pushed the button that corresponded to the calling room. "Front desk," he said groggily.

"You gotta—" a scared female voice began. "There's someone—" A hand muffled the receiver for a second, and he could vaguely hear two people arguing. A man's voice took over.

"This is Aaron Falk in 115."

"I know that. What do you want?"

"The people in the room next to us are—well, there's shrieking. And moaning."

"Yeah, this is a hotel. People tend to do that when they're fucking. Wait—your neighbors were complaining about you last night, weren't they? Yeah, 115. Well, revenge is sweet. I hope they keep you awake all night." He hung up and smacked his lips. A Coke. That's what he needed. A little carbonation to cut through the sticky mass of saliva that had accumulated while he had dozed, and a little caffeine to cut through the brain haze. He went to the mini-fridge and opened the door. The phone rang again.

"Front desk."

"No, man, not moaning like lovemaking moaning. I mean screaming bloody murder like someone is seriously getting hurt over there!"

Tony found a Mountain Dew and frowned. It would do, but it wasn't really what he wanted. He cracked the seal with the pull tab and took a long pull at it. It was surprisingly yummy. Yes, this would do just fine. He decided to play with Mr. Falk, just a little bit.

"Okay, on a scale of one to ten, how loud is the...noise?"

"It's an 11! Listen, it's happening again!"

Tony stood up straight. He heard it, all right, coming through the telephone as loud as Falk's voice. Louder. "I'll be right up," he said, and grabbing his baseball bat, he headed for the door. "Goddamn fucking college kids," he mumbled. "Goddamn spring break."

His mumbling turned to outright curses when he rounded the corner that brought him within sight of 115 and its surrounding units. All of the furniture from 113 had been moved out to the parking lot near the door. The television sat in its entertainment cabinet at the head of one of the parking spaces as if it had just driven up and parked there. Not far away, Tony saw the dresser, two chairs, a little desk, the nightstands, and the shoddy metal clotheshorse.

Whoever had done it had been careful not to take up more than one parking space, which was very considerate since parking was always in short supply at Berkeley's Flamingo Motel. On the other hand, the furniture was also out in the open where anyone could just wander up from University Avenue and carry it off. Tony was so shocked by the sheer implausibility of it he almost forgot to be mad. The anger returned, though, as he pounded at the door.

The door opened a crack, revealing a room ablaze—every light in the place was on, including a couple not native to the room. An eye peered out at him and glanced around him, this way and that. "What the hell is going on here?" he yelled at the sliver of light coming from the door.

The door opened a little wider, and Tony found himself face to face with a stocky, balding man dressed like a priest, a purple stole dangling from his shoulders. "Hey, dude. How you doing?" the man said and passed a pudgy hand over his forehead, clearing away a large amount of accumulated sweat. He held the sweat-soaked hand out for shaking. "Ah'm Father Dylan. Nice to meet ya."

Tony ignored it. "What the hell is going on here?" he yelled again.

"Uh..." Dylan looked behind him and then turned back to the doorway. "Waal, to be honest, it's an exorcism. Ever seen one? It ain't pretty." The man's broad, sweaty face smiled at him.

Just then, a howl emerged from the room that sounded like a thousand children screaming in unison. "Yah know," the priest said, "this really ain't a good time."

Just past Dylan, Tony could see a naked man tied to the bedposts with ropes of stout hemp. As he watched, the foot of the bed swung up and struck the wall and then fell to the ground. Then it swung up again and fell again, in rapid succession as if it were a Murphy bed that was possessed. The sheetrock near the top of the wall was thrashed, and little puffs of plaster dust showered through the air.

Another figure—also a priest?—short guy, Asian-looking, stood back a couple of feet, book in hand, patiently waiting for the bed's acrobatics to cease.

"Can ya come back later?" the priest at the door asked again in what was clearly a Southern drawl. "We're kinda busy right now, you know, what with the demon and stuff." Then an idea seemed to strike him. "Unless you want to help. You look strong. Are you shriven?"

"What?" Tony simply could not take his eyes off the man on the bed.

"Are ya Catholic? You look kinda Eye-talian."

Absently, Tony nodded.

"You been to confession lately?"

"Huh—oh no."

"Oh," the priest looked momentarily disappointed. "You should probably go back to work, then, dude."

Tony just stared at the stout man, completely unsure what he should do.

The priest passed a hand over Tony's eyes and said dramatically, "These are not the droids you're looking for. You want to go back to the front desk and have a refreshing beverage." Then he slammed the door in Tony's face.

9

BISHOP TOM MÜELLER cursed as he strode to his motorcycle. He had had a long, difficult day at work and had dutifully procured all the items his wife had requested on the grocery list she had texted him earlier that afternoon. All except one—tampons.

"God*dammit*," he said out loud, kicking at the shrubs that lined the walk to the one-bedroom apartment they shared with twelve of their closest feline companions. His wife did not drive, and so was totally dependent upon him for the running of what seemed like innumerable errands.

Tom felt tired, hungry, angry, and depressed. The feelings were all so strong and so thickly intertwined that he could not easily sort them out. He just *felt*—intensely, and bad. He jammed the helmet onto his head so hard it hurt, and he took momentary pleasure in the way the pain cut through the tangled mass of emotions.

Finally, for a fleeting second, here was a feeling he could *identify*, one that would end. Sure enough, as soon as he raised the kickstand, it was gone. He punched his leg, once, twice, and reveled in it. He knew that a bruise would most likely result, but he didn't care. He waited until the pain subsided and the thick and confusing mass of emotion rushed back to fill its space. Then he gunned the engine and swung out onto the wet, dark Seattle street.

"Goddamned tampons!" he shouted at the gnats hitting the shield of his helmet. Why hadn't he run away from the seminary with Stephen when he had a chance, all those years ago? *Stephen wouldn't be sending me out into a Washington storm for fucking tampons*, he thought, racing around the cloverleaf of the freeway onramp. Stephen would wrestle him to the ground before a roaring fire, would lick at his face like a dog until they were both randy and hard. Stephen would peel off his T-shirt and lick his armpits, grabbing the hair in his teeth and growling like the beautiful animal we was.

Bishop Tom was so lost in this fantasy that he didn't see the crappy Ford Pinto with the missing headlight. The impact seemed quiet, almost distant, not at all like he had ever imagined it would be. His body flew up, and he tumbled in free space, end over end. Halfway through this aerial ballet, he stopped screaming, "Oh shit!" and started saying the rosary. Three lines into it, he hit the pavement. A split second later, a Prius took him out.

10

"Good one, Ben Kenobi," said Terry, marking his place in his *Roman Ritual* with a ribbon. "Is he gone?"

Dylan stood on tiptoe to fit his eye to the peephole. "Nah, he's just standing th...No, there he goes. He looks really disoriented...Okay, now he's gone." Dylan turned back to the room. "Think he'll call the cops?"

"Nah," Terry said. "Old Scratch, here, performed on cue pretty well."

Dylan set his hands on his hips and surveyed the mess. "Ah hate these distractions, dude."

"Tell me about it. I think I just had the Voice emerging."

"Ah heard it. How much ground did we lose?"

The man on the bed blinked and tried to sit up. "Is it over?"

"Oh shit, Doug's back," said Terry, his hands on his hips. "Square one."

"It's not over?" The naked man asked again, with not a little bit of despair cracking his voice.

"Sorry, man," said Dylan, flopping onto the floor. "It's not like we're not glad to see you or anything, but we had a bit of a setback just now."

"Sweetie," cooed Terry, sitting on the edge of the bed, "how conscious are you when the demon is...well, pulling your strings?"

"Not," he said. "It's like I'm asleep."

Terry nodded and looked up at Dylan. This kind of thing varied quite a bit from case to case. He was hoping that the man would have "heard" the demon's name—as that would have sped the ritual along immeasurably.

"That demon isn't going to give up his name, dude," said Dylan, knowing exactly what Terry was thinking. "He's smarter than some we've seen."

Terry nodded. They had expelled some pretty dumb demons, but this wasn't one of them. The infernal hosts, in their experience, varied as much in intellectual prowess as humans did. And though none of them were big on self-improvement, many of them had formidable street smarts, as one would expect from beings who had several million years of experience behind them. Sometimes they lucked out and got a being with the IQ of a slab of cheese, but not today. Today, they were fighting someone as smart as they were. Maybe smarter.

"Okay, let's try something different," Terry decided, rising from the bedside and heading for his kit bag. "Let's do the sigils while the invader is dormant."

"You got it," Dylan said and grabbed a grease pencil and a well-worn copy of *The Lesser Key of Solomon* from his kit bag. He opened the grimoire to the appropriate page and began to copy one of its sigils onto Doug's chest.

"What are you doing?" Doug asked.

"Relax, man, this isn't going to hurt. Terry, dude, you explain. Ah'm busy."

Terry stopped studying his *Ritual* and turned his attention to Doug. Real compassion shrouded his features as he spoke. "It's hard to command a demon if you don't know its name."

"I thought you said his name was Scratch."

Terry laughed. "That's just a traditional nickname—like calling Germans Jerry. They're all Old Scratch until we know better. We need to know his *real* name. But this is a pretty smart demon, so he's not going to just hand us power over him like that. The next best thing is to figure out who he works for. If we can figure out his boss's name, then we've got a leg up. Understand?"

Doug nodded.

"Demons are arranged into—well, they're like military companies, same as angels. We call them hosts. Every host has a big, extra-nasty demon commanding it. If we can figure out what host this demon inside you belongs to, then we can bind his boss, his commander. That'll weaken his hold on you, and we should be able to drive the demon into the mice."

"Mice?"

"Doug, meet Castor and Pollux." Terry held up a Chinese food box from which squeaking was barely audible.

Dylan scowled. "You named the mice?"

Terry smiled, looking distinctly elfin in the harsh light. "Just now. They've been Castor and Pollux for about three seconds."

"Just don't become attached to them, dude," Dylan warned. To Doug he said, "If everything goes right, they'll be demon food soon."

"Those poor mice." said Doug.

Dylan smiled as he wiped grease away with a handkerchief and began to draw another sigil. "At least we know we're really talking to Doug here." He winked at the naked man. "Demons ain't big on compassion."

"Better the mice than you," Terry added, nodding.

"Ah heard that," Dylan agreed. One by one, he copied each of the sigils, waited a couple of seconds, and then wiped Doug's chest clean and began on the next one. "Good thing you're not hairy—this would be a *lot* harder if you were."

"How many of these...sigils...are there?" Doug asked.

"Waal, fifteen hundred years before Christ, when Solomon wrote his *Key*, he knew of seventy-two of the buggers—the demon generals, I mean," Dylan said.

"We don't know what the job turnover rate is, so no one has an up-to-date or complete set of sigils," Terry added, "although the occult blogosphere is full of speculation."

"I saw a Satanist selling a 'complete set' on eBay, dude," Dylan said.

"How much?"

"Twenty thousand dollars."

Terry whistled. "That's a lot of money for crap."

"That's how Ah like my grapes, too, Ter—good and sour. You're probably right, though. Satanists are not generally renowned for their veracity."

"So anyway," Terry continued, "no doubt some of the sigils no longer work because some demon generals have been breakfast cereal for Beelzebub—and some of them we don't know because some demons have been promoted since the *Key* was written. But we do know that a lot of them *do* work. If we're lucky—"

"Bingo!" Dylan said and jumped off the bed to stand next to his friend. The sigil on Doug's chest flared and glowed, filling the room with an eerie light that seemed to put all the blazing lamps to shame.

"Parrillon," Dylan said. "He's in Parrillon's host."

"No wonder he's smart," Terry said, skimming a passage from the *Key*. "Parrillon is one of the demon generals that can grant intellectual prowess—especially in the arts and sciences—and those that serve under him are no slouches, either." Terry put down the *Key* and picked up his well-worn copy of the *Priest's Ritual*. He straightened his stole and asked, "Do I need a new stole? This one is getting ratty, don't you think?"

"Just a sec, 'afore we get started again," Dylan said and lit a joint. He puffed until it was going good and held it to Doug's lips. "Here, dude, this will help ease the shock when the demon comes out. Trust me."

The man gave Dylan a dubious look but took a drag nevertheless. He coughed and grimaced against the acrid taste of the pot. "Take one more, man, but that's it. It's strong shit." The man did as he was told and visibly relaxed as the THC hit his brain.

Dylan took another drag and held it out to Terry. The shorter man shook his head in refusal, as he nearly always did, and Dylan flipped the joint into the sink. "Let's do this thing," he said resolutely.

Terry wiped the sigil off Doug's chest and placed a crucifix there. He held a larger one in his hand in front of him as he faced the possessed man. He crossed himself and took up his *Ritual*. "Holy Lord! All powerful! Father! Eternal God! Father of our Lord Jesus Christ!" He read with a voice of forceful entreaty. "You who destined that recalcitrant and apostate tyrant to the fires of Hell; you who sent your only son into this world in order that he might crush this roaring lion: Look speedily, and snatch from damnation and from this devil this man who was created in your image and likeness. Throw your terror, Lord, over the Beast who is destroying what belongs to you. Give faith to your servants against this most evil Serpent, to fight most bravely. So that the Serpent not hold in contempt those who hope in you! Let your powerful strength force the Serpent to let go of your servant so that it no longer possesses him whom you designed to make in your image and to redeem by your son..."

The demon was not long in surfacing again. Before Terry had finished the first prayer, the damned spirit was thrashing with super-human strength against the ropes that held it.

"Second base, dude, in under ten seconds," Dylan noted. "Ah think that's a record." He was referring to the six stages of exorcism, which the friars typically referred to using baseball metaphors, partly because it was easy for them to do so and partly because it was confusing to the demons.

"Wouldn't have been so fast if we hadn't already gone over this ground earlier," Terry reasoned.

"Prolly true."

The lights started winking off and on, and the bed began to rattle and shake. Doug's body thrashed and pulled against its bonds and made the sound of an angry and caged animal.

"Unclean Spirit!" Terry intoned in his high, sweet tenor. "Who-ever you are, and all your companions who possess this servant of God, by the mysteries of the incarnation, the sufferings and death, the resurrection, and the ascension of our Lord Jesus Christ: By the sending of the Holy Spirit and by the coming of our Lord into last judgment, I command you to obey me in everything, although I am an unworthy servant of God. Do no damage to this possessed creature or to my assistant or to any of their goods."

"Damn straight, asshole, you are unworthy!" The demon fully surfaced into consciousness and spat at him. "You're a fake! You're not even a real priest! And you're"—the demon looked Terry over carefully, and cocked Doug's head—"you're *gay!*"

Utterly unperplexed, Terry and Dylan began to sing, cheerfully and in unison,

"NOT A PRIEST, *not a priest,*
    but Rome is quite explicit.
    All of us Old Cath-o-lics are
    valid but illicit!"

TERRY STRUCK a pose with one hand on his hip. "And prettier than you ever thought of being."

"*You,*" the demon screamed at Terry, "you have no right to judge me, or to cast me out! You are a sinner!"

"You'll get no argument from us on that," Dylan said confidently. "Ah'm a sinner and no mistake. But lucky for me, and unlucky for you, Ah don't cast you out by mah own authority, or mah own power. It's the power of Jesus you gonna have to worry about."

The demon looked confused. It had hoped to unsettle the priests, to shake their resolve, to overwhelm them with uncertainty. Yet despite its efforts, the exorcists seemed not only unperplexed, but they seemed to be...enjoying themselves. "I know you, Priest!" It tried again, upping the ante. "You suck the cocks of little boys!"

For the first time, Terry looked taken aback. "He was eighteen, I swear it," he said with a look of mock affront. Then he placed one index finger against his cheek and winked. "At least he *said* he was eighteen!"

Realizing that he was being mocked, the demon roared and bucked his hips against the bed, trying to gain some leverage against his restraints. With a loud "pop," every light bulb in the motel shattered. As the room sank into darkness, the Voice emerged. "WE WILL EAT YOUR SOULS IN HELL, FAKE PRIESTS. WE WILL SEE YOU THERE, AND WE WILL DEVOUR YOU."

"Third base," Dylan's voice emerged from the darkness. Then he clicked at his lighter, and as their eyes adjusted to the little flame, he began to sing a song from his childhood. "*This little light o' mine, Ah'm gonna let it shine...*"

Dylan kept singing as he lit a candle. Terry approached the possessed man and touched his forehead with his stole as he intoned, "I exorcise you, most unclean Spirit! Invading enemy! In the name of our Lord Jesus Christ: Be uprooted and expelled from this creature of God. He who commands you is he who ordered you to be thrown down from Heaven into the depths of Hell. He who commands you is he who dominated the sea, the wind, and the storms. Hear, therefore, and fear, Satan!"

The sound of frying and the smell of burning flesh filled the air as a burn mark appeared where the stole touched the man's head. The Voice howled its rage. As if it were hurling nothing more than a rag doll, Dylan was thrown off his feet, into the air, and was slammed backward into the wall. There he remained, pinned by an unseen force.

"Ah really hate this part!" he yelled above the howl of the Voice. "Next time, dude, can you throw Terry? Ah've got a bad back." The howl renewed its intensity, sounding like a cross between a thousand human screams and the wail of tortured animals.

Dylan pried himself free of the wall. Terry screwed his face up in a grimace of pain as the demon battered at his brain for entry. He felt Dylan place his hands on him—one on his shoulder, the other on his head—and he knew that his friend was praying for him with all his might.

Terry fought to clear his mind of all the images that the demon imposed upon him—rape and murder, decapitation, his own damnation, and other horrors too foul to dwell upon. Instead, the priest looked up, opened his spirit wide to Heaven, and spoke the words provided to him from an unseen and holy source, "I bind your power, Parrillon, most evil captain of demons, in the name of the Lamb most immaculate who walked unharmed among dangers, who was immune to all evil spirits. I bind you and banish you and all your minions from this room. I command you to bid your servant of corruption to depart from this person. Depart from the church of God. Fear, and take flight at the name of our Lord whom the powers of Hell fear, to whom the powers and virtues and dominions of Heaven are subject, whom the cherubim and seraphim praise with unceasing voices, saying: 'Holy! Holy! Holy! Lord God of Hosts!'"

Terry's shoulders deflated, and he waited. At the invocation of the demon's general, there should have been a final howl of rage, a rattle of bones, and the flight of the demonic presence. Instead, in the light of the flickering candle, Dylan saw only the unholy grin of pure, unbounded Evil. It was a malevolent smile, void of real cheer, but full of both contempt and victory. And then, with a Voice that shook their very souls, the demon began a chillingly childish song of its own.

"*I know something you don't know...*"

"That should have done the job, dude," Dylan said, a worried tone in his voice. "What just happened? Did ya *feel* that?"

Terry nodded. He felt as if someone had just pulled the plug on all the warmth in his body. He shuddered as the singsong Voice of the demon played with his head.

"Someone you love is dead tonight." The demon used Doug's face to screw into the most pained and fiercely perverse smile Terry had ever beheld. It was a smile of victory.

11

Bishop Preston swirled his scotch and looked out over the magic carpet of lights that was San Francisco by night. From his easy chair high in a Hyatt penthouse, the scene was alluring, mesmerizing.

Governor Ivory stepped up to stand beside him. "It's beautiful, isn't it?"

Preston nodded reluctantly. "Deceptively so," he said, taking a slug of the whisky. "Hiding behind that façade of beauty is blatant corruption. Make no mistake about it, this is the most sin-sick city in the world. Don't let the pretty covering fool you."

The governor harrumphed and rocked back and forth on his loafers. "That's why you and I get along so well, John. We both see right through the bullshit."

"Damn straight," the bishop agreed. "And we're not afraid to say so." He downed the rest of his drink and headed for the wet bar to pour another. "I'm glad this worked out—I'd been hoping to talk to you soon."

Ivory was in town in preparation for the Republican National Convention, starting in just a few days. The organizing committee, which he chaired, had chosen San Francisco in order to highlight its new "gay-friendly" positions, much to Ivory's own disgust and against his stern protests.

"So, let's get to the straight talk, then, shall we?" Preston said. He pulled the stopper out of a crystal decanter. The whisky glowed like gold in the light from the fireplace.

"Okay, but you first. You never told me you were going to be in the running for bishop of California."

Preston smiled, handing a fresh glass to Ivory. "Didn't know it myself. I was planning to stay only so long as necessary, until Cindy was better, or...not better." He swirled the whisky in his glass again and made his way around to the easy chair. He sat down with an audible sigh. "Not getting younger, that's for sure."

"So, what made you think, 'Hey, I think I might want to do this job'?" Ivory asked.

"David, this is a diocese on its way down the drain. It's run primarily by feminists and faggots. It needs a strong, uncompromising hand to save it. And I think God has called me to be that hand."

"If the diocese is being run by perverts, John, how in hell do you expect to get elected? It simply isn't going to happen."

"Well, we'll know tomorrow night, won't we?" Bishop Preston said with a twinkle in his eye. "I will emerge from the diocesan convention the bishop-elect." He held out his glass as if to make a toast. "You just watch." He took a slug.

Ivory lit a cigar and twirled it, standing near the window and considering his friend. "How can you possibly be so confident?" he asked.

"Let's just say I have found *the means*. God gave me the means, and not to use the means would be...well, it would be ungrateful." He grinned a large, victorious grin. "How about you, David? You haven't announced yet. When?"

The governor swayed back and forth, holding the cigar in his teeth. He took it from his mouth and curled his lip. "We are still considering," he said.

"Bullshit," the bishop laughed. "You'll run. The Republican Party can't survive the next election without you. You know it's true."

"I know it, and you know it," Ivory said, punctuating the air with his cigar. "But if *they* don't know it, it isn't going to do us a damned bit of good."

"The only one out there that can beat you right now is Ridgeway, and he's a train wreck on foreign policy."

Ivory nodded but stared into the fire.

"The way the Middle East is heating up right now, Ridgeway's conciliatory tone would be disastrous, and you know it."

"You're preaching to the choir, John," Ivory said. "What if I lose?"

"You can't lose," said the bishop.

Ivory frowned. "What do you mean, I can't lose? You saw how Obama trounced Romney."

"I am aware of that tragic result. You cannot lose, my friend, because I am supporting you."

"Okay, John, I think my kids call this a reality check. There was a time when the Episcopal Church held a lot of sway in this country. But that time has passed." He sat down in the chair adjacent to Preston's. "I'm grateful for your endorsement, John, but in the grand scheme of things, it isn't going to make a lot of difference to the outcome."

"But there's where you're wrong," said Preston, not seeming the slightest bit offended. Excitement danced in his bleary black eyes. "I tell you what, let's look at the diocesan election tomorrow as a test case, shall we? You're right: There's no way in hell the feminists and faggots are going to elect me their bishop. So, tomorrow at this time, when they *have*..." he patted his friend's hand. "You get ready to throw in your hat."

"There's no way I'll get the nomination this late in the game, John."

"Ah, but there's where you're wrong. You forget—I believe in miracles."

12

THE TEAKETTLE BEGAN ITS HOMEY, shrill song, and Brian got up to remove it from the stove. He filled two cups, plopped in tea bags, and carried both to the table where Susan sat with her hands folded. Brian noted the red patches on her knuckles where she had been picking at her skin. "Okay, Honey, spill it. What's with you?"

Susan looked surprised.

"Don't give me that," Brian said. "You were awfully short with Dylan earlier. It's not like you. What's going on?"

Susan pulled her teacup closer to her and flicked at the tea bag's paper tag. It spun, slowed, and began to spin the other way. "I'm worried about him. And pissed at him. He seems to have no self-control right now." She looked up at Brian, and he saw real worry in her eyes. They were a little wet, and a long crease stretched across her forehead. "He lights up before he even gets out of bed, and he's hardly without a joint in his hand. The only time he abstains is on Sunday before he says mass—and only because Bishop Tom told him he has to."

Brian nodded. "He's always been a pothead."

"But not like this."

"What do you think it is?"

"I think it's Richard." They both nodded at the truth of it. Susan continued, "Richard's a born leader. Despite his quirks and faults, any of us would follow him into Hell and back if he asked us. But Dylan's a follower. I think he's lost without Dicky to give him direction."

"That's not good for the rest of us if Dylan's supposed to be in charge."

"Don't I know it?" she said.

A powerful thudding came from the ceiling above them. Brian looked up. "Should we turn a hose on them?"

Susan smiled despite herself. "C'mon, Brian, it's nookie night! Just 'cause you and I aren't getting any doesn't mean they shouldn't. I'm *glad* someone's fucking like bunnies around here. It gives me hope."

"The relationship is young yet," Brian said. "You wait, six months from now, Mikael and Kat will be down here having tea with us."

"I certainly hope not." Susan pushed out her lower lip. "Not that I wouldn't want to share tea with them. Just that..."

"I know. We all want love to be eternal."

For several minutes, neither of them spoke. "Life is sad," Susan said at last.

The doorbell rang. Tobias roused himself from the couch in the living room and barked. "Who the fuck could that be?" Brian asked, swinging his leg over the broad bench.

Susan looked at the clock. "It's nearly eleven."

Brian trotted out of the kitchen toward the foyer. He pushed Tobias out of the way and looked through the peephole. A distorted, elongated face stared back at him. He debated whether to open the door. "Who is it?" he called, loud enough to be heard on the other side. Tobias barked again.

"My name is Charlie...although you'd probably know me as Charybdis. I'm a member of the Lodge of the Hawk and Serpent. I'm a friend of Richard's. Can I come in?"

Brian hesitated for a moment and then opened the door and stood aside, grabbing at Tobias's collar while Charlie stepped inside. He was about the same height as Brian, with wispy brown hair and an angular face. In Brian's experience, magickians were either emaciated or obese, with few representatives in between. And they all smelled like they hadn't bathed in a week. Charlie was no exception.

"Susan and I were just having a cup of tea. Would you like one?" Brian asked, taking the magickian's coat. Tobias's tail wagged fiercely, and he stuck his nose directly into the young man's crotch, relishing the pungent new smells.

"Sure," Charlie said, pushing the dog's nose away.

"Sorry about that," Brian said. "Magickians are cat people."

"Um...that's pretty much true," Charlie agreed as he followed Brian into the bright kitchen. He paused and gave a stiff little bow in Susan's direction. "I'm Charlie...my magickal name is Charybdis."

"Susan," she said, offering her hand. "I've heard all about you. Actually, the boys speak quite well of you."

Charlie smiled a pained smile. "I hope that's true. Is Richard here?"

Brian looked at Susan, and their eyes met. It was a sad exchange. "No, Charlie, I'm afraid not," Susan said.

"He had to find new accommodations," Brian added. "For reasons that are...well, complicated, he can't stay here right now."

"How about Dylan?" Charlie asked hopefully.

"Out fighting demons," Brian said, placing another steaming cup on the table. He pushed it toward Charlie. "So is Terry."

"And Mikael and Kat are...indisposed," Susan added. As if on cue, a headboard banged in the distance.

"Oh," Charlie said, a bit sheepishly, and blushing visibly. "We don't have that problem at the lodge."

"You mean no one gets laid?" Brian asked.

"Eh...right," Charlie nodded, blowing on his tea.

"What brings you out tonight?" Susan asked him. Brian noted that, far from being annoyed at the interruption, she seemed genuinely interested.

"I've been doing a lot of thinking, since"—Charlie put the cup back down—"you know, since the whole Dane thing." He was referring to the events of several months ago, when a local sociopathic tycoon had employed the Lodge of the Hawk and Serpent to carry out his plans to wipe all the children from the face of the Earth.

"Well, I should hope so," Brian said. "Talk about hitting for the wrong team."

"Brian," Susan warned, "please. No need to kick a man while he's down."

Charlie shot her a thankful glance. "Yes, well, that's a good description of how I've been since then. I keep thinking of what my mother would have said if she were alive and knew...well, knew what I'd done. Or helped to do. I'm quite ashamed, really." The young man looked ready to cry. Susan put her hand on his arm and gave it a reassuring squeeze.

"I don't want to get myself into that situation again," he said. "Larch is..." He trailed off. "Oh, he's not a bad guy. But he's *driven*. And he's persuasive. And I'm just not...well, I can't stand up to him. And I'm afraid..."

"There's nothing wrong with being afraid," Susan said.

"'Fear is the beginning of wisdom,'" Brian quoted. Susan scowled at him. "Okay, 'Fear *of the Lord* is the beginning of wisdom'—thank you, Miss Literal."

"Brian's right, though," she said, smiling at her friend. She turned her eyes back to Charlie. "You should trust that fear. It's telling you the truth."

Charlie nodded. "I know it. That's why I'm here."

"Say more," Susan said, sipping at her own tea.

"Well, I don't think I'm strong enough to resist Larch by myself. He is the leader of the lodge, and...well, I'm not." He blew over the tea but set it down again without tasting it. "I think my only choice is to leave. But if I do that, where do I go? The lodge has been my life since I was sixteen. I'm afraid I'd get sick or homesick or lonely or mugged or whatever and end up right back there. I need help."

Brian leaned back. "Oh my God," he breathed. "You want to join the Order of Saint Raphael."

"Yes," said Charlie. "Yes, I do. If you'll have me."

13

"HOLY SHIT, Ter, what is this fuck talkin' about?" Dylan asked in a near-whisper.

Terry crammed his stole onto the possessed man's forehead again. It emitted no hiss, and no burn resulted. "Fuck," Terry said. He felt confused, out of control.

"Okay, Ah think we need a time out." Dylan grabbed his friend by the sleeve of his surplice and steered him toward the door. He shot the possessed a glance over his shoulder and spoke to him as if he were a dog. "Stay! We'll be right back."

When they emerged from the motel room, it was as if they were entering another world—one where hope and beauty and traffic noise had a place. Sanity and order had a foothold here, in spite of the wino passed out on the sidewalk. Dylan steered Terry into one of the chairs in the parking space and then sank himself into the other. "Dude, you okay?"

"Who do we know that could sap our power like that?" Terry asked, still glassy-eyed. "He or she would have to be—what? Indisposed? Distracted?"

"Dead?" Dylan said the word Terry was avoiding.

Terry held his hands up to his face and flexed them, studying his palms. They had, only moments ago, been filled with energy. Now they felt tired, even arthritic. He felt old beyond his forty years. Something was gone. Something he knew the demon had no power to take away.

"It has to be Bishop Tom," Terry said sadly. "You know it. There isn't a single other person I can think of that could—throw the switch like that."

Dylan looked at his feet and nodded. "Yup," he admitted.

"Call Bishop Tom," Terry said. "Call him now."

Dylan whipped out his cell phone and speed dialed the Bishop's home. He hit the speakerphone button with his thumb. Gretchen answered with a musical "Hellooo..." and Terry could hear the mewing of cats near the phone.

"Gretch, hi, it's Dylan. Is Tom there?"

Dylan and Terry locked eyes as they waited. Terry willed himself to hope. For the sake of their friend, he *had* to hope.

"You just missed him, Honey. He is so fucking forgetful some-times. You know, I texted him a whole list of things to pick up from the grocery, and he got everything but tampons! Can you believe it? What am I supposed to do, shove paper towels up my twat? I swear, the man would forget his dick if it wasn't attached. How are you, Sweetie?"

Terry spoke up. "Gretch, Terry here. We're not doing so good. I want you to listen to me. I want you to call 911 and report..." What? What could have happened? A mugging? A heart attack? "Gretchen, we think something might have happened to Tom. I know this sounds crazy, but you need to call a cab, or get a neighbor to drive you, and go wherever Tom was going. Bring a cell phone if you have one. We're afraid you might need to call an ambulance." He stopped and listened for a minute. Terry could hear Gretchen getting hysteri-cal, but he couldn't make out her words.

"Gretchen?" Dylan said, trying to sooth her. "Gretchen, you've got to focus. We don't *know* if anythin' has happened. Don't panic. There's just somethin' we can't explain any other way, so we have to check it out. It's probably nothing. So...focus, Honey Pie. Do you have a cell phone? Your neighbor does? Good. Okay, well, can your neighbor go?" Dylan asked. A moment later, Gretchen was talking again. "Uh, okay, Gretch," Dylan said, "but call us if...if anything happened...We don't know, we just think it's *something*. Call us, please." He closed the phone. "Whatever happened, it *just* happened."

"He probably *is* dead, Dyl." Terry cradled his head in his hands and fought against the knowledge that was dawning on him. It won.

"If Tom is dead, Ter, then we're through here."

"If Tom is dead, we're out of business until we get another bishop." It sounded callous to say it like that, as if Tom could be so quickly replaced. He couldn't, of course.

"Okay, Terry, let's pull ourselves together. We'll have time to grieve for Tom tomorrow. Tonight, though, we got a naked man tied to a bed in a motel room, throwing feces like a bonobo and tossin' us around like kitchen rags." He squirted some holy water into the air and then tossed the plastic squirt gun onto the pavement. "So, what are we going to do about it?"

"I guess we untie him," Terry said in a daze.

"Are you nuts? That Doug guy is, like, really counting on us, not to mention his family, who have already made a very generous donation..."

"So, we return the money, we say we're very sorry, and we refer them out."

"Refer them out? To who? The Episcopalians? They'll send him to a Jungian analyst! The Romans? The Romans will send him back to us!"

"We could refer them to the Armenian Orthodox. Father Asmon has done a couple."

"Yeah, and almost got half a city block destroyed before we intervened. Ah don't think so, dude."

They sat there in stunned silence for what seemed like an eternity, feeling paralyzed. Just then Dylan's cell phone rang. Before he hit the Talk button, Dylan saw that it was from Susan. "Hi, Honey," he said, his voice betraying his despair.

"Oh, Honey, you sound wiped. Are you two still at it? Must be some demon." She sounded cheery, with a mild note of concern.

"Susan, Baby Doll, who all is home?"

"Baby, you okay? Uh…everyone's home except you guys—and we have a visitor. I'll tell you more, later, but it's not important now. What's wrong?"

"Call the others, and put us on speakerphone, will ya?"

Dylan heard shuffling as she walked to the back door and called out. "Brian! Kat! Mikael! Emergency call! Come quick!"

Terry heard a voice he recognized but couldn't place in the distance. "Should I duck out?"

"Who is that?" Terry whispered to Dylan. Dylan shrugged. "Sounds familiar." Dylan shrugged.

Terry heard the clack of toenails on the linoleum and knew that the excitement had summoned Tobias from his canine slumbers.

"What's up?" asked Brian's voice, coming from the tinny speaker.

"Can you merge Richard in on this?" Terry asked.

Dylan nodded. His fingers flew as he speed dialed Richard's number. In a moment, they heard his bleary voice.

"Fuck," Richard said.

"Richard, is that you?" Terry asked.

"I have a splitting headache," said Richard's voice. Dylan punched a final button, and they heard Tobias shake his coat.

"Uh…" Dylan started but couldn't continue.

"It's stopped working," Terry said.

"What's stopped working?" Susan asked. They heard Richard moan.

"The mojo," Terry said. "We can't cast him out."

"'This kind only comes out by fasting and prayer…'" Richard mumbled.

"No, it's not the method. We're not doing anything out of the ordinary…for us. It's like someone turned off the power. Like they yanked the extension cord right out of the wall. *Nothing is working,*" Terry clarified.

"Plus, the demon said someone was dead," Dylan added.

"What?" asked Susan's voice. "Who's dead?"

"There's only one person's death I can think of that would have this effect." Terry paused to give the notion time to sink in.

"Holy shit," came Richard's voice, clear for the first time. "Bishop Tom?"

"That's what we're afraid of," Terry admitted.

Just then, Dylan's phone buzzed. "Uh...it's Gretchen," he said.

"Can you patch her in?" asked Terry.

"Uh-uh," Dylan said. "Ah think Ah can only merge two calls."

"Put us on hold," Richard said.

Dylan did.

"Gretchen?" he asked.

A wail rose up from the phone's tiny speaker. She was keening in grief.

14

As soon as Richard was passed out drunk, Duunel slipped in between and summoned his master. Within a few moments, the mists cleared, and the demon prince Maaluchre glowered down upon him with the red eye of doom, his talons scratching with impatience.

"My master," Duunel said, falling on his face.

"Rise and report," the prince boomed.

"It appears that something has gone right, O Prince," Duunel said. "My host's conspirators were singularly unsuccessful last night."

"That is good news. Yes, I just got the report from Mugwort in Seattle. Seems a little black cat was in the wrong place at the wrong time. Terrible tragedy."

Duunel looked away so as not to see the skin pull back from his master's beak in a grotesque approximation of a smile. *Some things,* Duunel thought, *are too terrible for even demons to behold.*

"Your plan was creative and efficient. Our Father will be pleased."

Duunel shook to his core. "You'll be reporting this to the Father *himself?*"

"It is not inappropriate for you to know this, as our plans are unfolding rapidly. We have a major event planned in the next few days in the City of the Cursed Saint. The fact that you have rendered our only opposition in this area helpless will not go unnoticed, or unrewarded."

"I am honored, my prince. And I am proud to have helped—even in my ignorance."

"Don't overdo it, snail." The red eye loomed and flared. "You know as well as I that all modesty is false, and you are a fool to think that I am easily played."

"Sorry, Master." Duunel tried to appear sufficiently cowed. "May I ask, my lord, what our Father has planned during this window of opportunity? After all, the friars are only out of commission temporarily."

"Well, let's just say our influence is about to spread exponentially," said the demon prince, stretching his beak again with his terrible attempt at a smile. "By this time tomorrow, every demon in Hell will be turned out onto the streets, looking for hosts."

"This calls for party hats," Duunel grinned.

SATURDAY

15

WITH AN ACHING HEAD and a stomach churning with nausea, Richard trudged up the hill on Cedar Street toward All Saints' Episcopal Church. Along the way, a motorcycle sped by. As he watched it pass, memories of Bishop Tom flooded through him.

Do you need a moment? Duunel asked.

"Fuck you," Richard said, starting up the hill again.

I've heard you'll boink anything that moves, Duunel teased.

Richard ignored him, and feeling a splash of moisture on his nose, he stopped and relished the cool wind on his face. He loved this time of morning—when the sun had just come up and the air was still charged with chill—although he rarely managed to see it these days. He pondered this when a voice in his head said, *It's the alcohol. You sleep until noon most days. That's because you suck.*

Richard sighed. "Can you please just go back to sleep?"

What? And miss your Rocky Mountain High? And who says I was sleeping?

"Fuck off. What did you think of the duck last night?" Richard was hoping to deflect his attention toward—well, anything that wasn't designed to wear down his self-esteem.

Nice try. You're an asshole, the demon responded. Then, a moment later, *I thought it was greasy.*

"What do you want? It's duck!"

The sauce was nice. And the wine. You should have had another bottle.

"Uh-huh," Richard said. He reached for the handle of the door leading off the parking lot and swung it open. The halls were dark, but he knew the way well. In moments, he was sitting outside Mother Maggie's office.

I don't like this place, Duunel said. *It gives me the fucking creeps.*

"Of course it does," Richard agreed. "It's a church. Good things happen here. You wouldn't like it."

Mother Maggie waddled into view, closing the door of the restroom behind her. Her squat, round frame was twisted by arthritis, but her spirit was unbowed. "Good morning, Dicky," she said, bending down slightly to where he sat and placing a kiss on his cheek. And then, slightly louder, "And good morning to you, too, Duunel, you cheeky little prick."

"You don't need to shout, Mags," Richard said. "If I can hear you, he can hear you."

"Quite right," she said, nodding vigorously. "Come in, both of you. Take a bonbon—everyone needs a wake-up chocolate, I say. And you should take two, of course."

"I'll pass," Richard said. "I'm afraid I'll hurl."

"Yes, but *he* wants one," she sang, "don't you, Duunel?"

I don't trust her, Duunel said in his head. *I don't trust her for a second.*

"I'd trust that impulse if I were you," Richard said.

Maggie ignored him.

"I was talking to Duunel," Richard explained.

"So I supposed," Maggie said, planting herself in her regular chair. Her dog, JoJo, raised her head to see what the fuss was, noticed it was only Richard, and put her head down again. In mere moments, she was snoring. "Let's take a moment to come into the presence of the Holy, shall we?" Maggie said as she lit a candle on the small table beside her.

Let's get out of here, pronto. Shall we? Duunel said forcefully.

Richard ignored him and relaxed his body. "*Veni Sancte Spiritus,*" he prayed, "Come, Holy Spirit..."

Not going there with you, Duunel said. *I know I said I wouldn't allow cocksucking activities, but given the choice...*

"Veni Sancte Spiritus..." Richard began to sing. Mother Maggie joined him. Together, their voices blended in the early morning air, until an unseen Presence surrounded them and held them.

Okay, that's it. Shit, I'm outta here. See you in—how long does this spiritual direction silliness actually last?

"See you in an hour, Duunel," Richard smiled at Maggie. She winked at him.

With Duunel either absent or dormant—Richard couldn't tell which—he was able to sink deeper into prayer. After about five minutes of rich, delicious silence, he opened his eyes and saw Maggie smile. It looked like a forced, pained smile, but he put it aside for the moment.

"Tom's dead," he said simply.

Her face fell. "Oh my God," she breathed. "You don't mean it?"

He nodded gravely. "Last night. Motorcycle accident. Killed instantly. That's what Gretchen said, anyway."

"Oh my God," she repeated. "Oh, Dicky, I'm so, so sorry."

"I know you met him once—"

"At dinner at the friary. He's...He was a lovely man."

"Yes, yes, he was," Richard agreed. He felt tears begin to burn at his eyes, but he forced them down.

"Are you doing a Requiem Mass for him? I'd like to come."

"Thank you, but we can't have a mass. We'll have a memorial service, but that's all."

She cocked her head, thinking this through, and suddenly her eyes got round. "Oh my dear. You can't have a mass because *you have lost your bishop...*" The implications came rushing in on her. Her mouth gaped open. "Oh my, Dicky, that means...if you go to fight a demon..."

"We're powerless, yes," Richard nodded. "We discovered that last night, much to our horror, and to the extreme discomfort of a man who should have been delivered of a demon today—but isn't."

"And you can't say mass, and you can't hear confessions, and you can't...Well, you can't do any of the sacraments."

"We're unplugged," Richard agreed.

"God help you," Maggie breathed.

"I don't see how he can." Richard shifted uncomfortably. "God gave us this structure—the church—a line of authority, a conduit of power, and it's broken. It was a gift, and now it's gone. 'The Lord giveth, and the Lord taketh away.'"

"Unless..." Maggie held up one gnarled finger.

"Right. Unless we put ourselves under the authority of another bishop."

Maggie's face fell. "Oh my dear. That is the last thing you need to be thinking about as you grieve for your friend."

"I know it. I just have to...compartmentalize. Actually, I'm doing a lot of that these days, what with Duunel in residence."

"How is *that* going?"

"He's the biggest pain in the ass imaginable. It's like having a hyper-destructive roommate handcuffed to you at all times."

"I can only imagine." Maggie nodded thoughtfully.

"So, there are two things before me—dealing with my feelings about Tom..."

"Not easy to do with a demon in your head making fun of you for loving people, I'm sure," Maggie said compassionately.

"True," agreed Richard. "And second, I need to find a new bishop."

"I wish you could find two," Maggie mumbled, looking at her gnarled hands.

"What was that?" Richard asked.

Maggie smiled. "Oh nothing. Let's start with Tom, shall we?"

They sat in silence for a few minutes. Finally, Richard said, "I don't know where to begin."

"Well," said Maggie, "I'm here, you're here, and Jesus is here. Surely, there's something that needs to be said."

Richard nodded his head. "It's so unfair."

"That's my boy!" Maggie slapped at his knee. "Tell us what's unfair."

"We do crazy, dangerous things all the time—the order, I mean. We go to fucking battle with demons, for Chrissake. We do it all the time. If one of us got killed, it would be sad, but it wouldn't be tragic."

"Why not?"

"Because we went into this knowing the risks, and we are all ready to die for something. We took up our cross; we followed Jesus. And if we die like Jesus, too, in order to help someone, well...it's not okay, but it's okay. It's fair. It's what we're called to do."

Maggie nodded, her face looking like a dried apple in the glow of the candle.

"But Tom...he was an accountant. The most dangerous thing he ever *did* was ride a motorcycle. There was no *meaning* in his death. He was going to the *store*. He didn't die *for* anything. He just *died*..." Richard's throat clotted up, and tears began to come.

"What do you need to say to Jesus?" Maggie asked.

Richard felt lost. He snatched a tissue from the box beside him and blew his nose. "I don't know. I haven't been able to pray."

"Why don't I pray for you, then?"

Richard nodded and bowed his head. Maggie stretched out her gnarled hands to Heaven and cried out with a clear voice, "Jesus, you son of a bitch! What were you thinking? Have you no heart? What did this poor man Tom ever do to you? He loved you! He lived for you! He was faithful to you! He gave friendship and love and support to Richard and his friends—your servants, your people, these folks who are supposed to be close to your heart! Don't you care? Are you powerless to save? What kind of God are you? If you don't save the ones who actually live for you and love you, they'll say, 'He's a *weak* god!' If you don't care, they'll say, 'He's a *heartless* god!' Don't trouble yourself on our account, Jesus, oh no, I'm sure you have *better* things to do—but how about your own? This kind of thing looks very bad, and I'm tired of trying to spin it for you. From now on: not my job. Do you hear? Not my fucking job!" Maggie's features, contorted with passion, softened again. "Thank you, Jesus, for hearing us and loving us even though it sometimes seems as if you don't give a fig. In your own sweet name we pray. Amen."

Richard was riveted. "If I were God, I'd be scared shitless of you."

She smiled and laid a twisted hand on his knee. "*Someone* has to keep him honest."

16

KAT SAW children playing and walked toward them. An ostrich crossed her path, causing her to look around. She seemed to be in a park, and she noticed that there were other large animals milling about with the people. In the distance, she saw the spire of a church and the dome of what might have been a mosque or maybe an Orthodox Christian church—she couldn't tell.

Just then, the ostrich ran straight up to her and looked directly in her eyes. "You're not saying," the ostrich said, and behind it an enormous ball of fire descended from the sky, enveloping the sacred buildings in the distance. She never heard an explosion, but the wind roared and tore at her clothes, whipping at her hair. A tarp blew into her, covering her face, and she fought to get it off.

When she woke, her top sheet was wadded around her upper torso, restricting her arms' movement. "Shit," she said to the ceiling. "Dream."

She sat up and looked out the window. The early morning sun was warm on her skin. Despite the dreadful panic of her dream, everything here seemed bright, clean, and good. She struggled to recall as much of it as she could, but the images were fading quickly. She remembered the ostrich. And the fireball. She shuddered. She breathed deep and tried to let it go. Then she got up and stumbled to the bathroom.

After a quick shower, the dream was mostly forgotten, and she felt much better—human, even. She shook out the wadded sheet and started to make the bed. Yesterday's concerns began to light upon her mind like crows on a high-tension wire.

"Jesus, I'm a little worried about Richard," she said, tossing one of the pillows aside.

Six months ago, she realized, she would have felt stupid praying like that—hell, she would have felt weird praying at all. But a lot had changed since that time, and rather quickly. She found herself praying a lot now. Not long after she had been baptized and petitioned to join the Order of Saint Raphael, Mikael had suggested she read a little book called *The Practice of the Presence of God* by Brother Lawrence.

She had been instantly enchanted by the medieval monk's friendly style, but even more so by the method of prayer he pioneered. She described it as "housework with Jesus." Just as Brother Lawrence had talked to Jesus while he did the monastery dishes, Kat began talking to Jesus—out loud—while she folded laundry, mowed the lawn, or did any of the other mindless chores that everyone pitched in with at the friary.

Sure, she had felt self-conscious at first, afraid that someone would hear her. Then one day Dylan walked by while she was ranting at Jesus about something she didn't even remember, and she had stopped short, blushing. Dylan had only nodded. "Brother Lawrence," he grunted and continued on down the stairs. She had sighed, and relaxed. It wasn't at that moment that she truly realized she was among friends, but it was certainly an affirmation.

"And the whole Bishop Tom thing. That was terrible. I didn't know him, but..." she trailed off. "You know, I'm just getting started here. It wouldn't be fair if everything just...crumbled now because of some stupid bishops-thingy." She stopped and stood upright. "Why do we need bishops?" Jesus didn't say. She made a mental note to ask Susan about that next time they took a tea break together.

Or she'd ask Brian. Since neither of them were Catholic, she valued both Susan and Brian. Their perspectives on the sometimes labyrinthine nature of the Catholic faith were invaluable to her as they were both respectful and no-nonsense at the same time.

"Anyway, Jesus, I don't want to stop now, not now—I just found these people. I just found Mikael. I just found you..." She stopped making the bed for a moment and stared out the window. "I don't suppose I'd lose you no matter what, though, right? I mean, that's what the baptism was for. Together forever, right?"

And in the silence, she heard a still, small voice. "Kat! Heeeeeey, *bitch*!"

Kat bolted upright. "Jesus?" she asked. The old Jesus—the Jesus she thought she knew about before she met the order would never call anyone "bitch." But now that she was coming to know Jesus as the order understood him, she wasn't so sure.

"No, not Jesus, you idiot! Over here!"

Kat could barely make out the words. In fact, she wasn't at all sure she was even hearing them. They were just barely on the edge of her awareness. She could be making it all up. She could be going a little crazy. It could be Jesus. And all of a sudden, she wasn't sure she'd be able to tell the difference between any of those things.

"Who's talking? Am I imagining this? Say something again!"

"I want a hamburger so bad I would sodomize Ronald McDonald to get one," said the voice.

"Where are you? *Who* are you?" The voice was a little louder this time and sounded vaguely familiar.

"The new mirror!" the voice shouted. "Come closer to the new mirror."

Kat had been moving in a cold direction, obviously. The mirror that Brian had found in the yard was about three paces from her. She nearly jumped to it and examined the frame. Rustic wood surrounded the mirror, and in it she saw the room reflected with tiny waves of distortion. And that's when she noticed him, sitting on the bed, waving his arms.

Her brother, Randy.

Kat gasped and turned around to look at the bed. It was empty. She spun again and looked at the mirror. Again, she saw Randy sitting on the bed. He waved at her like Queen Elizabeth. "Hi, Sis," he said.

"Randy..." Kat breathed, not comprehending. "What the fuck?"

"It's good to see you," he said, flashing her his old, goofy smile. The last time Kat had seen him conscious and cheery like this was before his attempt to destroy the archetypal avocado through demonic magick. "Of course, it's even better seeing you with your clothes on."

"What?" she mouthed. He pointed behind her to the bed, she turned and looked at it, and then turned back, her eyes wide. She and Mikael had made love last night...with the newly found mirror hanging in its current place.

"I never. Ever. Want to see anything like that again as long as I live," Randy said with undisguised and unfeigned revulsion. He shuddered. "I kept thinking, 'Someone, please, stab out my eyes with an ice pick!'"

"You could have shut your eyes!" Kat said, feeling herself getting angry. She was red as a beet, and fighting back waves of shame.

"Yeah, I hid in the closet there," Randy pointed to the reflection of the closet door in the mirror. "But that didn't stop the noise." He banged against the wall with his fist and made rhythmic grunting sounds punctuated by animal shrieks. It sounded disturbingly like their lovemaking. Kat had no doubt that Randy had experienced just what he said he had. She felt faint, so she backed up and sat on the bed.

Unfortunately, she was now too far from the mirror to hear him well. So after a few moments, she stood, somewhat shakily, and approached the mirror again. "I'm sorry, Randy, I had no idea. I thought we were alone."

"Don't sweat it. But I am curious. Do you always shriek the Portuguese word for bunny rabbit when you come?"

"I swear to God, I'll smash that fucking mirror," Kat said.

"Does Jesus know you pray with that potty mouth?" he asked. He leaned in closer, a worried look on his face. "Aaaaand, what is up with the Jesus stuff, anyway? You never used to talk to Jesus. You're a witch, aren't you?"

"Yeah, I am," she said. "So is Mikael."

"And who the fuck is this Mikael?"

"Oh, it's a long story," Kat sighed. "The most interesting thing is, though, that it's all your fault."

"I doubt that," he said, looking affronted.

"Believe it," she said firmly.

"Okay, what happened?"

"As I said, it's a loooong story," she repeated.

"Do I look like I'm going anywhere?"

Kat moved the mirror onto the bed and sat down. When she looked for her brother, she found him clinging to the ceiling with a terrified look on his face. She looked up and realized that, lying where it was, the mirror could only reflect the ceiling, and therefore the ceiling was the only place Randy could be. "That looks uncomfortable," she said.

"Do you think?" Randy asked shrilly.

She propped the mirror up against the headboard, and—at least in the reflection—found herself sitting on the bed with her brother. "Well, it started when I got to your house and found you passed out on the floor..." she began.

17

"THAT'S ABOUT OUR TIME," said Mother Maggie, looking at the clock. She smiled at him. "Shall we set a time for our next meeting?"

Richard flipped out his iPhone, and they agreed upon a date. Richard gave her a hug and turned to leave, but she caught at his sleeve. "Richard, dear, are you...in a hurry?"

Richard noted the hesitation in her voice. "I have a lot to do today, but none of it is tied to the clock. What's up?" He sat back down and faced her with concern.

"You're not the only one with bishop problems," she said cryptically.

"What do you mean?" Richard said. "Wait...the Episcopal Diocese of California is having its diocesan convention now, isn't it? Aren't you voting on a new bishop?"

She nodded. "That's the trouble. We did three ballots last night, and I expect the final one will be today sometime. I'm on my way over as soon as we're done." She lowered her voice apologetically. "It's why we had to meet so blasted early this morning."

"I didn't mind," he assured her, although his visible hangover and bed hair told a different story. "Who's winning?"

"That's what scares me," she said. "We had three candidates for bishop, and we've done all the vetting and interviews, and any of them, I think, would have been excellent."

"So, what happened?" Richard asked.

"There was a nomination from the floor—from Reverend Felicia Dunne, over at Saint James's."

"That's up in the Berkeley Hills—a pretty conservative congregation, right?"

"That's the one," Maggie agreed. "I know Felicia. I know her partner. Which is why I don't understand why...how she could possibly have nominated this man."

"What man?"

"A retired bishop by the name of John Preston," she said, spitting out the name like poison. "He literally came out of nowhere. No one has done any interviews, no one had ever even mentioned him as a possibility until yesterday, when Felicia raised his name as a tie-breaker."

"Where does the vote stand now?"

"Three votes shy of the needed two-thirds majority," she said tensely.

"In favor of...?"

"Preston," she said the name like it was a curse.

"So, tell me about Preston," Richard said, pulling out his iPhone to take notes. His thumbs flew over the virtual keyboard as she spoke.

"Before he stepped down as bishop of South Carolina, he encouraged most of his churches to continue using the 1928 prayer book. He never did ordain a woman even though there were plenty of eligible candidates in his diocese. He's a homophobic, xenophobic misogynist, and he's just plain cruel besides."

"He certainly doesn't sound like a good fit for the Diocese of California." Richard looked up from his keyboard with a frown.

"That's putting it mildly," she said. "I've heard he actually advocates the death penalty for gays and lesbians—privately, of course. Make no mistake, Richard, if this man wins, the most conservative bishop in the Episcopal Church will become bishop of the most liberal diocese. It will be open war on everything we stand for."

Richard stared at her, his mouth open. "So how could he possibly be winning?" he asked.

"That's what I don't know. I'm hoping everyone comes to their senses this afternoon. But if they don't...I might be asking for your help."

"Do you suspect demonic activity? At a diocesan convention? That seems unlikely." Richard furrowed his brow.

"I don't know. I have no idea. I literally have no explanation for this." Mother Maggie leaned back, and Richard could see just how concerned she was. "Let's just pray we won't need to look into it further."

18

KAT ENTERED the kitchen in the midst of typical breakfast activity. She had missed morning prayer due to her unexpected conversation with her brother, but no one seemed to be scowling at her. Dylan padded in and took his place at the table, next to Susan, already blowing on her tea.

The phone rang, its sound loud and jarring even from down the hall. "Damn!" said Susan. "That's the third time it's rung this morning!"

"What's going on?" Dylan asked her.

"Hell if I know," Susan said. "We just got a referral from the Roman Catholic Archdiocese of San Francisco, and another call from the Swedenborgian Church in El Cerrito. I'm afraid to listen to the voice mail on this one."

Mikael smiled at Kat from the doorway to the foyer, where he was leaning—sexily, she noted. Brian was shouting orders to no one in particular, and Tobias was already begging. Terry breezed past Kat, "Hey, are you okay?" he said to her. "It's not like you to miss prayer."

"Um...yeah. I have something to show you," she said. In her right hand she gripped the rustic frame of the mirror. Carefully, she set it on a chair and removed a random picture from its nail. Then she hung the mirror in its place.

Brian stopped mid-shout, spatula in hand, his eyebrows akimbo. "I think that looks better up in the bedroom where I put it."

"I agree," Kat said. "It doesn't go here. I just wanted you to see it."

"Uh...that thar's a very nice mirror," Dylan pointed at it with his knife, which was dripping butter. "Where'd it come from?"

"I found it in the yard," Brian said.

"In the yard?" Terry asked suspiciously.

"Leaning against the side of the house," Brian finished.

"Anyway, we can't hang it in the bedroom anymore," Kat said, unsure about how to broach the subject.

"Why not?" asked Mikael. "It's a handsome enough mirror."

"Because I don't want my brother watching us every time we have sex."

It was like someone had yelled "freeze!" in a childhood game. No one spoke. No one moved. Everyone just stared at her. Kat shifted uncomfortably. "You remember my brother, Randy?"

"Idiot magickian," Terry answered, "Comatose. Not fond of avocados, as I recall."

"That's him," Kat nodded. "Except that he's not comatose. Anymore." She pointed at the mirror, looking vaguely like a prophet of doom in a Greek tragedy.

Nobody moved. The phone rang. Susan rolled her eyes. "Make it stop!"

"Ah don't get it," Dylan said to no one in particular. "Why is Kat pointing at the mirror?" He eyed Kat suspiciously. "Is this a test? 'Cuz Ah suck at tests."

"No, just look closely at the fucking mirror!" Kat said, on the verge of losing her patience.

Terry was the first to approach it. He leaned in and squinted slightly, then jerked back suddenly. Kat saw her brother waving at Terry—at all of them.

"Hey, it's the Addams family!" Randy called, his voice barely audible.

Terry leaned in again. "Randall fucking Webber," he breathed. "Alive and kicking. Sort of." He shot a look at Dylan, then at Brian. "He seems to be trapped in the mirror."

One by one, the others got up and peered closely at the mirror. Randall met each of them with a grin and a wave.

"How is that possible?" asked Susan, resuming her place.

Terry rubbed at his chin, still not able to take his eyes off Randall. Brian turned back to the bacon, apparently just in time to save it. "Sorry," he called, "bacon's a little crispy. I got distracted."

"Ah'll say..." said Dylan, throwing his leg over the bench again, back in his place. "Can we eat yet? Did anyone say grace?"

"Grace," said Terry, waving at Dylan. "Eat. Eat. We gotta figure this out."

"The Lord don't need to do nuthin' to make me grateful for what Ah am about to receive," Dylan said, and tucked into his eggs.

Terry speed dialed Richard and hit the speakerphone button. "Richard here," came the familiar voice.

Terry spoke quickly and efficiently, bringing Richard up to speed. Richard whistled. "Okay, so it sounds like Randall's spirit is trapped in the glass," he said. "That's why people used to cover mirrors whenever someone died, to keep that from happening."

"I think I know what happened," Brian said, leaning on the table and speaking up so Richard could hear. "We sent the angel's spirit back to Heaven in that mirror, remember? When it transferred to its old body, Randall's spirit must have traded places with it."

"Huh...I guess that frame does look familiar. So, who brought the mirror back?" Terry asked, still puzzled.

Tobias barked.

"Has he been fed?" Susan asked.

Brian nodded. "He has. I...huh..." Brian paused and considered. "Okay, this might not seem relevant, but hear me out. I've been meaning to tell you all this, but every time I've tried I got interrupted. Tobias has been acting...strangely lately. Not sick, just...weirdly clever."

Tobias barked and nosed at the back door. Brian pointed at the door with the spatula. "Don't ignore him. Go watch him. Tobias, go to the backyard."

"The screen door is shut," Dylan said.

"Just watch," Brian said.

"Hey, idiots!" called Randall from the mirror. "What, do you guys have the attention span of gnats or what? Don't you think this is odd? Aren't you going to help me?"

But no one heard him. Their attention was riveted on Tobias, who went up on his back legs, felt at the door handle with his paws, and fell forward as the door swung open.

"Well, Ah'll be..." Dylan breathed.

Mikael picked up the cell phone on his way to the door and briefly described to Richard what had just happened.

Once outside, Tobias ran to where the angel's body lay, barely depressing the grass beneath it. The yellow lab circled the body and barked.

"He did that yesterday, too," Brian said.

Kat watched as Terry approached the spot where Tobias circled and held out his hand as if feeling for energy signals—which, she realized, was probably exactly what he was doing.

"What do you see, Terry?" asked Susan. Of all of them, Terry was the most sensitive to spiritual phenomena, often able to see and interpret auras. That had made Kat nervous at first, until she realized it wasn't some kind of supernatural lie detector talent.

"There's a shimmering field here." He traced an outline around the grass. Terry stepped back and tried to see it from different angles. Finally, he knelt down and extended his hand to the grass. "*That* tingles," he said.

"What is it, dude?" Dylan asked, still munching on a handful of bacon clutched to his chest.

"Dylan!" Susan slapped at his sleeve. "Now you've got to change your cassock. I swear to God."

"Well, I could be wrong...but I don't think I am," Terry said. "I think what we've got here is a rotting angel corpse. It's almost gone, in fact."

"Wait, what?" Kat asked. "Can angels *have* corpses?"

"Well, what would you call an angel's body when it dies?" Terry asked.

"I..." she was momentarily flummoxed. "I guess I didn't think that angels *died*. Don't they have eternal life?"

"Nope," Terry said, getting up and wiping his hands on his jeans. "Just very, very long lifespans. Unless they get sick or are struck down."

"What happened to him?" Kat asked.

Terry shook his head, "Can't say."

"So how do you explain Tobias's behavior?" Richard's voice called from the iPhone's speaker.

Terry watched the dog and narrowed his eyes. A look of shock came over his face. He knelt down again. "Toby, come." The dog trotted up to him and licked his face. Terry looked into his eyes and felt at his head. Finally, he stood up.

"Okay, don't freak out..." he said.

"Ah am not freakin'," Dylan said. "But go ahead and say somethin' trippy."

"Wait, let me try something first." Terry faced the dog again. "Toby, *noromi ol vonpho a-ai-om*?"

Instantly, Tobias lay down, silent.

"Toby," Terry called again, "*noromi oiad a-ai-om*?"

At this Tobias leaped up and began barking excitedly.

"What did you just say, dude?" Dylan asked.

"Well, first I asked him if a demon was in our midst." Terry shrugged. "I think the lying down and playing dead was a no."

"That's how I'd read it," said Brian, hands on his hips.

"Next, I asked if an angel were among us, and he...Well, you saw him. I'd say that was a yes."

"Wait, are you suggesting that Toby can answer yes-and-no questions?"

"Well, he can if you speak Enochian."

"Let's try English," Mikael said. "Toby, do you want a bath?"

Tobias looked at Mikael but only cocked his head.

"Here's what I think," Terry said, starting to make his way back to the house. "I think an angel brought the mirror back to us—probably because it contains Randy's spirit. It was an act of mercy, of kindness. But before the angel could return, it died." He stopped and looked back toward where the angel's body was slowly fading out. "Or he was struck down." A dark look crossed his face. "Maybe he disobeyed orders in bringing Randy back to us. Justice is swift for angels."

"And Toby?" Kat asked.

"I think the angel knew that his body was dying, and he decided to possess the most complex living creature around at the moment."

"Mah Toby," said Dylan with wonder in his voice.

19

LARCH BREATHED deep of the incense, waving it over his body as part of his purification ritual. He felt like a high school kid with a first crush. Pim filled his every thought. He knew he was obsessed; he just didn't know what to do about it. Well, if he were honest, he did know a couple of things he could try, but the truth was, he didn't want the feelings to go away or to diminish in any way. She thrilled him, and he hungered for her like he had hungered for no human woman. Not ever.

His hands shook as he removed the velvet cloth and settled into his meditative pose. His eyes unfocused, he gazed into the viewing stone and waited for the images to take shape. "Pim, come to me," he called. His hands were shaking and they radiated cold.

He caught a glimpse of her gauzy shift, and he saw her ankle flash by. An ear. *She's playing with me*, he thought. Giggling, she finally emerged into full view. The slit in her dress tormented him. He would have traded his soul for her to be flesh. The danger, he knew, was that she was probably aware of that. *What is her real form?* The thought was fleeting, and he pushed it away forcefully.

"Pim, it's so good to see you," he gushed.

"Hi there, handsome," she winked at him.

"I did what you asked me to do," he said. "I said an octave of invocations to the twenty-four guardians. It was supposed to open the gates. Did they open?"

"What do you think, Sweetie?"

"*I think* I did everything right."

"You did everything just *perfectly*." She blew him a kiss.

"Did it please you?"

"Oh, poop, it isn't me you have to please, silly," she waved him away. "Let's just say the guardians were pleased, and when you please them, it's *always* good for me."

Larch thought he was about to cry. He would do *anything* to please her—anything to make her grateful to him. He wanted her to feel about him the way he felt about her. Desperate. *Is that even possible?* he wondered.

"And now I suppose you want something from me?" She looked down and twisted one leg fetchingly. "A little *knowledge*, perhaps?"

"Um...I'm just happy to have pleased you. But well, sure, if you have some knowledge you'd like to give me." *What am I, a pimply teenager?* he scolded himself. *Could you possibly be any more uncool?* The truth was, he wanted to use her in two very *different* ways—ways that were in conflict with each other.

"I spy with my little eye," she said, "that one of your birds has just flown the nest."

"What does that mean?" he asked, his brow furrowing. But she just winked, and that was all.

20

CHARLIE—THE magickian formerly known as Charybdis—knocked on the door of the friary, his bags piled on the porch next to him. He turned to watch as the cab driver pulled away, no doubt still grumbling at the lack of a tip.

No one answered. He knocked again. Still no answer. He walked to the large picture window and, shielding his eyes, peered inside. He saw the living room, and the chapel in the distance, but no living soul was stirring.

Hesitantly, he tried the front door. It opened with a soft "click," and the heavy door swung open easily. He shrugged as he started to move his bags into the foyer. "I *guess* I can come in," he said to himself. "I live here now, after all."

Intuitively, he gravitated toward the kitchen, the main hub of activity in most houses. No one was there. Food was laid out, and places were set. It looked as if an entire household of people had been raptured in the middle of breakfast.

Not sure what to do, Charlie sat with his back to the wall and just waited.

"Charybdis?" said a tiny voice near his ear.

He turned his head but saw nothing.

"Charybdis...Charlie, it's me. Randy."

Charlie's head spun, trying to discover the source of the voice. Finally, he caught motion in the mirror. Randy was there waving at him, standing by the stove. He turned and looked at the stove, but Randy was not there.

He looked back to the mirror. "Randy?"

"I am, it seems, only in the mirror," Randy smiled at him, but it was a pained smile. "I didn't expect to see you here. Actually, I didn't expect to see a lot of things I've seen since I got back. But what are *you* doing here?"

"Why are you in that mirror?"

"Um...I don't really know. I think it's this or death. So, while I'm not happy about it, I think I prefer *this*."

Charlie nodded, not really understanding, but understanding enough to agree.

"And you?" Randy asked. "My sister has apparently fallen in with a bunch of Jesus freaks who are turning her brain to mush. I'm really not happy about it. So why are *you* here?"

"I'm moving in. I'm...I left the lodge."

Randy looked shocked. "Larch must be furious."

"He will be when he finds out."

"But why are you moving in *here*?"

"I'm going to join their order."

"What? Are you fucking crazy?" Randy put his hands on his hips, looking angry. "Have these people put a spell on you and Kat? Are they magickians or witches?"

"I think that's a complicated question when it comes to them," Charlie said. "But no, I don't think they've put any kind of a spell on us. In fact, I'm sure of it."

"So, what are you and Kat *doing* here?"

"Um...I can't speak for your sister, but my guess is that this is the only place in the world where she feels safe right now. I know that's why I'm here."

"Safe?"

"Oh, Randy, you have no idea what we went through after you... well, you went to Heaven, I guess. How was that, anyway?"

Randy rolled his eyes. "Oh my God, it was unbearable. Very uncomfortable. I have to say, I'm bummed to be stuck in a mirror, but I'll take that to being in Heaven any day."

"Was it Heaven that was so uncomfortable, or the fact that you were in a body that you...well, that you weren't made for?"

Randy thought about that, but he didn't have time to answer before the back door slammed open and Tobias rushed in, the housemates immediately behind him.

"Charlie!" Susan called and gave him a hug. He stiffened, not used to affection. "Are you here for breakfast?"

"I'm here." He didn't know what to say. "I'm here." He left it at that.

"Well, if you're here, you're eating," Brian said and put a fresh plate in front of him.

"Okay, so I've got a question," Kat said. "If the angel is inhabiting Toby's body, why is he happy and active? When that other angel was inhabiting Randy's body, he could barely move for days."

"What? Who was inhabiting my body?" called Randy from the mirror, but only Charlie heard him.

"The situation is different," Terry explained. "Toby is still in there; the angel is residing as a guest. Hanging back and watching most of the time, I'll wager. I mean, Toby is still really excited about kibble and belly rubs, which, I would imagine, the angel would not be."

"It's kind of like my situation with Duunel," Richard's voice emitted from the speakerphone.

"Right," said Terry. "So, it's the angel that knows how to work the door handle and understands Enochian. But it's Toby that wants to sniff your crotch."

"I don't know," objected Brian, goosing Terry's butt. "We know very little about angel fetishes."

"That sounds like a great fantasy for nookie night," Terry said, leaning up and planting a wet kiss on Brian's lips.

"Oh for God's sake," moaned Randall in Charlie's ear.

Mikael resumed his place in the doorway, but Charlie could see he was scowling. Suddenly, he perked up like he had an idea, and a moment later could be heard pounding up the stairs.

"We need a plan," called Richard's voice from the speakerphone.

"Right!" Terry said, sitting back down at the table and picking up a piece of toast. He spread jam on it while he spoke. "Who's doing what today?"

Everyone looked at Dylan. He shrank back as if someone had just brandished a torch in his face. "Okay, stop looking at me that way!" he yelled.

"It's your job to make assignments, *mon capitaine*!" Terry said.

Dylan stared at the remnants of his breakfast, apparently paralyzed.

"Okay, fine, I'll do it," Terry said. "Someone has to plan Bishop Tom's memorial. I'll do that this morning. This afternoon, I have pastoral visits to make for Trinity North Church. Richard, you find us a new bishop."

Mikael walked back into the room, holding a small guitar amplifier and some wires. "That's harsh," he said to Terry. "Who died and made you prior?"

"Dylan is falling down on the job, so someone has to take up the slack," Terry said defiantly. "Things have to get done. It's sad that Bishop Tom is dead and we need to mourn him properly, but if we don't get episcopal oversight immediately, we're out of business here. Now, true, we own our building outright, but we have bills to pay, and property taxes are due in a couple of months. So, we need to get cracking."

"So, you're just taking over?" Mikael said. "Shouldn't we vote on this?"

"Look, it's not my fault our bishop died and your ordination got delayed—" Terry snapped.

"This has nothing to do with my ordination!" Mikael slammed the guitar amp on the bench.

Charlie felt the tension in the room rising fast. Terry said nothing. Mikael closed his eyes and took a deep breath. Then he moved to the mirror, affixed a suction cup mic to the back of it, and plugged it into the guitar amplifier. With swift movements, he made adjustments to its controls, plugged it in, and turned it on. Suddenly, the tiny voice yelling complaints in Charlie's ear was loud enough for all to hear.

"Fucking *Mutiny on the Bounty*?" Randy's voice finished.

"What was that?" asked Brian, looking at the mirror.

"I said, is this going to turn into fucking *Mutiny on the Bounty*? 'Cause if so, I want popcorn."

"How are you going to *get* popcorn in there?" Kat asked him.

"I don't know, set it on the stove?"

She watched in the mirror as Randy picked up a piece of bacon from the kitchen counter and put it in his mouth. A look of wonder came over his face, and he began to shovel in all the bacon that was left.

"Hungry?" asked Brian.

"I had no idea how hungry I was. Am. Ravenous," Randy said. "Is there any more?"

Brian started moving plates of food to the counter where Randy could get to it, and he tucked into a proper breakfast for the first time in weeks. A squeal of feedback cut through the air, and Mikael adjusted the knob on the amp until it subsided.

"Okay, so if you're not going to take assignments from me," Terry said bitterly, "and Dylan *won't* make them, who's going to make them?"

"Can't Richard do it over the phone?" Kat asked.

"Nope. I really need to be in the room for that," Richard answered from the iPhone. "Besides, you can't trust me right now. You don't know for sure that it's me talking."

All eyes gravitated to Susan. She looked around incredulously. "Don't look at me. I'm not actually a member of the order. I'm not even Catholic."

Richard's voice was soothing. "I think Terry has made some good suggestions. Dylan, don't you think so?"

Dylan nodded.

"He's nodding!" Mikael called to the speakerphone, "but he still has that wildebeest-in-the-headlights look."

"We're going to have to figure this leadership thing out, but for now, let's go with Terry's...suggestions." Richard was reasonable and confident. Everyone sat up a little straighter while he was talking. "Mikael, you're working at Mitochondrion Music today, right?"

"Yeah, noon to six," Mikael said.

"Good," Richard agreed, "someone needs to be pulling in some money. Terry has pastoral visits filling in for the UCC minister this afternoon, and I could really use some help lining up interviews with bishops."

"Okay," Terry shrugged.

"Dylan, why don't you start planning a liturgy for Bishop Tom? Of all of us, you connected with him the most, so that makes sense to me. Brian, do you have time to do some training on working the inner planes for Kat?"

"Sure. But we have a new oblate, too. Charybdis, er, Charlie."

"You're shitting me," Richard's voice fell.

"Hi, Richard," Charlie said timidly.

"Hoo boy, okay. Sure, Brian, can you do some training?"

"Aye-aye," Brian agreed. "And I'll set Charlie up with a room."

"I've got one lead I can follow up on for episcopal oversight," Richard said.

"What does 'episcopal' mean?" asked Charlie.

"It means anything pertaining to a bishop," Terry said, sulking a little since Mikael's slap-down. "An 'episcopal arrangement' means we need a bishop to connect us to the apostolic succession; otherwise, we have no mojo."

"Really? You can't cast out demons now?"

"To our ever-lovin' shame," Dylan finally piped up. "No."

The phone rang again. "Oh for God's sake!" Susan shouted. "Will somebody besides me get that, please?"

"I will," said Mikael, and he moved swiftly to the hall.

"And what about Randy?" asked Kat.

Everyone looked at the mirror. "Yeah, what about me?" Randy asked, loud enough now for everyone to hear him clearly.

"Actually, that's not such a bad place for him," Brian said. "He'll have community because we all meet here. He has access to food since we're in the kitchen."

"Wait a minute," Kat asked. "Where have you been going to the bathroom?"

Randall looked sheepish. "Uh, well, when I was hanging in the bedroom, I went in a pile between your bed and the wall."

"Ugh," said Kat. "Didn't it get noxious in there?"

"You do what you have to do," Randy said, matter-of-factly.

Brian snapped his fingers. "This," he said, setting a stew pot with a lid near the stove where Randall could reach it, "is now a chamber pot. When people are out of the room, avail yourself of it. Once a day, I'll move you into the toilet where you can empty it and rinse it out. Sound okay?"

Randy, red-faced, nodded.

"Be safe out there today, people!" called Richard from the cell phone in full *Hill Street Blues* mode, and the call ended.

21

KAT AND CHARLIE were waiting for Brian in the chapel. He appeared, wiping his hands on a towel. He opened the lid on a window seat and pulled out three zafus, handing one to each of them. He settled on one and closed his eyes, grounding himself and visibly relaxing. When he opened his eyes again, he smiled. "Let's start simply," he said, "with the correspondences between the chakra system and the Kabbalistic Tree of Life."

"That's simple?" asked Kat.

"Why are *you* teaching us?" Charlie said disdainfully. "Aren't you the cook? You're not even an order member, are you?"

Kat gasped. "Charlie! You have *no* idea—"

Brian held up his hand. "It's okay. I'm a Talmudic scholar, and I'm Jewish. I'm also the housemother here. *And* I'm your teacher today." He smiled patiently.

"I know all this stuff already," Charlie said. "Larch taught us."

"Good. Then it'll be easy for you. And a refresher course is always helpful when you're dealing with...powerful forces," Brian said firmly.

Charlie sighed and crossed his arms. "This is baby stuff."

Brian answered in an even tone. "It is foundational material, certainly. But my guess is that you learned it from Larch as an academic discipline. You learned *about* it. But did you *encounter* it? Did you *work* with it?"

Charlie uncrossed his arms. "Well, no..."

"Then this will be a natural next step. The first chakra is *Muladhara*—it is the root of all of our emotions. All of the involuntary psychological forces that drive us reside here—"

"Like neuroses?" Kat interrupted.

"Exactly—Muladhara is where they live. Our sexuality lives here, too. Passion, right? This chakra is material, chaotic, impure. Which sephirah do you think it corresponds to?"

"Sephirah?" asked Kat.

"Baby stuff." Charlie rolled his eyes.

"The Jewish mystics mapped the universe using the metaphor of a magnificent tree," Brian explained. "It's essentially a Jewish derivative of Gnostic thought that posits a multiplicity of worlds, which are progressively rarefied the higher up you go."

"So, lower worlds are more material?" Kat asked. "And higher worlds are more...spiritual?"

"Exactly," said Brian. "The lowest sephirah—the lowest world—the Kabbalistic term for this is *Malkuth*; it means, 'kingdom'—it refers to the physical universe. Can you see the connection between Malkuth and Muladhara?"

"Yeah, I think so," Kat said. "They both start with M..."

"That's a good start," said Brian, laughing.

"But it's our passions that unite us to this material plane. Right? The material plane gives us pleasure, and pain, too, of course. But it inspires greed and lust—"

"And love," Brian added.

"Right. I didn't mean to demonize it."

"Lots of people do, but I'm glad you're seeing the danger in that," Brian said. "So, why don't we do a meditation and actually explore the connection?"

Kat noted that at this, Charlie perked up. She realized that the experiential piece must be new for him. She was relieved because she was finding his belligerence tiresome.

"Close your eyes, and bring your attention to your genitals," Brian began, sitting up straight on his zafu. Kat settled in on hers, closed her eyes, and breathed deep. In her mind's eye, she pictured her womb and felt a warm sensation deep in her belly.

"Imagine a multicolored spinning disc right there. Imagine that it is expanding—not far, just as far as your belly button." Kat did as he said and was amazed at how real the image in her mind seemed to her. The warmth in her belly grew hotter and larger. She shifted on her zafu in surprise.

"Can you see it?"

She nodded.

"Good," Brian said. "Now, bring your awareness inside it. Note carefully what you see."

In her imagination, Kat moved into the spinning ball of energy. She entered it with the sound of quickly passing flame and found herself underground in a place filled with heat and lit by fire. In the corner, she saw a figure huddled against the wall of what seemed to be a cave. Cautiously, she moved toward the figure and saw that it was a young girl. The figure was shaking beneath a blanket. "Hey," she said to the figure. "Hey, don't be afraid." She pulled back the blanket and saw a much younger version of herself weeping and scrambling in terror.

"No, it's okay. I'm not going to hurt you," Kat said. "*No one* is going to hurt you."

Two words dropped from the girl's mouth like lead. "Too late."

Kat jerked back as if she had been slapped. "What *happened* to you?" she asked.

The girl backed away from her, hugging the wall. "No knowing! No knowing!" she screamed.

Kat followed her, making calming gestures. "What do you mean, 'no knowing'?"

"The blanket covers you," she said, cowering beneath it. "If you look under it, you'll be sorry. No knowing!"

"What could be so bad?" Kat said. "We had a wonderful childhood."

"You don't know, then."

"Don't know about what?" Kat asked.

"You have forgotten," the girl said with a sadness that cut at Kat's heart.

"What have I forgotten?" Kat asked.

"Countless lifetimes of horror," the girl said and then she pointed behind Kat.

Kat turned around and stood up. Before her stretched countless galaxies. Somehow, she beheld each star, and at the same time, the gossamer web of the whole. Every planet spun within her knowing, every creature, every act.

And it was terrible. Fangs tore into the flesh of a billion beasts, their end to be only prey. Pain ripped through the brains of a billion more, from the slash of claws and the quick jerking snap of the neck. She beheld the fetid corrosion of bacteria, the fall of countless beings to disease and decay, and felt every stab and collapse within her own body. Kat screamed.

Suddenly, Brian was shaking her and talking softly. "Come back, Kat, come back. Tell me what you saw." She opened her eyes, and after a moment of vertigo she clutched at his shoulders, her right hand cupping the lump of his hunched back, and she loved it. She burst out crying.

"Talk to me, Kat. Talk your way back. Talk to me now!" Brian commanded.

Kat quickly relayed what she had seen, and as she spoke she saw Brian nodding. "Yes, that's Malkuth, in all of its glory. You see how you used the chakra to gain access to it?"

Kat nodded, still faint. She felt weak, and she continued to clutch at him.

"Susan!" Brian called. In a moment, Susan appeared in the doorway.

"Oh my God," she said, seeing Kat. "Is she okay?"

"Malkuth shock," Brian explained. "Can you bring me some ice?"

"Wrapped in a towel?" called Susan, who had already run into the kitchen.

"Yes, please," answered Brian.

In a moment, Susan reappeared, handing Brian a robin's-egg-blue towel full of ice. Brian took it and put it on the back of Kat's neck. "Okay, Kat, listen to me. I want you to move your consciousness away from the Muladhara chakra. I want you to concentrate on the coolness of the ice on your neck. Can you do that?"

Kat nodded and felt less disoriented almost instantly. The fire in her belly had diminished, and she tried not to think about the vision. Quickly, her eyes were focusing normally again, and she could orient herself in space. She was in the chapel. Brian and Susan were there, each of them were touching her and speaking to her soothingly. She felt their love and concern. She felt safe. She straightened up and nodded.

"Okay, that was intense," she breathed. "So that was baby stuff, huh, Charlie?" She looked over at Charlie, but he did not answer.

"Oh shit," Brian said. He slapped Charlie. "Charlie, come back, dude. Come back!" Charlie slumped forward and then fell over. Brian caught him and pushed his hair back from his face.

"More ice?" Susan asked, getting ready to run for the kitchen.

Brian scowled. "I don't think so. He's rigid—I don't think this was a Malkuth experience. Put a small potato in the microwave, please, four minutes."

Susan nodded and ran to the door.

"Ground, dammit!" Brian shouted at Charlie. Frantically, he pulled off Charlie's shoes and pounded on his feet with his fists.

"Ow!" Charlie screeched.

"Pinch his legs," Brian commanded. Kat did as she was told.

"What happened to him?" Kat asked.

"I won't know for sure until I talk to him, but my guess is that he didn't follow directions," Brian said, a note of bitterness in his voice. "Too simple for you, you stupid fuck?" he shouted at Charlie. He pounded on his left foot.

"Ow...ah ha ha!" Charlie screamed and sat up. "Stop hitting my feet!"

"Then you come back down now, and you ground yourself!" Brian said. "You get those feet on the ground, and you put some energy into them! Whatever energy you've got flowing up here"—he gestured to Charlie's head—"you force it down to your feet. Do it now! Now, dammit!"

Charlie closed his eyes, apparently concentrating. Kat saw his feet twitch then grow still. Charlie's breathing slowed, and his eyes snapped open. "I don't feel good," he said.

Susan rushed in with the potato, and Brian passed it from hand to hand, weighing its heat. He nodded, apparently having made a decision because he grabbed at Charlie's belt.

"Hey," Charlie said. "You're undressing me."

"I'm trying to save what's left of your nervous system, asshole. Raise your hips so I can get your pants down."

Charlie looked unsure but acquiesced. Brian put the potato in his hand. "Take this, and put it in your underwear. Position it right underneath your scrotum."

"But it's hot!"

"Damn right it's hot. Hopefully, it'll be hot enough." Brian watched impatiently as Charlie tried to position the potato. Finally, Brian grabbed at the crotch of Charlie's jeans and held the lump that was the potato firmly against his perineum.

Discomfort showed on Charlie's face, but it quickly passed. Within moments, he seemed calmer, and when his eyes opened, he seemed cogent.

"I'm *here*..." he said with a bit of wonder.

"Yes, HaShem be praised," Brian said. "What I want to know is, *where were you*? Because you very clearly did *not* focus on your Muladhara chakra. What sephira did you try to access?"

"*Kether*," he said.

"You're a fucking idiot," Brian said, almost spitting.

"Malkuth is baby stuff."

"Fuck you," Brian said. "You could have blown out your whole nervous system."

"I don't think so," Charlie said, feeling at his arms.

"No, because you wouldn't be talking to me now—you'd be dead." Brian took the ice pack from Kat's neck, examined her skin beneath, and patted her shoulder. Then he threw the ice pack against the chapel wall. Pieces of ice flew up and struck the giant patchwork mural of Christ that overlooked their daily prayers. "Sit up."

Charlie did so, moving his fingers in front of his eyes. "The colors were...pretty," he said, smiling.

"What's Kether?" Kat asked.

"It's the highest sephirah," Brian answered. "Ideally, we'd work up to that, doing a *lot* of intensive spiritual and psychological work along the way to prepare you for it. Mr. Reckless here just jumped from the first grade to graduate school without any preparation. He's lucky he didn't completely fry his crown chakra."

Charlie looked around at them with wonder. He pointed at Susan. "You have big boobies."

Susan raised one eyebrow at Brian.

Charlie pointed at Kat. "You have teeny boobies."

"Hey!" Kat protested.

"Okay," Brian said testily, "I think we've established that some actual damage was done."

"No kidding," Susan said, wrapping her sweater more tightly around her bosoms.

"He's lost some impulse control, that's for sure."

Charlie's finger pointed at Brian next. "You are *sooooo* gay."

22

RICHARD WAS SURPRISED that Bishop Clem Parkison was able to see him so quickly. He had only left a message about an hour previously, and now he was in the order's dilapidated Geo, turning left from Telegraph Avenue onto the 24 on-ramp toward Walnut Creek.

You hate this guy, said the voice in his head. *And now you're going to kiss his ass?*

"I don't hate him," Richard said, gunning the motor to get up to speed, merging carefully. "I just...intensely dislike him."

He's a prick, Duunel said.

"How do you know? Have you ever even met the guy?"

No, but I have access to all of your memories—and believe me, if it were possible for my kind to be traumatized—

"Fuck you," Richard laughed. "So, you've seen everything I've seen on this guy. And you concur?"

Prick. No doubt about it.

"How unusual for us to be on the same page," Richard smiled.

Au contraire, mon ami—

"I am soooo not your ami."

We both loved breakfast this morning. Smoked salmon on a toasted garlic bagel with espresso and beer.

"Breakfast of champions," Richard agreed. "See, but what I don't understand is why you're not fighting this effort to get a new bishop."

What do you mean?

"Well, as it is, we're powerless against your kind. No bishop, no power. No power, no casting out Hades-Americans."

Oh, I like that, Duunel said. *I'm a Hades-American. We can hire lobbyists now.*

"So, why aren't you fighting me tooth and nail?"

What does it matter? Duunel said. *Any setback would be temporary. You'll eventually hook up with the Enemy's power source again—it's just a matter of time. I'm kind of a go-with-the-flow guy. I'm just enjoying tormenting you in the moment.*

"You certainly have that down."

And the food is good. Better than that nasty stuff they were feeding Old Man Dane, Duunel said, referring to his last host, an aging man who had not been fit for solid food.

Richard thought about Bishop Parkison. From his blog perusings, he had gleaned that Parkison had not openly opposed the order at the last Old Catholic Synod of the Americas meeting. But then again, he had not supported them, as Bishop Tom had. Hell, Bishop Tom had championed them. Richard felt a wave of grief over his friend's death. With effort, he refocused his thoughts on Parkison.

He was an insurance salesman—an Allstate agent—with an office in a trendy Contra Costa high rise. At first, Richard was surprised that Parkison kept office hours on a Saturday, but then he realized that it made sense—working people did a lot of their shopping on Saturday, after all. Parkison had an eleven o'clock opening in his schedule, and Richard was just going to make it. He gunned the engine again, looking at the clock.

When he finally parked and breezed into the office building, he was already two minutes late. His black Anglican cassock always garnered stares, but he was in too much of a hurry to notice. He fairly danced in place waiting for the elevator, and when he entered the office, he was apologetic.

"Fr. Richard Kinney here to see Bish—er, Mr. Parkison, please. So sorry I'm late."

The receptionist looked him over curiously. Then recognition dawned. "Oh yeah," she whispered conspiratorially. "I know about his...*other* life."

"Other life?" Richard asked.

"His *Catholic* stuff, you know," she nodded as if it were a fetish or an illness that shouldn't be public knowledge.

"Of course," Richard said, feigning complicity.

She made a quick phone inquiry then said to Richard, "You can go right in."

"Thank you," Richard said and opened the door to Parkison's office.

Bishop Parkison was at his desk when Richard walked in, head down, going over some papers. He did not look up.

Richard stood and waited. Two minutes passed. Richard shifted uncomfortably from one foot to another.

Prick, Duunel said in his head. *You should kill him.*

"I'm *not* going to kill him," Richard mumbled under his breath.

"I know you're there," said Parkison, still not looking up. "You'll have to wait until I finish this up."

There's a baseball bat in the corner, Duunel said helpfully.

Finally, Parkison looked up and took off his glasses. He pinched at the bridge of his nose and leaned back in his chair. "What do you want?" he said.

I want you to rip your anus in an elephant gangbang, Duunel said. Richard ignored him. "I'm sure you heard about Bishop Tom."

Parkison pursed his lips. "Very sad," he said. "Tampons, wasn't it?"

"I think it was a Prius," Richard said with a grim smile. "Anyway, we're having a memorial service for him at the friary. You're most welcome to join us."

Parkison gave a quick shake of his head. "We'll have a Deanery Mass in his honor. You can come to that."

Richard said nothing.

Interesting little power struggle, Duunel noted. *What do you have planned for an encore?*

"May I have a seat?" Richard asked.

Parkison nodded. "Help yourself."

"Thanks." Richard sat on the edge of the seat. "I'll come right to the point—"

"I wish you would."

Say 'You're a prick,' Duunel suggested.

"Bishop Tom was our link to the apostolic succession. Without him, we're...well, we're cut off from the power we need to do our work."

"You mean casting out demons."

"Yes."

Parkison swung his chair slightly from side to side. His face looked like he'd been eating unripe persimmons. "I don't believe in demons," he said.

Oh, this guy's not so bad after all, Duunel cooed. *We like him now.*

"I can understand your position," Richard said diplomatically. "A lot of people agree with you. And yet people consistently express a need for a deliverance ministry, and by and large, people are happy with our work. I believe what we bring to the church is valuable, even if it is not well understood."

"Hmph," Parkison said. "So why are you talking to me?"

"Well, you're one of the few Old Catholic bishops in the East Bay. We're not asking for permanent shelter—we're simply hoping you can take us under your authority temporarily, until we can find a permanent bishop."

"How could I possibly support a ministry that I don't believe in?" he asked. He began to pick at his eyebrow.

"Uh...I suppose you could have faith that we're doing something good," Richard suggested.

"Faith?"

"Yes, faith."

I don't understand that word myself, Duunel commented.

Parkison picked at his eyebrow some more. "I'll consider it on one condition. If you are under my authority, you are also in my service."

"We'd be happy to serve your diocese whenever they need deliverance—"

"Forget that. Once a week you can have...what's her name, the fat one's wife? Busty girl..." He looked up, trying to remember.

"Are you talking about Susan Melanchthon, Dylan's wife?" Richard put his hands on his hips, hoping he wasn't hearing what he was hearing.

"Yes, that's her. Blonde woman. Once a week, she can come to my house in Lafayette and give it a good cleaning. And the fat one can come with her and cut my lawn."

Richard's mouth was open.

Your mouth is open, Duunel told him.

Richard shut his mouth but couldn't find words. "Are you *kidding* me?"

"Why would I kid you?" Parkison said. Richard could see that he was serious. "No need for *you* to come, or the little gay one, or the tall stringy one with weird hair."

You could still kill him, Duunel said helpfully. *Bat in the corner.*

"Bishop, that's appallingly offensive."

"How so? It's a barter. Service for service. Sounds like a bargain to me."

"Is there any way you might *reconsider* that...condition?"

"There is not."

"Well then, sir, I thank you for your time." Richard stuck out his hand, but Parkison ignored him.

"I'll send you an invoice for the time," Parkison said and turned back to his papers.

23

TERRY CHECKED his phone to be sure he was at the right place. He had forgotten how time-consuming making pastoral visits could be, but on public transit it was doubly so. He straightened his hair and made sure his cassock was straight before knocking on the door of the modest ranch house.

The door swung open, and a friendly face soon appeared. "You must be the rental father!" an old woman exclaimed in what sounded like a Cockney accent. She shook his hand furiously.

"Something like that, yes," said Terry. "Are you Mrs. Brickle?"

"I *was* Mrs. Brickle, but Mr. Brickle died," she smiled naughtily. "But *you're* sure handsome." The woman was dressed in a velveteen track suit and adorned with a bright pink scarf. She was wearing way too much makeup—Terry could see it caked up in her wrinkles. A large peacock feather stood straight up over her head, its quill stuck in the bun of her hair, evoking images of Egyptian deities in Terry's imagination.

"I'm sorry," Terry said, "about Mr. Brickle."

"Oh, don't be, it was ages ago, and he was an old fart anyway. Come in, and have some tea!"

Terry entered a house that was in every way a pre-war English cottage. Terry wasn't surprised that some of his visits were with British expats since Reverend Oberlin was British himself. He was charmed by the décor.

Terry settled himself in an overstuffed chair and waited as Mrs. Brickle set the tea service in front of him. He noted with a sinking feeling in his stomach that the cups on the tray were either extremely stained or unwashed altogether. He shifted in his chair nervously and felt a bead of sweat break out on his forehead.

"Will you take milk, dear?" Mrs. Brickle asked, poised with the creamer.

Terry had to stop himself from recoiling as he noticed the clumps in the milk. "No, thank you. Just some sugar, please."

"Oh, I forget. You Yanks don't put milk in your tea." She spooned some sugar into Terry's cup and poured the tea in. With a smile that made her whole wrinkled face bunch up like an elastic hair band, she handed him the cup and saucer.

Terry looked at the cup suspiciously. *Lord, honor the sacrifices of thy servant*, Terry prayed silently as he took a cautious sip of the tea. It tasted sweet, hot, and good. He relaxed a little.

Just then, Terry noticed an enormous cat on the chair near his own, sitting stock still. It was white with fur radiating out in all directions. Its eyes did not move.

"Father, I'd like you to meet Captain Fluffy. He's the naughtiest kitty in the room, and that's saying something," she said, glowering at the cat playfully.

Terry looked around, and despite his best efforts, could not discover *any* other cats in the room.

"It's good that you're here, Father. Captain Fluffy has a confession to make, don't you, Captain? Don't be shy, dear, Father looks very congenial."

Terry looked at the cat. It did not move. Not sure what to say, Terry took another sip of his tea. Something he could not identify rose to the surface in it. He swallowed and put the cup and saucer down on the side table.

"Captain Fluffy has been going to the Berkeley Farmer's Market and picking pockets, haven't you, Captain?"

Terry shifted his eyes, thinking that if he did not look directly at the cat, it might move. It didn't. "Um...that's definitely bad," Terry said, trying to sound normal. "How do you know...Captain Fluffy... has been picking pockets?"

"I caught him in the act!" she exclaimed, her eyes growing wide. "One paw in a man's coat pocket, and when the man noticed, he scampered away!"

Terry looked again at the cat. It was large, for a cat, but didn't stand knee high. "How did...how did Captain Fluffy reach the man's pocket? Was the man lying on the ground?"

"Don't be daft!" the woman laughed, waving a hand at him. "Don't underestimate Captain Fluffy—he is one resourceful puss!"

"Oh, I don't doubt that," Terry said. He looked at the tea tray again, at a little plate of English digestive biscuits. He picked one up, but as several ants climbed onto his finger, he set it back down again.

"I was shocked, I tell you!" she said, leaning forward. "A common thief, living under my own roof; can you believe it?"

Terry wanted to say yes, but he refrained.

"So, I confronted him with it, and he made a paltry excuse about the National Health Service, and I told him to go right to bed." She leaned back, tsk-tsking. "Oh!" She leaned forward again. "And then you'll never *believe* what I found in his room!" She leaped up and ran out of the room.

"He has a room?" Terry asked, mostly to himself. He stared at the cat again, willing it to move. It didn't. He turned his attention to the tea again, hoping to identify whatever might be floating in it. It seemed to be hook-shaped, of biological origin. More than that he could not surmise.

"Here we are!" sang Mrs. Brickle, approaching the sitting room again. Terry snapped back into his former position, hands in his lap, and waited as Mrs. Brickle entered carrying a large wooden box.

"Take a look at these!" she said, setting the box at Terry's feet. Inside, Terry saw what looked like nearly a hundred billfolds, in leather of every color, as well as nylon and even one wallet that appeared to be made from duct tape. "I was cleaning the other day, and I found *this* under his bed." She pointed at Captain Fluffy. "That is one naughty, naughty cat!"

Terry felt a sinking feeling in his gut and only then realized that he was out of his depth. He fished for something to say. He came up empty.

"Well, aren't you going to say, 'That's a pussy who needs to go to confession'? That's what Pastor Oberlin always says."

"Um...that's a pussy that needs to go to confession?" Terry said hesitantly, unsure of what was supposed to happen next.

"Well, confession needs privacy, doesn't it, dear?" She patted his hand and turned to leave the room. At the doorway to the kitchen she paused and turned back. Pointing a finger at Captain Fluffy, she scolded, "And don't leave anything out! I'll not have the wrath of God fall upon this house on account of your like!" Then she flashed Terry a smile and left the room.

Terry panicked, but with an effort of will, mastered himself. He had not done a lot of pastoral visiting, but he had not encountered anything like this. He was beginning to feel wistful for a good, straightforward demonic encounter.

Something about the cat sparked Terry's curiosity, and he leaned in to inspect Captain Fluffy more closely. Hesitantly, he reached out toward the cat, ready to withdraw it should he hiss or attack. The cat was completely motionless, however, no matter how close his hand got. Finally, he touched the cat, which was cold and hard. Leaning in, Terry used both hands to separate the fur, and saw the telltale marks of an expert taxidermist.

"I'm waiting to hear the penance!" Mrs. Brickle called from the kitchen, where, Terry realized, she must be standing just out of view. "Because I will hold him to it, by God!"

Terry quickly got out his short stole and pulled his *Book of Common Prayer* from his back pocket. Quickly, he turned to the Rite of Reconciliation. Glancing nervously at the kitchen to make sure Mrs. Brickle was still out of sight, he loudly intoned, "Now there is rejoicing in Heaven; for you were lost, and are found; you were dead"—at this Terry gulped, but plunged ahead—"and are now alive in Christ Jesus our Lord. Abide in peace. The Lord has put away all your sins."

"Thanks be to God!" called Mrs. Brickle, emerging now from the kitchen. "Thank you, Father Nancy," she said, giving Terry a kiss on the cheek. Terry struggled not to recoil from the woman's icy touch. "Pastor gives him confession every time he comes to see us. He's a dutiful man. He's very patient with Captain Fluffy, but just between you, me, and the bears, I think that's because the captain is such a generous donor to the Church."

"Well, Mrs. Brickle, thank you so much for the tea," Terry said, removing his short stole and standing up. He put the prayer book back in his pocket.

"So nice of you to come, Father Nancy," she said.

Terry narrowed his eyes at the "Nancy" bit, but he ignored it. With resolve, he turned toward the door.

"Do be careful, Father. I've heard we've had a rash of burglaries in this neighborhood. You don't *live* in this neighborhood, do you?" she asked.

Terry did, but he wasn't about to tell her that. "I live...a ways, so I'm sure it's fine," he said vaguely.

"Goodbye, dear," Mrs. Brickle said, holding the door for him. "And do come again soon. Captain Fluffy is almost obsessive about the Rite of Reconciliation."

"Pastor Oberlin is set to return in just a couple of weeks," Terry said without commitment. "But do call if you have an urgent need." He handed her his card and walked out of the house with a great sigh of relief.

It was only after the door had shut behind him and he had walked across the street to the bus stop that he realized his wallet was missing.

24

RICHARD DROVE BACK through the Caldecott Tunnel in a black haze of worry. It was only after he emerged from the tunnel, seeing the foggy beauty of the Oakland Hills spread out before him, that he realized how tight the knot in his stomach had become. He willed it to relax.

You should have killed him, said the voice in his head.

"And that would have accomplished what?" Richard said out loud.

You would feel better.

"No, I would feel terrible. *You* would feel better, though." He almost smiled. Richard wracked his brain for what to do next. There was no shortage of Old Catholic bishops in the Bay Area, of course, and he and Terry had both left numerous voice mails. He felt fortunate to have lined up two meetings so quickly. "One down," he said out loud. "One to go."

He felt no more hopeful about his next candidate, however. She taught feminist theory at the Pacific School of Theology, and had come into Old Catholicism via the Roman Catholic Womenpriest movement. Through the grapevine, he had heard that they had chucked her out for being so strident that she was impossible to work with. Richard's own few encounters with her in the past left him dreading any future contact. Just thinking of meeting with her tomorrow made his teeth hurt.

You could kill her, Duunel suggested.

"You are not helpful," Richard said.

I'm not actually trying to be helpful, Duunel confessed.

"I didn't think you were."

His phone rang, the Casio-like tones of "Here I Raise My Ebenezer" piercing the air. Keeping his eyes on the road, Richard fished for his phone and punched until he hit the speakerphone button.

"Richard here," he said in a business-like fashion.

"Dicky, it's Maggie," said a frail-sounding voice.

"Uh-oh, I don't like the sound of this," he said.

"You've got that right. It's terrible news, I'm afraid. Preston was elected on today's second ballot."

"No way," Richard breathed.

"Unbelievable, I know," Maggie said. "Everyone here is walking around like the living dead, shaking their heads."

"I'm so sorry, Mags," Richard said, steering onto the Telegraph Avenue off-ramp.

"I'd like to schedule a meeting with you and the other friars. Tonight, if possible," Maggie said, her demeanor uncharacteristically business-like.

"Of course. We can't meet at the friary, though."

"I know, it's fine. We can meet at All Saints'. Is 7 p.m. all right?"

"I'll check with the others and get back to you if it isn't. If you don't hear from me, we'll see you then."

25

SUSAN SLAMMED down the telephone in frustration. Brian was in the bathroom, so she yelled loud enough for him to hear. "That's the second call from the Episcopal Diocese of San Joaquin today!" She heard him whistle. "This isn't a coincidence, Brian. This is a fucking epidemic!"

Just then, the doorbell rang. Brian called from the bathroom. "Can you get that?"

Susan sighed and headed for the door. "Sure thing!" she called. She stretched her arms and moved her head around in a wide orbit, feeling painfully the kinks in her neck. She opened the door to find a scruffy-looking young man wearing a stained striped tie.

"Yes?" Susan asked, sporting a polite, business-like smile.

"Are you"—he looked at his papers—"the Order of Saint Raphael?"

"No, but this is the order's friary."

"Uh...I guess that's good enough." He handed a light blue bundle of papers to her. As soon as she took them, he said, "You have been served."

Susan felt like she'd just been slapped. The young man turned and scampered away toward a rusty VW that looked like it was not long for the road.

Stung suddenly now with curiosity and rising anxiety, she opened the bundle and started reading. A moment later, she started screaming, "Shit! Shit! Shit!"

Heaving herself into motion, she flew upstairs and threw open the door to the room she shared with Dylan. There he was at his desk, under a bright window. A stack of liturgy books was to his right, his laptop was directly in front of him, and an enormous bong was to his left, still trailing wisps of smoke. He was snoring.

She slapped at his back. "Dylan, wake up."

He bolted upright, but the only word that leaped to his lips was, "Waffles."

She brandished the light blue papers. "Dylan, we just got served."

He peered up at her as though through a misty haze, seemed to recognize her, but then laid his head back down on the desk, smiling. "Ah love me some waffles."

"Dylan! Up! Honey, this is serious!"

But Dylan did not stir.

"Aaahhhh!" Susan shouted in frustration. She slapped at his head.

"Wha—?" Dylan grimaced. "Why are you hittin' me?"

"We're being sued, Dyl! Sued!"

"A boy named Sue...bum-ba-ba-bum buh-da bum-ba-da-bum..." he mumbled out a rockabilly rhythm. Then he began to snore.

Susan stood there, feeling helpless. She looked at the papers. She looked at Dylan. Then a steely look of resolve crossed over her face, and she snatched open the closet and grabbed Dylan's kit bag.

She headed down the hallway toward the back stairs, and saw Kat out of the corner of her eye, putting on a sweater.

"Hey, whatcha doing?" Kat called.

"I'm going to kick some demon ass!" Susan called over her shoulder.

26

THE DOOR SWUNG OPEN, and Bishop Preston stepped into the room
that would soon be his office. Carefully, he leaned his crozier against
the wall. The rich, red carpet was soft beneath his feet, and the wide
windows looked out onto a stone labyrinth and the entrance to Grace
Cathedral.

A security person held the door as he looked around. Softly, not
wanting to break the mood, she said, "Bishop Ryder's family cleared
everything out when he died. It's pretty much ready for you to move
in." She smiled.

Preston nodded, still taking in the grandeur of it. "Do you mind if
I...take a few minutes alone?"

"Of course, sir," the security guard said, hunkering slightly and
looking sheepish. "I'll be right out here if you need me. Oh, and sir?
Congratulations." She bowed nervously and shut the door
behind her.

It had been a long time since Preston had been the recipient of
such deference. "I could get used to that," he said to himself. On the
far side of the room was a large desk of dark wood with a leather
office chair behind it. He walked around the desk and sat in the chair,

wheeling up into a working position. "Oh yes," he said, "this feels good."

Set into one wall was a TV, and on his desk was a remote. Lured by curiosity and pride, he switched on the television and flipped to the news. He grunted with satisfaction, having caught a story about his election. He scowled a bit as he saw himself on the screen—he never could get used to seeing himself without his hair. In his mind's eye, he would always be thirty-five, with a thick, healthy pile of hair on his head. It had been twenty years since that pile had dissipated to a scraggly shadow of its former glory, but it still stung his pride to see it.

He allowed himself to revel in his victory, though, as he watched images of the diocesan convention flash on the screen. The commentator came on and made some remark about "the controversial nature" of the selection, but he knew *that* was coming. He glanced at his tall, oversize crozier and smiled a grim smile.

Soon, the news story had passed, so he switched to another channel. He wasn't so lucky this time. Last night, the commentator was saying, Iran had experienced two earthquakes in unlikely places. NATO security experts questioned the nature of the earthquakes, saying they were more likely to have been underground nuclear tests. The Israeli prime minister was almost hysterical. Preston's eyebrows bunched up, and he pursed his lips in concern.

His private cell rang. Very few people had that number, so he fished it out to see who it could be. He smirked with satisfaction to see that the call was from Governor Ivory. "David," he said, flipping open the phone.

"John, I can't believe it. I'm watching it on CNN, but I can't believe it," the phone made the governor's voice sound thin, but he spoke with gusto.

"Believe it," Preston said. He passed the phone to his other hand and put his elbows on the desk. *His* desk. "I told you I had this thing in the bag."

"You sure as hell did. But what I don't understand is *how*."

"It takes power to get power, my friend."

The governor laughed. "You know, not all of my preacher friends are so cryptic."

"I'll let you in on my little secret later—are you still at the Hyatt?"

"Yup, two more meetings tonight, God help me. The week before the national convention is always an endurance test."

"Let's get together for a little victory drink soon, then, and I'll tell you all about it. In the meantime, we have a dark horse candidate to promote."

"This morning, I would have said you were crazy. But now..." Ivory's voice trailed off. "Do you really think we can do this, John?"

"I think we *have* to. Did you see what's happening in Iran?"

"Goddamned Persians," Ivory spat. "Can you believe it? We're *this* close from seeing Israel go up in a mushroom cloud. If we're not careful, those little brown people are going to be running the world."

"And you know damn well that the pansy Democrats aren't going to do a damned thing to stop it. And neither are the two Republican candidates you guys are putting forward next week—Calver and Pinopscott. Too cautious, both of them." Preston sighed. "We've got to face facts, David, you are the *only* person with the resolve to stand up to the Persians—and the Arabs. The fate of the world hangs on you getting the nomination next week. And by God, you *will*."

"How can you be so sure?" Ivory was still incredulous.

"Because I just *tested* it. I just ran an impossible upset, right here at granola ground zero. I *won*, David. Consider this the trial run. Next week, we'll pull off the real coup."

"You really believe that, don't you?"

"My friend, you literally *cannot* lose." Preston sat back and put his feet on the desk. That felt pretty good, too. "But you know what we need now is a show of strength—something to put you on the map, to get people's attention. Something to get people talking, saying, 'Hey, this Ivory guy is the answer.' Especially now, with things hotting up in the Middle East."

"What do you have in mind?" Ivory asked.

"Remember that threat you made about Dearborn?" Preston asked.

"Yeah—that was just hot air. I was trying to get attention."

"You want attention? Make good on it. Not today, though," Preston chuckled. "Wouldn't want you to steal my thunder. Wait 'til the next news cycle. Do it tomorrow."

27

WHEN LARCH HEARD about Charybdis's "defection," he smashed a replica Babylonian pot his aunt had bought for him from the New York Antiquities Museum. Then he started throwing books. Eventually, he had slumped—panting—into a dusty, overstuffed Victorian chair that had probably been in the lodge's sitting room since such chairs were all the rage, certainly before the earthquake and fire of 1906.

He was not a rash man. He was not a vindictive man. So, why were his fists clenching? Why were his teeth gnashing? Why was he dying to punch out a neophyte?

He went to the bathroom and splashed water on his cheeks. He looked at his haggard face in the mirror. "I barely recognize you, old man," he said to his image. *Could Pim be enchanting me?* he wondered. *This isn't how I act. It's not how I normally feel. I like Richard and his crew. If Charybdis feels called to walk a Christian path, well, power to him. Right?*

His gut churned. They'd had a lodge meeting last night. The others had joked about it. They made fun of Charybdis; there were "good riddance" and "serves those monks right" statements. Larch had listened with a face like stone.

He had to talk to her. He had to see her. He had to know why he was acting this way. A part of his brain resisted. *You're like a heroin addict*, he told himself. *You're not in your right mind. You're going to make a mistake, and it is going to fuck you up.*

But the other part of his mind didn't care. He lit the censer and placed the incense on the charcoal as soon as it turned gray. After a few moments of concentration, the object of his obsession danced into view. She bowed ostentatiously, quite intentionally permitting him a maddening view of her cleavage.

"I feel like we're in a relationship," he told her. Instantly he regretted it. It was like saying "I love you" too early. It could ruin what they had—whatever that was. *If only she was a succubus*, he thought.

"Did you find your wee little lamb?" she asked teasingly.

"I know where he is," he said. "But it's his choice. I don't own him."

"Don't you wish you did?" she tilted her head.

"Uh...well, no, actually, I don't," he said, uncertain and uncomfortable disagreeing with her about anything. But if he were honest... no, he didn't want to command anyone. Not anyone *human*, that is. Or did he? He closed his eyes and checked in. She seemed to notice.

"Why don't you go to that order's house and confront them? Why don't you tell your *practicus* to come home?"

"Those monks will laugh me right back to the Bay Bridge, and Charybdis with them." Larch noticed that his voice sounded bitter. He didn't like the sound of it.

"Not if you're commanding an army, they won't." She smiled from that mouth that was just a little bit too wide. A mouth that invited fantasies.

"What army? How?" he asked.

"What if I told you that you could command hundreds of occupied people?" she asked him.

"Occupied?" Then realization dawned on him. She meant *possessed*.

"Every one of them would obey only you. You would so impress your lodge members that they, too, would follow you anywhere. And that lost little lamb"—she leaned in and licked her lips—"would come scampering home faster than you could say 'mint sauce.'" She leaned back and turned in a circle, playfully allowing her skirts to swing in wide arcs. She was tantalizing his gaze, and he was dying to see more.

Larch shook his head, trying to break the spell she was weaving over him. Power—was that what he really wanted? Well, yes, if he were honest. That's what any magickian was after, really. But power over other people? He would need to think about that. Demons were one thing; people were another. But if you put people and demons together...he wasn't sure how he felt. And yet he heard his mouth utter the word: "How?"

28

"WHAT? WHO'S SUING US?" Kat asked as Susan pulled the cherry-red Corolla onto Vine Street. She headed downtown.

"That botched exorcism that Terry and Dylan didn't do," Susan said angrily. "The man is suing us for breach of contract."

"We don't sign contracts, do we?" Kat asked, sitting up straighter in the passenger seat.

"No," Susan answered. "Which is why we can probably beat this in court. But I'm hoping it won't get that far. If we can nip it in the bud now, we should."

"But..." Kat wasn't sure how to phrase the next sentence. "But you're not..."

"A member of the order? Right. Precisely why I might succeed where the boys can't right now."

"I don't understand," Kat said. "Have you ever *done* an exorcism?"

"Nope," said Susan, turning left on Shattuck.

"So, why is it you think you can succeed when Dylan and Terry—who have done tons of them—couldn't? And Susan, please"—Kat touched her shoulder—"I'm not putting you down. I'm just trying to understand."

Susan managed a smile. "You're a dear, and it's fine. The boys are Catholic. I'm not."

"But you're all Christians."

"Yes. But Catholicism is conceived in terms of a medieval monarchy—power flows from the top down through 'approved' channels. The power is real, and it's strong, but it's mediated."

"Okay, I can see that. Is that why we need a bishop?"

"Right. The bishop is the link to the power source—to God. The...*mojo*—as the guys like to call it—flows from him to his subordinates, the priests and deacons. Then they give it to us—the 'little people.'" She smirked. "Sorry. It's hard for me not to laugh."

"But it works, right?" Kat asked.

"Oh, it works all right, to countless demons' shame and humiliation." Susan turned right onto University Avenue.

"But, I'm guessing not just for demons," Kat said, pursing her lips.

"Right. Any sacramental mojo works that way," Susan affirmed. "That's why only bishops and priests can preside over the Eucharist—the bishops give the power to the priests, and the priests 'confect' the grace-bearing gifts and distribute them to the people."

"Trickle-down grace?" Kat asked.

Susan laughed. "Pretty much, yeah."

"So how does it work for...You're Lutheran, right?"

"Right."

"It's hard for me to keep all the varieties of Protestants straight," Kat admitted.

"It's a rat's nest, that's for sure," Susan agreed. She dodged a delivery van and made a left on Sacramento Street.

"So, how does it work for Lutherans?" Kat asked.

"Pretty much the same as it does for all Protestants. The power is democratized. Luther preached 'the Priesthood of All Believers,' meaning that every baptized Christian has direct access to the mojo—no bishops required."

"So, it's not a hierarchy," Kat reasoned. "So, what provides the connection to God?"

Susan smiled, "The Holy Spirit—who resides in everyone—*is* the power of God, *is* God. Protestants just tap into that Power directly."

"Isn't the Holy Spirit in Catholics, too?" Kat asked, cocking her head.

"Oh yes," Susan replied. "I think the Holy Spirit is in everyone, no matter what their religion."

"So why can't Catholics tap into it directly, like Protestants do?" Kat asked.

Susan leaned over and whispered conspiratorially. "They *can*. They *do*, all the time."

"So, why couldn't the guys do this exorcism?" Kat asked.

"That's easy," Susan said, pulling along a tree-lined curb and parking. "It's because they didn't *think* they could."

"You make them sound like *The Little Engine That Could*," Kat laughed.

"Well, more like *The Little Engine That Couldn't*," Susan agreed. "Do you mean that Terry hasn't given you his 'paradigmatic contextualization' speech yet?"

"No," Kat said, her eyebrows raising. "Should I be glad?"

"No," Susan said, opening the car door. "You'll think it's cool."

"I take it we're here?" Kat asked, opening her own door and stepping out.

"This is the address on Dylan's contacts file." Susan opened the trunk and pulled out Dylan's kit bag.

"Do we have a plan?" Kat asked.

"Knock on the door. Remind God of his promises. Kick demon's butt," Susan said.

"What do you mean, 'remind God of his promises'?"

"God promised to deliver us from evil," Susan shrugged.

"Why do you need to remind him?" Kat asked. "Doesn't God know everything?"

"Well, you'd think so," Susan said. "But in actual practice, sometimes God needs a kick in the head."

"Really? That sounds...weird." Kat looked skeptical.

"It is. But Luther did it a lot. You've got to call God on his shit sometimes. It's part of having a real relationship with him."

"Aren't you afraid of...pissing him off?"

"What kind of relationship would we have if I couldn't say what I think, or get mad, or tell him off now and then, especially if he's slouching?" Susan asked.

"Okay..." Kat breathed, marveling at how disorienting life in the order could be sometimes, even after six months. "And you've never done this...exorcism thing...before?"

"No. So?"

"And you're not afraid?"

"What's to be scared of?" Susan said calmly. "I know exactly who I belong to."

Kat slammed the trunk closed and looked up at Susan, mouth agape. "Dude, you so *fucking* rock."

29

TERRY'S NOSTRILS flared as he fought his own internal recoil at the smell. Nursing homes always had this effect on him. He signed in at the desk and gave the nurse seated behind it a friendly wave. He knew that with his tonsure and black cassock no one would question him. He glanced at the room number on his smartphone and picked a direction at random to seek it out.

It was not hard to find, and in a few moments Terry knocked on the wood of the open door. "Madeline?" he called.

An old woman was sitting up in bed, an oxygen strap beneath her nose. She had been looking at the green outside the window, but now she turned to Terry. "Have you come to take my food away?" she asked.

Terry didn't see any food, so he shook his head. "No, Sweetie. I'm just here to see you." He sidled up to her bed and gave her arm a gentle squeeze.

"Are you God?" she asked.

Terry laughed. "I hope not! If I am, we're all in trouble."

She seemed confused by this, as if she weren't sure whether to be comforted or disturbed by the news. Terry noticed and spoke quickly to reassure her. "I'm Father Terry. Pastor Oberlin is away—he's had a family emergency—so I'm here instead. Is that okay?"

She seemed pleased by that. "You're very nice," she said.

"I do try," Terry said, giving her a wink.

"I didn't want to come back," she said.

"What do you mean?" Terry said. "Didn't want to come back from where?"

"I was going to the movies," she said. "All my friends were there already." She looked toward the window and held her hand up as if trying to touch someone.

"When was this?" Terry asked, thinking that it had probably been a very long time since Madeline had been sufficiently ambulatory to go to the movies.

"Last night, of course," she said as if he should know better.

"Of course," he agreed, feigning a look of being chastened.

"But the man at the door wouldn't let me in," she said, dropping her voice in what could only have been sadness and disappointment.

"Why not?" Terry asked.

"I didn't have a ticket." She looked up at Terry and he noted that her eyes were watery. "I wish I had a ticket. They were all waiting for me."

Terry opened his mouth to ask Madeline if perhaps she had dreamed this, when the true significance of what she was saying hit him. He closed his mouth and took her hand in his. He swallowed hard and fought back his own tears.

"Oh my dear," he said. "It's just *fine*. Your friends are waiting for you, but they're not impatient. They are having a great time, and they will be eager to see you *whenever* you get there. And I happen to know that when the time is right, you *will* receive your ticket." Now the tears came for real. He couldn't stop himself. He didn't try.

"Do you promise?" she asked him, squeezing his hand like a vise.

"I promise," he said. "I have some experience with...this kind of thing. In fact"—he leaned in and whispered—"I'm on a first-name basis with some angels." He squeezed her hand back. "So, I can tell you with some authority that there's nothing you need to do but just relax and give thanks." He sat on the edge of the bed, adjusting his cassock.

She let go of his hand and patted it. "Good, because the plays here are pretty good."

"The plays?" Terry asked. "They have plays here? In the nursing home?"

"Yes!" she said, her eyes growing wide. "They're *silent* plays. I got to play a role. They star in them, usually." She pointed to her roommates, two of whom were either in comas or in a very deep sleep. Terry didn't think it likely that any of them were up to engaging in the thespian's craft.

"So...what happens in the plays?" Terry asked.

"Well, in one there was a campfire, on a low dais. And on the stones was a coffee pot, like the kind that cowboys use. And it was turning veeeery slowly." She moved her head in slow circles, obviously following the turning of the coffee pot in her mind's eye.

"And that was it?"

"It was profound."

"Uh...okay. Tell me about another one."

"She was there"—she pointed to her roommate, an elderly woman with a breathing tube coming from her mouth—"slicing up these huge wheels of cheese. The staff was all there; everyone was eating cheese."

"And that was the whole play?"

"It was delicious," she nodded.

Terry understood the symbolism of the first dream, or vision, or whatever it had been. But the plays baffled him. He wrinkled his brow and patted her hand again. "Madeline, dear, what did those plays mean to you?"

For the first time, she looked him directly in the eye, and he saw within her a keen intelligence that had been hidden only moments earlier. She smiled as if to pity his blindness. "Well, I think it's obvious."

"I'm thick, apparently," he said, wincing in an exaggerated way. "Tell me what *you* think it means."

"It's about the most important things in life."

"Which are?" Terry held his breath.

"Cowboy coffee and cheese," she said with a confident smile. "Wisconsin cheese, of course."

"Of course," Terry agreed.

30

SUSAN KNOCKED ON THE DOOR. A moment later, she knocked louder.

"Oooh, you *are* mad," Kat said under her breath. She listened closely and soon heard sounds coming from the house. A minute later, the door opened a crack.

"What do you want?" a man's voice said curtly.

"That depends," Susan said, jutting out one hip and holding up the court papers. "Who am I speaking to? The fucking demon or the asshole who sent us these?"

The man's eyes grew wide, and Kat could almost hear him gulp. *Go, Susan*, she thought.

"I am...I did. I...sent the papers," the man almost stuttered.

"So, you're Doug Fairfax?"

"Yeah."

"Did you think to ask *why* the friars weren't able to deliver you of your...*visitor*?"

"Um...no. I just assumed—"

"What? You assumed *what*, asshole?" Susan struck the screen door with her fist.

The man jumped. "Uh...that they were...fraudulent. Using me. I don't know. Making fun of me." He opened the door wider and leaned against the doorpost. He did not move to open the screen. "You know, they didn't *act* like monks."

"They're not monks," Susan and Kat said together, "they're friars." Kat could see Susan trying not to laugh. She struggled to pull a straight face herself.

Susan continued, "The reason they failed in your exorcism is because their bishop was killed in a motorcycle accident—while they were with you. They're Catholics—no bishop; no mojo. They did not intentionally mislead you or try to trick you. They did their best, and they couldn't do it because their *machine* is broken. Do you understand?"

"Machine?"

"It's a metaphor, jerk."

Doug winced. "You don't have to be so nasty."

Susan held the papers up again. "That. Makes. Two of us." She slapped the papers against the screen.

Doug recoiled slightly and looked chagrined. "Look, I'm sorry about what happened to your friend."

"Is he still in there?" Susan asked.

"Who?"

"The *demon*." Susan put both hands on her hips. "Are you even paying attention?"

"Oh yeah. He is."

"How does he manifest himself?"

"Uh..."

"Do you think it could *possibly* be something we haven't seen before?"

"Sex addiction. Whenever I get into a...situation, I black out, and he...takes over. I've hurt people—*he's* hurt people, I mean. I don't like it."

"Neither do those *people*, I'm sure," Susan said. "Do you still want to get rid of it?"

"Yes, of course!"

"I'll make you a deal," Susan said. "We make the demon go away, and you make *this* go away." She held up the court papers again.

"Yes, okay," Doug said immediately.

"Where do you want to do this?" Susan asked.

"Uh...I guess we could go back to the motel."

"Not necessary. We just need privacy for about five minutes."

Kat looked at Susan warily. "*What?*"

"None of my roommates are home now," Doug said. "Come on in, then." He unlocked the screen door.

Susan followed Doug into the house, and Kat followed. Inside, the living room was bright from a large picture window. The furniture was cheap IKEA stuff, but the rooms were fully appointed. Not artsy, Kat mused, but not granola, either. She'd feel comfortable living here.

"Please, have a seat," Doug said.

"I'll stand," Susan said. She dropped Dylan's kit bag on the floor. "You sit."

Doug obeyed. "Wait—how come you can do this when the...er, the friars...couldn't?"

"Short answer: I'm a Lutheran. Are you ready?"

Doug looked around uncertainly. "Five minutes? Really?"

Susan placed her hand on the man's head and said, "Peace on you, my brother, from God our Father, and from our Lord Jesus Christ." Then she stood back. "Hey, demon!" Susan shouted. "Hey, asshole! Let me tell you who we are: We are the ones who believe in one God, the Father, the Almighty, maker of Heaven and Earth, of all that is, seen and unseen. We believe in one Lord, Jesus Christ, the only son of God, eternally begotten of the Father, God from God, Light from Light, true God from true God."

In a clear, loud voice, Susan rattled off what Kat recognized as one of the creeds. As she spoke, Doug looked back and forth between Susan and Kat, unsure of what to make of them. His eyes rested on Kat, and his face looked almost pleading. Kat waved at him and offered a weak smile.

Finishing the creed, Susan said, "Pray with me, Kat. Our Father, who art in Heaven..."

This one Kat knew all of the words to, and she joined in enthusiastically. Even Doug started to move his lips, although Kat couldn't hear his words. When they had finished, Susan placed both hands on Doug's head and prayed, "O God, through Jesus you told us that whatever we ask of you in his name, you will do. You have commanded us and encouraged us to pray in his name, saying 'Ask and you shall receive.' You also told us, 'Call on me in your time of trouble, and I will deliver you and you will give me glory.' So, that's what I'm doing. I'm a fuckup and a sinner—but I'm *your* sinner."

With her psychic eye, Kat could see energy rising around Susan. Her voice got louder and, keeping one hand on Doug's head, she held the other up to Heaven. "I'm relying on these promises of yours, I'm obeying your commands, and I'm praying for your mercy with as much trust as I can pull together right now. I ask you to be kind to this man, to free him of the evil that plagues him, to break the hold that this demon has over him. I ask this in the name of Jesus Christ our Lord, who lives and reigns with you and the Holy Spirit, One God, world without end. Amen."

With that, Susan dropped her hands and opened her eyes. Doug looked around, waiting for something to happen.

"That's it," Susan said. "See you tomorrow." She picked up Dylan's kit bag and headed for the door.

"What?" Doug asked. "That's it?"

"That's it until tomorrow," Susan said. She turned and looked at Kat, "Are you coming?"

Kat's mouth had dropped open in disbelief, but she quickly closed it and scampered after Susan. Doug rose and followed them. "Is this a trick?" he asked.

"Did I ask you for any money?" Susan turned to face him, just shy of the door.

"Uh...no," Doug said.

"Did I do some kind of hocus-pocus?" she asked.

"No."

"Where's the *trick*?" she asked.

"But...you didn't do anything," Doug said.

"Bullshit. I prayed for you, you ungrateful prick."

"But nothing happened," Doug complained.

"Are you always so impatient?" Susan asked. "Because if you are, you'd be a bitch to live with."

"Be patient," Doug said, almost as an affirmation.

"Be patient. And chuck the porn, pronto—you obviously can't handle it," Susan said. "We'll be back tomorrow. I'm going to do exactly the same thing. And the day after that. And, if necessary, the day after that."

"But when will you drive out the demon?" Doug asked, looking hopeless. Kat's heart went out to him, and she wished Susan would temper her responses to him. She reached out and touched Susan's arm, willing her to be kinder.

She must have received the message because Susan did seem to soften. "Look, I won't *ever* drive out the demon," she said in a more patient tone. "I don't have the power. God will drive it out, but it will take some time."

"Okay, so when will *God* do that?"

"Basically, when he gets tired of hearing about it from me. I plan to pester him until he delivers you."

"Will that work?"

Kat saw Susan smile. "Yes, strange as it seems. Pretty much every time." She put out her hand and touched Doug's shoulder. "Those who trust in God lay hands on the sick, and they recover. I said I'll be praying for you, but actually I'll be bugging God every hour on the hour. Kat will, too. And we'll see you tomorrow."

The man just stared at them as they descended the steps to the street.

31

RICHARD BLINKED in the harsh light of the fluorescents as they flick-
ered on. To his great annoyance, one continued to flicker. Mother
Maggie had just waved them into a meeting room at the All Saints'
parish, and Dylan, Terry, and Mikael filed in dutifully. Richard found
a seat and watched Maggie with concern. Her hands were rubbed red
and raw, a sure sign she was distressed. As soon as everyone was
seated, a large man about Richard's own age appeared in the doorway, clutching a laptop to his chest with one hand and holding a
projector in the other.

"Friars, this is Davy Shannon, the diocesan communications officer. Davy, I'd like you to meet my friends, and the nicest exorcists
you're ever likely to meet." Quickly, introductions were made, and
Davy hastened to set up his equipment.

"Are you really exorcists?" he asked. "I mean, is that real?" He
plugged the projector into a port on his laptop.

"The real deal," Terry said with a tinge of pride. "And we have the
paid invoices from the Episcopal Diocese of California going back
seven years to prove it."

The man's eyebrows jumped. "That's not common knowledge, is
it?" He looked at Maggie.

"No, dear," she said, "but it's not a secret, either."

"It's just something that most people don't want to think about," Richard said.

"Where's Kat?" Dylan asked, mostly in Mikael's direction.

"Beats me," Mikael said. "I just got off work."

"She's with Susan," Terry said. "Brian said he overheard something about a lawsuit."

"*That* can't be good," Richard said. "Well, we'll just have to fill her in. Why didn't you bring Charlie?"

Mikael laughed. "Because we completely forgot about him!"

"Probably best," Terry said, a wide smile on his own face. "He's a bit...under the weather."

"There!" Davy announced. The diocesan logo filled up a mostly blank white wall.

"Okay, Maggie," Richard said. "What's happening? I've never seen you so jittery."

Maggie nodded at Davy. A picture of an older man in episcopal regalia filled the screen. "This," she said, a note of venom in her voice, "is Bishop John Preston, who is now, I am very sorry to report, the bishop of the Diocese of California."

"Yeah, Ah saw him on the news," Dylan said. "Good old boy. Georgia boy."

"He's a good old boy, all right," Maggie said. "He retired from the Diocese of South Carolina in 2005. Do you want to know how many women were ordained in that diocese during his tenure there?"

"I'm guessing zero," Terry said.

"You would be guessing correctly," Maggie said. "Do you know how many were ordained the year after he left, in 2006?"

"Tell us," Richard said.

"Twenty-six," she answered, her eyes hardening into little black pools of poison.

Richard whistled. "That's quite a backlog."

"No kidding," Maggie spat. "But wait, there's more. The Defense of Marriage Act? Preston had a major hand in drafting the language on that. He's...well connected in Washington."

"How about his treatment of gays and lesbians when he was in South Carolina?" Terry asked.

"What gays and lesbians?" Maggie asked. "As far as he's concerned, they don't exist, and when he finds them, they are rooted out."

"You mean, he's defrocked clergy?" Dylan asked.

"Far worse than that. I mean he's literally walked into parish offices and deleted parishioners from the parish rolls. He's unsealed pledge records and *returned pledges* to gay and lesbian parishioners."

"You're shitting me," Richard said.

"God's honest truth," Maggie said. "Davy, play that clip from CNN."

Preston's face filled the wall of the meeting room. He was confident, and his eyes shone. "There's no place for perverts in a Christian nation!" he bellowed, speaking to what looked like an enormous crowd. A roar went up, and Preston held up a hand to quiet them.

"Who's he speaking to?" Mikael asked.

"A Tea Party rally in Tennessee," Maggie answered.

"Thet's mah home state," Dylan said, deflating in his seat. "Ah needs me a doobie. Can Ah light up in here?"

Richard slapped the back of his head playfully.

"Ah *was* polite enough to ask," Dylan complained.

Preston was speaking again. "We need to return to biblical standards of morality!" The crowd cheered again. "And to do that, we must return to a biblical standard of law. We should not be a *tolerant* people. We should not *tolerate* wickedness in our midst. We should not *tolerate* wickedness where it can reach our children, where it can influence them, corrupt them, hurt them!" The cheers trebled in volume. "Gay behavior should be punished in our day as it was in Moses's! Perverts should be put to death—no ifs, ands, or buts. No years of supporting perverts in our prisons as they exhaust their appeals. It should be quick, public, and merciful." The crowd cheered again, but there was an edge of hesitancy in it. "Because we are a merciful people, what we must recognize is that perverted people are in pain—moral pain, psychological pain, existential pain. For people such as them, death is a mercy. And the fact that Hell awaits them is between them and God, and is none of our affair." Davy paused the file so that Preston froze with his mouth open and his forefinger raised to Heaven.

Terry's eyes were wide. "And this is the man who is bishop of California *right now*?"

Maggie nodded gravely. "That's why we're here."

"What Ah don't understand is why the good people of *this* diocese would want someone like *him* to be their bishop," Dylan wondered. Then he added, "Are there snacks?"

Maggie ignored his second remark. "That's what I don't understand, either. Davy, play the file you shot on the convention floor."

A new file sprang to life on the wall. The camera followed Preston as he wandered, in full regalia, around the floor. A voice boomed. "We'll proceed with the results of the new ballot. San Francisco Deanery?" The camera whizzed across the room in a messy blur of color and lit upon a frumpy, middle-aged woman with librarian glasses. "The San Francisco Deanery voted 27 to 5 for...Bishop Preston."

"Stop!" Terry said. "Can you roll that back a little? Watch the guy behind her."

Davy restarted the file. Behind the woman speaking, a man in a blue suit was shaking his head vigorously. Suddenly, however, his eyes focused on one spot, and his shoulders sagged. "That's not right," Terry said. "Can we see that again?"

Davy played the file again. Richard nodded in unison with the others as he watched the man carefully. "I'd sure love to see the actual numbers on those ballots, to see if they match up with what was reported," Richard said.

"Ah am with you there, buddy," Dylan said, his head resting on his hands as he squinted at the wall.

"What is Preston doing while this is happening?" Mikael asked.

"Near as I can tell, and there are a number of cameras rolling—smartphones, mostly—he's wandering through the crowd. Here's a long shot of the convention floor." He played a different file. The sound was muted, but they could still make out what was being said.

"Look at that"—Terry said, pointing at the blurry figure that was Preston—"he's travelling from deanery to deanery as they take their votes."

"Okay, what do we think is going on here?" Richard asked. "Ideas. No judgment, just brainstorming."

"It could be demonic," Dylan drawled, "but the apparent need for proximity makes no sense. He wouldn't need to be anywhere near a demon for it to do its work."

"It could be a glamour variation," Mikael said. "A spell. The people think they're voting for one person but actually writing down a different name—or the name that appears, that is read by the person reading, is different from what's actually on the paper."

"That would explain the reaction of the man behind the woman reading the deanery results," Richard nodded.

"But it wouldn't explain his zombification immediately after-ward," Mikael said. "Boom! Fuckin' zombie."

"Point," Richard conceded.

"An influence spell?" Mikael offered.

"You're the expert on spells, Mikael," Terry said, his eyes narrowing as he thought. "Is proximity important?"

"Well...no. That doesn't fit." Mikael's shoulders sagged.

"Okay," Richard said, getting up and writing on the chalkboard. "Let's list what we see. Proximity is an issue. Mind control of some kind is going on. And in more than one person. And it's not blanket, but targeted; otherwise, both this guy and this woman would both be...zombified at the same time."

Richard could see nods all around. "So, what could it be?"

No one spoke.

Richard put his hands on his hips. "Really? We got nothing?"

"Waal...look on the bright side," Dylan said, "we know what it's *not*. Now we just have to look at what we haven't ruled out yet."

"It's not a spell. It's not a demon..." Richard discovered he was chewing on the chalk. He spat it out.

"Thet thar stuff comes in bubble-gum flavor, too, dude," Dylan said helpfully.

Richard wiped his mouth and turned back to the chalk board.

"Talisman?"

All eyes turned to Terry. He squinted. "Show us that file again, please, Davy. Let's watch what he's doing."

They watched as Preston moved through the crowd, clutching at his crozier and holding it forth whenever the results were being read for a particular deanery.

"Bingo," Richard breathed.

"It's the crozier?" Mikael asked.

"Davy, do you have a clearer shot of him in the crowd?" Richard asked.

"Yeah, a couple of them. There's the one we saw at the beginning, before we panned over to the vote." He played that one again. They saw Preston stop and close his eyes. Then the camera zoomed away in a wash of color.

"And here's another one shot with a phone." A grainy file jumped to life on the wall and quickly focused on the bishop. He pressed one hand to his forehead, closed his eyes, and held forth his shepherd's crook.

"That's very curious," Richard said. "It's like Moses holding his staff up during the battle against the Amalekites in Exodus 17."

"As long as he held it up, the Israelites won," Terry remembered, nodding. "But as soon as he lowered it, the Amalekites started winning."

"Riiiiight," Dylan nodded.

"So, what's so special about that crozier?" Terry said, leaning in for a closer look.

"It's big," Richard noted. "Oversize. It's bulky. It's weird."

"It sure is..." Terry breathed.

"Whatever it is," Richard said, "it allows him to control people. Lots of people. Whatever that crozier *really* is, it allows him to completely have his way."

"Zero accountability," Terry whistled. "Zero democracy."

"And that's just about as dangerous as church people can get," Richard agreed. But a sinking feeling in his gut told him that it wasn't true. It *could* be more dangerous. He just didn't know *how*.

32

LARCH LIT a candle for mood and called the meeting to order. The assembled magickians of the Lodge of the Hawk and Serpent lumbered up to the table almost reluctantly, each of them focused on something else. Fraters Purderabo and Turpelo were locked in a heated argument over the relative efficacy of two medieval grimoires, while Frater Eleazar stared off into space, almost terminally distracted.

Frater Khams emerged from the kitchen with a veggie tray that seemed to be unusually heavy on bell pepper wedges. Larch scowled. He hated bell peppers. But there were also Fritos. Khams next emerged with guacamole and a large pitcher of iced tea, which he placed on the table.

Larch frowned at the guacamole. "Trying to send a message, Frater?" he said, raising one eyebrow in Khams's direction.

"Far from it. Sale on avocados at the Nob Hill Market." He held his hands up in a *don't shoot me* gesture. Larch let it go. Nobody else seemed to even notice. In fact, no one seemed to be paying much attention at all. Larch picked up a spoon and tapped at his water glass until the grimoire conversation abated.

"Gentlemen of the Light," Larch began with his ritual greeting, "brothers and comrades in the service of liberation—let us bring our meeting to order so that we may efficiently direct our energies for the transformation of mankind."

"Hear, hear!" they all shouted, banging on the table.

Larch turned to Eleazar. "Master Secretary," he addressed the officer, "what is at the top of our agenda?"

"Frater Purderabo has moved that we change the wording of our ritual greeting from 'the transformation of mankind' to 'the transformation of humankind,'" he said, looking at his papers.

Larch sighed, wondering just how much transformation would be assisted by this motion. Nevertheless, he acquiesced to duty and pointed at Purderabo. "Please state your rationale, Frater."

"It's time for the magickal community to come into the twenty-first century and to be sensitive to women's issues. Use of exclusionary language in our proceedings and rituals is insensitive and damaging to women," he stated firmly.

"That sounds reasonable," said Khams, nodding.

Larch looked around the table and pointed out that there were only men present. "We are in precious little danger of offending any women tonight," he said.

"But that's just the problem. Women might want to join us if we used more inclusive language," countered Purderabo.

"Master Secretary, in the seventy-five years since the founding of our lodge, how many women have petitioned to join us?" Larch asked.

Frater Eleazar did not need to consult any papers. "None, Frater." Then he raised a finger. "Although Frater Dubois in 1975 did undergo a sex change operation...that didn't end well..." he trailed off.

"But if one *should* wish to join us..." Purderabo began hopefully.

"A motion has been made to change our deliberative and ritual language in the alleged interests of hypothetical females," Larch stated authoritatively. "All in favor?"

Khams, Purderabo, and Turpelo raised their hands.

"All opposed?" He looked over at Eleazar, who shifted nervously. "Uh...I'm against it? If you're against it, that is," he smiled obsequiously. Larch shuddered inwardly and turned back to the rest of the table. "The ayes have it," he said with a disappointed note of resignation in his voice, "Let the mythical women clamoring for admittance rejoice."

Purderabo slapped Turpelo on the back. He, in turn, was congratulated by Khams. "This is a great day for the magickal community!" Purderabo announced, raising his glass.

"Yes...a red-letter day for the worldwide occult community," Larch said darkly. "Next on the agenda?"

"New aprons!" Eleazar read. "This is my item. I mean, I suggest we discuss it—but only if, of course, you all deem it necessary."

Larch ran his fingers through his thinning hair and wished he could be...well, almost anywhere else. *The endodontist's?* he mused. *Yes, I'd much prefer to be at the endodontist's.* "New aprons, Frater Eleazar? I am on the edge of my seat. Pray, give us your rationale."

"Our old Masonic aprons are getting a bit ratty," he said. "And what with the bit of a windfall we got from the Dane affair—"

"The proceeds from the Dane affair are going for repairs on the lodge house," Larch declared firmly. "There will be no discussion regarding other uses for those funds."

"Uh..." Eleazar fussed with the front of his shirt, his flat, puffy features looking lost for a moment. "Yes, of course. Well, regardless of how we pay for them, we need them."

"I've never noticed that our aprons were getting ratty," Khams said.

"Mine is starting to fray," Eleazar said.

"Then maybe you should replace your own damned apron," Khams said. "Mine's fine." Heads nodded all around.

"Mine has a soup stain." Frater Turpelo raised his chubby hand.

Larch bunched his eyebrows together momentarily. "Frater, how on earth did you get soup on your Masonic apron? There's no food allowed in the temple—you know that."

"It happened at that Thelema Camp party," Turpelo said thickly. "We came in ritual gear to give them our blessing—"

"Oh yes, that was grand," Khams nodded.

"And then...well, I don't remember much of what followed. But when I woke up the next morning, my apron was stained."

"Not to mention your reputation," whispered Purderabo. Khams tried to stifle a giggle, but this only caused tea to erupt from his nose in two tiny streams. Turpelo scowled.

At which crossroads in his life, Larch wondered, had he made the wrong turn? Which precise decision had brought him here, and how might be possibly correct it? As the meeting wore on, Larch felt his mood grow bleaker. Finally, they had worked through all of the agenda items—the most portentous seemed to be a motion to hold a summit meeting with a recently formed Gnostic group in Hayward. When Frater Eleazar finally announced, "New business," Larch held up his hand.

"I have something very important to present," he said. He rose and began to pace back and forth at the head of the table. "As some of you know, I have been trying to recreate some of the John Dee workings in my private temple." There were nods all around. "During these sessions, I have made contact with a spirit named Pim." It seemed odd to utter the sound of her name aloud. His stomach did a little flip-flop, which, he was grateful to note, was invisible to his assembled fraters.

"I have heard of her," Purderabo said. "The occult bulletin boards say that she has succeeded Madimi."

"I thought she *was* Madimi at first," Larch acknowledged. "And she appears to be in every way like her."

"Has the contact been regular?" asked Purderabo, who seemed keenly interested.

"It has," Larch said.

"And what has she offered you?"

Larch was struck by the question. "How do you know that she has offered me something?" Larch asked.

"Because that is what she *does*." Purderabo waved his chubby hand in an *of course* gesture.

"Well...yes, she has offered me something," Larch said. "But I have not yet accepted it...because I'm not sure I trust her."

"That's very John Dee-ish," Eleazar pointed out.

"Yes, thank you," Larch said dismissively. "If I aspired to be John Dee, I would be flattered."

"Wonderful," Eleazar bent to write that down in the minutes.

Larch sighed. "I have brought the matter before you to ask your assistance in a discernment. Pim has offered me an army. My question to you is, were I to lead an army, what would I do with it?"

A look of wonder came over the faces of all those gathered at the table. Frater Turpelo paused with a chip halfway to his lips. Eleazar began to salivate on his notepad.

"Uh...what *sort* of army?" Purderabo asked, a suspicious look on his red, puffy face.

"An army of the possessed. It is gathering even now," Larch said.

"*Where* is it gathering?"

"I...don't know. Pim just said it was gathering."

"You're taking a lot on faith with this Pim," Purderabo said. "You know that she's a cocktease, yes?"

For some reason, this made Larch angry. Purderabo might just as well have asked if Larch knew the sky was blue or that Kraft Macaroni & Cheese was yummy. Larch wanted to shout, "Yes, I know she's a cocktease, you idiot—the buttons on my 501s are so strained they're in danger of blowing like champagne corks," but the imagery was simply too close to home. He kept his mouth shut.

"What should I do with an army?" he asked again, this time through gritted teeth.

"Larch—" Turpelo began.

"Magickal names, please!" Eleazar scolded. "I'm writing that infraction down."

Turpelo took no notice but continued his sentence, "You seem... irritable. Are you quite all right?"

He wasn't, of course. Larch stopped pacing and wavered visibly as if he were a bowling pin that might or might not topple. Purderabo nudged Turpelo. "Someone's *enchanted*," he said in a low, singsong voice.

Larch wanted to say, "Fuck you," but he didn't. He wanted to scream, to bash heads, but he didn't. Instead, he wavered, his eyes large, his hands behind his back. He looked into the beady black eyes of Purderabo. "Help me," he said weakly.

"Oh, I don't think we're going to do *that*, exactly," Purderabo was rubbing his hands in delight. "Let's figure out what we're going to do with that army of yours."

SUNDAY

33

DYLAN HAD a hard time concentrating during morning prayer. This being Sunday, they were supposed to be having Eucharist. But without a bishop, none of them could say mass. As a result, this Lord's Day was beginning just like any other.

Dylan woke frustrated and tense. Two decent bong hits before rolling out of bed had relaxed and fortified him to face the day, but now, as he tried to focus on the words of the Psalm, the meaning seemed to be like a rope, slipping away whenever he tried to grasp at it.

But the actual prayer part was different, and he was able to pour his heart out to God in the silence. He held his ample belly in his arms and rocked back and forth, baring his soul and laying his fears and faults and hopes before Jesus. When Terry rang the bell to call them back for the dismissal, he felt loved and encouraged.

And there was the smell of bacon. If the world possessed a more potent restorative, he did not know what it could possibly be. Thicker than coffee, sweeter than sugar, the smell of bacon wafted through the house, tickling his nose, calling him by a secret name no other foodstuff knew. He rose, he worshipped, he followed.

Dylan sat in his usual place, kissing Susan on the cheek and gratefully accepting a mug full of steaming coffee from Brian. Terry and Mikael followed soon after, and Kat joined them momentarily, apparently after making a short pit stop. Charlie had, it seemed, been there for a while, grinning stupidly.

"Don't mind him," Brian said. "We're working on it."

"What does *that* mean?" Mikael asked.

"We had a little training mishap yesterday," Kat said. "Mornin', Randy!"

"Mornin', Sis!" Randy called from the mirror.

In the office, the phone rang. "That's it!" Susan said, throwing up her hands. "I'm taking the fucking thing off the hook!" She stormed into the hall toward the office.

Everyone froze in the wake of her angered outburst until Brian ordered, "Say grace," and turned to the stove. Dylan's nostrils flared. Bacon acomin'. Tobias stuck his nose in his crotch and wagged.

"Oh. Right. Let us pray." Dylan pushed Tobias away and held his hands up in the *orans* position. "Lord, the game's afoot, and we're gonna need your help with it all. Do not forsake us, O Lord our God. Oh, and bless this food, please. Thanks and amen."

"Amen," they all replied and tucked in with gusto. Susan sat down next to Dylan again, without missing a single plate as it went by. No business was discussed for several minutes as potatoes were passed, bacon was distributed, juice was poured, and broccoli dished out.

"I've never thought of broccoli as a breakfast food," Kat commented.

"Try it with the maple-cheese sauce," Dylan suggested. "It's plenty breakfasty."

"It's runny," said Charlie. Dylan noticed there was maple-cheese sauce running down Charlie's chin. He made a mental note and tried not to look.

When the urgency of the first helpings subsided, a more leisurely pace kicked in. Terry pulled out his cell phone and dialed. In a moment, Richard's voice was wishing them a cheery good morning.

"Mornin' to you both," Dylan said.

"Duunel is still sleeping, apparently," Richard's voice said wryly. "He hasn't incited me to a single felony yet this morning."

"That's gotta be hard to live with," Kat said, her brows furrowing momentarily.

"You're telling me!" Richard agreed. "Actually, it's not much different from the voice in your head anyway—just snarkier and turned up to 11."

"First things first," Dylan said, making a sincere effort at leadership. "Brian, how's training going for our oblates here?"

"Well," Brian said, uncharacteristically taking a seat beside Terry, "not well. We did a simple Malkuth exercise, and I'm pleased to say that Kat had a vivid and very normal experience. Pretty much what we were hoping for."

"And Charlie?" Dylan asked.

"Charlie didn't follow directions." Brian allowed himself a glower as he looked in Charlie's direction.

"She has big boobies." Charlie pointed at Susan.

"I'm going to kill him," Susan said to no one in particular.

"You may have to stand in line," Kat responded.

"Thet's not right..." Dylan commented, pointing at Charlie.

"Exactly," Brian said. "He did the exercise all right, but he focused on Kether instead."

"You are an idiot," Randy announced in Charlie's direction. Mikael adjusted his volume on the guitar amp.

"My anus is sticky," Charlie said.

Brian rolled his eyes. "I've been doing reiki on him, and Terry can confirm that I've almost closed the breach in his crown chakra. We've still got some repair to do, but I think we can get his impulse control back in a day or so."

Dylan nodded. "Thet sounds like a plan."

Terry asked for the jam, then said, "I have a pastoral visit scheduled for this afternoon, but I'll begin Void training with them this morning."

"Do you think Charlie is in good enough condition for that?" Susan asked.

"He's alert, and there's no chakra work involved," Brian said. "He may say inappropriate things to the Sandalphon, but he's in an impressionable place right now, which can only help. At least he won't be arrogantly thinking he knows it all. I think he's actually more teachable now than he was yesterday."

"Okay, dude, thet sounds like a plan," Dylan said to Terry with a nod.

Susan patted Dylan's knee. "A for effort, dear," she whispered in his ear.

He wasn't sure how to take that, but he smiled appreciatively, which was always a safe default.

Richard's voice piped up. "Susan, what's this I hear about an exorcism?"

Susan filled them in briefly on the previous day's events. Terry whistled. "Will that even work?"

Susan shrugged. "Worked for Luther," she said, "and we have to do *something* or we'll lose our house to lawyer's fees—even if we win the lawsuit."

Richard's voice was grave. "Susan, thank you. You've really stepped up in a big way here. And I'm glad you're taking Kat along. At least *someone* is showing her the ropes, since we're out of commission."

Terry reached for the potatoes. "I didn't even know Luther had a method of exorcism."

"Absolutely," Susan said. "Just because the Catholic Church went away doesn't mean the demons did."

"Word," Dylan agreed.

"His method is less dramatic. And it takes longer. But as for effectiveness"—she shook her head—"we'll just have to see. I'm praying hard."

"Me, too," Kat added.

"What's the plan, then?" Dylan asked his wife.

"Kat and I are going to go over every afternoon until the demon is gone," Susan said.

"You've got a busy day, then," Dylan said to Kat. "Training in the morning and demons in the afternoon."

"Can't wait," Kat said, hoisting her orange juice as if making a toast.

Dylan turned toward the phone. "And dude, what's up with the bishop-hunt?"

"I struck out," Richard said. "Parkison is an asshole. Can you believe that he offered us episcopal oversight only on the condition that Susan come over once a week and clean his house, and Dylan had to mow his lawn?"

Susan's jaw dropped. "You are fucking kidding me," she breathed.

"God's honest truth," Richard answered. "Even Duunel was floored. He tried to get me to kill him."

"Good thing I wasn't there," Susan said. "I would have done it for you."

Terry cleared his throat. "So, let's talk about the main item of business, can we? Preston?"

Kat's shoulders slumped. "I was sorry to miss that meeting," she said. "Can you fill us in?"

Terry did, and Brian beside him started nodding. "Looks like I know what I'm doing today," he said. "Sounds like I'm researching talismans that can do mind control."

"Thet sounds like an excellent plan," Dylan nodded. He snuck Tobias a bit of bacon, but Brian saw anyway. Dylan flashed an apologetic smile.

"I did some web searching when we got home last night," Mikael said, taking an iPad out of his shoulder bag. "Check this out." His fingers sought the web page he was after.

"What is it?" Kat asked.

"It's Bishop Preston's acceptance speech after his election," Mikael said. He held the iPad up and started the YouTube video.

Bishop Preston's fleshy visage filled the screen, looking triumphant and grim at the same time. The file stuttered, then started to play. Mikael turned up the volume.

"I want to give thanks to our Lord Jesus Christ for this opportunity to serve him in this way, and thanks to the good people of the Diocese of California for placing your trust in me. I assure you that I will be a faithful head pastor to you.

"This commitment is implanted deep in my bones. It is, in fact, my heritage. My family traces its lineage all the way back to the first Christian community among the Mongols. On my father's side, I am directly descended from Prester John, the terror of the Moors. You will perhaps remember that when the Crusaders' cause was failing due to poor leadership and sinful, licentious behavior, Prester John arrived in the nick of time—he rooted out the rot in the Crusaders' ranks, and he led those Christian soldiers onward to victory!

"Today, I willingly shoulder his mantle. The times are wicked, but God has not failed us. It is no accident that he has sent me to you, today. The years you have suffered under poor and unfaithful leadership are at an end! The time of sinful, licentious behavior among your clergy is over! I vow to root out the rot in this diocese, and I will lead the true soldiers of Christ in this diocese to victory—victory over sin! Victory over the twin dragons of liberalism and relativism! Victory over the homosexual and feminist agendas that have torn our church apart and guttered her sacred mission."

There were a few hoots and scattered applause, but mostly the crowd watched in hushed, horrified silence—as did the friars. Mikael clicked off the iPad.

"Holy Christ," Terry exhaled. "Richard, did you get that?"

"Most of it. I'm pulling up the file on YouTube now to give it another listen."

"What the fuck?" Susan asked, her mouth gaping open.

"Who is Pres...Prester? John?" Kat asked.

"My scrotum itches," Charlie announced.

Brian ignored him. "Prester John is a legendary figure in Christian history."

Terry piped up. "Some say he was a Mongol prince; some that he was Indian. All agree that he was a terrible warrior—terrible as in 'a holy terror,' quite literally. His army destroyed the Muslim forces in Egypt during the Fifth Crusade."

Richard's voice continued, coming from the tinny speaker. "Later, he was thought to rule a kind of Christian Shangri-La, except that no one knows exactly where it was. 'Prester' comes from 'priest'—Prester John was a priest-warrior-king, which was kind of a medieval ideal."

"The stuff romances are made of," Susan said. "Er...that would be *medieval* romances, not Harlequin romances. Just clarifying 'cause I read the medieval ones...not...never mind. So, what does this mean?"

"Ya mean, other than Bishop Preston is delusional?" Dylan asked.

"He's more than delusional," Richard said. "He's dangerous. He just pulled off an impossible coup. Basically, he just hijacked the most liberal Episcopal diocese in the country. Why? What's in it for him?"

They all stared at their plates. Terry got up and carried his plate to the sink. "So, let's find out—" He froze.

Dylan narrowed one eye, noticing Terry's sudden arrest. "Dude, what's up?"

Without looking down, Terry set his plate into the sink and leaned toward the window. "Um, guys...why are all those people out there?"

Almost as a single person, everyone jumped up from the table and crowded around the kitchen window. Sure enough, across the street, about twenty people were gathered. Some were milling about, but most were just staring—straight at them.

"So...why are they there?" Terry repeated. "Aaaaand, why are they staring at *us*?"

Mikael straightened up. "Let's go ask them." And before anyone could stop him, he was gone.

The group stayed huddled by the window as they watched Mikael set out across the street. They couldn't see his face, but he certainly didn't act scared. He stuck his hands through the slits in his cassock into his jeans pockets and sauntered across the street in an unhurried fashion. About five feet from the curb, he pulled his right hand out and gave a little wave. He was obviously talking to them, or trying to.

No one even saw the first punch coming. When it connected with Mikael's jaw, they saw his head whip around, and a stream of spit and blood flew to the street. Kat gave out a shriek, and Susan moved to wrap her arm around Kat's chest, pulling her close.

"What's going on?" Randy called from the mirror. "Someone tell me what's happening!"

"Randy, what are they doing?" Richard's voice called from the phone.

Another attacker stepped up, but by this time Mikael had sprung into the classic *hanmi* stance—the position in which aikido artists meet their attackers. Dylan gripped the edge of the sink as he watched his friend repeat what he had done in competition very recently—take on multiple attackers with speed and grace.

"We've got to get out there!" Brian called. "Through the back, grab shovels!"

Tobias barked, and almost as a single unit, they filed into the back yard. Brian was ahead of them, handing out garden tools and pushing open the gate. Tobias leaped to the fore, barking and running full out. Dylan puffed as he ran, but he did not lag. He saw Mikael artfully dodge every swing, almost dancing as he pushed the blows past himself without allowing them to connect. And bit by bit, Dylan noticed that he was backing up toward them.

Tobias surged past Mikael and barked a blue streak at his nearest attacker. The man hesitated and backed up a step. The barking and snarling were fierce, and the other attackers likewise halted their approach.

"Mikael, run!" Dylan called, and with relief watched as Mikael did just that, retreating behind the line of his armed friends.

In a surprisingly neat formation, the friends stood with tools radiating outward, moving back toward the house with slow but steady progress. Tobias continued to bark, but he kept pace with them, backing up but remaining their point guard about six feet out.

Terry called, "Okay, everyone, if this is demonic, we'll know as soon as we hit the curb—because they won't be able to follow past the halfway point in the street. That's where the wards are set—and they should still be good since they were made before...you know."

Dylan saw Susan stumble as she tripped over the curb, and he grabbed at her forearm to steady her. She clutched gratefully at his shoulder and righted herself. A moment later, they were all on the curb, and Toby was past the halfway point, still barking furiously. But their attackers continued to advance. All held their breath as the horde approached the middle of the street—and stopped. They released their breath in a storm of relief.

Lowering their garden tools, the friends stood in a gaggle facing off against the crowd. Tobias seemed to sense that the danger was lessened, and his barks grew less insistent, replaced by a worried whine as he nuzzled at Dylan's hand for reassurance.

Dylan saw Kat fighting back tears as she examined Mikael's face. His lip was cut, and he held his mouth open. He was talking, though, and reassuring her.

"Okay, we've got a real problem on our hands," Terry said. "Those aren't zombies, but they're damn close."

"Are they possessed?" Susan asked.

"I think it's highly likely," Terry nodded. "They're either possessed or demonically compelled. Mikael, did any of them say anything to you?"

"No," Mikael said, and Dylan was relieved that his jaw didn't seem to be broken. "It's like the lights are on but nobody's home."

Terry nodded. "That's what it looks like to me, too."

"What does that mean?" Susan asked.

"It means that all those people are probably possessed by demons who are front-and-center, meaning they've taken over the bodies. The people are still in there, but they're being actively suppressed. And the fact that these demons aren't saying anything tells me that they're not used to possessing humans. Look at them; they're barely upright."

"They sure didn't know how to fight," Mikael said. "Well, that first one got off a good punch, but I was able to pull away from the worst of it. The rest of them move with the grace of geriatric mummies."

"Like that angel who took over Randy's body—he didn't know how to work it," Kat said, making a connection.

"They're not *that* clueless; they've probably had some training, just no experience. But you're right, same principle," Terry agreed.

"So, what do we do?" Brian asked.

All eyes turned to Dylan. He began to sweat. "Holy Christ on a stick, don't look at me!" Dylan shouted at them. "Ah have no clue what to do here! Ah'm not Dicky, and Ah'm never gonna *be* Dicky!"

"Honey, this is no time for a tantrum," Susan scolded.

Doobie, Dylan thought, and the compulsion cut through every other concern. *I needs me a doobie fucking NOW.* He fumbled at his cassock and pulled out a battered fattie. Shielding his lighter from the wind, he lit it. The ritual action of it steadied him, and by the time he had it well lit, a season of calm rested on him. "What *can* we do?" he asked, mostly in Terry's direction.

"Until we get a bishop, there's nothing we can do," Terry said. "And someone knows it because I've never seen that many possessed people in one place in my life. And there's more of them every minute —look!" He pointed down the street, where two more people—a woman in a muumuu and floppy hat, and a man in an electrician's uniform—were walking toward them, their faces twisting with rage, their steps uncertain and plodding.

Dylan took another long drag, feeling every moment calmer and more in control. But he still didn't have a clue what to do.

"Even if Susan's Lutheran method of exorcism is successful," Terry went on, "it's too slow to handle all of these. We have *got* to find a bishop, and I mean *yesterday*. Because unless I miss my guess, this"—he gestured at the loitering assembly of the damned—"is just the tip of the iceberg."

34

MADIHAH RAN TOWARD THE SANDBOX, squealing.

"That's far enough, Habibi," her mother called. Fadilah Zaman pulled her hijab away from her face. It was early summer, but the heat was already beginning to get to her.

Sitting on the park bench where she could watch her daughter playing, she chewed at a fingernail. Looking to the west, she saw her neighbor Eshal coming up the street, pushing a stroller. Fadilah waved and smiled despite the nerves that caused her stomach to tighten into a dense, hard ball of fear. "*Assalamu 'alaykum,*" she said, when Eshal was close enough to hear—"Peace be upon you."

"*Wa alaykum us salaam,*" Eshal responded with a weary smile —"And peace be upon you, too."

Eshal was her mirror opposite. Where Fadilah was bone thin, Eshal was a large and fleshy woman. Fadilah was reserved, while Eshal gushed about everything. Fadilah's family went to the progressive Sufi mosque, while Eshal's family were of the conservative Wahhabi sect.

"My feet are like barking dogs," Eshal said, dumping herself with a huff onto the park bench next to Fadilah.

Fadilah knew that Eshal's husband would not approve of their friendship, but it wasn't like she was asking them over for supper. She thought of Eshal as her playground friend, and she figured that Eshal thought of her in the same way. She was fond of Eshal, certainly, but never thought of deepening the friendship. Things simply were the way they were, and Fadilah was content.

But there were plenty of things about which she was not content. The conflict in the newspapers regarding their community scared her. She eyed Madihah nervously and forced herself to smile when her daughter looked over at her and waved.

"Did you see the papers?" Eshal asked.

"How could I not?" answered Fadilah. They spoke, imperfectly, in English, since their families were from different countries. They shared some Arabic phrases, but Arabic was not Fadilah's first language, and she barely understood it when it was read aloud at the mosque.

"Samir calls it a crusade," Eshal said, shaking her head.

That sounds exactly like something Samir would say, Fadilah thought, even though she had never met Eshal's husband. She knew the *type*.

"I think it's just political grandstanding," Fadilah said.

"What does your husband say?" Eshal asked.

Fadilah wanted to snap at her and say something like, *Who cares what my husband says?* but she held her tongue. She cared what her husband thought, and she agreed with him. She was just jumpy today. No need to take it out on poor Eshal. "He thinks the same."

"My husband thinks we should go away," Eshal said.

"Back to Saudi?"

"No, silly, just to Canada for a couple of weeks. He has some vacation coming, and we have cousins in Toronto."

"That sounds nice," Fadilah said, feeling herself relax a bit at the fantasy of going to Canada. She liked Canada. It was clean and bright. It was certainly less...bleak. Michigan was rich, compared with Iran, but—having acclimatized herself to America—she had begun to see how it was also...dumpy, struggling—ugly, in some ways.

Eshal fussed in the stroller. Leaning over, Fadilah saw her baby looking around, his dark eyes filled with wonder. For a moment, she forgot about everything and was filled with wonder herself.

In the distance, she heard a whine she couldn't place. Looking up, she saw a streak of light in the sky. "*Ya Allah ehfadnaa*," she breathed —"God save us." Jumping up, Fadilah rushed to where Madihah was playing and snatched her up in her arms. She dropped to the ground and covered her daughter with her own body. The flash of light came first, so powerful that she never felt the earth heave beneath her.

35

TERRY OPENED the door to the bathroom and smiled at Susan, at work at her desk. "Is the phone still off the hook?" he asked.

"Yes, but I'm writing down the voice mails." Susan looked at a clipboard behind her. "Seventy-two calls in the past two days," she said, looking back at him grimly. "That's a record, several times over."

Terry whistled. "And I'm guessing every Roman Catholic and Episcopal diocese in the state is represented."

"At least twice," she said, "plus seven Independent Catholic jurisdictions and the Lutheran Missouri Synod."

"You're shitting me," he said. "You should tell them about working Luther's method."

"They won't talk to *me*," she said, "I'm ELCA. I'm with *the Devil*."

"Bastards," Terry smirked. "Let's pray Richard has some luck. In the meantime..."

"You have students waiting," Susan smiled at him. "Relax, Honey, we'll get through this. We always do."

KAT SAW Terry step into the chapel, and she grinned broadly, excited about their next lesson. She felt bad about Charlie's mishap last time —but not *that* bad. After all, he had done it to himself by not following directions.

She saw Charlie scowl at Terry, but he said nothing. Terry grabbed a zafu and sat in front of them, making himself comfortable.

"Okay, peeples, this morning I'm going to introduce you to the Abyss."

"That sounds scary," Kat said.

"That's baby stuff," Charlie said.

Terry pointed at him and squinted dangerously. "That's enough of that. Unless you want to fry your nervous system again, you're going to do *exactly* what I tell you, exactly *when* I tell you, exactly *how* I tell you. Am I clear?"

"Yeah..." Charlie said sullenly.

"Yes *what*?" Terry asked.

"Yes...*ma'am*?" Charlie raised an eyebrow.

"Close enough," Terry conceded. "Okay, we're going to go into vision again, but instead of climbing the Tree of Life, we're going to enter the Void. This is going to take us to a desert, which we'll have to cross on foot."

"Why don't we just imagine us up a couple of ATVs?" Charlie asked.

"Are you through?" Terry said impatiently.

"I'm just asking," Charlie said. "As long as we're doing imaginal work, why not save us the trouble *walking*?"

"Because, strange as it might seem to you, there is value in the walking," Terry said. "Plus, you're going to encounter *beings*. You're going to talk to the beings while we walk."

"Beings," Charlie said skeptically. "What sort of beings? Demons?"

"No, not in the desert. Not usually, that is," Terry said. "But you never know. The desert is kind of like a hotel lobby. It's a waiting place and a going-through place. Are you ready?"

Kat felt a little tug of fear, but she mastered it. "Ready," she said.

"Then close your eyes," Terry said, "and picture before you a black window into nothingness. Can you see it?"

Kat sensed that no one was looking at her, but she nodded anyway. What she saw was like an enormous cat's eye staring at her, unblinking and oddly voracious.

"Okay, I didn't tell you exactly what it looks like, so if you're really seeing it, you'll notice some things about it," Terry said. "Like how it's narrow at the top and bottom but wider in the middle. It's shimmering all around the edges. You'll also see little ripples in it as if you're looking at the surface of a pond."

Kat leaned in and examined it in her mind's eye. She definitely saw the shimmering. She also saw the ripples, although they were faint.

"Okay, being careful not to touch the edges of it, step into it, one foot at a time," Terry said. "I'm going to go first. Watch how I do it in your mind's eye. I'll see you on the other side. It will seem less imaginal once you go through."

She watched as Terry lifted one foot and placed it inside the black slit of the cat's eye. He balanced carefully, and once his foot was firmly planted on the other side, he carefully drew up the other leg. Then he disappeared.

She looked at Charlie. "Do you want to go next?" she asked.

She saw him scowl, and it seemed to her that he seemed frightened. She stepped over to him and reached for his hand. "It's okay, Charlie. We're doing this together."

He snatched his hand away. "I'm not afraid! Bitch..." She recoiled as if he had struck her.

She breathed deeply to regain her center. When she spoke, her voice was measured and calm. "Charlie, I'm on your side here. I don't know if you've really noticed yet, but if you're here, you're *loved*."

He cocked his head as if he did not understand the word. She sighed. "Well, I hope you'll find that out sometime." She motioned toward the Void. "After you."

He grunted and stepped toward the black wedge shimmering

before them. Just as Terry had done, he placed one foot over, then drew up the other. Then he winked out of sight.

"Hoo, boy," Kat said, drawing in a huge breath and then letting it out. In two short steps, she covered the distance to the Void and lifted her left leg inside. It was like stepping into a warm bath. She felt a breeze on her ankle, but it was not a cool one. She found a firm footing and, feeling like the Karate Kid, she placed all her weight on one leg and lifted up her right leg, pivoting it up, drawing it in, and turning slightly. "Form of the Drunken Crane," she said to herself.

She turned and gasped. A hot wind brushed at her face, and the vision before her looked like the surface of Mars—a vast desert, vaguely red in color, with distant mountains looming over a dry, parched plain. Terry took off his sweater and motioned for them to do the same. "You're not going to need these here," he said. He took their sweaters from them and threw them into the Void, which looked the same from this side as it did from the other.

"Let's go," Terry said. "This way." His short legs began to work quickly, and she had to run briefly to catch up with him.

Terry was right, she noted. The sense that she was watching something on the screen of her mind's eye was gone, replaced by a dreamlike physicality. She had the sense that she was really here. She punched at her leg. It hurt.

Terry didn't even look back at her when he said, "If you keep that up, you *will* have a bruise when we get back."

"Are you serious?" she asked.

"I've tried it," he said. "It's uncanny, I know." Terry seemed to notice that Charlie was lagging. "Hup! Catch up, and stay up, Charlie!"

Charlie jogged to match him, but Kat could see that he was struggling to match Terry's pace.

Frankly, she thought, *so am I.*

She looked around. Every few hundred feet, she saw what looked like a large tumbleweed, or a cocoon or something. She pointed at one of them. "Terry, what *are* those things?"

"Some of them are angels. Some of them are demons. Some of

them are...something in between. Whatever you do, don't touch them."

"Why not?" Charlie asked.

"Because they're safe right where they are. And *we're* safe if they're right where they are. They'll be released eventually. When their time is right."

"Who will release them?" Kat asked. Just then, she had the vague, creepy feeling that someone was standing just over her shoulder. Terry stopped and pointed behind her. "They will."

Kat froze and turned around. She found herself staring into a wall of hair. Or fur. The wall came to an end about a yard on either side of her gaze. So she looked up. Hovering over her was a creature about twelve feet tall covered tip to tail in white fur. Its legs were large and powerful, and longer than she was tall. Its body arched like a banana, ending in a face with large eyes, sad and wise. It possessed no mouth, however—nor, it seemed, arms. Looking around, she discovered there were about four of them, all looking very much alike to her.

"Kat, Charlie, I'd like to introduce you to the Sandalphon," Terry said.

The creatures bowed slightly in greeting.

"Holy shit, how did you sneak up on me?" Charlie asked, his voice quaking.

The creatures did not answer.

"They don't really talk," Terry said. "They might place a thought or an image in your mind if it's really important. Otherwise, they're just here to see us safely to the Abyss."

"Um...hello, Mr. Sandalphon," Kat said. She stuck out her hand to shake, then, remembering that the being in front of her didn't actually *have* hands, she placed hers in her back pocket, feeling stupid.

"Okay, let's go," Terry said, trudging off in the same direction they'd been travelling, straight between two mountain ranges. The Sandalphon lumbered after him.

"Uh, Terry," Kat said, following. "What *are* they?"

"They started out as the archangels assigned to Malkuth, and some of them still work that gig," Terry said. "But they're all from archangelic stock, as you can tell by the way that they communicate."

"Oh. Of course." She looked at Charlie and shrugged.

"But the ones that work here are kind of caretakers of the desert. They also protect travelers, like us. Their name comes from the Greek *synadelphos*, which means 'coworker,' or more literally, 'brother with me.' You can call them anytime, anywhere in the phenomenal universe—anywhere in Malkuth, that is. They'll come running. They don't say much, but they're fiercely protective. And they are good guys. You can trust them with your life. In fact"—he flashed a smile over his shoulder—"you're doing that now."

Just then, right in front of them, a wolf leaped into view, seeming to drop out of the sky. It seemed disoriented and unsteady on its legs. Terry stopped short, and the Sandalphon, moving more quickly than Kat would have thought possible, placed themselves between the wolf and the three human travelers. The wolf looked down at its own legs, seemingly beholding its own body for the first time.

For some reason, Kat wasn't scared. Instead, she was certain that what she was viewing was an expression of abject sorrow. And horror. The wolf curled up in a ball and began to whimper.

From the corner of her eye, Kat saw a fifth Sandalphon move quickly toward the wolf. She watched in wonder as the long body bent down, nearly to the earth, like an enormous, animated bass clef. The fur of its face touched the fur of the wolf's face. The wolf looked up, and Kat was sure she saw fear in its wide eyes. But then she saw it soften, and she imagined that the Sandalphon was communicating something comforting to it.

Hesitantly, the wolf got to its feet, and tail between its legs, it followed after the Sandalphon in the direction of the mountains.

"Okay, what did we just see?" Kat asked.

"I have absolutely no idea," Terry said. "I've seen something like that before, but only once, and years ago. I have no explanation." He turned to the Sandalphon nearest him. "Can you tell me what just happened?"

Terry must have received an answer because his brows knit together in confusion.

"What did he say? She say? Wait, what are they, male or female?" Kat asked.

"Neither one. They're androgynous. But I usually default to he. Anyway, he said something like, 'The Children of the Prophet await judgment.'"

"That's all he said?"

"That's it."

"Do you have any idea what that means?"

"Nope." He turned back to where the valley split the two mountain ranges. "Let's keep going."

They hadn't gone ten steps before a pig fell out of the sky, squealing like it was running from death itself. It hit the ground, rolled, and took off running.

Before they could even process what was happening, a horse fell out of the sky, screaming with terror. Its legs kicked and flailed, until it was able to roll upright. Hesitantly, it got to its feet, and another Sandalphon moved toward it. It took off running, the Sandalphon following at a respectful distance.

Suddenly, the four Sandalphon traveling with them surrounded them and leaned their heads in together to form a kind of tent over them. Then the black desert sky began raining terrified animals. Frogs, coyotes, lemurs, dogs, gerbils, elephants, sparrows, pandas, butterflies, giraffes—animals in greater variety and number than Kat could take in, all at once began to pepper the desert plain, all screaming in terror—a wild and deafening cacophony.

36

SUSAN SIGHED, watching Terry, Kat, and Charlie in still repose on their zafus. As much as they looked like they were meditating, she knew they weren't. She knew they were *elsewhere*, and she took pains to be quiet so as not to intrude on the reality they were experiencing.

Her teacup was empty, so she went to the kitchen for a refill. As she waited for the kettle to boil, she gazed out the window at the milling mob just across the street. They were about thirty strong now. She felt a chill run down her back as she watched them, staring straight at her, working their mouths in some kind of distressed compulsion.

She had to remind herself that they weren't zombies massing for an attack. They were ordinary people, and if all went well, would be again. They were just…"temporarily hijacked," she breathed. She said a short prayer, and then poured the steaming water into a fresh cup.

She pulled her sweater more tightly around herself. She felt alone and scared. She wanted to be held, to be reassured. She looked over at Randy, but he seemed to be asleep—at least, she couldn't see him anywhere in the mirror. Tobias was asleep, with all four paws in the air underneath the table. She smiled at the sight of him.

Where is Dylan? she wondered. She turned toward the back staircase and quickly and quietly ascended. She passed quickly down the hall to their room and opened the door. Dylan was in much the same pose as Tobias, spread-eagle on the floor, a half-unsmoked blunt firmly wedged between two fingers. Her heart sank. She knelt by him. "Oh, Baby," she said. "Why are you so weak? We need you to be strong right now." She took the blunt from his hand, wondering at the size of it.

She did enjoy a hit now and then. It was especially helpful if she was experiencing hard PMS. She wasn't puritanical about it. It would have been impossible to live with any of the guys if she were. But she hoped for more for her husband. She knew he truly enjoyed marijuana, and she didn't begrudge him that. But he also used it to hide, to numb out. The more stressed he was, the more compulsively he smoked. Right now, with all that was going on, he seemed completely powerless. No doubt after their close call this morning he had come directly up here and smoked himself into oblivion.

She felt a difficult mixture of emotions—pity for him, and for herself, anger, and gobs of frustration. "I don't know how to help you right now, Dylan," she said, stroking his hair.

One of his eyes opened. "Hey, cutie," she said. "Good to see someone is in there." His eyeball moved around, taking her in, but otherwise he did not move. "Honey, I hate to say this, but it needs to be said: You're an addict, and it seems to me that you are completely powerless to pull yourself together. The problem is, we all need you right now. We need you strong and clear-headed and brave. We need you to be the best Dylan that is in there, and I know *that* Dylan is in there because that is the Dylan I married."

The eye sagged, his body relaxed, and he began to snore. Susan sighed. Then, without even thinking about it, she grabbed the trash bag out of the little can in the corner, opened Dylan's stash cabinet, and emptied every bud, every joint, every roach, every brownie, every capsule that she could find into it. Then she thought for a moment, making a mental checklist of all of Dylan's stashes throughout the house, and systematically, she emptied every single one.

Stepping down the back stairs again, she saw Tobias on the

landing waiting for her with broad swoops of his tail. "Hey, baby dog," she said to him, feeling sad and scared. "Your papa's not going to be very happy with me when he wakes up." Toby licked her hand. She opened the back door and walked to a large metal trash can. She was amazed, as she poured the contents of the trash bag into the can, how much Dylan had accumulated. Then she reminded herself that this was about how much he consumed every month. She shook her head, opened the lid on a bottle of lighter fluid, and doused the pot. Then she struck a match and watched as the metal can erupted in flame. Susan stood back and Tobias barked.

"Careful, there, Toby," she said. "Don't breathe too deeply. We don't want you passed out all afternoon, too."

37

RICHARD STOPPED and caught his breath walking up the steep hill toward the Graduate Theological Union. In a moment, he was trudging on again. He checked his phone and stepped up the pace, not wanting to be late. When he called to set up the appointment, Bishop Mulgrew had been curt: "My office. Two thirty." Then she hung up.

Another day, another bishop, Duunel said in his head. *Will this one be a prick, too?*

"Probably," Richard said, puffing. And it was probably true. She always had been, every time he'd met her in the past. It was a long shot, but he had to take it. Mikael had filled him in on the frightening assembly of the possessed. He was running out of time, and he knew it. How many more Occupied Americans would be encircling the friary by sundown? He shuddered to think of it.

You know that saying, "If you can't beat 'em, join 'em?" Duunel asked. *I don't think you can beat us. There's just too many. Even if you find a bishop this afternoon.* If a disembodied voice could smile, Duunel did. *And you know what, boobie? You've already joined us. You're no different from those poor sods lining up outside your house. Not even a little bit.*

Richard ignored him. It was a skill that he had almost perfected.

Instead, Richard mulled over what he knew about Bishop Mulgrew. She held the Mary Daly Chair of Feminist Theology at the Bay School of Religion. She had been ordained and later consecrated as part of the Roman Catholic womenpriest movement, but had jumped ship to the Independent Catholic movement about three years ago.

She was not well liked in Old Catholic circles. She never attended clergy meetings, and she kept her distance from any local church communities. Richard didn't know why. He didn't even have a guess.

He was sweating as he stepped onto the campus. Even though it was Sunday, several students were sunning themselves on the lawn, and most were studying. On his right was a large medieval-style manor house that was home to the oldest part of the school, looking for all the world like a wing of Hogwarts. Straight ahead was a 1950s Disneyfied version of a Tudor house, where many of the students lived. To his left was a 1960s modern-art chapel, all sharp angles and glass. It was an architectural mutt of a place, and Richard could never quite figure out what to make of it. *What were they thinking?* he wondered to himself as he made for the enormous dark wooden doors of the castle-like manor house.

Straightening his cassock, he ran his fingers through what remained of his hair and approached the front desk. Being Sunday, however, there was no one there. He rang the bell just to be sure. A very butch woman with a nose ring and a blue Mohawk scowled at him as she passed by. "Closed. It's Sunday."

"Um...and yet, I have an appointment with Doctor Mulgrew," he said cheerfully. "Do you know where her office is?"

"Second floor, office 234," the woman called over her shoulder, not bothering to stop.

"Thank you," Richard said, and turned toward the stairs.

Is that how they're cranking out Christians these days? Duunel asked. *'Cause that was a little disconcerting, even for me.*

"Some of the students here are what I would describe as 'post-Christian,'" Richard said.

Look, we demons have whole bureaucracies devoted to inventing doublespeak like that, and even I don't know what that means. I thought this was a Christian seminary, Duunel said—sounding remarkably perplexed.

"Well, it's a seminary that encourages questioning. Deconstructing the Christian faith is definitely high on the agenda. Ideally, reconstructing should follow."

That "deconstruction" sounds like something we could get behind, Duunel said, and Richard could almost see him rubbing his hands together. *I feel a sizable bequest coming on.*

"Where from?" Richard said. "You're no longer inhabiting a tycoon, or have you forgotten? You are now rooming with a penniless friar."

Don't have to, Duunel said.

"No indeed. Please leave anytime you like," Richard said.

And where would I go?

"How about a nice herd of pigs, perhaps somewhere near a cliff?"

I love your little biblical allusions. They're quaint.

"I didn't know you read the Bible," Richard said.

Read it? Dear boy, I have it committed to memory.

Richard was somewhat taken aback by this news and didn't know what to say. Fortunately, he didn't need to respond because he found himself at the threshold of office 234. He knocked.

"Hold your horses!" came the loud response. In a moment, the door swung open. A very large woman appeared, who seemed to loom over Richard. At six feet two, Richard had met few women capable of this, but here, without a doubt, was one.

"Doctor Mulgrew, thanks so much for seeing me," Richard held out his hand.

She ignored it, narrowing her eyes at him. "In this office," she said as if instructing a child, "we eschew the rituals of the patriarchy. Who are you?"

"Oh. Sorry. I'm Father Richard Kinney, of the Order of Saint Raphael. We spoke briefly."

"And we'll speak briefly again." She did not budge from her doorway. Richard had expected to be invited in, so he shuffled in the hallway uncomfortably.

"Um...could we speak privately?"

She looked up and down the hall. "I don't see anyone. And I don't allow males into my inner sanctum. You will pollute the sacred womb energy that my sisters have worked so hard to establish here."

Richard wasn't sure what to say to this.

"Perhaps you don't understand," she said, speaking slowly and deliberately as if to a slow child. "This is a patriarchy-free zone, so I will thank you to keep your testicles as far away from me and my office as possible."

Ah! said Duunel in his head. *Bet you a fifth of Maker's Mark she runs with wolves. Probably naked. At the new moon. Perhaps she'll speak to you at length if you consent to being castrated. I think that's a fine idea, don't you?*

Richard ignored him. "Could we perhaps have some coffee in the cafeteria?"

"There's no food service, only drinks," she scowled. "Sunday."

"That's fine," said Richard, a little too cheerily. "I'll spring for coffee."

Mulgrew looked uncertain about this. "All right," she said. She closed the door to her office, leaving Richard outside. After a few minutes, she reemerged wrapped in an autumnal shawl. She locked the door after her and set off down the hall without a word.

Richard fell into step behind her. She was a giant wall of a woman, standing half a hand taller than Richard and extending to fully twice his width. Her gray hair was styled in a drill sergeant buzz-cut, and tiny twin-edged axes hung from the lobes of her ears. As he caught up to her, he noticed a button pinned to her shawl. It had a cartoon picture of the pope's head, with x's in the place of his eyes and his tongue hanging out. The letters underneath spelled, Starve the Patriarchy.

Stepping out into the summer sun, Richard pushed himself to keep up with her. She did not deign to speak to him as they rushed across the commons toward the cafeteria. Once inside, Richard paid for himself—Mulgrew apparently had a meal plan—and grabbed himself a mug of coffee. He found the professor in a corner table at far remove from any of the other diners. He sat and forced a smile.

"What do you want?" she asked, arms crossed over her bosom.

"I don't know if you've heard, if you read the ISM listserv or not, but Bishop Müeller was killed a couple of days ago."

Richard was expecting a rude retort to this somehow, but none came. Instead, she looked sad and a little concerned. "How is Gretchen?" she asked.

"You know Gretchen?" Richard asked, surprised.

"She was a student. And later, we were...friends."

The pause indicated to Richard that they had been something more than just friends, but he didn't pry. Of all people, he understood the pull that former lovers could exert on the heart, the sad sweetness that can issue from memory and longing. "I'm sorry," he said.

"I should call her," she said.

"She's very upset," Richard said. "I'm sure a friendly voice would help. She's pretty isolated."

Mulgrew nodded. "How did Tom die?"

"Motorcycle accident," Richard said. "I don't have the whole story, but Gretchen says he swerved to avoid a cat."

Mulgrew almost smiled. "They were obsessive about cats," she said.

Richard laughed. "Yes. Yes, they were. I remember once I stayed overnight, and they had seventeen of them in their one-bedroom apartment."

"I hope you're not allergic," she said, looking at him for the first time.

"I am, in fact," he winced visibly. "It took me a week to recover. I think I cornered the market on Benadryl."

Mulgrew laughed out loud. As her smile faded, she looked him in the eyes. "So, you didn't come to bear bad news, I assume."

"No. Tom was our bishop. Do you know about the Order of Saint Raphael?"

"I've heard the name, but I don't know anything about you. Are you local?"

"Yup. Our friary is just a few blocks away, in the Gourmet Ghetto," Richard answered.

"What is your charism?"

"We're exorcists," he said plainly.

"Exorcists."

"Yes," he affirmed.

"Is this a joke?"

"No, no joke. That's what we do. We handle about seventy demonic deliverance cases a year, give or take. We regularly receive referrals from Roman Catholic and Episcopal dioceses. We're actually on their speed dial," he chuckled.

"Is this a joke?" she repeated.

This time, Richard just shook his head and looked her in the eyes.

"There are no such things as demons," she said.

Oh, I do like her, Duunel said.

"Yes, well, that's what they'd like you to believe because then they can practice unopposed."

"Young man," Mulgrew began, causing Richard's eyebrows to shoot up, as he hadn't been called that in many years. Mulgrew continued, "Have you ever been picked up on a 5150?"

"Uh...no," Richard said, not liking the sound of that. "Isn't that a Van Halen CD?"

"It's code for involuntary psychiatric hold, for observation," she said. "Did you know that I'm also a psychologist?"

"No," Richard said, beginning to squirm. "Look, we're not crazy. We cast out demons in the name of Jesus Christ. That's our calling. It isn't delusional; it's real."

Slowly, Mulgrew reached for her phone.

Richard plowed ahead. "But Tom was our bishop. Without him, we're cut off from the apostolic succession. Our power line has been... severed. Ever since he died, we can't command the demons. They just laugh at us."

Mulgrew's eyes narrowed. Richard continued. "That's why I'm here. We need temporary episcopal oversight to get us back in business. We've got a demonic crisis brewing right here in Berkeley, and if we don't tend to it, like, yesterday, a lot of people could get hurt. A lot of people are getting hurt now."

"First of all," Mulgrew said, waving his arguments away, "you are delusional. There are no such things as demons. They are entirely a figment of your imagination. Second, your theology of apostolic succession is a twisted patriarchal distortion of the tradition. You don't need a bishop any more than I need testes. And third"—she leaned in and narrowed one eye on him—"the Roman Catholic arch-diocese isn't the only one with speed dial. The ambulance will be here in about five minutes."

Just then, someone screamed. Richard looked around but couldn't identify the source. Mulgrew bolted out of her chair, appar-ently keen to investigate. At the same time, Duunel distracted him by with his own screaming, confined to his own head, and regarding how they *had to get the fuck out of there*, but he ignored him.

"She's not really going to call 911," he said.

Wanna bet? Duunel asked.

"How do you know?"

She's batshit crazy, Duunel said. *It's—what do you call it —projection?*

"What makes you say she's crazy?" Richard asked under his breath.

Um...'womb energy'? Duunel answered.

Another student screamed, and Richard rose and joined Mulgrew beside a tiny gaggle of students, all looking up at a television set in the corner. Richard saw the CNN logo, then a picture of a mushroom cloud erupted across the screen. The caption read, Dearborn Bombed.

"Holy shit," Mulgrew said, clutching at a stone goddess hanging from her neck. Not daring to breathe for fear of missing some words, Richard strained to hear the tiny television speaker. Then one of the students found a remote and turned it up, much to his relief.

The scene cut to a press conference, and the caption told them that Michigan governor David Ivory was about to address the public. By this time, everyone in the cafeteria was crowded around the television. Richard discovered he was holding his breath. It was so quiet he could hear Mulgrew's faint wheezing beside him.

Oh, this is going to be good, Duunel said. Richard ignored him.

"My fellow Americans," Ivory began, looking both grave and confident. "In the last twenty-four hours, my office received incontrovertible evidence of no less than seventy sleeper cells concentrated in the city of Dearborn. Both state and federal intelligence agencies affirm that these cells were organized and poised to strike at more than a thousand US targets simultaneously.

"The projected date for the attack would have been...tomorrow, in part to coincide with the first day of the Republican National Convention, and in part to commemorate the death of the Indian Islamic terrorist Abdul al-Siddhar.

"My office was faced with an impossible choice—we had a very narrow window between learning of the planned attacks and the hour at which the cells would be mobilized. In fact, that window was less than four hours. I made an executive decision, and an hour ago, I ordered the Michigan State Militia of the National Guard to drop a 1.2-megaton thermonuclear bomb on the city of Dearborn.

"I am well aware that this is the first time that a nuclear device has ever been used as a weapon on US soil. I am also aware that this is the first time a nuclear bomb has ever targeted US citizens, and I grieve this decision deeply. They say heavy is the head that wears the crown, and never has that been truer than it is today. For today, the decision fell to me to choose between the lives of the innocent people of Dearborn and the lives of hundreds of millions of Americans all across this great land, had the terrorists not been stopped.

"No, I had to act, and act quickly. And I did the only thing that would stop *all* of the terrorists in their tracks. And we stopped them *cold*. We *stopped* their evil and nefarious plans before they ever got off the ground. We paid a terrible price to stop them, to be sure, but allow me to assure you—the innocent people of Dearborn did *not* die in vain. They died heroically. They died so that *you* could live.

"Critics are going to say that we should have waited for federal authorities to make this decision. Would you have taken that risk? I don't know about you, but I know how Washington works. They would have dickered and argued and wrung their hands until the window of opportunity had long passed. And I don't need to tell you about the *deliberative* nature of this administration. So yes, I could have waited, and tomorrow, *you* could have been burying your loved ones.

"Instead, let us mourn for the good people of Dearborn, all of us. Let us honor them as heroes. And let us be grateful for our crack intelligence agencies, and the brave soldiers of our National Guard, who did not waver in their dedication to preserving American lives. God bless you all. God bless you as you enjoy your tomorrows, safe from the murderous plans of Islamic terror. And God bless America."

At that moment, a siren cut through the stunned silence of the cafeteria. A police officer entered, followed by a paramedic. "Oh shit," said Richard.

38

AS THE SKY continued to rain terrified, screaming animals, Kat covered her ears with her hands and backed up so that she was pressed tight against the solid, furry body of the Sandalphon nearest her.

An ostrich ran in crazy circles but then began to run directly for her. Ice ran down her back as déjà vu washed over her. "You were in my dream," she said as the ostrich suddenly wheeled and scampered off in a different direction. Other animals ran by, too close for comfort. When a hyena landed two feet away and began shrieking and lashing out, she screamed and buried her face in the Sandalphon's fur.

She kept moving, farther and farther into the fur, until she realized that she had somehow passed into the Sandalphon and she was surrounded by a warm, black, quiet, womblike presence that was calming and comforting. She slowed her breathing and had the same feeling that she had had as a girl when her mother combed her hair at the end of a long and tiring day of play.

Soon, her heartbeat was normal again, and so was her breathing. A large, gentle hand seemed to nudge her, and she realized that she was being encouraged to step back out into the desert. Once on the outside again, she saw that it wasn't a hand at all but the Sandalphon's other foot. She smiled at this for some reason and stretched out her hand to touch the fur, not wanting to lose contact with its comfort and protection.

She looked around her. Terry and Charlie were still crouched with their hands over their heads, but they, too, were starting to straighten up and look around. Beyond the circle of the protective Sandalphon, she saw that the rocky surface of the valley floor was dotted with thousands—no, tens of thousands—of disoriented animals. No zoo on earth could hold even a fraction of a collection of this size. She gaped in wonder at the sight of it. Like triage nurses, hordes of looming Sandalphon seemed to float across the plain, comforting, leading, sorting the distressed beasts.

"*Children of the Prophet*," Terry repeated the words of the Sandalphon, shaking his head. "I have no idea what we are seeing." Their own Sandalphon, perhaps perceiving that the crisis had passed, straightened up and, like Australian shepherds, seemed to be herding them back into motion. "Well, whatever it is, it doesn't seem to concern us. Let's get moving."

Terry once again set his face toward the space between the mountain ranges and trudged on. Kat was shaken by what they had witnessed, but she steeled herself and fell into step behind Terry. She was determined to share in everything this community faced, and she knew that she must muster courage on a regular basis to do that. She rallied that courage now.

"I'm tired," Charlie complained.

"You're only tired because you think you should be tired," Terry said. "If you tell yourself you're energized and rested, you will be."

"Next I'm going to tell myself I'm a wish-granting fairy," Charlie said acidly.

"Works for me," Terry said, flashing them a grin.

After what seemed like an hour of walking through dry and empty waste, Terry halted just short of what looked like an enormous pit. It was about a half mile across, and Kat could see no bottom to it.

No light escaped from it, but wisps of smoke or vapor wafted from it, only to dissipate into the dry desert air.

Terry walked over to the nearest Sandalphon, and joining his hands in a Namaste gesture, he bowed slightly. The Sandalphon all bowed in return, turned around, and began to lumber back toward the desert in the direction that they'd come.

Terry faced Kat and Charlie. "My friends, I welcome you to the Abyss." He made a sweeping gesture toward the pit. "When you want to get rid of demons, this is where you go. The Abyss will take them right back to where they belong. If you want to access other spiritual powers or principalities, this is the elevator that will take you there. In fact, there are few places in this universe or any other that you can't access here." He turned and whistled. Facing them again, he said, "In a moment, you'll see a giant hand hovering over the pit. We're going to step on it and say where we'd like to go. Got that?"

"Just out of curiosity," Charlie said, "what would we have seen if you hadn't just told us that?"

"That, sir, is a very excellent question, and I'm glad you asked," Terry smiled a proud smile. "My guess is that we all would have seen different things. I would have seen a giant hand because that is what Richard told me I'd see when he trained me all those years ago. But you might have seen an elevator car, because I'd just used that as a metaphor. Or maybe you would have seen a pterodactyl. Who knows? The important thing is that we'll be able to share the experience better if we're accessing it through the same symbols."

"Is that how religions work, too?" Kat asked. "They provide symbol sets for real things that can't be perceived except through symbol and metaphor?"

"Right," Terry said. "And symbol sets are more or less arbitrary. We can have cultural and emotional attachments to them, of course. But if we ever confuse the metaphor or the symbol for the thing that it points to...well, there's a word for that."

"What's that?" Charlie asked.

"Idolatry," Terry said.

Just then an enormous human hand appeared, the size of a football field across. It seemed to be floating in free space. Its surface rose to match the level of the plain they were standing on, and without hesitation, Terry stepped onto the thumb, walking across it toward the open palm. He waved them in. "Don't just stand there—he's not going to wait for you all day," he said. "And don't stand too near the edge—it's not safe."

Kat gulped and jumped onto the thumb, although she didn't really need to jump. Charlie apparently saw that because he simply stepped off and walked more or less normally. In a moment, they caught up with Terry, who turned to face the place they had just come from.

"Abaddon," Terry called, "please take us to Hell."

Instantly, the hand began to plummet at a dizzying speed. Kat fell to the heel of the great hand and held on to a fleshy fold for dear life. Charlie struggled to gain his sea legs, but Terry stood confidently, his feet set apart at an odd angle as if he were surfing. His hands were behind his back, and a hot wind whipped through his stiff black hair. He smiled at them reassuringly. "You'll get used to this. The Abyss is something we make frequent use of. Abaddon is the angel of the Abyss. It's his 'hand,' as it were," he explained. "Or his elevator car, or magic carpet, or whatever it is the user sees. The point is, if you want to go somewhere, you ask him."

"And does he automatically take you wherever you want to go?" Charlie asked, his eyes lighting up.

"Automatically?" Terry scowled. It seemed to Kat that Charlie was just a wee bit too eager. "No. He's not a machine. You ask. If it's permitted, he'll take you there. If it isn't, he won't."

"And us going to Hell is permitted?" Kat asked, not at all sure about this.

"Sure," Terry said. "There's nothing to be scared of in Hell. You'll see."

After what seemed like an overlong carnival ride, the hand eventually slowed and finally stopped level with a stone outcropping. They seemed to be in a cave, carved from long-dead lava. Kat expected to smell sulfur, and she was not disappointed. In fact, she was nearly knocked over by both the heat and the smell of rotten eggs.

"Come on, Abaddon's a busy cuss," Terry said, hopping onto the ledge. Kat and Charlie followed him, and his little legs worked quickly as he scurried down a main shaft cut into the rock. Waves of heat poured over them, and were it not for some fluorescence native to the rocks surrounding them, they would have been in complete darkness. "This way!" Terry called to them. "You don't want to lag here."

In a few minutes, the darkness dissipated to a haze that was vaguely reminiscent of twilight. They emerged from the shaft of the cave into what seemed like a city street. Kat looked up and saw skyscrapers disappearing into a pink sky obscured by clouds. Cars and buses were everywhere, but they were still. In the distance, a single man was visible—sweeping the street.

Terry shook his head slowly. "Okay, this is not good."

"Is that guy a demon?" Charlie asked, pointing at the street sweeper.

"No, just a human," Terry said. He turned a 360, taking in all that he could. "This is the bureaucratic district. This should be as bustling as the business districts of New York City or Chicago. We should be seeing demons *everywhere*." Terry looked around him uncertainly. "I do *not* like the look of this," he breathed.

"Let me ask a question," Charlie said. "Would these demons be wearing suits and ties and carrying briefcases?"

"Well, yes. You've been here before?" Terry said.

"No...I...just wondering," Charlie said, looking uncertain himself.

"Oh, I see what you mean," Terry said. "Again, what you see would be determined by paradigmatic contextualization. If you were from a medieval Arabic culture, this would look like a *souk*, a "marketplace." You'd see the same peop—er, demons, but they'd be wearing different clothes and riding in different kinds of transport. If, that is, there were any demons to see."

"How does this change our lesson, Terry?" Kat asked.

"Well, I guess it doesn't. It's just...strange, that's all. Another day, another mystery, I suppose," Terry said, intentionally brightening. "Let's press on."

They walked past street after empty street. Newspapers blew in lazy patterns through alleyways, and bars and shops were locked up tight. Every now and then, they saw a lonely person doing menial work. Kat waved at them, but they did not look up or even take any notice of them. Kat stared at the odd color of her skin, caused by the pink ambient light that filled the place.

"So, Terry, if this place was crawling with demons, like it's supposed to be," Kat asked, "why wouldn't we be afraid of them?"

"Because their focus is elsewhere—they're strategizing and wheeling and dealing for influence on Earth and other planes—market share, I guess you could call it. You're not a threat to them here, and, truth is, they barely notice you. After all, they can't tell the difference between you and one of the human damned. They're always underfoot as far as these guys are concerned. We're just servants and peons."

"There's no, like, immigration control?" Charlie asked.

"Uh...Hell isn't trying to keep anyone *out*," Terry said over his shoulder with a grin. "And it's not like you're going to run into any *police*."

"Then how do they keep order?" Kat asked. "Because the infrastructure here is incredible. It's not chaotic."

"Strict hierarchy. Get out of line, and the next guy up just toasts you. No questions asked. Believe me, it works."

"How does he toast you, exactly?" Charlie asked. Kat wasn't sure she wanted to hear the answer to this.

"Souls are not eternal," Terry asked. "They can be destroyed...eaten."

"Ho-o-kay," Kat said, feeling a little lightheaded from panic. "So, why don't they eat us now?"

"Because they don't really crave *nourishment* like we do," Terry said. "They crave *influence*. Power. If they destroy you, they can't rule you. If they eat you, they end up hungrier for what they *really* want."

"Oh."

"And that's the real pull of Hell," Terry said. "It's rarely actual *evil*. Evil is a byproduct. It's almost always the lust for power, and often it's disguised by an impulse toward philanthropy."

"You mean, people tell themselves that they want power so that they can do more good in the world?" Kat asked.

"Exactly," Terry said. "It's a Moebius strip. You start out on one side, and it twists around to the other. There's no getting around it."

"Is that *always* true?" Kat asked.

Terry stopped and faced her. "Yes, 100 percent of the time," he said, looking her straight in the eyes.

"Then why do we have a prior?" Kat asked.

"To marshal us through dangerous situations where one person needs to call the shots. All the important decisions are made by consensus when we have the leisure and safety to discern together," Terry answered.

"Pussies," Charlie said.

Terry ignored him. But Kat didn't. "Charlie, if you feel that way, why do you want to join us?"

Charlie didn't say anything. But some kind of dam had broken in Kat, and she continued. "We've been nothing but sweet and welcoming to you, and in return you've been surly and sarcastic and bull-headed. Surely, you know that we are all going to *vote* on whether to let you in, right? And we don't vote in assholes!"

Charlie looked humbled and a little hurt. "I...don't know. It's just so *different* from how it is at the lodge. At the lodge, no one says that they love each other—I don't know how to respond to that kind of stuff. It makes me...queasy. It feels weird. And I feel insulted that my previous training isn't being given its proper due. I feel like I'm being put back into kindergarten, like I'm being punished for some reason. It makes me mad."

Kat touched his arm. "Okay, that's honest. Thank you." She gave him a hug.

Terry nodded. "That's what I figured was going on, Charlie. It's okay. But we're starting you from the beginning because we are grounded in an entirely different set of assumptions than the lodge is, and you need to see how those work from the ground up."

"Such as?" Charlie asked. "What assumptions are you talking about?"

"Such as—love being stronger than power," Terry said.

"That's just crazy," Charlie said. He looked disgusted.

"Well, hold that thought," Terry said. "You'll see in a minute." He continued to walk quickly, and soon they came to an ornate archway over the sidewalk. But the wall into which the archway was cut was ancient. "This was formerly the great wall of Dis," Terry said, waving a hand toward the crumbling wall.

Kat could see that at one time there were enormous gates hung to her left, but the gates were long gone, and the pillars that had held them were little more than rubble. It reminded her of pictures she'd seen of old temples in Greece.

She focused again on the archway. On this side was a city with soaring buildings, paved as far as the eye could see. On the other side of the arch was a rolling plain that looked like high desert—brown and still and lovely. Footpaths crisscrossed the hills, and although there were plenty of trees, they were void of leaves, their branches reaching toward the pink sky like desperate, spindly fingers.

"Welcome to the tombs," Terry said.

"This is kind of nice," Charlie said. "It's beautiful, in fact."

"It reminds me of Arizona or something," Kat agreed. Terry stepped out onto the main footpath, and they followed eagerly, looking around with dazed interest.

"So, what happened to the flames and eternal torment stuff?" Charlie asked. "I wasn't expecting this."

"Propaganda," Terry said. "This place has had a lot of names—the Greeks called it Hades, the Jews called it Sheol. At one time, everyone came here when they died. And you're right, it's not so bad. It's just not...fulfilling. People here are kind of isolated. There's no community to speak of. The most you'll find is people who live here but work over in the bureaucratic district, just to stay vibrant."

"What do you mean, 'vibrant'?" Kat asked.

"Well, Hell is not eternal despite what the propaganda says. After a few decades here, a soul eventually just...fades out—usually when the last person on Earth who remembers him or her dies." Terry pointed straight ahead. "Okay, take note when we go near this hill. Look closely at it. What do you see?"

Kat squinted and peered carefully at the approaching hills. Black dots appeared all over the hillside. As they grew nearer, she could see that they were caves. Closer still, she saw that over each cave mouth was an iron grill.

"They're...prison cells?" Kat asked.

"Yes, that's exactly what they are," Terry said. He walked directly toward a cluster of them. But instead of getting too close, he sat down on a rock. He gestured to the rock, inviting them to join him. They did, and he turned to Charlie. "So, in answer to your question about love being stronger than power, this is a fundamental Christian teaching."

"Since when?"

"Since the beginning," Terry said. "I'm not saying we've done a good job of living it, or preaching it, but it's always been there."

"How so?" Charlie asked, seeming to be interested. Kat understood. There was a lot about the friars that just didn't make sense on the surface of things.

"Christians teach that Jesus is God—and that, out of love for us, Jesus emptied himself of all his divine power, and became a simple, vulnerable, fallible human being, with all the frailty and danger that comes with that."

"If he was really God, he could have zapped anyone, anytime he wanted to," Charlie said. "He did all those miracles, after all."

"No, he couldn't have zapped anyone. Remember, those miracles only worked when the people he was ministering to *trusted* that they would work. The power came from them, not from Jesus. Jesus didn't just *seem* to be human. He *was* human."

Terry leaned back and took a deep breath of the hot, dry air. "And so are we. This tells us something really important about God—God is opposed to coercive power. God never forces anyone to do anything. God's power is persuasive, not coercive. The Holy Spirit is always whispering to everyone, trying to nudge them in the right direction, but ultimately, we all have free will. To take that away from anyone is violence. It's evil."

"Is that why we study magick but don't practice it?" Kat asked.

"Yes, that's it exactly," Terry nodded. "In terms of power, we are called to be celibate. That's why we make our big decisions by consensus. That's why we don't do magick. If we follow Jesus, we have to do what he did. We have to reject coercive power." An impish look came over his face. "Fortunately, we're celibate only in terms of power, not in terms of sexuality. Thanks be to God!"

"Amen to that!" Kat laughed. If she'd had a glass of wine, she would have toasted.

"So, getting back to Jesus," Kat said, "he gave up all his power—his divine power, that is. I think he had a lot of power as a leader, as a speaker."

"He had moral authority," Terry agreed. "And he exercised persuasive power very well. But there's nothing wrong with persuasive power."

"But, so, is that how they could kill him?" Kat asked. "I mean, he couldn't stop it, right? If Rome decides to kill someone, they just kill someone. And Jesus got caught in their crosshairs somehow."

"Right," Terry said, nodding. "But it's deeper than that. Rome was coercive power personified. It is the very definition of coercion, of tyranny. As such, it is antichrist—it stands against everything that Jesus stood for. Rome stood for coercive power, and Jesus stood against coercive power. And coercive power stomped him and ground him into dust."

Kat's eyes were wide. She knew about the crucifixion, but she'd never heard it talked about in exactly these terms before. Suddenly, the story was taking on vast, revolutionary dimensions.

"Fortunately, that's not the end of the story," Terry said. "On the third day, God raised him up, breaking the power of death forever. But more than this, the resurrection was a big, fat 'fuck you' to Rome."

Kat laughed, "Okay, they *never* told me this at catechism class, not even once."

Terry smiled but went on. "Rome did its worst; it did what it always did in order to coerce people into staying in line—it terrified them by killing anyone who dared to say 'boo' to them. Well, Jesus said boo, they smashed him, and then he got up and said, 'Ha ha, you lose.'" Terry paused for a moment, looking reflective. "Power did its worst, and Power didn't win. Love won. And in the end, it will win every time, no matter how big or bad or scary Power seems to be. Jesus met the worst of it, and death was powerless to hold him. And for those of us who have been joined to him—what do we have to fear? Death? Poop on death. It's been beaten. Demons? Demons are silly beings who are in total denial of reality. People? Okay, people can be scary sometimes, but in the end, Love still wins."

Charlie didn't look like he was buying a word of it. "Okay, so where do those come in?" He pointed at the prison cells in the hillside.

"What did Jesus do when he died?" Terry asked. "I mean, while he was dead, where did he go? Any guesses?"

"To Heaven?" Kat asked.

"This is ridiculous," Charlie said. "Oz. He went to fucking Oz— where he had a cheeseburger with the fucking Easter Bunny. And then he and the Easter Bunny picked up some babes."

"Um...close, but no." Terry grinned at him. "He came here."

"Here?" Kat said. "Are you saying that when Jesus died, he went to Hell?"

"That's exactly what I'm saying," Terry nodded. "Although it wasn't called Hell then. It was just the place of the dead." He dusted off his hands. "Jesus stood right here, right where you're sitting."

Kat looked around her, feeling a momentary wave of awe.

"Do you want to know what he did while he was here?" Terry said.

Kat nodded, entranced. Charlie scowled skeptically.

"Well, he started out in one of these cells, as everyone who goes to Hell does. But the cell couldn't hold him. Do you know why?"

"Because...he was God?" Kat asked hesitantly.

"Right. So, he broke the lock and walked right out. Want to know what he did next?"

"Tell me," Kat said, breathless.

"He smashed the locks on every prison cell in the whole place. Then he went over to that big wall that we just passed—the one that separates the tombs from the bureaucratic district—the wall of Dis. And he smashed the doors off it. Boom, he destroyed it."

"Wait a minute," Charlie said, "How can Jesus give up power but then come down here and kick ass like that? Isn't that displaying power?"

Terry sighed. "Religion is a heaving mass of paradox. Roll with it."

"So, after Jesus...busted the place up, what happened to everyone who was here?" Kat asked.

"Everyone who wanted to just walked right out. The locks were busted; the walls were down. Jesus led everyone who wanted to go straight to Heaven." Kat could see that Terry was enjoying this. "Here, come and see," Terry led them to the nearest cell. Sure enough, through the bars hung an ancient-looking chain. A padlock hung from one of the links, looking like it had been smashed with a rock or a sledgehammer.

Charlie peered into the cell. "It actually looks kind of homey."

"And the person who was a prisoner here?" Kat asked.

"Gone. Followed Jesus right out," Terry said. "But look, here." He walked a couple of hundred feet to their left. As they approached another of the cells, Kat could hear crying and snuffling. It sounded like an old woman. Kat lowered her hand over her eyes to try to see better into the dim recesses of the cell. In the far corner, she saw a figure covered in rags, huddled against the wall, rocking back and forth.

"Okay, you said, everyone who wanted to could leave," Kat said. "So, is this a person who *didn't* want to leave?"

"Well, she only died about twenty years ago, but in Jesus's time there were lots just like her. There still are. Jesus destroyed Hell's coercive power, but people can still *choose* to stay."

"Why in the world would she choose to stay?" Kat asked.

"Beats me," Terry said. "Ask her."

Kat examined the door. The chain was slack, the lock busted, just like the other one. "There's nothing keeping her in there," Kat noted.

"Right," Terry said.

"Hey, Honey!" Kat called to her. "Come out! We'll take you to a much better place!"

"Go away, devils! You can't trick me!" the woman's voice shot back.

Kat looked at Terry. "That's so, so sad."

Terry nodded. "I know it. And there's nothing you can do."

Just then, Kat noticed that only she and Terry were standing at the cell. "Where's Charlie?" she asked.

Terry's eyes flashed with panic. "Oh shit," he said. "Charlie!"

"You said there was nothing to be afraid of," Kat said.

"Well, there isn't...exactly," Terry said.

"And...not exactly?" Kat asked.

Terry followed the trail along the hillside until he came to the first cell. Inside, huddled against the rock, was Charlie.

"Charlie, you idiot, what are you doing in there?" Terry asked.

"It's safe here," Charlie said.

"Charlie, come out right now!" Terry called, swinging wide the door. "Look, there's no reason for you to be in there! Come on!"

But Charlie shook his head and hugged the rocks. "It's dangerous out there. It's peaceful here. For the first time in my entire life, I feel like I'm home."

"Charlie, you're *not* at home. You're in fucking Hell!" Kat felt a moment of hysteria bubble up in her. She forced it down.

"Go away," Charlie said defiantly. "I'm staying."

39

As soon as he saw the policeman and the paramedics' uniforms, Richard ducked behind the wall that separated the main cafeteria area and the kitchen. Students were allowed there—it was where they dropped off their soiled dishes and silverware, and also where they picked up fried food and condiments. A window graced the south wall, and without thinking, Richard jumped up on a counter, opened the window, and pitched himself through.

Do you have any idea how far a fall this is? Duunel asked as he was doing so, but Richard didn't hesitate long enough to answer. He was relieved to find that he only fell about three feet before hitting the corrugated fiberglass roof of the porch below. Richard crouched there, gaining his bearings. He shuffled to the edge of the roof and lowered himself to the ground.

Is this really necessary? Duunel asked. *I mean, a psychiatric hold could be just the kind of break that you need. Like a mini-vacation, with interesting friends, lots of professional pampering, and it would keep you off the sauce.*

Richard did not grace this with an answer. He'd landed near the offices of the Swedenborgian House of Studies. He thought of going in, but Hearst Street was just a few quick paces away. He scurried across the street, trying to look inconspicuous. He crossed the street again, heading toward the GTU library, when a voice called out after him. Without looking back, he started sprinting past the library.

The Episcopal seminary was on his left, just across the street. Instinctively, he ran for it. He pushed past the double doors, ran past the front desk, and opened the door to the basement where the restrooms were. Once in the stairwell, he drew off his cassock, rolled it up, and stuffed it beneath the stairs. Once again he heard voices, just upstairs. He rushed to the bottom of the stairs, opened the stairwell door, and ducked into the women's room.

Fortunately, it was empty. He entered a stall and crouched, feet out of sight on the toilet seat should anyone check. He fought to control his breathing. *This is certainly exciting*, Duunel commented. *I haven't been a fugitive from the law in years.*

"I'm not a fugitive," Richard whispered under his breath.

*Walks like a duck...*Duunel almost sang.

Just then, Richard's cell phone vibrated. He said a short prayer of thanks that it had been on vibrate mode and hadn't just given them away with a rousing chorus of "Here I Raise My Ebenezer." Carefully, he drew it out and checked it. There was a new email. Richard opened it, his curiosity piqued.

Before he could read it, however, the bathroom door opened. Richard froze. *Your nose itches*, Duunel said in his head. *It itches so bad you're about to sneeze.*

Richard ignored him. He counted to twenty, and at about fifteen the door closed again and Richard heard heavy shoes clomping back up the stairs. He let out a huge sigh of relief.

So, that was a bust. I like Mulgrew's style, though, I must say. She would have been a hoot to work for, don't you think? Duunel said, for some reason suddenly chatty. *I hear the Muslims are recruiting, if you strike out with this whole bishop thing.*

Something about that comment gave Richard pause. Then the news report came rushing back to him. The attack on Dearborn, and the Michigan governor's statement. It was almost too much to get his mind around. A heaviness came over him, and he closed his eyes and quietly lowered his feet to the floor. Then he looked back at his cell phone.

This morning he had sent out a message to the old-cath listserv, urgently but discreetly announcing a need for emergency episcopal oversight. He hadn't really expected anyone to respond to a note with such sketchy details, but here was one. The email address read bishop@noexit.com, which Richard did not recognize.

He scanned the message. "Richard, long an admirer of your work. We can probably work something out. Must visit in person." A street address in Riverside, California, followed. It was signed, simply, Bishop.

Who is Bishop? Duunel asked. *Is that a title or a name?*

"I have no idea," Richard said.

He sounds like a nut, Duunel said.

"That message is too short for him to sound like anything," Richard retorted.

I'd delete it if I were you, Duunel suggested.

"I'm going to do no such thing," Richard said. He stepped out of the stall and listened at the bathroom door. Nothing. Cautiously, he opened it and made for the service door.

Where are we going now? Duunel asked.

"We've got to pack," Richard said, speed dialing Brian. "We're going on a road trip."

40

MIKAEL TURNED the key in his PO box and grinned to see the slip of paper indicating that he had a package waiting. He was almost jumping up and down as the turbaned Sikh proprietor handed him the package. Mikael noted that he was not his usual cheery self. "What's up, Gus?" Mikael asked.

"It is too bad about Michigan," he said, shaking his head. Mikael was mystified. Did Michigan State just lose a championship? He knew Gus was a sports fan. That must be it. He shrugged and picked up his package. "Take it easy, Gus. Give my love to Radha." Gus forced a brief smile and waved.

The Post Box Place store was only a few blocks from the friary, and Mikael traversed it easily. The package was only about two feet on its largest side, and it wasn't heavy, so he felt no burden. The summer sun felt good on his hair, and a trickle of sweat ran down his back. He relished it.

Nearing the friary, he noted that there were about fifty people across the street now. His brow furrowed at this, and he pressed on to the next street and turned right, walking to the house directly behind theirs. To the side of the house was a small footpath. Mikael turned onto it, and, not for the first time, wondered to whom the path belonged—the city? The Murphys, whose house was directly behind theirs? Or was it some liminal no-man's-land that had simply been grandfathered in without being questioned?

Whatever its status, he was grateful for it now as he lifted the latch on the gate to the friary's back yard and entered. He was grateful that no one was around. He saw the remnants of a fire in the trash can, which he definitely thought was odd, but he didn't stop to investigate. Instead, he opened the door, patted Tobias, and headed up the back stairs. Once in the narrow window-laden room he shared with Kat, he closed the door behind him. With his thumbnail, painted black a week ago and now beginning to chip a bit, he sliced through the packing tape and opened the box. He discarded the packing material and held up a jet-black cowl.

The official habit of the Order of Saint Raphael was the Anglican cassock, which has no hood. Mikael liked the cassocks as their double-breasted cut was smart-looking, and of course, black was classic. But for what Mikael had in mind, a hood was imperative. And a cowl...well, that was just plain *cool*. He put the cowl over his head and noted with satisfaction that it blended into the cassock seamlessly. It was *exactly* the same color, and close enough to the same fabric that unless you looked carefully in good light, it would be impossible to tell that it was not the same.

Smiling in satisfaction in the mirror, he opened the dresser drawer that held his socks. Fishing around in the back, he found another prize—a black mask. He put it on and then looked at himself in the full-length mirror fixed to the back of the door. A feeling of excitement and pride welled up in him. "Meet *the Confessor*," he said to his image in the mirror.

It was a dashing image if he did say so himself. The cassock flared just a bit at the waist, and his hair radiated in a mane, barely contained by the hood of the cowl. The mask hid any identifying features. "Foemen beware," he said dramatically.

Then the door opened. Kat was there, looking disheveled. Her eyes were wet and red, and her hands were shaking. She ran to Mikael and fastened her arms around his waist. She sobbed into his chest. Mikael put his arms around her reflexively, wondering at her state. "What's wrong, kitten?" he asked, stroking her hair.

She poured out the details of their journey in one long, sobbing sentence. Mikael didn't grasp all of it, but the general contours eventually took shape. He made comforting shushing noises whenever she dissolved into sobs, and waited patiently for her to resume. Finally, she finished, recounting how she and Terry had hiked back from the Abyss in stunned silence. Then she sank to the bed and stared blankly out the window.

Mikael handed her a tissue from a box on the windowsill. She grabbed at it gratefully and blew her nose. She took deep breaths, broken by occasional staccato catches, but eventually her breathing became steady and she looked like she was more aware of the room around her. When her eyes finally lit on him, he smiled.

"You look ridiculous," she said.

"Thank you," he said. "The great advantage of being in intimate partnerships is the mutual support, I always find."

"Is this for the steampunk convention next month?" she asked warily.

"Do you see any goggles?" he shook his head.

"Mikael, I don't have it in me to guess right now. Why are you dressed like that?"

He shifted uncomfortably. "I kind of thought...well, I'm good at getting people to talk."

"Since when?" She raised one eyebrow. Then she blew her nose again.

"Okay, I *aspire* to getting people to talk," he said. "I'm forming a secret identity."

"You mean as in a *superhero* identity?" Her face screwed up in a ghastly look of pity.

"Um...kind of?"

"Oh, Honey, that's so...weirdly pathetic, I don't even know where to begin," Kat said, her voice sounding genuinely sad.

"How about, 'Great idea, Honey! You'll be one more arrow in our quiver as we seek to fight the forces of evil!' or something like that."

"Not even Terry talks like that," Kat said.

Mikael looked downcast. He took off his mask.

"What are you going to call yourself?" she asked.

He brightened up a bit, hopeful that she might be showing some genuine interest. "The Confessor."

"And what's your superpower?"

"Uh...I don't really have a superpower. Although I am good at aikido," he said.

"Excellent. So, when you exhaust the forces of evil, you can get them a glass of milk and tuck them in for a good night's sleep."

"I get the feeling you're not taking this seriously," he said, a little hurt.

"All right," she said, rolling her eyes. "What does The Confessor do, exactly, besides tuckering evil out with his stunning aikido moves?"

"Well, he's kind of like the Sandman comics—"

"You look just *like* the Sandman!" Kat said, smiling. "Sexy."

"No...I mean...thank you, but I mean the other Sandman. Not Morpheus from the Gaiman books, but like Wesley Dodds from the Matt Wagner books. You know, the *Sandman Mystery Theater*." His eyes lit up with little-boy excitement.

The look of pity came back into Kat's eyes. "Honey, I have absolutely no idea what you are talking about."

"Wesley Dodds is this millionaire in the 1930s—"

"Ah...I see the resemblance, now." She gave him one of her looks.

"At night, he puts on a trench coat and fedora and a gas mask. He has a gas-shooting gun that makes people tell the truth. And he solves crimes by sneaking up on bad guys and making them...tell the truth."

"And you're going to make people tell the truth...how?"

"Well, I'll be a priest, soon. The moral force of talking to a priest... people will feel compelled to tell the truth...won't they?"

"Okay, Honey, it's obvious that you did *not* grow up Catholic. Nobody tells the truth to the priest. Not even priests tell the truth to priests." She looked at him like she was genuinely worried. "Please do me a favor, and put the mask away. It's...it's just silly."

Mikael felt his heart sink. He didn't agree, but there was no reason to debate it now. He could see that despite the welcome diversion of their conversation, Kat was still in shock. He took off the mask and the cowl and replaced them in his dresser, then he sat on the bed next to her, held her, and rocked back and forth. She clung to him.

41

"Do I hear stirring?" Susan wandered out of the back office. She saw Terry sitting hunched over Charlie, who seemed to be taking a nap. Then she saw Terry's shoulders shake. "Oh, Honey, what's wrong?" She put her cup down on the altar and knelt by Terry, encircling him with her arms. Terry turned and buried his face in her neck. She felt the hot water of his tears and hugged him tighter to herself. Eventually, his sobbing stopped, and he pulled back, wiping his eyes on the back of his hand. "We left him there," he said.

"You left who, where?" Susan asked, shifting so she could sit more comfortably.

"Him, Charlie." Terry's face screwed up like he was about to cry again. "We went to Hell. You know, a day trip. He went into one of the tombs, and...he felt at home. We couldn't lure him out."

Susan was horrified. She leaned back. "Fucking drag him out!"

"I can't do that. You can't force anyone into Hell, or out. People get to choose. Always."

"What would happen if you tried?" Susan asked.

"I'd violate the most sacred values I have!" Terry said, a note of ferocity entering his voice. "We don't coerce."

"Fuck your values. Go back and get him!" Susan said.

"It's not like that, Susan. It's just not. Not even Jesus could force people out of Hell. I certainly can't."

"*Won't.*"

Terry looked away. "Look, let's not fight. It's a setback, not a tragedy...not yet. He's safe where he is. And his...body...isn't going to get up and go anywhere." He looked down at Charlie, who seemed to be napping. "We can brainstorm our options at the table when everyone is here."

"What is it with us?" Susan said, shaking her head. "I mean, what is this, Comatose Magickian Central? A few months ago, it was Kat's brother, and now Charlie?"

"One by one, we seem to be catching the members of the Lodge of the Hawk and Serpent as they fall," Terry agreed. He pulled out a handkerchief and blew his nose.

"Well, let's make him comfortable, and then we should probably call the paramedics," Susan said.

Terry looked up in surprise. "Paramedics?"

Susan put her hands on her hips. "He needs hydration and food. He needs to be fed intravenously. Unless, of course, your plan is to simply sit by and watch him starve to death."

Terry said nothing. Susan placed one of the zafus under Charlie's head and, opening one of the choir benches, pulled out a quilt. She spread it over him and stood back to consider him. "He sure is a prick," she said.

"You shouldn't speak ill of the comatose," Terry mock-scolded.

"Maybe a part of him will hear me," Susan said. "Someone needs to tell him the truth."

"What did we do wrong?" Terry said.

"You want my opinion?" Susan asked.

"Yeah, of course," Terry said. He tried to fix his hair. He gave up.

"Insufficient catechesis."

Terry froze. "Say more."

"You've been training him to do all this inner work, and he isn't even a Christian, is he?"

"Uh...I didn't ask. I just assumed that if he wanted to join us that he already was."

"We didn't assume that of Kat," Susan pointed out.

"No, but it was clear from the outset that she *wasn't* a Christian. Plus, she didn't show up and say, 'Hey, I want to join your order.'"

"So, it seems pretty important to *establish* his status from the outset, don't you think?" Susan said, trying not to sound too judging. She knew she was failing. She plunged ahead anyway. "Maybe instead of starting with the Tree of Life, you should have started with the Apostle's Creed? Or a children's Bible? Or we could have had a hymn sing, and between every song we could have taken turns talking about what Jesus means to us. Loving Jesus is a relationship, and helping Charlie build that relationship should have been our first agenda item."

Terry looked down at his hands. "You're right. You're always right. I feel like an idiot."

"Oh, Honey, I'm not always right," she leaned over and kissed his cheek. "Most of the time, but not *always*. We'll brainstorm this. We'll pray about it. We'll figure it out. We always do. God has never abandoned us. He's not about to start now."

He reached over and squeezed her hand. She squeezed back. "Oh, Terry. Something happened while you were...down under. Something terrible." She told him about Dearborn.

Terry stared at her, open-mouthed. "Oh my God," he breathed. "The Children of the Prophet..." he said, a distant look on his face. He clutched at his head and drew his knees up. "That's...unthinkable."

"That's Republicans for you," Susan said.

"We've got to call Nazim at the Islamic Cultural Center and see if we can help. They're going to need grief counselors," Terry said.

"Good idea," Susan said. "Oh, Terry, there's one more thing I need to tell you. Any minute now, Dylan's going to wake up."

"And that's a problem why?"

"Because I burned all his pot." Susan pursed her lips and waited for the penny to drop.

Terry almost burst out laughing. He caught himself and pressed his hand to his mouth. "You didn't!"

"I did. He's going to be furious."

"Then it's a good thing that we both have places we need to be this afternoon," Terry said.

"That's exactly what I was thinking," Susan said.

"The sooner, the better, I say," Terry said. He looked down at Charlie. "Think he'll be okay?"

"Um...sure he will," Susan said. "What could *possibly* go wrong around here?"

42

TERRY RODE the bus up into Kensington in a daze. The news about Dearborn left him jittery, and he felt like he'd been up for days. Yet he was sure he couldn't sleep. The sight of the possessed gathering outside their house as he walked to the bus stop left him with the same feeling that he'd always had waiting for the results of a medical test—in the background, foreboding, never quite out of consciousness, and yet life rolled unmercifully on.

Terry was so lost in his own thoughts that he missed the bus stop. Mentally, he kicked himself, got off at the next one, and walked back to the house he was seeking. Kensington wasn't much of a town. It was, in reality, a Berkeley bedroom community perched high in the East Bay hills. A rambling assemblage of arts-and-crafts-style architecture, tiny pubs, and boutique restaurants, it was the kind of place that only the impossibly rich could afford—*although one could say that about Berkeley in general*, Terry mused. He felt lucky that the friars had been bequeathed their house years ago as none of them would ever be able to buy it or even rent it.

Checking the address on his phone again, he found himself outside a beautiful two-story fairytale Victorian. Pastor Oberlin's notes said that he was to go around the side and knock on the basement door. Terry let himself in at the gate, wary of dogs, but as none seemed to be around, he relaxed. He knocked on the basement door, and in a few minutes it opened. An elderly gentleman greeted him with a warm smile. He was wearing dark pants, loafers, a smoking jacket, and a bright lavender ascot. "You must be the replacement pastor," he said in a faintly British accent.

"I must be," Terry said, smiling broadly. "And you must be Mr. York."

The old man nodded. His hands shook with the telltale signs of Parkinson's, but his gaunt face was cheery. His few thin wisps of hair were neatly cut and, it seemed, almost plastered into place. *He's doing the best he can with what he's got,* Terry said to himself. He was struck with the momentary vertigo of a man looking at himself in thirty years' time—an old queen whose partner has died. Terry shuddered and resolved to do something to make Brian feel very special when he got home. He knew *just* the thing.

"Please come in, the kettle is warming now," the man swung wide the door. Terry stepped into what was obviously a basement apartment, but one which had been appointed with much care. The low ceilings and odd angles were offset by the elegance of overstuffed Victorian chairs and the rugged wood of mission-style tables. It was patchwork, thrift store décor—but done with such attention and verve that the effect was immediate and pleasing. Terry not only admired it; he envied it, and this, he realized, meant that Mr. York was *successful*, at least as a decorator and a homemaker.

The man waved Terry into a seat at the table in his tiny kitchen. A teapot with a knitted cozy was in front of him along with a full china tea set. The little bowls of sugar cubes and the elegant creamer were chipped, and Terry could see where Mr. York—or someone—had glued them back together and repainted. The new paint did not quite match—it was too bright, and inexpertly applied. There was something about the attempt, however, that was so sweet that he reflected on the fragile dearness of the things he loved—how precious were useless things of beauty. A lump arose in Terry's throat, and he found himself blinking back tears.

Mr. York poured hot water from the kettle into the teapot and carefully placed the lid on top. Wisps of steam brought the smoky odor of lapsang souchong to his nose, and he closed his eyes, basking in the loveliness of it. He swallowed as his salivary glands kicked in. "That smells delicious," Terry said.

"An old lover of mine—he's a Nepalese importer, you know—brings this tea to me. It's from Bhutan, actually. It's like nothing else I've ever tasted. I hoped you'd like it." He set a plate of lemon custard cookies in front of Terry, and then he took a seat himself, wafting into the chair with grand, exaggerated gestures that Terry understood all too well. They were gestures that said, "Don't let the squalor of my conditions fool you—I am a creature devoted to beauty." Mr. York paused as he poured out the tea. "Now tell me, Father, are you partnered?"

Terry blinked in the face of such a cheekily personal question. *Nothing wrong with his gaydar*, he thought. "Um, yes. Nearly ten years, now. His name is Brian. He's a Talmudic scholar."

"Oh, now that *is* promising. But in my experience, scholars can go one of two ways. They can either be dreadful bores who need to show everyone how much they know, or they can be exciting, lovely people who are so in love with their subjects that it's infectious—and of course they are *not* bores because they are keenly aware of how much they do *not* know, and they are not embarrassed about that fact. Now, which one is your Brian?"

"Well, he doesn't fit neatly into your categories. He's not pedantic, and he's plenty humble, but he's not exciting, either. He's...solid."

"He's an Old World German *frau*, is what you're saying." York winked at him. Terry was saying no such thing, but he realized that he was talking to a man too old to care what anyone in the whole fucking world thought of him. He liked that *immensely*.

"How long have you been at Trinity North Church?" Terry changed the subject.

"Oh, nearly twenty years, I should say. I followed Pastor Oberlin there from Saint Irenaeus's, I'm sure you know the story."

Terry didn't. He shook his head.

"Ah, that's a grand tale. Pastor Oberlin—he was *Father* Oberlin, then—was running a Christian-Buddhist *sangha* in England when he was approached by the search committee from Saint Irenaeus's Episcopal Church in Oakland—you know the one."

Terry did. It was a stone's throw from Ted and Mary's, the best breakfast joint in the East Bay. York continued. "They were the most conservative parish in the diocese at that time, and they wanted a real English rector, so they found Pastor Oberlin and brought him and his family over here, promising him the world."

"This sounds like it doesn't have a happy ending," Terry said warily.

"Noooo...conservative parish, he running a sangha...you can see the trouble coming, I'm sure. Two weeks into his ministry there, he had Indian temple dancers baring their midriffs to the strains of a sitar during the offertory. Myself, I think he *barely* escaped a lynching."

Terry laughed out loud but then caught himself. "Oh. My. God. That sounds *so* Oberlin. I can just see it."

"Yes, so the bishop booted him out, and about a hundred people left the parish with him, myself included." His face looked momentarily sad. "We felt...responsible for him, after all. We brought him over here; we couldn't just abandon him."

Terry nodded. There was real love there.

"Soon, we were renting space at the little UCC church on Cedar, and within a couple of years, the two communities merged."

"And that's how Berkeley got its one and only Anglican-Rite United Church of Christ congregation," Terry smiled.

York sipped at his tea, pinkie finger prominently extended. "Only in Berkeley," he affirmed. "Which isn't to say I don't stay connected to the diocese," he said. "I have too many roots there to completely let it go. I keep a toe in the water."

Terry had no idea what he meant by that, but he didn't inquire.

His eye lit upon a striking poster of a rearing horse bearing a rider in a cowboy hat and a brightly woven poncho. The text was in Spanish, and the word Gaucho! was splashed in blood red across it. "What's the story behind that picture there?" Terry pointed to it.

"Oh my dear, you would ask about that, wouldn't you?" His eyes took on a dreamy quality, and Terry could see his thoughts were retreating to the distant past.

"I was in Argentina in 1972. I was madly in love with my traveling companion, Larry Bern—you've probably heard of his 1980s incarnation as Swami Gitananda."

Terry's ears perked up. "He wrote *Don't Be Here Now, Just Be*, right?" Terry remembered. "That was a great introductory text."

"*I* came up with that title," the man said, touching his own chest proudly. "Anyway, we were making our way across South America living off our psilocybin sales."

"Excuse me, your what?" Terry asked.

"We had three suitcases filled with 150 pounds of dried magic mushrooms," he said as if he were reporting on a news item. "It was one of those heavenly hedonistic periods that your generation resents but mine looks back on with the hazy nostalgia born only of selective memory." He paused and seemed to savor the memories. "I can't say that I remember *much* of that trip, but I do recall the *feeling* of the trip, and it was far more fun than ecclesiastically permitted.

"Anyway, we ended up in Buenos Aires, at a sex party with a visiting Brazilian bishop and half of the local diocesan staff in attendance. The beautiful blond über-Aryan I was fucking said that he had a proposition for me."

"Excuse me, did you say 'Aryan'?" Terry asked.

"Um...yes. Second-generation Nazi...refugees, let us say. Did I mention that he was beautiful?" He sighed, his eyes focused on a distant, dreamy horizon. "Anyway, I told him I wasn't sure I could handle another proposition, especially if it worked out as well as his last one. He said he'd trade us the Third Reich's most sacred relic for one of our suitcases.

"At the time, I had about as much interest in sacred relics as I did stewardesses, and he was proposing to walk off with fifty pounds of premium 'shrooms." York sat back and shook his head. "It was more than I wanted to think about since those 'shrooms were all that stood between us and pimping ourselves out on the street—not that I haven't been *there*, truth be told. Anyway, I told him to shut up and hold still so I could make good on his *first* proposition before I went limp, but he went over my head. Larry jumped at the offer, and we walked away from that party with massive hangovers, three sexually transmitted diseases, and one religious relic of dubious provenance. We also left deprived of one suitcase of psilocybin, a fifth of hideously expensive English gin, and our girlish innocence, which has never returned." He grinned wickedly. "But I'm sure you know all about *that*."

Terry returned the smile and turned up the wickedness just a touch. "Oh, I think I *do*."

"Unfortunately, the bishop's little dog got hold of some of the mushrooms and ate God knows how many of them. That fucking Pekingese was vibrating so fast that he rose into the middle of the air like a hummingbird."

Terry choked, sending some of the rich, smoky brew up his nose. When he recovered, he asked, "Just out of curiosity, what *was* the relic?"

"Oh, it was a little stub of a spear. Little more than an arrowhead, really. Made of iron. I thought the thing was going to crumble away in my hand, but the damnedest thing happened to us. Ever since we made that exchange, we just breezed right through every border crossing in Latin America. No one asked us any questions; no one searched our bags. All we had to do was say we wanted something, and people just gave it to us. It was like we were blessed. So, who knows, maybe there was something to it after all."

"A spear...and no one opposed you..." Terry was suddenly lost in thought, an excitement welling up in him. "Mr. York, where is the spear now?"

"Well, after we came back to the States, Bern took up with a shrill bitch from Brooklyn and became an insufferable prick. So, at a New

Year's Eve party"—he waved at Terry playfully—"so many parties—I snuck into his sock drawer and took it. I came out to California—this was, oh, 1976, yes, because of all that bicentennial brouhaha—and I began a torrid affair with the rector of Saint James's."

"That's an Episcopal parish, in Berkeley, right? The one up in the Hills?" Terry asked.

"Yes, that's the one. And they called David—*my* David—to be their rector." He sighed deeply. "We were Abelard and Heloise..."

Terry was about to ask which was which, but he held his tongue as other, more evocative questions occurred to him. In what *way* were York and his David Abelard and Heloise? Did angry relatives or social convention keep them apart? Or had one of them been castrated in a midnight raid?

Terry's mind reeled as the questions spooled out in his mind. But before he could ask any of them, York continued. "We placed the relic in the tabernacle one night after we made love in the chancel. Oh, those were wild times." His eyes lit up. "It's the memories of him that keep me going, you know. We were together for twenty years before he finally succumbed."

"To..." Terry started to ask, but then he stopped. "Oh. Of course." No one succumbed to anything in the gay community except for AIDS. People endured everything else—triumphed over everything else—but they only succumbed to *that*.

"And as far as I know, it's still there," Mr. York smiled. "I've thought about going to see if it's still there, but then I think, why bother? More trouble than it's worth. I don't know anyone there, now. And besides, being in that building brings up too many...memories." Terry could see the moisture in his eyes, and he reached across and took York's hand. The old man squeezed it, and then held on, no doubt hungry for human touch.

"Now...I've been an old fool talking about myself far too much. You didn't come to hear about me."

"Well, actually, that is *exactly* why I'm here," Terry said, still holding tightly to the man's hand.

"Tell me about yourself," York spoke brightly, but tears coursed down his cheeks. Terry debated whether to inquire further or to honor the man's request to change the subject. He opted for the latter.

"I fight demons," Terry said simply.

"Oh, that *does* sound exciting," Mr. York said, letting go of Terry's hand and dabbing at his eyes with a bright red handkerchief. "Tell me all about *that*."

43

KAT WAS RELIEVED when Susan grabbed her for their exorcism visit. As comforting as it had been in Mikael's arms, her brain circled obsessively around the image of Charlie huddled by the back wall of the cave. The distraction, the invitation to do *something*, was welcome indeed.

Both of the women seemed lost in their own thoughts on the way over, however. Susan looked over at her. "Did Mikael...do you know about Dearborn?"

Kat shook her head. "No, what about Dearborn?" Susan told her, and as she did, Kat's eyes grew wide. "Oh my God," she said. "I *dreamed* that."

"What?" asked Susan.

"I totally dreamed that. Yesterday morning," Kat slumped in her seat. "There was the ostrich that we met in the Void—"

"Ostrich? What?" Susan raised an eyebrow in her direction.

"There was a church, and another building that looked...Eastern. Then there was this fireball. Then the animals were running around, just like we saw on the plain in vision today. The ostrich ran up to me, and then I saw the flash. I didn't hear the explosion, though. I guess I still didn't, in real life."

"So it was a capital-D dream?" Susan asked.

"It had to be," Kat nodded. "I mean...it came true."

"I guess it did. What do you think it means?"

"I don't know. I don't have these for nothing. I mean, not usually." For several streets, neither of them said anything. Kat's musings reminded her of a question that had been bugging her lately. "Sue, is Satan really real?" Kat asked.

Susan looked over at her and seemed to be gauging the seriousness on her face. "Define *real*," she answered.

Kat sighed. After several seconds, she said, "Why is everything in the religion biz so maddening? Even my dreams. I mean, why is everything so obscure?"

Susan smiled grimly. "Do you want the long answer or the short answer?"

"Forget it." Kat looked out the window, drew her legs up, and hugged her knees. "How long before Charlie fades out?" she asked.

"That's a Terry question, I think," Susan said. "But I'm pretty sure as long as someone remembers him, he's safe."

"Safe," Kat repeated. "I'm not sure what that word *means* anymore." She looked over at Susan. "Do *you* feel safe?"

"That depends on what you mean by 'safe,'" she said.

"Oh, fuck you all," Kat said, burying her face in her knees.

Susan laughed a hearty, stress-shattering belly laugh and patted Kat's shoulder. "You'll get used to it, Honey. Religious life means living in a constant state of not knowing. The rest of the world can be sure of things—at least people can tell themselves they're sure of things. You know, as long as you eat packaged foodstuffs before the printed expiration date, you won't get sick. The sun will definitely come up in the morning—that kind of thing. But we religious folks can't be sure of...well, of almost anything. We have trust, not knowledge. It's crazy-making, I know. Consider it a lifestyle choice."

"*Why* would I choose that?" Kat pleaded with the windshield.

"I don't think you did. I think *it* chose *you*."

Kat thought about this for a while. "I don't understand the power thing."

"What power thing?" Susan asked.

"Well, as a Wiccan, we were always doing ceremonies where we raised power and then sent it out to do healing. But Terry said that Jesus gave up power, and so we should do the same. I don't really understand why that's good."

"It's not."

"What? I thought that was a Christian thing." Kat's eyebrows nearly met in confusion.

"That's a Christian *guy* thing," Susan said. "Look, if you are of a privileged class who *has* power, then you imitate Christ by giving it up. As in, if you're a *white man*."

"And if you're *not* a white man?" Kat asked.

"If you're not a white man and you're being told that in order to be a good Christian you have to give up even the power that you *don't* have, you're being exploited." Susan bit at a nail. "You know what I want? Frosting. Cream cheese frosting. Right out of the can." She turned to Kat. "You want to split a can of frosting? I promise I won't tell the guys if you don't."

"No. Eww." Kat pushed Susan's face toward the far window. Susan laughed. Kat scowled, still thinking. "Okay, so how does someone who isn't already privileged with power follow Jesus?"

"By doing what Jesus did. He was a poor peasant and probably didn't have the money or education to be a legitimate rabbi, right?"

"If you say so…"

"So, he became a rabbi anyway—he didn't let them keep him down. And then when that woman was about to be stoned for adultery, he stood up to that whole angry crowd of privileged men with rocks in their hands, just itching to throw them. He stood beside her. He didn't lord power over anyone, but he took the power that he had and used it to help someone else. He was always doing that. He acted in solidarity with every sort of disempowered person in his society. He may not have had a lot of power, but he made what he had count. Not for himself but for others."

"Is that what Luther says?" Kat asked.

"Yeah, more or less." Susan squirmed in her seat. "Okay, here's the thing about Luther. I love him dearly, but I don't always agree with him." Susan pulled the car into a space and shut off the motor. "For instance, Luther says that if that guy there"—she pointed at a pizza delivery guy with a heater bag—"if he were charging at me right now to attack me—"

"Armed with a deadly pizza," Kat added.

"Assuming I'm gluten-intolerant," Susan agreed. "Luther would say that I could not defend myself. If, however, the pizza guy were charging at you with murderous intent—"

"Death by anchovy," Kat said.

"I'd be free to do anything in my power to stop him, in order to protect you. I could even kill him, and it wouldn't be a sin."

"That's extreme," Kat said.

"He works for Extreme Pizza," Susan pointed out. "We're here, aren't we?" Kat opened the door.

"You don't have to come in," Susan said.

"No, I want to. I'm just a little overwhelmed. I've already lost one friend today."

"You mean Charlie? First, you don't know that he's lost. And second, he wasn't much of a friend. And third, I'm not in any danger." Susan smiled at her. "It's *just* a demon." Susan opened her own door and got out.

Together they walked up the steps to the door. Susan knocked. In a few moments, the young man from the day before opened the door just a crack, but it wasn't his voice that emerged. "You cunts can get lost. We've got him, and we're going to keep him."

Susan looked at Kat and narrowed her eyes. Then, faster than Kat could see what was happening, she snatched open the screen door and kicked at the wooden door with her wide, beefy legs. An "oof" sound emerged from inside the house as the young man was flung to the floor. Susan followed him, and Kat scooted quickly to catch the door before the screen slammed shut. Going inside, she saw Susan standing with her foot on Doug's throat. "Remember me, asshole?"

Susan said. "I'm the one who believes in one God, maker of Heaven and Earth." As she rattled off the Apostle's Creed, Kat looked around to make sure they were alone and wouldn't be interrupted. No one else seemed to be around.

"You have no dominion over us!" the young man shouted, clutching at Susan's leg and writhing on the floor. Once Susan had finished the Creed, she answered. "No, I don't. Never said I did. But the one to whom I belong *does*. And it is he who sent me. And you'll obey me, or you'll answer to *him*." She pressed more firmly on the man's throat.

"You're not a priest—" the demon complained.

"Every baptized Christian is a priest, and more than enough to deal with something like you," Susan countered.

Doug's body yanked on her ankle, and Susan went down, hitting her head on the hardwood floor. She shook it off, undaunted. She rolled on top of the man and pinned his arms under her sizable legs.

"You don't have any holy water!" the demon within the young man spat. "You don't have any vestments! You don't even have a ritual book!"

"Oh yes, that's what you'd like, isn't it, you stuck-up piece of shit. You'd like a ceremony, wouldn't you? You'd like me to make a big production of casting you out, so that at least when you're squeezed out of his body like the little turd you are, you can feel like you've put up a brave, dramatic fight. Well, fuck that. You don't get a ceremony. You don't get to wear a party dress, and you don't get balloons. And you don't get any satisfaction from the drama of it all." She looked over at Kat. "Worse than Terry," she grinned.

The sight of her grinning while riding that possessed man like a bucking bronco was deeply unsettling. Kat felt sick.

"Our Father," Susan began. Kat joined in as they prayed the Lord's Prayer. About halfway through, her stomach settled. When they'd finished the prayer, Doug had stopped struggling.

Susan placed her hand on the man's forehead, "Jesus, hear your sinner. Drive out this demon, and deliver this man, and give him the grace that he may choose a better life." Then she rolled off him, stood up, and wiped her nose on her arm. "I'm not going to give you what you want," she said to the possessed man. "No ceremony. No big to-do. I'm just going to come back, day after day, and I'm going to keep praying for you. And I'm betting I can keep it up longer than you can. Because it's easy for me, and you are fucking suffering." She kicked Doug in the head and made for the door. "C'mon, Kat. Done here for now."

Kat followed silently, realizing for the first time that Susan hadn't even bothered with a kit bag this time. Outside the house, the sunlight seemed brighter than she'd remembered it. The leaves on the tree above her were shockingly green. It wasn't until they'd started the car and driven a couple of blocks that Kat spoke. "Did you really need to kick him in the head?"

"Was that a little rough?" Susan asked uncertainly.

"You know, I've been meaning to ask if your little friend is paying you a visit right now?" Kat looked at her warily.

"Because...?"

"Well, you're a little irritable. Make that a *lot* irritable." Kat braced herself for an angry response. But none came. Instead, Susan pressed her lips together until she found a parking space. Then she rested her head on the wheel. When the sobs came, they burst out violently.

"Oh, Susan. I'm sorry. I didn't mean to..." Kat was flummoxed. She waited until Susan's heaving subsided.

"It's not you," Susan said, her voice shaky and weak. "It's Dylan." Briefly, she told her about burning his stash.

"Oh boy," Kat said. "Yeah, that's not going to be any fun at all."

"Let's not go home," Susan said, head still on the wheel but turned now to see Kat out of one bleary eye. "Let's go drinking."

"Oh. Okay. Let's get drunk because you made it impossible for your husband to get high." Kat frowned. "That makes no sense."

"He's going to be furious at me."

"Did you think of that before you did it?" Kat asked.

"I wasn't thinking. I just did it. I was pissed at him. Frustrated. Whatever."

"Susan, here's what we're going to do. We're going to go home, and you're going to face whatever wrath Dylan can muster. And I'm going to stand beside you."

Susan sniffed, choking back a sob. "Because that's power," she said.

"That's power," Kat agreed.

44

BRIAN PULLED into the parking lot at All Saints' Episcopal and parked. To his right, Tobias panted noisily. He punched at the horn on the cherry-red Corolla, and Richard, who had been sitting on the steps near the back entrance to the church, looked up and waved. He stuffed a paperback into his shoulder bag and headed for the car.

"You brought me the *good* car," Richard said when he was close enough to be heard.

"Yeah, I'll probably catch hell for that, but Susan had the clunker today, so it's not my fault," Brian responded, giving Richard a brief hug. "She's going to need gas," he continued. "But you've got everything you need: There's a duffle bag with three changes of clothes and your summer cassock. You'll need that if you're going south. Oh, and I packed your iPad and a charger."

Richard ducked to look into the car. "I see you've also brought me a dog," Richard said. Tobias seemed to be smiling at him in the way that yellow Labs do. Richard straightened up and gave Brian a puzzled look. "Why do I have a dog?"

"He insisted on coming." Brian shrugged. "He barked until I let him in the car, and he doesn't seem to be budging. My guess is that Toby—or the angel that's in him—is determined to go with you."

"All the way to Rages…" Richard said quietly, thinking deeply.

Brian passed a hand over Richard's eyes until he refocused. "You okay to drive?"

"Oh yeah. Just thinking. Um, how is Dylan going to take this?" Richard asked.

"You mean his dog just taking off on a road trip?" Brian asked.

"Right," Richard said.

"Believe me, Dylan is thinking about other things right now."

"Such as?"

"Susan burned all of his pot."

"Oh Jesus. I am so glad I'm leaving now."

"I actually think Toby has the right idea. If I had half a brain, I'd go with you, too." Brian slapped at his back. "Godspeed. Bring us back a bishop."

"I'll do my damnedest." Richard snatched the keys from his hand.

45

THE CROWD of the possessed was about a hundred strong when Susan and Kat approached the house. They parted like the Red Sea before them, and Susan was glad for the car's protection, dilapidated as it was. Once within the warded area surrounding the house, they parked and got out. The damned stood lining the street as if they were a choir about to sing. It occurred to Susan that since some stood in the street and some up on the curb, it was as if they were standing on risers. *What would they sing, if they* did *sing?* she wondered. "I Feel Possessed" by Crowded House seemed too obvious. Some of them were even working their mouths in wild, obscene motions as if lip syncing to a soundtrack only they could hear.

"There's more now," Kat said. "Where are they all coming from?"

Susan just shook her head.

"Hey!" called a voice. Susan looked at Kat, who was also looking around. Then a woman broke free from the pack of Occupied Americans. Susan expected her to hit the wall of the warding when she got to the middle of the street, but she didn't. She just kept coming, her face flushed and her hands on her hips.

"Do these belong to you?" she asked Susan, gesturing at the possessed.

"No," Susan answered. "You live across the street, right? I'm Susan."

"I don't give a *fuck* who you are. I want these...*animals* off my lawn. Now!"

"Have you tried saying 'Please don't stand on my lawn'?" Susan asked.

"Have *you* tried talking to them?" The woman barked the question, one red vein straining to burst free from her forehead. "Make them go away!"

"I can't make them go away," Susan said.

"Then tell those weird monks to make them go away," the woman demanded.

"The *Blackfriars* can't make them go away, either," Susan answered. "We don't know why they're here. We don't know what they're doing. And right now, we can't do anything about it."

"I'm calling the police, and you're going to answer for it!" the woman said. "And you're going to replace my lawn!" She turned on her heel and walked back across the street.

"Does she know that she's walking into a horde of possessed people?" Kat asked.

Amazingly, the possessed shuffled to either side to let her pass unmolested.

"Even *they're* scared of her," Kat said, clearly impressed. "You handled that well."

"That's nothing," Susan said. "It's my husband I'm worried about."

Kat squeezed her arm. "Let's go face the music."

Susan blew air out of her cheeks and followed Kat to the front door. Once inside, she saw Mikael sitting by himself in the chapel, his eyebrows so high he looked as if he'd just had a facelift. With his eyes, he indicated the kitchen. He was very still and very quiet. "Oh shit," said Kat. She padded over to Mikael and kissed him.

"Maybe you should wait here," he suggested in a whisper.

"No," Kat said. "Gonna stand with my sista."

"You're a braver man than I," Mikael said.

Susan joined them, wiping the sweat from her palms onto her jeans. "How bad is he?" she whispered.

"Well, he's stoned, so he's not in too bad a shape," Mikael said. "But he's mad as hell."

"How could he be stoned?" Susan asked. "I was sure I got all of his stashes."

"Dregs," Mikael said, wrapping his arms around Kat's waist. "He's scraped every wooden pipe down to the new wood, and every metal bowl in the house looks as shiny as the day he brought it home from the head shop. He's also smoked a couple of roaches so old I think they came from joints rolled by Junipero Serra. They ought to have been in a museum."

"Oh Jesus," Susan breathed. "I didn't think of any of that."

"It's all gone now. I give him a half hour before he's smoking turnip tops and catnip."

Kat disentangled herself from Mikael's embrace and took Susan's hand. "Let's go, Honey," she said. "Power."

"Power," Susan repeated. She squeezed Kat's hand and did not let go. Together they walked toward the kitchen. Kat went through first, and Susan followed, seeing Dylan in his regular place at the table. Terry was massaging his shoulders. Dylan looked over his shoulder, saw Susan, and stood up, sending the bench flying behind him as he turned. Terry righted it and stood back.

"You betrayed meh!" Dylan shouted, stabbing in Susan's direction with a chubby, accusing finger. "How could ya do it? How could you do this to meh?"

Susan expected to be cowed before his wrath, but the injustice in Dylan's accusation stopped her short. Months of accumulated resentment and neglect rose within her. Bitterness at his blindness and selfish obsessiveness burst through her sense of propriety. Reacting, unthinking, she stood to her full height, puffed out her chest, and advanced on him. She slapped at his chest. "What did I do to you, Dylan?" she asked, "Love you? Care about you?" She slapped his face, hard. The sound of it reverberated throughout the kitchen. "What did I do *to you*, Dylan? Refuse to see you be dragged down by your own weakness? By your *stupid* addiction?" A huge red welt rose up on Dylan's cheek. She slapped at his thinning hair, and her voice began to lose its certainty. "What did I *do*? What the *fuck* did I *do*?"

As the tears rose up, the volume and ferocity of her voice rose as well. Dylan held his hands over his head to ward off the blows, but Susan, screaming now, just kept coming. "I stood by as you sank deeper into this *fucking* pit you're in." She slapped at the top of his head. "I supported you; I *enabled* you in your *stupid* habit. I stood by and *watched* as it claimed more and more of your life and you had less and less for me and for your friends and for God!" She struck at his neck. Dylan stumbled, and he went down. Susan fell on him with her knees, pinning his chest.

"And now I'm taking you back, you ungrateful shit! You do *not* belong to yourself. You are *not* an island. You are *not* your own master. We are married—I have a claim on your life! And I'm not the only one—you are the fucking *property* of Jesus! And you have obligations to this house and this order! We have stood back and let you retreat further and further into yourself." She slapped him, then she slapped him again. "No more! I won't let you go, not one more inch. Because I"—*slap!*—"fucking"—*slap!*—"love you"—*slap!*—"asshole!"

She got up and turned her back, leaning on the table and choking up sobs so deep she thought she might vomit. She was almost lying over the table. Dylan crouched by the stove in the fetal position. No one moved.

Just then, they heard the sound of the front door opening. A moment later Brian walked in. "Sorry supper is la—" He stopped short as he took in the scene. "So, *this* is awkward," he said, his shoulders lowering so much that his hunchback was far more pronounced than usual. "I'll just...stand over here." He sidled in alongside Terry and squeezed his shoulder.

"So, listen up! This is how it's going to be," Susan said, turning around and facing them all. One of Dylan's eyes stared at her from behind his hands. Red welts peppered every inch of his exposed skin. "*You* are going cold turkey!" She pointed at Dylan.

"*You*," she pointed at Terry, "are going to strategize order affairs and dole out assignments, and no one is going to complain about it." She looked directly at Mikael. "Got it?"

As if they were one body, everyone in the room nodded their assent. Then Susan turned, drew her elbows into her gut, and let out a rage-filled wail that shook the timbers of the house. Then she pounded out of the room.

"Well, *that's* power," Kat said under her breath and followed after her.

46

As soon as Susan had left the room, Dylan rolled onto all fours and tried to stand. Mikael steadied him as he rose.

"Oh, man, she did a number on you," Mikael said. "Sorry, dude."

Dylan's face flushed red again, but this time out of shame. The effect was a more unified field of red that made the welts less noticeable. Strands of Dylan's remaining hair hung at all angles, and he caught at the kitchen counter to steady himself.

His mouth worked in pained gyrations, making sure he wasn't physically hurt. His jaw seemed to be all right. His eyes were glassy and watery, but he was damned if he was going to cry. He made for the back door.

"Dylan, where are you going?" Terry called after him. Dylan didn't answer. The screen door slammed, and he let himself out at the gate.

He went directly across the street, heading straight into the mass of the possessed. His face glowered, and he was so red he almost glowed. The damned seemed to notice and kept their distance—a wedge opening up in their ranks through which he passed.

Some distant part of his brain registered how dangerous and stupid his actions were. But in the moment, he was so angry and ashamed that he would have been almost relieved if they had fallen upon him and eaten his brains. *They're not zombies*, he reminded himself. *They're just possessed. Fuckin' actin' like zombies, though.*

He had no idea where he was going. *Find pot*, a voice in his head was screaming. He could already feel the effects of the dregs he'd smoked waning, and the desolation of sobriety already beginning to settle into his bones. He turned left onto Cedar Street and began up the hill toward the Berkeley campus.

Did he have his medical marijuana ID card with him? He did. Did he have money? He didn't. Did he have his ATM card? He did. Was there any money in his account? There wasn't. Could he borrow any from the common funds? He hesitated. Surely, the guys would understand. They would, right? But now Kat was part of the equation. Where would she stand? And how much was in the common fund, anyway? It couldn't be much. And Susan would skin him alive. Again.

He looked at his feet and stopped. A wave of grief washed over him, and he steadied himself against one of the trees lining the street. Had he lost his Susan? Did he deserve to? Tears welled up, and he leaned against the tree and allowed gravity to take him down into a pile. There was no one to see him now except for the anonymous drivers passing by. He wailed, and sobs gobbed up through his throat.

When he was calm enough to talk again, he noticed the cool of the air. "Jesus," he spoke out loud, "Ah ain't got much of a prayer in meh. So Ah'm just gonna say *help*." In that moment, he felt a tiny flame of comfort emerge within him. Not judgment, or shame. Just a paradoxical warmth countering the cold wind. "Ah wouldn't blame you if you just took off," he said, but the warmth did not retreat.

"Ah'm such a shit," he said. "Every word Susan said wuz right. Ah got no cause to be mad at her." His pride was hurt worse than anything she had done to his body. He was aware of this. He also knew that he had neglected her. But he hadn't allowed himself to acknowledge it until that moment. Fresh tears spilled out on his cheeks. "Ah'm sorry, Honey!" he wailed. When he was emptied of wails, he said quietly, "Ah'm so sorry, Jesus."

It was colder now, and it stung at him. He no longer felt hungry, and he thought this odd. He stood up and debated. Should he go home? No. There was pot to find.

47

IN THE KITCHEN, Brian, Terry, and Mikael sat at the table and stared at the wood. "Shall I order us a pizza?" Brian asked. No one said anything, so he got out his cell phone and speed dialed the pizzeria. That done, the table returned to silence. A minute later, Kat entered. "She wants to be alone," she said and sat down next to Mikael, leaning against him slightly. He put his arm around her comfortingly.

Finally, Mikael spoke. "Terry, I'm sorry I was such a shit to you a couple of days ago."

Terry looked up and couldn't hide the hurt look that passed over his face. He nodded. Mikael continued. "I just...sometimes you're critical and quick to judge, and it just felt like you were trying to take over—"

Terry's eyebrows raised. He leaned back and said imperiously, "Sorry, was this an apology?"

Mikael pursed his lips together. "Yeah. It's an apology. And you're right. I was frustrated that my ordination got put on hold. It was selfish. I'm sorry."

"Apology accepted," Terry said. "Mikael, I know I can be hard to take. It's just my style. You can push back. It's okay. Brian does it all the time." As if to illustrate, Brian pushed him over. Terry sat back up. "See? All is well."

"You're a prick," Brian said, smiling.

"Don't push it," Terry warned. His smile faded, and he looked at the grain in the wood again. "I know I get on people's nerves. I don't mean to. And I wasn't trying to take over. I was just trying to...get things done."

"I know. I know," Mikael said. "And I think you should. You're a type-A detail person, which is exactly what we need without Dicky here. I mean, he's a type-A detail person, too, he's just..."

"Less irritating?" Terry asked.

"I wasn't going to *say* that."

"You were thinking it," Terry countered.

Mikael didn't refute him. Instead, he said, "Can we, like, have a meeting? I mean, I know everyone isn't here, but...there's a lot of stuff to talk about."

Terry nodded, but nobody said anything. Then Terry got up from the table and left the room. In a moment, he came back with a yellow legal pad and a pen. "Let's take stock," he said. "We've got a growing nation of possessed people on our doorstep, and we can't do anything about them without a bishop."

"And Richard is on that," Mikael said.

"And Toby," Brian said. They all looked at him. "It's true. Toby insisted on going with him—or the angel did."

"Hokay," Terry scrawled that last bit of info. "Do we have any idea *why* we've got a growing nation of the possessed congregating around our house?"

"Nope," Kat said.

"Intimidation?" Brian asked. "Normal people would be intimidated by such things."

"Normal people?" Terry asked. "Who would want to intimidate us?"

"Anyone with cloven hooves and a tail?" Mikael suggested.

"Point," Terry said. "But why?"

Brian drummed his fingers. "Could it be misdirection?"

"You mean, keep us focused on the slobbering horde so that we miss something more important going on?" Mikael asked. "But what would that be?"

"If we haven't noticed it, then maybe it's working," Brian said.

"That's a frightening thought." Kat said. No one disagreed.

"Maybe we just haven't put it together yet," Terry said. "Maybe we have all the pieces, but we don't see how they connect."

"Or most of the pieces," Brian corrected.

Terry shrugged. Then his eyes got a faraway look. "Something odd happened while we were on our way to Hell this morning," Terry said.

"That sounds like the beginning of a joke," Mikael grinned.

"We were crossing the desert on our way to the Abyss, when it started raining animals. Like I told Kat and Charlie, I saw that happen once before, but it was only one animal then."

Kat leaned in. "There were thousands of them today—maybe *hundreds* of thousands," she said. "I thought they were going to crush us."

"If it weren't for the Sandalphon, they would have," Terry said.

Brian's head snapped up. "Just a minute," he said, going out through the back door. A minute later he came back, pecking furiously at an iPad. "Okay, listen to this, from the medieval Islamic theologian Al-Ghazali: 'On the Day of Resurrection, meanings are bared. Then form takes on the color of meaning. If a person had been dominated by passion and greed in the world, he will be seen on that day in the form of a pig. If he was dominated by anger and aggression, he will be seen in the form of a wolf.'"

Terry nodded. "There were lots of other animals, too."

"Well, there are ninety-nine names of Allah—all of them represent a divine attribute which is also manifested in human beings. It's what it means to be made in the image of God, according to Islamic theology. Any one of the attributes out of balance with the others renders it a vice, and whichever vice is dominant is represented by a different animal. Al-Ghazali suggests that everyone is out of balance somehow and so will manifest as an animal while awaiting judgment."

"But is *this* the Day of Resurrection?" Mikael asked.

"Resurrection happens in various stages," Brian said. "First, there is the manifestation of the attributes—I think that's what you saw today. Next is judgment, where each soul will be weighed and assigned an eternal destiny. It could be that there are thousands of years separating the different stages."

"So, we saw an Islamic resurrection?" Kat asked. "Does that even make any—"

"Dearborn," Brian said. They all looked at him. "Dearborn has the highest concentration of Muslims in the United States."

"Had," Terry corrected him.

"Exactly," Brian nodded slowly. "You were in the desert at the exact same time that the Michigan governor bombed Dearborn. You witnessed all of those souls—"

"Coming through the other side," Terry nodded, getting it.

Kat held her hands up to her mouth, not daring to breathe. "Oh my God," she said. "That's horrible."

Mikael nodded. "That must be it," he said. "But what do *we* have to do with that? There's nothing we could have done; no way we could have known it was coming; no way we could have stopped it."

"I don't know," Terry admitted. "It's just...sad."

"It makes me angry," Kat said, her hands balling up into fists. Mikael pulled her closer to him, and she leaned her head on his shoulder.

"We've got two other threads in play, here," Terry said. "We shouldn't forget that we have a commission—we still have no idea how Bishop Preston could have won election to the Episcopal Diocese of California. Brian, you were researching talismans, yes? What did you find?"

"I found three possibilities," Brian said. "Two of them are lost, but that doesn't mean anything. Magickal artifacts don't like to stay lost, as we all know, and they surface regularly. Anyway, there are two Talismans of Sedephora—that's the demon that rules psychic phenomena. The talismans were made twenty years apart, when one of them had been stolen. I'm thinking it must be one of them since it has a limited range.

"The third option is a glorified glamour—the Stone of Tsarit. It's a stone—a piece of volcanic resin, actually—that makes it *appear* as if people agree with you. But there's no range—its effects can be world-wide. The stone hasn't been seen since 1277, and the older Talisman of Sedephora disappeared around 1942, purchased by Jack Parsons, of all people. He used it to lure into his circle...well, let us say, several science fiction writers, one of whom would go on to found one of the most nefarious cults the world has ever known."

"And the younger talisman?" Terry asked.

"Sold by Coventry Magickal Supply just last month," Brian checked his iPad. "For a cool 1.3 million dollars."

Mikael whistled. "I think that's our baby."

Terry felt something nagging at him. "Brian, what about the Spear of Longinus?"

Brian jerked upright. "Where the fuck did *that* come from?"

Terry smiled. "Humor me, Honey Pie. Could the Spear have done this job?"

"What's the Spear of Long...How do you say it?" Kat asked.

"It's the spear that was used to pierce Jesus's side during the cruci-fixion," Terry said. "It's coated with the bile containing the sins of the world."

"Okay, that sounds...evil."

"It is."

Brian's face screwed up in thought. Tapping the table with his fingers, he said. "Maaaybe the Spear could do it. It wouldn't have been my first choice—and still isn't."

"Why not?" asked Kat.

"Because it's counterintuitive. It's like using a jackhammer when a butter knife will do."

"So, the Spear is more powerful than what we saw on those diocesan convention videos?" Mikael asked.

"Waaaaay more powerful," Brian said.

"What about proximity?" Mikael asked. "If it's so powerful, why is proximity an issue?"

Terry slapped at the table. "User proficiency!" He looked hopefully at Brian. When he saw him nod, he pounded the table again. "Yes!"

"It could be that Bishop Preston is just figuring out how to use it. He'll get better, though, trust me. *If* it's the Spear, that is." Brian held up a finger. "I still want to know why you brought it up."

Briefly, Terry told them what he'd heard at his visit with Mr. York. Mikael whistled. "I think we need to establish whether the story is true."

"How are we going to do that?" Kat asked.

"A little breaking and entering," Mikael said.

"Is this a job for The Confessor?" Kat asked slyly.

"For who?" Terry asked.

"Nobody," Mikael said. "Terry, are you up for a little nocturnal visit to Saint James's?"

Terry nodded, looking Mikael in the eye.

"Can I come?" Kat asked. Before Mikael could answer, she held up a warning palm. "Consider carefully, as you have already witnessed more feminine fury tonight than the male constitution can comfortably tolerate."

A glimmer of fear came into Mikael's eyes at that. "Eleven o'clock?"

"Fine," Kat said.

"Kat, how did that Lutheran exorcism go?" Brian asked.

"Slow. Susan kicked him in the head."

"Was that effective?"

"I think it was effective for Susan. She's pretty frustrated." Kat smiled, but it looked more like a grimace. "We'll go back tomorrow. Stay tuned."

"Okay, is that it, then?" Brian asked, ready to get up. He was already looking around at all that needed to be done in the kitchen.

"Wait," Terry said. "There is one more thing. Charlie is in Hell."

"Charlie's in Hell?" Brian asked.

"Yeah," Terry said, slouching. "Just an educational field trip. He took to it."

"He's at home," Brian said, nodding.

"He's at home," Terry agreed.

"Well, who are we to judge?" Brian said. "He knows how to get back. He can walk out anytime he wants to."

"I feel so bad about this," Terry confessed.

"Where's his body?" Brian asked. "Is it breathing?"

Terry nodded. "Alta Bates Hospital. We called the paramedics earlier."

"Poop," Brian said. "Just what the world needs—"

"I know, another comatose magickian."

Just then, Kat's cell phone vibrated. She pulled it out and checked it. A look of shock came over her face. "What is it?" asked Terry, noticing.

"It's an email...from my brother." She looked at the space on the wall where his mirror usually hung. It was empty. "Where the hell is my brother?" Panic forced her voice into an almost painful pitch. Her phone buzzed. She looked down at it again. "I'm in the bathroom," she read. "It's boring in the bathroom. At least I can surf the web." Kat looked up. "What??"

Brian said, "Ah. Just a moment." He got up, walked to the back bathroom, and returned moments later with the mirror. He hung it in place and plugged in the suction cup mic.

"Hi, Sis," Randy said, waving. "Thanks for leaving me in the bathroom *all day*, Brian."

"Sorry," said Brian.

"It *sucked*."

"Sorry."

"How were you able to send me email?" Kat asked.

"The bathroom door was ajar," Brian said. "Part of Susan's office was visible in the mirror when I went to get him. My guess is that he was able to access the internet in the reflection of her computer."

"Yeah, you might want to close those windows," Randy said, shuffling his feet. "Susan will not appreciate all the porn that is open on them now."

"Jesus Christ, Randy," Kat said.

"No, this is really important," Brian acknowledged. "Knowing that Randy can get online can substantially contribute to his quality of life."

"What he said," Randy agreed. "Only less geekily."

"Randy, I'll leave a laptop or an iPad or something on the kitchen table whenever I can. Remind me," Brian said to the mirror.

"Will do," Randy saluted.

"So, what can we do about Charlie?" Kat asked.

"Wait, so did I hear this right? Charlie's in Hell?" Randy asked. "Why is Charlie in Hell? Has anybody ever told you people that *you are not safe* to be around?"

Terry ignored him. "There's nothing we can do, Kat. He walked in willingly—we all did. And he can walk out, too. He just doesn't want to."

"Can I go in and drag him out?" Kat asked.

"No," Terry said.

"What's stopping me?" she asked.

"Any one of about a thousand demons," Terry said.

"What demons?" Kat asked.

Terry's eyes opened wide. "Holy shit, she's right. There were no demons there. Brian, why were there no demons in Hell?"

"There were no demons?" Brian scowled. "Well, I have a theory."

"Hit me," Terry said.

"I don't think there are any demons in Hell," he said, getting up and going to the window, "because they're all *out there*. And there will be more of them every hour until—hey!"

"What?" Terry asked.

Brian looked up and down the street. He turned back and faced them, a look of confused concern on his face. "Uh...guys, that horde of the possessed we were just talking about? They're all gone."

48

As Dylan walked, he went through a short checklist of scoring possibilities. There was a medical marijuana dispensary on Telegraph, but that would require money. There would also be boho kids camped out on the sidewalk smoking—it was conceivable that he might bum a hit off the odd splif. That was especially likely in People's Park. He made a slight course correction and headed for the UC Berkeley campus.

Telegraph lay just on the other side of campus, so the shortest way there was simply through. Dylan shivered as the dusk settled over Berkeley, bringing with it a foggy chill, even in summer. He hugged his arms around his chest for warmth.

He'd just stepped onto the campus when he saw movement out of the corner of his eye. He looked to the right and stopped in his tracks. Walking down Hearst Street was a mass of at least a hundred people —probably more. Berkeley was ground zero for street protests, so the sight was not unusual, but there was something odd about this particular group that caught Dylan's attention. There were no signs. No one was singing or chanting. There was not even a hint of the party atmosphere that accompanied most protests.

Dylan cocked his head. He looked south across campus in the

general direction of Telegraph Avenue. Then he looked west after the marching group of people. He looked south. He looked west. "Awwww, dammit all to Hell!" he swore and began walking west after the crowd.

He hadn't gotten far before he realized that he recognized a couple of them. They had been gathered outside the friary. These were the possessed. With that realization, he hung back and hid behind a plumber's van.

Looking from side to side, Dylan debated internally what to do. He was simply too recognizable in his cassock. But it was nippy, and the temperature was dropping. "Shit," he said out loud and pulled the cassock over his head. He rolled it up, tucked it under his arm, and set out again at a slight jog to catch up with the lumbering horde.

Reaching the rear flank, he stopped jogging and matched the steps of the possessed. He noted with some alarm that many of them were carrying garden tools or bricks. Since none of them were paying any attention to him, he double-stepped to move through the crowd, hoping to gain some sense of where they were going, and why.

The group had reached Oxford Street now and was stopping traffic, stepping out to make an enormous group left-hand turn. Watching carefully to see who was leading, Dylan almost tripped when their point person came into view.

"Larch. Well, Ah'll be damned." Dylan had been curious before, but now he was fairly champing at the bit. He didn't feel cold anymore, nor was he thinking about scoring. He kept Larch in his line of sight but was careful to keep a prudent distance since he did not want to be recognized. Weaving his way through the crowd, Dylan saw a few of the other lodge members walking near the front of the advancing horde.

At Allston, they made a right and stopped. Dylan knew the place —it was the Maccabee Museum of Jewish Art and Life, a cultural fixture in Berkeley for nearly half a century and a place where Brian lectured regularly on Jewish mysticism and magick.

Dylan was sure it must be closed, but that didn't seem to stop them. Dylan ducked into a recessed doorway of a nearby building to watch as Larch and his lodge cronies hung back. The possessed lumbered forward and brought the bricks and tools to bear on the long, frosted windows facing the street.

The glass shattered with a crash that Dylan could hear nearly a block away. The possessed draped themselves over the exposed shards of glass to provide safe passage so that the magickians could climb over them and into the museum. Others of the possessed followed. Dylan heard gunshots coming from within the museum, and he heard the roar of sirens.

He'd seen enough, and as he didn't really feel like being detained for questioning, he walked nonchalantly past the possessed bodies draped over the cut glass, now bleeding and still. Deftly, he snagged a wallet out of the back pocket of one of the dead. He patted the man's butt uncomfortably, muttered, "Sucks to be you, dude," and made a quick left at Shattuck.

A block later, he headed due east, making for the UC campus again. Once across the street, he pulled on his cassock and examined the wallet. Inside were four twenty-dollar bills—exactly enough for a quarter ounce of medium-grade smoke. He stuffed the wallet into his pocket and headed as directly as he could for the dispensary.

49

THE SUN WAS DIPPING out of sight just as Richard took the south-bound ramp to I-5, toward Los Angeles and ultimately, Riverside. Tobias sat in the passenger seat, alert and erect, eerily as a human might. Richard, having never been on a road trip with the dog, didn't know if that was just Tobias, or the influence of the angel somehow.

Then it occurred to him that it didn't really matter. *When are we going to stop for dinner?* asked the voice in his head.

"We haven't even been driving for an hour. What are you, six?" Richard responded.

More like six hundred thousand, asshole, so don't be snotty. If I'm hungry, you're hungry, and you are hungry, Duunel answered.

"Yeah, but I want to make some time before we slow down," Richard said. "After all, I don't plan to drive all night. It's not safe."

Why not? There's two of us to keep us awake, Duunel argued.

"Because I don't trust you not to run us off the road into a gas tanker just to watch the pretty lights," Richard said.

You are harsh. And hurtful. Duunel's voice sounded almost like he was pouting.

Just then, the radio began to hiss static. They had travelled beyond the reach of KFOG, San Francisco's classic rock station. Richard punched a couple of buttons on the radio, trying to home in on the signal a little better. "Fucking newfangled radios," he said. "Give me a dial anytime."

You are old, Father William, quoted Duunel.

"You are a pain in the ass, fuckhead," Richard responded, nearly automatically.

Do you pray with that potty mouth? Duunel asked.

"Anyway, there are plenty of country music stations around," Richard said mock-cheerfully.

If I could die, I'd say "Kill me now," Duunel complained.

"Ah, but there's hope," Richard said. "See what I've got here?" He held up his iPhone.

It's a phone, Duunel deadpanned.

"Yes, but it's also holding every CD Amy Grant ever made," Richard said.

Who? Duunel asked.

"So, since we've got a long trip, I say we start at the very beginning, with the eponymous album," Richard said.

I should be worried about this, right? Duunel asked.

Richard jacked the iPhone into the stereo, keeping one eye on the road. "No, seriously, you'll love this," Richard said. "Brown Bannister's production is so sweet, you'll be raising your hands and praising Jesus before side one is over."

I knew you were a pervert and an alcoholic, but I didn't think you really had a cruel streak in you, Duunel noted.

"You're making me blush," Richard said, and a moment later the syrupy strings and horns of "Beautiful Music" filled the car. Instantly, Richard started singing along.

You really know all the words, don't you? Duunel asked.

"So do you, then, right? C'mon, access 'em, and let's have us a sing-along. It'll be fun!" Richard began to mimic the strings part.

So...country music isn't so bad, right? Duunel asked hopefully.

"Toby seems content," Richard said.

Toby's idea of aesthetic value is gauged by two questions: Is it dead, and can I roll in it? Duunel said.

"*Now* who's harsh?" Richard asked.

Halfway through the *My Father's Eyes* album, Richard noted a rest stop approaching and indicated a lane change to catch the off-ramp.

Oh good, Duunel said, rousing finally. He seemed to have gone into hibernation halfway through the first Amy Grant album. *Your bladder is starting to become painful.*

"You're free to leave anytime," Richard said. "Look, there's some cows."

No, thanks.

"Mmmm...cows are comfy. So calm. So noble. So much yummy cud to chew."

You know, eventually I will leave this cesspool of a brain of yours, but you are trapped in here for life, Duunel said.

"The sooner, the better," Richard said. He pulled into a space and got out. He stretched and then called to Tobias. "C'mon, big boy, there are weeds that need watering here. Come, and do your duty."

Tobias leaped from the car and began sniffing around the little patch of grass that separated the parking lot from the restrooms. He seemed excited to find the picnic table. He investigated it thoroughly then lifted his leg on it. Then he leaped off, running back and forth with abandon.

"Okay, big guy, back in the car before I burst," Richard called. Tobias jumped up in the car, and Richard shut the door. The dog leaped into the backseat and lay down, scratching his back against the seat, all four paws in the air.

Richard walked quickly to the small building, trying not to dance. He unfastened the Velcro of his cassock as he did so and made a beeline to the urinals. Sweet relief flowed over him as he released his bladder.

Ah...that's better than sex, Duunel said.

"I'm not going to dispute that one," Richard agreed.

Urgency past, Richard washed his face and took a turn in the stall, just in case. He tossed the wadded paper towel into the trash and turned back into the warm Central Valley night.

He walked back to where he'd parked the car but then stopped short about halfway there. The parking space was empty. The car was gone.

50

Mikael parked about a block from Saint James's. Terry peered out the back window. "All clear." The church was isolated from the road by a wall of trees, located as it was in the posh Berkeley Hills. Trees rose up all around them, separating them from city lights and stars alike. The church was visible only in silhouette, a featureless black hole set deep in a copse. Mikael opened the door and got out.

There was no one to see him. He motioned to Kat and Terry, and they, too, got out of the car and stood beside him on the sidewalk, facing the church.

"Looks pretty dead," Terry said.

"That should make it easy, then," Mikael said.

"Don't count your chickens," Kat cautioned.

Mikael nodded and motioned for them to follow. "It looks like we've got three primary entrances: the front doors to the sanctuary, what looks like a kitchen door on the fellowship hall, and there's got to be a back door to that building, too, more than likely. The two buildings are joined, there, so if we get into one, we can get into the other. First, let's see if anyone left the main doors ajar. I'll take the back; Kat, you take the front doors; Terry, kitchen." He paused to see them nod. Kat started forward, but he caught at her sleeve. "Oh, wait. We're only a stone's throw from Oakland, remember, so look for signs of an alarm system, too."

Noiselessly, they scattered to cover the various doors. Mikael wound through the trees to the rear of the fellowship hall. Just as he had expected, there was a back door. Mikael approached and examined it. It looked typically institutional—metal with a narrow, wire-reinforced window. He tried the horizontal bar-style handle. It didn't budge.

He didn't expect it to, really. But first things first—he would have felt silly looking for a window to crawl into if there had simply been an open door. Having eliminated that, he began to scout other methods of entry. There was a row of basement windows. He was too big to fit in any of them, but Kat probably wasn't, he reasoned. He stooped to examine them. One of them was slightly loose, but the others were fast.

"Tsshhht," he heard. He looked up. Terry was peering around the sanctuary at him, waving him to come. Mikael straightened up and, stepping carefully so as not to trip in the dark, moved quickly to where Terry was standing. He pointed up. Mikael squinted to see where Terry's finger was indicating.

"Sacristy window," Terry whispered.

"Looks like it," Mikael agreed. "And it looks like it's slightly ajar, too. Here, let me give you a leg up, then you can stand on my shoulders."

"Oh jeez, I *hate* the acrobat stuff," Terry complained.

"Hup!" Mikael whispered and hoisted Terry up so that he was standing in his cupped hands. "Okay, sit on my shoulders." One foot wiggling uncertainly in Mikael's grip, Terry swung his other foot up and over Mikael's neck. Steadying himself against the building, he straightened so that he was indeed sitting squarely on Mikael's shoulders.

"I can reach the window," Terry said. "Hold still!" Mikael looked up and saw Terry reach for the window, swing it out wide, and get a solid handhold on the sill. Then he drew his knee up and placed his foot on Mikael's shoulder. Then he heaved.

Mikael was almost thrown by the recoil of Terry's motion, but he caught his balance and held it. When he looked up again, the bottom half of Terry's body was snaking into the tiny window. The distant sound of breaking glass heralded the tiny priest's arrival. A moment later, Terry's cherubic face filled the window. "I'm in. Go to the kitchen door with Kat. I'll let you in there." Then he disappeared.

Mikael jogged off around the back of the building to the kitchen door. There he found Kat climbing a tree, about three feet shy of reaching a ventilation screen. "Terry's in," he whispered up the tree. "Come down; he's going to let us in!"

"Thank God!" Kat whispered back. "'Cause I didn't really think that was going to work."

The kitchen door creaked open. "There's an alarm, but I figured out the code."

"How did you do that?" asked Kat, scrambling down the tree.

"Well, it's an Episcopal parish, so it can only really be one of four possibilities."

"As in 1549, 1662, 1928, or 1979?" asked Mikael.

"Exactly," Terry nodded. "Years the prayer books were published."

"So, let me guess," Mikael said, impressed by Terry's logic. "1928?"

"Bingo." Terry winked at him.

"I guess we know where their loyalties lie," Mikael said.

"Let's go," Terry said, just as Kat jumped the final length to the dirt.

Mikael and Kat scurried inside, and Terry swung the door closed behind them. Mikael breathed deep. "Okay, that was the major hurdle. We can't turn on any lights, but we can probably talk normally now."

"Okay where is this thing?" Kat asked, "What is it, a spear?"

"Not just any spear," Terry said. "*The* Spear. And it's supposed to be in the place where the holiest things are kept."

"Which is?" Kat asked, her eyebrows and voice raising.

"In the tabernacle," Mikael answered, "where the body and blood of Christ reside between services."

In a line, they followed Terry through the fellowship hall to a hallway in a much older building. The hall ended in a door, which Terry pushed open gently. As it swung, Mikael saw the dim sanctuary come into view, looking otherworldly and forbidding in the ghostly glow cast by the moon and distant streetlights bleeding through the stained glass. The silence seemed almost loud to Mikael, and he resisted the urge to start singing just to drown it out.

Once all three of them were inside, Terry headed for the altar. It was a grand, freestanding marble table with a halo of gold hovering about three feet above it, suspended by tiny wires. The combined effect of the finely carved stone altar and the halo was one of majesty and mysticism intertwined—a perfect evocation of the Mystery of the Incarnation.

Walking past it, Terry approached the tabernacle—the finely wrought gold box in which the consecrated elements were stored for later use. A sanctuary light hanging beside it indicated that the Lord's body was indeed present inside.

Terry bowed respectfully to it then turned the golden key to open the door. Inside, Terry saw only a silver ciborium. Opening it, he saw just what one would expect to see—consecrated hosts.

Terry replaced the ciborium and considered the tabernacle. "There's a lot of wasted space here," he pointed out. Mikael stooped, hands on his knees, to get a closer look. "See, the shelf ends here, but the tabernacle extends for another six inches."

"I would think that was just ornamental," Mikael said.

"Well, it could be," Terry said. He felt around the edges of the tabernacle, and then his breath caught. "A latch," he breathed.

Mikael watched Terry's face flinch as he tugged at the latch. But his facial contortions were mostly in anticipation of a resistance that did not, in the end, materialize. As if the door had already been opened recently, the latch flipped without resistance, and the door swung open easily.

Then Mikael was blinded as the sanctuary lights blazed to life. "Don't move!" a voice boomed in the empty sanctuary. Shielding his eyes, Mikael saw a tall figure coming toward him. But his eyes could not adjust quickly, and the figure just looked like a walking tree, coming near and bending close.

51

DYLAN SALUTED the bouncers guarding the door of the medical marijuana dispensary. They held the door for him, and as he entered, he breathed deep of the skunky, verdant aroma. There were only a couple of people in line ahead of him, and the menu above the counter boasted some of his favorite varieties. Unfortunately, the ones he loved the most—such as the Jack Herer and the Violet Bubblegum—were pricey. He wanted to make the small amount of cash he had go as far as possible, and that meant the medium-grade Skylab.

He resigned himself to it but salivated as he approached the counter and saw the THC-laden candy and cookies. "Oh mah," he said to himself as he finally approached the counter. *One of the fruits of the Spirit is self-control*, he reminded himself, and ordered a quarter ounce of Skylab.

His next stop was the convenience store across the street for a pack of rolling papers and a twenty-ounce plastic bottle of Mountain Dew. Having procured these, he turned North on Telegraph and walked the short block to People's Park.

The park was a part of Berkeley history and the cause of almost constant friction between the mostly vagrant park "residents," their advocates, and the University of California regents. Dylan was conflicted on the issue. On the one hand, the property belonged to the UC, and they should be able to use it in whatever way would benefit the school most.

On the other hand, it was more than just a vacant lot—it was a symbol of the rights of the disenfranchised to simply live, to have a place to be. Dylan was reminded of the ancient code of the Jews to leave the seed dropped while harvesting so that the poor may have something to gather. The park was society's "leavings," and the homeless felt that they had a right to it.

Overall, Dylan was just glad that it wasn't him making such decisions. Entering the park, he saw a circle of people gathered around a barbecue pit. One cradled a drum and every now and then would light into a wicked pattern. Mostly, though, there was just convivial talking. "Mind if Ah join yas?" Dylan asked. "Ah've got a joint t' share."

The guy with the drum waved him into the circle, but several of them eyed him warily. It was a diverse crowd. About four of them were street punks—homeless kids who at one time might have spent their days following the Grateful Dead but now just drifted, idealizing the 1960s counterculture and Jamaican style in equal measure. Three others in the group were older, what Dylan thought of as "the hardened homeless," who gave no thought to style or pit bull puppies on rope leashes but only to filling their bellies another night.

Generally, the kids were convivial, the older group sour and suspicious. But everyone warmed up as Dylan pulled out a bag of weed and rolled up a fat splif. Once it was done, however, it seemed unnaturally heavy in his hand.

A part of his brain told him he should go home right now, apologize to Susan, and hold her. The other part of his brain rebelled—he was angry, his pride was wounded, he wanted to strike back. This splif, heavy as a baseball bat in his hand, was his instrument of revenge. It felt good, it was satisfying, it was inevitable.

He was too hurt to resist the comfort it promised. He cupped his hand around its end to shield it from the wind and struck at his lighter. In a moment, green acrid warmth was filling his lungs, and a lovely woolen blanket of calm was pulled over his brain. Instantly, he felt a deep relief, but at the same time, a stab of guilt. He pushed it away. He exhaled slowly and passed the joint to his left.

"Hey, man, why are you dressed like that?" the kid with the drum asked him.

"Mah name is Dylan."

"That's a weird restaurant uniform," the kid persisted.

Dylan exhaled the rest of the smoke into the cold night sky. He shivered a bit and hugged his arms to his chest. "It's a uniform, but not fer a restaurant. Ah'm a priest of the Old Catholic Order of Saint Raphael."

"And you smoke weed?" The kid raised one eyebrow.

"What's yer name?" Dylan asked him.

"Craig," the kid said.

"Are you a good person?"

"Yeah," Craig answered quickly.

"Do you smoke weed?" Dylan asked.

"Well, yeah, but I'm not pretending to be a *holy* person."

"Ah'm not pretending to be a holy person, neither," Dylan shot back. "So-called holy people are just as fucked up as anyone else, and anyone who tells you they're not...Waal, not only are they *not* holy, but they're just garden-variety hypocrites. Let me tell you somethin' that Jesus said once—"

"Oh Jesus, here it comes," one of the older homeless guys said. "I've got to take a piss." He got up and left the circle.

"A bunch of religious hypocrites came up to Jesus and said, 'Dude, why don't your followers wash their hands before they eat?' 'Cause back then, if you didn't wash your hands, you know, in a ritual fashion, you weren't a good person," Dylan explained.

"Sounds like my mom," a girl of about sixteen said. "She's a religious whack-job."

"Ah'm sorry about that; there's a lot o' them," Dylan said quietly to her. "What's yer name?"

"Jenny," she said, smiling sweetly at him. She seemed touched that he'd asked.

"So, you know what Jesus said?" he said more loudly, to the whole circle.

"No, what?" Craig asked.

"He said, 'It ain't what goes into the mouth that makes us bad; it's what comes out of it.'"

"You mean, like, vomit?" Craig asked, confused.

"No, dude. I mean like telling lies, or yelling, or judging people. Smoking a joint doesn't make you a bad person, but harshin' on a dude you don't even know, well, that's just not cool."

Craig nodded, looking mildly impressed. "Jesus said that, huh?"

"Matthew, chapter 15," Dylan said. The joint had passed around the circle and had come back to him. He reached for it and took another long drag. He passed it on and blew the smoke out over the flames. From his perspective, it seemed to fill the sky until the wind whipped it away.

"So, what are you doin' here?" Craig asked him.

"Awww..." Dylan looked down at his feet. "Had a fight with my ol' lady."

"I know that one, right?" Craig pointed at his friends, and their heads nodded up and down like bobble-heads, big grins growing on their faces.

"Wait, how can you be, like, a priest, and have an old lady?" one of the older homeless guys asked.

"An' you are?"

The man pointed to his chest. "Chip."

"Well, Chip, sir, Ah'm an *Old* Catholic priest, and we can be married...or gay, or whatever," Dylan said, matter-of-factly.

"No way!" Craig held his head like it was about to explode. "That's not right!"

"It's only *Roman* Catholics that have to pretend they don't have privates," Dylan said, nodding. "And they'll come around, you'll see."

"In a hundred years," Jenny said. "And even longer before girls matter."

"Waal, yeah," Dylan agreed, sadly.

"So, what do you do all day, like, pray?" Craig asked.

"We fight demons," Dylan said. He smiled. He knew he had them hooked from that moment forward, and he regaled them with some of their more recent adventures. The moon rose high in the sky as he talked, and before long he was rolling another joint, and taking a sip from a bottle of wine that was passed around.

Eventually, he, too, had to pee. He brought his tale to a stopping point, excused himself, and lumbered off toward the freestanding restroom a couple of hundred yards away. He passed a few more fire pits, and several more ad-hoc gatherings of lost souls. His heart went out to them, but he recognized that just being with them was valuable—because only then did they stop being "the homeless" and become real people—like Craig and Jenny and Chip. They were people that mattered, to him and to God, rather than simply a problem to be solved, or worse, gotten rid of.

Dylan navigated inexpertly in the dark, nearly tripping over the uneven, torn-up ground that passed for a lawn at the park. He found the restroom building and wasn't surprised that it wasn't lit. That seemed unfair—surely even homeless people deserved to see what they were doing when they went to take a dump. He chalked it up to valuable experience as he approached the urinal. He swept the folds of his cassock aside and unzipped his jeans.

Behind him, he heard a rustle. A voice, rough and sickly, came from directly behind him. "Don't turn around. I want you to drop your wallet and your pot on the floor. Do it now."

Dylan couldn't have stopped the stream of piss if he'd tried, so he just continued to pee as he reached into his back pocket and tossed his wallet behind him. With rather more regret, he reached into his front pocket and pulled out the still-nearly full baggie of Skylab. He dropped that, too.

Before he could even zip up, he heard a sharp intake of breath behind him. Then he felt a sharp blast of pain between his shoulders. A wash of red filled his vision, then he fell as everything went black.

52

"WELL, SHIT," said Richard, sitting down on one of the picnic table benches. It was wet, so he stood back up again. "Shit," he said again, feeling the wetness on his ass. Richard fought down a feeling of panic. He had his phone. He had his wallet. He wasn't in West Borneo. As he clicked through his mental checklist, he realized he was only really worried for Tobias's sake.

Well, this is a pretty pickle, said the sinister voice in his head.

A picture of pickles in drag flashed through Richard's mind. He squeezed his eyes shut to banish them. "Could you suggest a *helpful* image, maybe?" he said. Richard paused. "Wait, did you know this was coming?"

What do you mean? Duunel sounded hurt.

"I mean, did one of your cronies tip you off that my car was going to be stolen, and you just kept quiet about it?"

You wound me, sir, Duunel said theatrically.

"Right," Richard said, growing angry.

Honestly, I don't relish being stuck out here in the middle of bumfuck California any more than you do. And besides, what makes you think that every transgressive human act is of demonic origin? Some people are just bad, Duunel argued.

"All people are just bad," Richard countered.

I'm not going to argue in favor of Catholic theology, but—

"But?"

But you can't blame me for your Calvinist anthropology, sicko, Duunel shot back. *As far as I'm concerned, the main problem with the world is that there actually are misguided, so-called good people.*

Richard said nothing. After a few minutes, he stood up. "We've got to do something." He reached for his phone to call the police.

I wouldn't do that, Duunel sang in his ear.

"Why not?"

Oh, I don't know. Something about a 5150 order hanging over your head, maybe?

"Oh shit," Richard said again. He put the phone back in his pocket. The night suddenly seemed oppressive. He felt completely alone.

Just as this thought occurred to him, Duunel piped up. *Relax, you're not alone. I'm here.*

"Oh yeah, that's a great comfort," Richard said.

Sarcasm does not become you.

"Sarcasm seems to be all that I have left," Richard countered, but the statement gave him an idea. He pulled out his cell phone. More than twenty apps shone out at him in the dark. Surely, one of them could be of help. He began flipping through them. Then he saw it.

"Find my phone," he said.

You're holding your phone, Duunel countered.

"But I'm not holding my iPad. My iPad is in the duffle bag in the backseat with Tobias." It took a few minutes for the app to load and orient itself. But then, to Richard's great relief, a little green dot appeared moving south on I-5. "South," Richard announced. He pocketed his phone and started walking, past the rest stop building and onto the freeway on-ramp.

53

As KAT's eye's adjusted, she saw a very tall African-American woman in a black peacoat hovering over Mikael, a large silver candlestick pitched over her shoulder like a baseball bat, ready to strike.

"Whoa!" Kat called out. "Don't hit him; we're no threat!"

The woman's head snapped up, and she seemed only then to notice Kat's presence. "I'd call burglary a threat!" she said. She kept the candlestick trained on Mikael, who threw up a hand in paltry defense.

"Please, ma'am," Terry said soothingly. "We're friars, from the Holy Apocrypha Friary in Berkeley. We're here investigating on behalf of...certain concerned members of the diocese."

The woman's eyes flitted back and forth, sizing up her three intruders. "Please," said Terry calmly. "As you can see, we're not dressed like thugs. We're all wearing Anglican cassocks. Of course, there *are* burglars who are eccentric, but this level of coordinated eccentricity is unlikely among criminals, wouldn't you say?"

The woman straightened up, lowering the candlestick a bit. Terry smiled and stepped forward, offering his hand. "I'm Father Terry Milne," he said. "And these are my order mates. Kat is an oblate, and Mikael will be ordained a deacon as soon as we...well, soon."

"Are you...Episcopalian?" the woman asked, uncertainly.

"No, Old Catholic," Terry said. "We've got a lot in common with Anglicans, though, and as I'm sure you know, in Europe we're close partners in ministry. We've done plenty of work for your diocese, though. We're from the Old Catholic Order of Saint Raphael."

The woman cocked her head. "You're the exorcists," she said, snapping her fingers. "I've heard of you." Her eyes narrowed. "Everyone thinks you're crazy."

"Envy," Terry waved, a little too fey in his movements. "The truth is, no one else has the guts to do what we do."

"Does that include breaking into churches?" The woman had fully lowered the candlestick to the floor by now.

"Apparently, it sometimes does," Terry shrugged.

Mikael hazarded getting to his feet and held out his hand. The woman took it hesitantly and studied him closely. "I know you," she said. "How do I know you?"

Mikael squinted at her. "You *do* look familiar."

"But why?" she said.

Kat was terrified that, at any minute, they were going to recall a one-night stand, but suddenly the woman snapped her fingers. "Doom Nipple."

"Wha—??" asked Kat.

Mikael grinned broadly and clapped his hands. "Yes!" he said.

"You were the bassist for Doom Nipple. I used to go to see you at 924 Gilman, back when I was in seminary."

"That was me!" Mikael said, nodding his giant black mane of hair. "Now I remember—you used to date that chick with the mo-fro."

"Uh, I *was* that chick with the mo-fro." She looked momentarily abashed.

"What's a mo-fro?" asked Terry.

"A mohawk cut from an afro," Mikael said, gesturing at his hair.

"Doom Nipple?" Kat asked. "You were in a band called *Doom Nipple*?"

"They weren't just a band. They were a *great* band," the woman said, excited. "I am so honored to meet you. When did you break up?"

"We never did officially. We just stopped playing out, and then the singer got sick. We've just been dormant for a while. We'll bounce back. You'll see."

"Doom Nipple?" Kat repeated. "I don't even know what that's supposed to *mean*."

"Please tell us your name," Terry said, "and...well, why you're here. Although I'm sure you're wondering the same of us."

"I'm the rector here, Felicia Dunne."

"Reverend Dunne, it's a pleasure." Terry made a little bow. Just then, a blue strobe light flashed through the stained glass. "Um...I'm wondering if you called the police?"

Her head jerked up. "Yes, actually." She smiled apologetically. "Why don't you explain yourselves concisely, and perhaps I'll send them away."

"Huh...okay." Terry rubbed his hands together and looked around nervously. "Well, some...representatives of your diocese approached us to investigate how Bishop Preston could possibly have won election to the episcopacy. They suspected supernatural means—and so, of course, they called us. We're following up on a lead. How's that for concise?"

Reverend Dunne looked like she'd been slapped. She looked down at Terry with a look of such abject sorrow and—was that guilt on her face? Kat couldn't be sure. In any case, it looked like she was about to cry. Without another word, she nodded, dropped the candlestick, and went to the front doors of the sanctuary. She let herself out, and in a few minutes, the blue lights receded and she entered the church again. She was shaking, Kat noticed, and she sat in the front pew, not daring to look at them.

Terry looked at Mikael and then at Kat, clearly concerned. He sat next to the rector and placed a tentative hand on her arm. "Reverend, it looks like we might have hit a nerve. Perhaps we can help each other?"

Reverend Dunne nodded and patted at his hand. "I started here a couple of months ago. It seemed like a great honor. I'm a girl from the streets, you know. My mama lived in the Episcopal Sanctuary in the City. The Episcopal Church saved my life. So, to be called here…"

"You mean, to such a conservative congregation?" Terry asked.

She nodded. "Exactly. It was like…a vindication. I think they saw it that way, too. Anyway, I'm ashamed to say it, but I committed a sin of omission when they were vetting me. I didn't tell them about my partner."

"You're a lesbian?" Terry asked. "You don't need to worry about judgment from us."

Reverend Dunne narrowed one eye at Terry. "Gee, do you *think*?"

"I'm not *that* flaming!" Terry mock-protested. Kat laughed.

"Anyway, Bishop Preston decided to settle in the diocese for a while. His daughter is sick. So, he came here, for obvious reasons."

"Is this a '28 prayer book parish, then?" Mikael asked.

"It is now that Preston's in place. Switched just last Sunday. But under Bishop Ryder we were using Rite I from the '79 prayer book."

Terry nodded, seemingly unsurprised. "So, what happened?"

"He caught us," she pressed at the bridge of her nose. It seemed to Kat to be an expression of either sinus headache or shame. Maybe both. "He caught us, and he threatened to expose me. Except…"

"Except…?" Terry asked.

"Except I had something he wanted." Reverend Dunne looked up at Terry, a fierceness on her face that Kat did not understand.

"I'm going to guess that you don't want to tell us what that was," Terry said. "Because I already know what it was, and I wouldn't want to tell anyone either."

Dunne's eyes grew wide. She nodded.

"It's a spear, isn't it?"

She nodded.

"And it was in the tabernacle until very recently, yes?" Dunne nodded, a look of amazement coming over her face.

"And now Preston has it," Terry finished. "Am I right?"

Dunne nodded again.

Terry looked down at his hands. "It took me a while to realize just why your name was familiar. You put Preston forth as a candidate, didn't you?"

She looked down, and her lower lip began to quiver. Kat wanted to move over to her, to comfort her, but she stood her ground. *Terry knows what he's doing*, she told herself.

"Did he threaten to expose you if you didn't?" Terry asked. "Or did he compel you by means of the Spear?"

"I don't think it works that way," she said. "He threatened me."

Terry nodded. "We're still trying to get a handle on exactly how it works. Now that we know for sure that it's the Spear, we can narrow our research. That's very helpful. Thank you."

"He's evil," Reverend Dunne said. "He's evil—and he's the worst kind of evil."

"How do you mean?" Kat asked.

"He's an evil man who thinks he's doing good," she said. "He thinks he's the reincarnation of Prester John. Did you know that?" Terry nodded. She looked back down at her hands. "He said as much at the diocesan convention. He's batshit crazy. But he's not just crazy; he's a crazy person with *power*." She looked up at Terry with a grim resolution in her eyes. "I want to help. I have to redeem myself. I'm partly responsible for this. I want to help *undo* it. Can you help me undo it?"

"That's exactly why we're breaking into your lovely church," Terry said, smiling impishly.

54

SUSAN STARED with horror at the empty frosting container. She put her hand to her mouth and felt momentarily dizzy. *Sugar rush*, she thought, and even though she was sitting down, she reached out and held on to the desk for support. Instinctively, she turned the container to see the nutritional information, to assess how many calories she had just consumed. But before she could see the astronomical numbers, she slammed it down on her desk.

"If you're going to sin, sin boldly," she quoted her beloved Luther. She opened a photo program on her large, 27-inch iMac and perused pictures of her life with Dylan. Here was their wedding day, before he'd grown his beard out. It was hard to believe he had ever been that trim. Here they were camping in Oregon; she had a garland of flowers in her hair, and her lips were pursed up to kiss someone just out of frame.

As she flipped through the pictures, her eyes became wet. She sniffed, and for the millionth time that night, regretted how she'd attacked Dylan. He maddened her at times, sure, but she'd never loved him more than she did now. Now, just as he was on the cusp of growing into the leader she knew he could be. Now, as he was being confronted by his own demons instead of other people's.

Time and again, she'd seen him and Richard walk side by side into situations so scary it'd make a cop faint. Her heart swelled with pride to think of it. He needed her support right now, not her judgment or her wrath. She felt small, petty, and out of control. "I'm *not* out of control," she said out loud. The empty frosting can stared up at her. She pitched her head into her hands and wailed. "Oh my God, I'm *so* out of control."

She heard movement behind her, and Brian poked his head into the office. "Um...are you...eating frosting out of the can?"

She didn't move her head from her hands. "Go away."

"Well, far be it for me to rain on anybody's guilt parade, but there's something I think we should watch. I just heard that Bishop Preston is about to be interviewed on *Washington Week*. Can you get a video capture on that?"

Susan took a deep breath and sniffed a little too loudly. She nodded, and her fingers flew over the keyboard, calling up the *Washington Week* website and starting an mp4 capture. "When's he on?" she asked.

Brian looked at his watch. "In about two minutes." He gave her a compassionate smile. "Do you want to talk about it?"

By "it," she knew he meant her *attack*. She felt ashamed. "Don't feel bad, Honey," Brian said, coming up behind her and putting his arms around her shoulders. "Terry and I have had our knock-down-drag-'em-outs, you know. Remember when Terry was going through his whole sex addiction thing?"

She nodded. Terry and Brian had almost split up over that. "I don't know if you remember, but I laid down the fucking law, and Terry didn't speak to me for a week. There were also some stitches involved." He grimaced. "But we got through it, stronger than ever. You will, too." He squeezed her. "Besides, you're my hero."

She burst out with a single sob at that. "Why do you say that?"

"Because it's true. It's not easy to be partnered with these guys, as we both know too well. I think we both struggle to give our men the freedom they need to do their ministries well and still have good boundaries. Sometimes I'm in awe of how well you're able to walk that line. I say to myself, 'I want to be Susan when I grow up.' I learn a lot just watching you."

"You're no slouch, Honey," Susan said, patting his arm.

He let go of her and turned so that he could look into her eyes. "I do what I do well in part because you're there. And that's the truth."

She reached over and squeezed his hand. With her other hand, she raised the volume on the computer. "It's on."

A square-jawed news anchor faced the screen, "Tonight on *Washington Week* we talk to a panel of newsmakers and experts about the recent bombing of Dearborn, Michigan, and the upcoming Republican National Convention—the initial ceremonies of which kick off tomorrow in San Francisco. I'm Block Jamison, and this is *Washington Week*."

A blast of synthesized trumpets heralded the start of the show, and Brian pulled Dylan's chair around to sit beside Susan. He pointed to the can of frosting. "Got any more of that?"

"Fuck off," Susan said. She squeezed his hand again.

"I'm not making fun of you; I'm serious."

"Back of the fridge, behind the pineapple," Susan said behind her hand, not looking at him.

"Just kidding. I am making fun of you," Brian said. "I can't believe you have another can of that gross stuff."

"Fuck off," Susan said again. She did not squeeze his hand.

"Good evening, America, and good evening to our panel," Block Jamison said, nodding toward a large table with a bluish-washed set behind it. "Mehilia Tanner is an attorney for the American Civil Liberties Union." A largish African-American woman with beautiful wavy hair spiraling out in all directions nodded, gold spectacles reflecting the harsh stage lights. "Tiffany Peet is a columnist for the *Washington Post* and a regular on our show."

A bone-thin, model-beautiful blonde woman with harsh, angular cheekbones waved and cracked a severe smile as she said, "Good to see you, Block."

Without bothering to acknowledge the greeting, Block turned to the other side of the table. "Returning to our show once again is the now newly elected Episcopal Bishop of California, the Right Reverend John Preston. Welcome back, Bishop." Preston dipped his head briefly in greeting. "And finally, environmental lobbyist and former press secretary for the Clinton administration, Cliff Arneson. Good to finally have you on our show, Cliff."

"Good to be here, Block. Persistence pays."

"Indeed it does," Block said with a chuckle. "First up, the whole world is talking about Michigan governor David Ivory's unprecedented nuclear strike on American soil. Mehilia, I'm going to put the first question to you: Did Governor Ivory overstep his bounds?"

"Block, we're way beyond bounds here. Governor Ivory is a criminal who needs to be removed forcibly from office and charged with genocide. He's a homicidal maniac, and the people of Michigan will not be safe until he is behind bars. And I personally will not rest until we get him behind bars."

"Feelings are certainly riding high about this incident," Block noted. "Tiffany, your thoughts?"

The slender blonde shook her hair before giving Block a smile so thin and sharp it could slice meat. "Governor Ivory doesn't belong behind bars, Block. He isn't a criminal; he's a hero. I've seen some of the documentation that his intelligence sources presented to him, and the evidence is incontrovertible—if Governor Ivory had not acted as he did, we would not be sitting here tonight blithely discussing it. Those of us who were still alive would be digging survivors out of smoking piles of rubble, and the liberal wonks would have been wailing about our feeble intelligence sources and the failure of Republican leadership in Michigan."

She shook out her hair again as if she were selling shampoo instead of giving a political opinion. Her smile as she spoke was confident and deadly serious. "Well, the liberal crybabies can't have it both ways. Governor Ivory saw the intelligence, and he pursued the one and only path open to him in order to save American lives. He struck at the root while it could still be stopped, and he stopped it. And millions of Americans are alive tonight because he did."

"I strongly disagree with that, Tiffany." Cliff Arneson leaned forward over the large conference table that served as *Washington Week*'s main set. "That intelligence has not been verified—"

"That intelligence is classified," Tiffany Peet countered.

"And even if it *were* reliable, something of this magnitude is the president's call, not the governor's. I contend that Governor Ivory *did* overstep his bounds. The National Guard is not his to command—"

"But the Michigan reservists *are*—" Peet interjected.

Block held his hand up to her. "Cliff, please finish your comment, then we can hear responses."

"And who gave the governor the authority to appropriate a thermonuclear device?" Cliff pounded the table to drive home his point.

"Bishop Preston, you've been uncharacteristically reticent in this conversation so far." Block swiveled in his chair to face the bishop. "Obviously, the loss of life in Dearborn was extreme. What is the Christian perspective on this situation?"

"Our Lord was innocent, and yet the Father was pleased to sacrifice him so that many might be saved. Christians have always understood that sometimes innocent people have to suffer if a great and powerful evil is to be stopped. I think our actions in the Second World War testify to this grim but necessary truth."

"You know what the problem is with him?" Susan asked.

"What's that?"

"He sounds completely reasonable. If I were just a tad more hawkish than I am, I'd buy his shit hook, line, and sinker." She shook her head in disbelief.

"That's the thing about evil," Brian said. "People wouldn't be tempted by crazy."

"Here's what I think, Block." The bishop placed both hands on the table and leaned forward, a look of grave resolve on his jowly visage. "David is my friend. I trust his judgment implicitly. If he says there were seventy Islamic terror cells ready to strike us this very day, then I believe him and I thank God that he was in a position to do something about it. Because not everyone would be. The Constitution is a noble document, but it must be kept in perspective. To paraphrase someone that I happen to hold in very high esteem, the

Constitution is here to serve people, people are not here to serve the Constitution. Given the choice between American lives and upholding every last jot and tittle of Constitutional law, I'm going to come down on the side of saving American lives. And I think anyone who says otherwise is either unpatriotic or a fool."

He sat back, and Block opened his mouth and began to turn toward Mehilia Tanner. But Preston held his hand up and continued. "I think the crisis in Dearborn is just the beginning. I think that Islamic terror is a worldwide phenomenon that is about to blow the lid off anything we've ever seen before. We just dodged a bullet, but there are more bullets coming—lots of them. I don't think we ought to be censuring David Ivory; I think we ought to be promoting him. I respectfully submit that the Republican leadership ought to wake up and realize just what a bold and necessary leader David Ivory is. And I suggest that he be put forward as the next Republican candidate for president of the United States."

Preston slammed the table with the flat of his hand. "The Republican National Convention begins tomorrow, and I intend to be there, speaking from the floor, and I encourage everyone who agrees with me to phone and email your Republican leadership and let your will be known. David Ivory was the right person, at the right time, in the right place to stop the Terror of Dearborn. He is the right person, right now, to lead this great nation."

"Oh my God," Susan breathed. "I did not see that coming."

"I think we have our missing piece of the puzzle," Brian said, unable to stop looking at the computer screen.

"If he didn't hesitate to nuke an entire American city..." Susan said, realization dawning on her slowly.

"Just what is he going to do as commander-in-chief?" Brian finished. "You know, I talked to Nazim today, down at the Islamic Cultural Center. He can use two of us tomorrow afternoon, for grief counseling, by the way. Anyway, he said that Ivory is a rabid Islamophobe."

"Great...just what we need." Susan shook her head.

"If that man gets elected," Brian said, "I can guarantee you that the whole Middle East is going to get bombed right back to the Stone Age."

"Then I guess we'd better stop it." Susan faced him gravely.

"Any ideas how to do that?" Brian asked.

"Not a one," Susan answered.

"You know what I need right now?" Brian asked. "Frosting. Straight from the can." He turned and walked from the room.

Just then, Susan's cell phone buzzed. She didn't recognize the number. "Hello?" she asked.

"Mrs. Mel...Mela..." a grim voice stuttered.

"Melanchthon," Susan corrected the voice. "This is she."

"This is Alta Bates Hospital. Your husband was just brought into emergency. Can you come down?"

55

IT WAS A PIECE OF CAKE, really. Jesse had zoomed through the parking lot of the rest stop in his pickup, and a late-model Toyota Corolla was there, all by its lonely. Tig jumped out, duffle bag over his shoulder, and tried the door. It was unlocked. He waved his baseball cap around—Jesse's engine roared, and he took off. "Too damn easy," Tig said to himself.

He jumped into the driver's seat and looked around. No keys, but he shrugged. There was easy, and there was *easy*. He pulled a cordless drill from the duffle bag and quickly drilled into the flap near the keyhole. In seconds, he had drilled through the lock pins, and he threw the drill back in the bag. Pulling a screwdriver from his back pocket, he jammed it into the keyhole, and the little car roared to life.

The tires spun momentarily on the gravel, but in a second they caught. Tig peeled out of the parking lot, making for the on-ramp, fast on Jesse's heels. He quickly got up to speed and merged onto the freeway, feeling the usual rush of adrenaline that was half the reward of boosting. The money would be nice, but this high was better than crack.

Then he sneezed. His nostrils twitched. He looked in the rearview mirror but didn't see anything. He sneezed again. His sinuses were swelling quickly, which could only mean one thing.

Dog.

He was fiercely allergic to dogs. He knew that if he didn't get away from the dog quickly—or get the dog away from him—his eyes would soon be too swollen to drive. He looked over his shoulder, and there in the footwell of the backseat, he saw it—a yellow Lab looking up at him uncertainly, tongue hanging out of its nasty little mouth, panting.

"Goddamned shit!" he yelled at the windshield and pulled over as quickly as he safely could. He so hated dogs. It wasn't that they were ever mean to him or anything; it was just that they made him suffer so. He was sure that they were very nice animals—for other people. He just wanted them kept away from him. When, a few months ago, there had been the very strange dog rapture, he was secretly glad, relieved, even. Finally, his years of exile from the homes of his family and friends—all of whom kept the filthy beasts—seemed at an end. Until, of course, they had all come back—redder, furrier than before, and strangely bearing advertising for the Pfizer corporation.

Jumping out of the car, he jerked open the passenger door. "Out, fucking mutt!" he shouted. The dog's ears drooped. The dog stepped out onto the blacktop—one infuriating paw at a time. Once the dog was clear of the car, Tig slammed the door, jumped back into the driver's seat, and roared off.

Tobias watched the car go and uttered a single whine. Then he sniffed at the wind. His eyes brightened, and he began to trot along the shoulder.

56

It was the licking that woke him. The huge pink tongue, hot and wet and rough as sandpaper, moved up over his broad, Melungeon nose again and again. "Wah," he said and rolled to the side to avoid another slobberous assault. He sat up but instantly winced at the pain in his lower neck.

He opened one eye. He was face to face with an enormous black jaguar, whose gold, unblinking eyes looked straight into his own. "Jaggy?" Dylan asked. The smell of that hot feline breath was unmistakable. Jaguar was his power animal, the spirit guide that had accompanied him on every shamanic journey he had ever made.

"Come," Jaguar spoke. "Old Leatherface has summoned you." Jaguar turned and began to walk away from him into shadow. Dylan looked around and discovered he was in the underworld. It was a place that was familiar to him. Whenever he wanted to consult with Jaguar, this was usually the place he came to.

It was a cave, deep underground, with a waterfall against a far wall. Between himself and the waterfall was a large outcropping of rock to his right, around which Jaguar usually appeared. It was around this wall now that Jaguar was walking...and disappearing. Dylan flinched, trying to rise. Gritting his teeth, he succeeded in getting to his feet. Stooping unnaturally and moving slowly, he followed after Jaguar.

After what seemed to be about ten minutes of subterranean walking, Jaguar led him out of the cave, into a field of wildflowers. Although it was brighter here than in the cave, it was dimmer than it should have been. The sun was visible, but it was a ghostly version of itself. A nearby rock, as tall as Dylan's knees, though solid, was eerily translucent. "Middle World," Dylan said. "Oh no, Ah'm gonna have to climb that damned tree, ain't Ah?"

Jaguar did not respond but just kept moving. To Dylan's chagrin, "that damned tree" appeared about a half mile ahead. It grew larger as they grew closer, its branches ascending higher than any tree had a right to go, twisting up into mist and disappearing.

Jaguar paused beside it. "You first," Dylan said. Jaguar did not respond but only swished his tail patiently. Dylan had never seen Jaguar climb, and he assumed that power animals didn't need to transport themselves by physical means no matter how metaphorical those means were.

"You know mah whole body aches like a motherfucker?" Dylan complained.

He heard the mildest growl from Jaguar's direction. "All right, all right, Ah'm goin'," Dylan said and reached for the lowest branch. He hauled himself up awkwardly and reached for the next. Every ascent caused a new stab of pain to course through him, and by the time he reached the top, he was exhausted and his body was fairly screaming with agony.

As his head cleared the cloud cover, Arnault reached out his hand. "I've got you, Father Dylan. No need to worry. You shan't fall."

Dylan relaxed and let Arnault pull him onto the foggy plain. Being in the Upper World always unnerved him at first. The ground seemed like it should be insubstantial, and he always feared falling half a mile to his certain death. Yet when he stood on it, the cloudy turf was solid. Sure, it had lots of give, like walking on a mattress, but it was stable.

Arnault helped him to his feet and sized him up. "Stay here," he said, and before Dylan could get his bearings, Arnault was gone. He didn't see where the Frenchman with the BBC accent had gone to, but he waited dutifully. He didn't see whence Arnault reappeared, either. He simply walked up from behind Dylan and offered him a cup of tea. "It's a restorative," he said. "You'll feel better once you get something warm inside you."

It seemed to be just regular black tea, but he was amazed how much better he felt after he'd had a cup. "Keep that in mind, Father," Arnault said, taking the emptied cup and saucer from him once he'd finished.

"Uh...keep what in mind?" Dylan asked, wiping his beard with the back of his hand.

"Tea. Good for the soul." Arnault smiled.

Strangely restored but still confused, Dylan thanked him and turned toward the valley where the teepees were gathered in a ring. Somehow, Jaguar was there, ahead of him, and moving with long, sleek motions over the cloudy firmament.

Jaguar descended into the valley, and before long they were stooping to enter the largest teepee in the center of the circle. Dylan's nose twitched at the familiar smell of sweet grass, sage, and venison. It made him feel simultaneously reverent and hungry. He started to salivate but swallowed hard.

Inside was a circle of grandfathers and grandmothers—Native American men and women—some of them waving at him playfully, the others taking no notice but chatting convivially. On the far side of the teepee sat Old Leatherface, the Grandfather to whom he felt the greatest degree of kinship.

He took his place next to him and waited. Old Leatherface began to hum. As the humming grew louder, the chatting and laughing subsided until a calm had descended on the circle.

Old Leatherface started to rock back and forth but eventually opened one eye, piercing Dylan with its gaze. The rocking slowed, and the Grandfather smacked his lips. "Sleeping Bear has returned to us."

"Where have you been, Sleeping Bear?" one of the Grandmothers asked.

"You neglect us," one of the other Grandfathers said. "Not good for you."

Dylan felt instantly chastened. It was true—he hadn't been on a journey since the Dane affair. He hung his head slightly and waited. He'd never been summoned by the Grandfathers before. He'd always sought them out. It didn't occur to him that they'd be calling him to a reckoning. He tensed up.

"Sleeping Bear fears," Old Leatherface said into the circle of elders. "He is right to fear. But, my grandson, it is not us you need to fear. We are always on *your* side."

For some reason, the Grandfathers and Grandmothers considered this a very funny joke. Many of them laughed out loud. They all smiled.

"But before we meet in council, let us have a smoke," Old Leatherface said.

"Thank God," Dylan said. "Ah could really use a smoke about now."

One of the Grandmothers pulled a peace pipe from her sleeve and lit the sacred tobacco. She passed it to her left. Each of the Grandfathers and Grandmothers puffed on the pipe then held it up toward Heaven before passing it on. When it came to Dylan, he put it to his lips, anticipating the green, acrid taste of marijuana.

Instead, his mouth filled with liquid. He spat it out. "What the fuck?" he swore. "What was that, tea?" The Grandfathers and Grandmothers laughed loud and long at this, but no one answered him. Eventually, Old Leatherface stopped chuckling and leaned over to speak to him, more or less privately. "Do not be concerned, Sleeping Bear. It is an omen. There is wisdom in this sign."

Suddenly, Dylan's vision spun, and the teepee was gone. He, Jaguar, and the Grandfathers and Grandmothers were sitting in an open field. The sun was shining bright and strong—not the shadow sun of the Middle World but the true and substantial sun of the Upper World.

In the center of their circle were two beasts linked by a chain. One was a dog, looking a lot like Tobias but much smaller, and so thin that Dylan could see his ribs through his skin. The dog's eyes were wild with fear, and he strained against the chain to get as far away as possible from the other beast. And no wonder—the other beast was a wolf, twice as large as a wolf had any right to be. His eyes were wild, too, but with fury and madness. A shackle was attached to his leg, too, but it had obviously been fixed there when the beast was much smaller because now it cut into the leg, the meat of it raw and swollen and angry.

"Ah Jesus," Dylan breathed. "That wolf is gonna kill that poor puppy."

Old Leatherface nodded. "Yes, that is what we fear. Wolf is good but has been given too much food. Too much leads to madness. Little Dog is a good dog. Loyal. Scarred in his mind, now, but still...he can love. He can make his master happy with him. But he will not last for long."

"We gotta *do* something," Dylan said. The wolf snapped at the terrified dog, foam drizzling from its fangs. The dog screamed and strained at the chain, scrambling to get away.

"What to do? What to do?" Old Leatherface shrugged. "You put on the shackles. You decided how much to feed to each of them. You tell us what can be done."

Dylan had no idea what he meant by this. He had no memory of shackling the two animals together. And he certainly didn't remember starving the dog or fattening up the vicious wolf. "Ah say kill the wolf," Dylan said. "An' do it quick!"

Although Old Leatherface nodded approvingly, he said, "Think carefully about what you say, Sleeping Bear. What will life be like without Wolf?"

Dylan looked at them, saw the wolf snarling and snapping at the little dog's legs. Dylan's heart leaped up into his throat. He spoke without thinking. "Ah don't love the wolf. Ah love the dog."

"I think you *do* love Wolf," Old Leatherface said. "I think you love Wolf more than Dog. That's why you feed Wolf and starve Dog."

"Ah would never *do* that!" Dylan shouted. "Do something!"

The wolf lunged and sank a fang into the little dog's haunches. Blood sprayed, and the dog screamed.

"*You* do something," Old Leatherface said.

Dylan didn't know what to do but reacted instinctually. With more alacrity than he'd known in many years, he sprang over one of the Grandmothers and ran to the two beasts. He snatched the little dog up in his arms and held it close to his bosom. Still not thinking, he crouched like a linebacker setting up for a play, the little dog held close in one arm, the other arm on the ground in a three-point stance. He faced the wolf and from the bowels of his being let forth the most terrifying roar he could muster. Its fury echoed off the far hills, and the wolf faltered, and retreated a step. But then its green eyes narrowed, and it began to advance on Dylan.

"Sleeping Bear will not survive his own wolf without medicine!" Old Leatherface called. Then Jaguar stepped up and stood between Dylan and the wolf. He turned to Dylan, standing nose to nose. Then, opening his massive jaws, Jaguar ate Dylan's head.

57

AFTER ABOUT AN HOUR OF WALKING, Richard began to get a cramp in his ankle. He tried not to limp. He also tried not to walk on the actual highway. The last thing he needed was to be stopped by the Highway Patrol, so he kept the highway in sight, but kept to the frontage road as much as possible.

You could hitchhike, suggested Duunel.

"And try to explain to someone why I'm a friar in full habit on an ill-equipped hiking tour through the Central Valley, and why we're not calling the police?" Richard said.

Well, when you put it like that, Duunel responded.

A faint glow on the horizon gradually became brighter as he walked. Eventually, he saw a gas station sign, and another sign sporting a buxom young woman straight off a 1950s pinup calendar promising homemade beer sausage and Breakfast All Day.

"Sounds like our kind of place," Richard said.

There are few times when we agree, my religiously misguided friend, but this is one of them, Duunel affirmed. *I'm famished.*

"You mean I'm famished," Richard corrected him.

And you want some beer, Duunel added.

"I would not say no to beer," Richard agreed.

Some pussy would be nice, Duunel said dreamily. *I like the look of that girl on the sign.*

"Don't get your hopes up," Richard said. "Remember that I am all you have to work with. I have *never* been accused of being a chick magnet."

It's all attitude, Duunel said. *It has very little to do with looks.*

"Fine, but getting laid is not my priority here," Richard said firmly.

You are not the center of the universe, Duunel said, sounding uncomfortably like Richard's mother.

"I am the center of my consciousness," Richard said.

I'll bet you never learned to share your toys as a child, Duunel accused.

Richard reminded himself that Duunel's goal was to make him crazy, and so he cut bait rather than taking it. Besides, they were almost at the diner. The lights were bright, and the activity surrounding the gas station, the fast food joints, and the little restaurant cheered him.

Richard opened the door and looked around. He spied an ATM machine and made a beeline for it. He took out more than he normally would, given the uncertainty of his situation. He might need a motel or a bus ticket or some such thing, after all.

Fortified with cash, Richard made his way to the diner's counter and sat on one of the stools. An old television had been placed atop a refrigerated display. On it, a panel of talking heads moved their mouths, but no sounds emerged. The closed captioning was on, though, and Richard quickly realized that the topic under discussion was Dearborn.

He had a bit of a jolt when Bishop Preston's face filled the screen. He squinted to catch the closed captioning as it flashed by, a little too fast for him to get a good sense of it. He cursed himself for being such a slow reader.

A few minutes later, a waitress hovered near him and waved a hand between his eyes and the television. "What'll ya have, sunshine?"

She called us 'sunshine', Duunel almost shouted in triumph. *Pussy is in the bag.*

Richard blinked and tried to focus on the young woman. She looked nothing like the 1950s pinup model, of course, and he wondered why he had expected her to. Instead, she was petite with red hair and a smear of freckle on her upturned nose. She was cute.

She was also twenty years his junior. He assumed a polite, detached air. "Sorry," he said, pointing to the television. "Hell of a thing, Dearborn."

"You mean all them Islams?" She scrunched her nose. "'Bout time." She had a vaguely Southern accent and somehow appeared to be chewing gum without having any gum in her mouth, so far as Richard could tell. *What a curious effect*, he thought.

Red pussy, Duunel prodded. *Best kind.*

Richard sighed, shook his head, and picked up the menu. "Well, coffee, obviously, please. Two eggs and some of that beer sausage. Sunny side up, if you don't mind."

"Comin' right up," the young woman said, writing on her pad. She paused and looked at Richard sideways. "So, you some kind of priest?"

"Yes," he said. "*Some* kind."

"What you doing out here?" she asked.

Richard didn't know what to say. Should he tell her about the stolen car? About his quest for a bishop? He opted for a short but simple truth. "I've lost my dog."

Her face scrunched up in a look of forced compassion. "Oh, that's too bad. Sorry."

"It's okay," Richard said. "He's a smart dog. If I don't find him, he'll find me."

It was a strange thing to say, but Richard realized that at least a part of him believed it. It was a comforting realization. Richard watched the bejoweled visage of Bishop Preston on the screen and caught as much of the scrawl as he could.

She's looking at us, Duunel said. Out of the corner of his eye, Richard could see that it was true. He refocused on the screen. He thought back to Preston's association with Prester John. His mind ran over what he remembered about the legendary Mongolian king. He was known as the Moor Hammer. It was a curious name, and it occurred to him that Prester John was not the only saint to whom that dubious moniker had been attached. Who was it? Who else had been called that? He scowled as he thought.

She's staring at us! Duunel announced with glee. Suddenly, it occurred to Richard that Duunel was not just horny but intentionally distracting him from—

Saint James. The Moor Hammer. Santiago. Richard sat bolt upright. He didn't know what it meant, but it had to mean something. He fished out his phone and texted to Brian: "Saint James and Prester John—both Moor Hammers."

The waitress waltzed over to Richard, her hips swaying in what might have been a mild exaggeration. She placed a steaming plate of eggs under his nose, and he almost swooned from the aroma. Duunel directed his eyes to her name tag: Sarah. Duunel tried to direct his eyes to her breasts, but Richard exerted discipline and met her eyes instead. He smiled and nodded his thanks.

The eggs were eggs, nothing remarkable. But the beer sausage was the best thing Richard had tasted in some time. He was tempted to order another round on the side but restrained himself despite Duunel's pleadings. "You're worse than a three-year-old in a toy store," Richard said under his breath.

I'm still hungry, Duunel said.

Richard ignored him. Sarah refilled his coffee and placed a check beside his cup. Richard picked it up and reached for his wallet. When he turned the check over, he found a Post-it note attached. It said, "Off in twenty. Meet me in the parking lot?"

Richard looked up. Sarah flashed a smile at him and winked. She turned her back and with a sway of her hips walked into the back room. *Score!* shouted Duunel in his head.

"I'm not so sure this is a good idea," Richard said.

Why not? You'll save money on a hotel, Duunel said.

"That's true. Okay, on one condition," Richard said quietly.

You're about to get your dick wet for free, and you're placing conditions on me? Duunel said, his mock indignation rising to full Shakespearean heights. *What is wrong with this picture?*

"Promise me you will not bash my head on the ceiling while I sleep," Richard said.

You are a hard man, Duunel said.

"Agree—or we walk out that door right now," Richard said.

You wouldn't dare, Duunel said.

"She's not really my type," Richard said.

You mean she doesn't dress like a lumberjack?

"Something like that."

She doesn't have a buzz-cut?

"Long hair is not my thing, yes."

No mustache?

"Now, wait a minute," Richard said, exasperated. "Are we still talking about women?"

I'm talking about women, Duunel answered.

"Oh. Well then, yes," Richard admitted.

You know, it just occurred to me that, being primarily attracted to lesbians, it must be very lonely for you, Duunel said, sounding uncharacteristically sympathetic. *No wonder you just normally default to faggots. Not so complicated. The rejection ratio—*

"Can we just change the subject?" Richard said, heading for the door.

We are getting laid, right?

"Yes, you horndog. We're just going to wait in the parking lot," Richard said.

Tell me you can get it up if she doesn't look like Rosie O'Donnell, Duunel insisted.

"I swear to God, if you don't shut up, I'm going to cast you into a truck driver and throttle you."

Promises, promises, Duunel sighed. *Why are we waiting out here in the cold? We could go back into the gift shop and look at the rack of* Penthouse *and* Hustlers.

"Do you *ever* fucking stop?" Richard asked.

58

WHEN LARCH EXITED the BART station, safely on the San Francisco side of the bay, with all of his fraters accounted for, he felt his muscles relax. It felt as if water was pouring out of his coat sleeves, or as if his arm was unspooling. He kept waiting for some policeman or federal agent to shoot at them—or, worse yet, to quietly clutch at his sleeve and whisper, "You'll be coming with us, now."

Instead, the Civic Center BART station was abuzz with tourists and locals, crisscrossing in chaotic patterns and jabbering in a wild profusion of languages. It was a safe chaos. The East Bay always made him nervous—he wasn't sure why. Too quiet? Too complacent? Maybe. It was hard to put a finger on it, but nearly everyone in San Francisco felt the same. It was easy to get someone from Berkeley to cross the bridge or take BART into the city. But to get a city person over to Berkeley? *Like pulling fucking teeth*, Larch reflected. He didn't understand why, but only that it was so.

He pulled his coat more tightly about him against the chill of the night as it was twenty degrees colder on this side of the bay. He dropped back, allowing the momentum of the crowd to overtake him, and with instincts proper to a sheepdog, began to nudge his fraters in the right direction by the sheer force of his approaching mass and scowling visage. Once he had successfully shepherded them up Market Street, he led them onto Haight and began making a beeline for their crumbling Victorian.

Once they were inside and safely upstairs, Frater Khams hurried to the kitchen to prepare drinks and snacks. Frater Eleazar asked, "Can we talk now?"

"Yes, we can talk now," Larch said, hanging his coat on a hook. "Thank you all for maintaining radio silence as we crossed the bay. All very well done, especially after such an exciting evening!" He felt ebullient. He raised his voice so that Khams could hear him in the kitchen. "Champagne, please, Frater!"

A few seconds later, Khams emerged with a platter of Triscuits, Spam cubes, and cheese. "Did you say champagne?" he said in Larch's direction as he set the platter on the common table.

"I did! Champagne all around! This is a cause for celebration!"

"We don't have champagne," he said. "But...I'll whip something up." He disappeared into the kitchen again.

The magickians, having scattered to shed clothes and tend to basic sanitary needs, began to settle into their regular places, their voices festive and jangly.

"Larch, that was *extraordinary*." Purderabo pounded the table with his puffy hands.

"Hear, hear!" Turpelo agreed. "I thought that that Pim of yours was leading you down a rabbit hole, but by the gods she came through!"

"An army, indeed!" Purderabo pounded at the table some more.

Khams emerged from the kitchen with a tray of drinks—a pitcher containing a bright red liquid and several Dixie cups.

"Our festive drink?" asked Eleazar hopefully.

"Yes," Khams said and began pouring. He passed a cup to Turpelo. He passed it to Purderabo, who sniffed at it curiously. "I'm guessing sangria?" he queried. He raised the cup to his lips.

"Cherry Kool-Aid and Everclear," Khams said.

Purderabo spewed the red liquid all over the table. Khams put his pitcher down and scowled at the frater, hands on his hips. "I dare you to scour that kitchen and come up with better, asshole!" Khams raised his voice.

"This sounds like a budgetary issue," Eleazar suggested appeasingly.

"If someone wants to buy us some fucking champagne, I'll fucking serve it. Until then, shut the fuck up." He stormed back into the kitchen.

"Khams is *on the rag*," Turpelo sang. Purderabo sniggered and began to mop up the spewed liquid with a handkerchief.

Larch tried the "festive drink" and puckered his face up as the bite hit him. He decided it was terrible in a variety of identifiable ways but drinkable. He took a guzzle and wiped his mouth on the back of his hand.

"So, Larch, let us see this prize that we risked our necks for tonight," Turpelo called, raising his cup in a toasting gesture. He did not, however, drink from it.

"Yes, and for which so many poor, possessed souls have given their lives," Purderabo added cheerily.

"Or at least their liberty!" Turpelo responded. "I think we passed two police vans by the time we hit the BART station."

"Oh!" Eleazar proudly raised his hand. "I saw three."

Larch drew a velvet bag from the inside pocket of his tweed jacket. Setting the bag down on the table, he trotted over to a bookshelf and pulled from it a small, tarnished silver platter. He carried this back to the table, and picking up the velvet bag once again, he carefully poured its contents into the tray.

There, on the tray, were two small stones, each about the size of a walnut. Silence fell over the room. Khams emerged from the kitchen, and, his offended pride apparently set aside for the moment, he leaned over the tray, nearly touching heads with his fraters as they all stared.

"Fraters, behold: the Urim and Thummim," Larch breathed. "These were the stones that were originally set into the breastplate of Aaron, the brother of Moses, and the first Jewish *kohen*. It was through these stones that the ancient Israelites determined the will of God."

"How did they do that?" Khams asked. "They just look like rocks."

"Look closer," Larch said. While the fraters were leaning in, Larch crossed the room again to a desk and returned with a magnifying glass and a flashlight. He handed the glass to Khams and shone the light on the ancient stones. "What do you see now?"

Khams peered through the glass and whistled. "I see letters."

"Right, Hebrew letters—but of the ancient Sinaitic style, not the modern. On how many sides do they appear?" Larch asked.

Khams picked up the velvet bag and used it as a glove in order to pick up the Urim and Thummim. He counted. "One of them has six sides, like a normal die. But the other one has...seven sides." He looked up at Larch. "Wait, is that even possible?" He counted again. Larch counted with him. Yes, there were seven sides.

"How did they use them?" Eleazar asked.

"They rolled them, you idiot," Turpelo said, unable to take his eyes off their haul. "It was what the ancient Jews did instead of reading tarot cards or casting I Ching coins or eviscerating animals to read their entrails."

"So, what do the letters mean?" Khams asked.

"Well, my guess is that each letter stands for a Hebrew word that gives some sort of direction. Like this letter *kaph*, which probably means 'yes'—since *kaph* is the first letter of the word *ken*, the Hebrew word for 'yes,'" answered Larch. "And this letter, *lamed*, probably stands for 'no.'"

"Those letters are on both stones," Purderabo noted. "So, what do the others mean, and why does one stone have six sides and one seven?"

"That's going to require some research," Larch said. "My best guess right now is that the seven-sided stone—the *divine* stone—represents God's *perfect* will, and the six-sided stone—the *human* stone—represents God's *permissive* will."

"What does that mean?" Turpelo asked, looking skeptical.

"Well, think back to the time of the judges," Larch explained.

"God's perfect will was that the Israelites should not have a king. But he permitted them to have one even though it did not please him. If the Jews had asked their God, 'Please, sir, may we have a king?'—"

Purderabo sniggered some more.

"—and then rolled the dice, my guess is that the divine stone would have said no, while the human stone would have said yes."

"Extraordinary," Turpelo said breathlessly.

"This is a fascinating bit of archeology, Larch," Purderabo said. "But of what use is this to us?"

Larch narrowed his eyes. "Are you really so dim?"

Purderabo narrowed his eyes right back. "Assume, for the moment, that I am."

Larch dropped his gaze and sighed. "My brothers," he said, "in a magickal circle, surrounded by the exiled and rightful citizens of Heaven, you and I all made a pact."

His fraters nodded. He went on. "We promised that we would use all of our skill, all of our art, to depose the tyrant on the throne of Heaven and to restore the exiled to their former glory."

"We did," Turpelo nodded. "What of it?"

"If you want to beat your enemy, you must know what your enemy *wants*," Larch said. He pointed to the stones. "Through these stones, the Israelites discerned the tyrant's will. We can use them for precisely the same purpose. Only we"—he leaned in and one by one looked them each in the eye—"will use that knowledge *against him*."

59

WHEN DYLAN once more emerged into consciousness, he found himself staring up into the enormous muzzle of Jaguar.

"Uh...hi there, Jaggy. Where are we?" he asked hesitantly. Rolling his eyes around, he saw that they were back in the underworld. In Jaguar's cave, it looked like. Dylan smiled at Jaguar. Then he frowned. "Uh, dude, you ate my head."

Jaguar said nothing. Dylan felt the hot breath of the great cat on his face, felt spittle from Jaguar's open mouth drip down onto his beard. "Where's the little dog?" Dylan asked.

"Ask your wife," Jaguar said. Then, without missing a beat, Jaguar brandished a long claw, lowered it to Dylan's chest, and cut into him. He cut a long swath from Dylan's throat all the way to his groin. With his great paws, he pushed aside the flaps of skin and dug into the abdominal cavity.

As Jaguar was cutting, Dylan's locus of consciousness rose. He now seemed to be floating just above his body, which appeared to be sleeping or dead. Dylan expected to feel a great deal of pain, but he only felt a vague, dull discomfort as if the pain was great, but far away.

Horrified but oddly detached, Dylan watched as Jaguar scooped out his entrails and placed them in neat piles next to his body. The Dylan-body twitched and grimaced as the great cat worked. Dylan was relieved to see it since he figured it meant that he was still—somehow—alive.

Once the scooping was done, Jaguar turned his attention to sorting. He gathered up entrails of one color and bound them with a colored string. Then he carefully placed them back in the Dylan-body's abdominal cavity. Next, he did the same with another pile of entrails, and then another. Each went neatly back inside the Dylan-body.

Dylan couldn't look away. He noted that there was a hollow place inside his body, about the size of a man's fist. Jaguar turned and faced the back of the cave, where the waterfall was. "Bring forth the gift!" he called.

After a couple of quiet moments, an old woman shuffled out from behind the outcropping of rock. Her hands were misshapen, and as she came closer, Dylan could see that they were mere nubs. The scarring of her face confirmed that she was a leper, and not a modern one in remission. Dylan realized he was seeing some manifestation of the archetypal leper.

In what was left of her gnarled fist, she clutched a worn burlap bag. She held it out to Jaguar, and he received it with a respectful bow. The woman turned and shuffled back to where she had come from. Jaguar, the toes of his paws more dexterous than they had any right to be, opened the bag and dropped its contents onto the floor of the cave.

What seemed to be a fluorescent ball of slime hit the floor with a sickening "thuck" sound. Whatever it was, it was glowing bright green. Jaguar, using both front paws, gathered it up and dropped it into the abdominal cavity of the Dylan-body. Then he began to close the great flaps of skin, sealing them together with his breath.

Once he was finished, the locus of Dylan's consciousness descended, and he was aware of his immediate bodily sensations once again. Dylan shook his head and sat up. "Uh, buddy, was thet really necessary? 'Cuz thet was intense. It's not somethin' that *friends* typically do to each other. You know, evisceration."

Jaguar sat back on his haunches. "How do you feel?"

"Ah feel weird."

"Weird how?"

"Queasy. What did you just do to me, Jaggy? What was that green stuff?"

"Your interior life had become disordered. I...straightened things up a bit," Jaguar said impassively.

"What does that mean?"

"I think you'll find that orderliness and discipline come a little more easily for a while," Jaguar said. "It will wear off if you don't cultivate it. It will give you a head start, though."

"Head start? On what?"

"The gift is another matter," Jaguar said.

"Are you talkin' about the green stuff now?" Dylan asked.

"Since you seem to have no power over your own appetites, the Powers have seen fit to begift you."

"Come on, Jaggy, begift ain't even a word."

"They have done this because you are important. Because your life and your ministry matter to this world. It is not for you."

"Ah get that. It's the message, not the messenger."

Jaguar gave a curt nod.

"So, how will Ah recognize this gift, and how do Ah use it?"

"There is nothing hidden that will not be revealed," Jaguar said. And with that, he turned and walked past the outcropping of rock, out of sight.

"Cryptic motherfucker," Dylan sighed.

60

GETTING INTO SARAH'S CAR, Richard was awash in regret. He didn't know why. A vague sense of unease filled him, a sadness, a poignant desire to have lived a different life. Richard was no stranger to such feelings. Generally, there was nothing to be done other than to focus on something else until they passed.

He watched her face as the streetlights passed overhead. Shadows crossed over in a quick succession of lines. She looked over at him and caught him staring at her. "I think someone's feisty," she said, her lip curling in a smile.

Richard noted that it must be projection since he was feeling little that could be termed "amorous." In fact, going home with her, cute as she was, was so far from the top of his list that he could barely stand to do it.

You think too much, Duunel said. *Stop thinking. Stop feeling, too, while you're at it. You're ruining the mood.*

Richard did not reply—partly because, curiously, Duunel only seemed to hear if he spoke out loud, but also because Duunel did not pause long enough for a response. *Do you know how long it's been since I've gotten laid?* he asked, and answered himself immediately, *Not since*

2002, just before I took up residence in the old Dane. Do you know how long it's been since I've had red pussy?

Richard wished he had a volume control. He didn't need to turn Duunel off, just down. Since that was impossible, he turned his attention back to Sarah. "So, you do this often?" he asked.

"What?" she asked.

"Bring customers home," he said.

"Whenever I get the itch," she said. "Or when I see someone...out of the ordinary." She scrunched her nose. "I get bored."

"Is that why you aren't partnered?" he asked.

"You know what? You talk funny," she said. "I'm guessing partnered is a San Francisco word. Very PC. Kinda like, equally applied to normal folks and faggots."

Whoo boy, Richard thought, sliding down in his seat. If there had been any lead in his pencil, it was gone now. He squirmed in his seat and began to panic about what he would do when they got to her house. There was no way in hell he could have sex with her. Her redneck attitudes repulsed him.

No fair, Duunel said, noticing his reactions. *You are not ruining this for me, asshole. I'll fucking take you over.*

"I'd like to see you try it," Richard whispered.

"What was that?" Sarah asked.

"Nothing. Um...how much farther?" he asked.

"You *are* randy. I like that in a feller."

The hair on Richard's neck stood up. He fought down a momentary feeling of panic. Something was not right about this. Sarah was acting like something out of a "Penthouse Letters" wet dream, not a real young woman. Of course, he knew that actual nymphomaniacs existed, but that they were also really rare. He also knew that the hookup culture among Sarah's generation was far more casual than anything he had known at her age. That *could* account for it—but he didn't trust it.

Jesus, something isn't right here, he prayed silently. *I need you to stand with me now. Give me strength and wisdom—because I don't trust what I've got.*

A couple of minutes later, Sarah drove through a gate that read, Rancho Ecbatana and pulled up to a small house set back a quarter mile from the road. In the flash of the headlights, Richard could see the outlines of a chicken coop and a large barn behind the house. Getting out, Richard noticed that there was not a single star in the sky. Intellectually, he knew that it just meant it was cloudy. Irrationally, however, the darkness around him seemed portentous. The fingers of his left hand started twitching, and his stomach was tied up in a knot. He willed it to relax. It refused.

"C'mon then, sunshine." Sarah waved toward the house. "I been runny for miles now."

Richard pursed his lips grimly. He didn't know how he was going to pull this one off. He supposed he could think of someone else while they were doing it, but he hated doing that and had never been good at it. Just as they got to the door, she placed one hand on his shoulder and with the other felt for his cock through his cassock. She had a hard time finding it. She looked at him uncertainly. "We gonna have a problem, here, cowboy?"

Richard just smiled in response, not sure what to say. He wanted to say, "Thanks for the lift. I think I'll just walk from here," but he knew Duunel would scream bloody murder, and he really didn't want to hear it. Logic dictated that with about twenty minutes of honest effort he could satisfy both the demon in his head and the curious moisture problems of this young woman, and he could then get what he really wanted—a good night's sleep, on the cheap, indoors. "Just gotta get the mood right," he finally said.

"Okay," she said uncertainly. "Now before we go in, I got to prepare you. I forgot to mention that I gotta introduce you to the family. My mama and daddy are pretty strict about such things. And my brother is a little...slow...so the rules are very important for him."

"You introduce your one-night stands to your family?" Richard asked, aghast.

"Them's Daddy's rules," she said. "It's the only place I got to bring you, so we gots to obey the rules. Daddy is the spiritual head of the family, after all, just like the preacher tells us."

"I...hadn't taken you for a religious person," Richard said.

"I've had my doubts 'bout you, too," she said. "Even if you do wear funny clothes."

Without bothering to unlock anything, she pushed the door open. The door squeaked on its frame, and it looked to Richard as if it might fall apart just by touching it. He followed Sarah into the house and was surprised to see that it was lit by kerosene lamps rather than electric lights. He wondered if this was a concerted effort on the part of the entire family to create an amorous mood for Sarah's dalliances or whether they really lived that way. Both options seemed incredible.

Sarah hung up her sweater on a coat rack and turned to face Richard. "I'm so happy to have you meet my folks!" she said and waved toward the couch.

And that was when Richard saw them. Two figures, hand in hand, leaning in toward one another on a couch that looked like it had been in place since the 1970s. The figures had old, weathered skin, stretched tight and dry as dust. The eyes had long since rotted away, and their mouths hung open in a perpetual scream of despair.

Nearly mummified now, the man looked far older than he must have been when he died. He was dressed in overalls and a plaid shirt. A gold-plated wristwatch hung limply from his bony arm. His wife wore a dress with a faded flower print. She must have been quite heavy in life, but decay had taken the cheese out of her, and Richard noted how her dress hung in bags around her.

"This is my daddy," Sarah said proudly. "He has one of them weird bible names—Raguel—but we just call him Daddy. You can call him Ragu, like the spaghetti sauce, or hey, just call him Daddy like I do." She turned slightly and curtsied. "And this is my mama, Edna. Mama, say hello to...what was your name?"

Richard could not look away from the couch. He could not speak. All he could hear was the voice of Duunel screaming in his head, *Get the fuck out of here!* There was a sane and oddly detached part of his brain that noted that if a demon is overwhelmed by a situation, it is a bad situation indeed. Richard said nothing. He felt nothing. His heart hammered in his ears.

"There's no reason to be rude," Sarah scolded him. "Mama and Daddy, this is a priest-feller I met at the diner. I asked him to come home for a little bit of hospitality. I knew you'd understand. Y'all have a good evenin', now." She took Richard's hand and pulled him deeper into the bowels of the house.

Run, you little shit, run! Duunel screamed.

"This way, sunshine." Sarah waved him on. At the thought of what was behind the next door, Richard's blood turned to water. He felt his knees buckle, and he grasped at a door handle to steady himself.

Run, fuck you all to hell! Duunel screamed. *Run, you bastard Christian cunt! Run!*

Richard mustered his will and sprang away from Sarah, toward the front door. Just as he was reaching for the handle, however, it opened by itself. Stepping into the frame was a hulking ox of a man, who scowled down at Richard with the amused curiosity of a child "experimenting" on an insect. His shoulders were misshapen, creating the effect that the man was the walking equivalent of a listing schooner.

"Sarah, is this your new beau?" he called past Richard.

"He is, Gabe. Do you like him?" Sarah appeared from the hallway.

Gabe studied Richard's face and clothing. "He's old. An' he's wearin' a dress." He apparently decided that was funny because he started snorting.

"He's also trying to run away," Sarah said.

"Nobody likes rejection," Gabe said, looking very disappointed in Richard. "You gonna make Sarah sad."

Do something! Duunel shrieked.

"You do something!" Richard responded.

"Who's he talking to?" Gabe asked Sarah.

Without thinking, Duunel raised Richard's body into the air. Watching him rise, Sarah's eyes grew large, and her mouth gaped open. Gabe jumped up and down and clapped his hands in glee. Unfortunately, Duunel raised Richard a little too quickly—his head struck the ceiling, his eyes rolled back, and his body fell into a crumpled heap at Mama's and Daddy's feet.

61

SUSAN RUSHED into the emergency room, with Brian struggling to keep up with her. She was breathless when she stopped at the desk. "Susan Melanchthon, here for Dylan Melanchthon. You guys just called."

The middle-aged brunette behind the desk pursed her lips and nodded. She looked down at her computer but then noticed Brian approach. Her eyes flitted to his hunched back and then to his eyes. Then back again to his back. "Do you...need to see a doctor?" she asked.

Brian straightened up in surprise. Susan turned to face him, and they looked at each other. Then they both looked at the woman behind the desk. "Uh, no," Brian responded. "Do you?"

This apparently confounded the woman, so Brian clarified. "I'm with her." He pointed to Susan. "Can you tell us where to find Dylan?"

The woman looked down at her screen again. "Room 27. But please stay in the waiting room—the doctor will want to speak with you before you go in."

Susan and Brian exchanged worried glances at this. Susan nodded, and Brian, his hand resting paternally on the small of her back, walked her to the waiting room. They sat, knee to knee, and Brian held her hands.

"He's going to be okay, Susan," he said.

"Please don't talk out of your ass," Susan said, struggling to keep her tears in.

"I'm sorry," Brian said, looking down. "I'm saying it because I need to hear it."

"I know. It's okay." Susan looked out the window. "This is an excellent time for spiritual practice."

"It sure is," Brian nodded. "What did you have in mind?"

"Trust," Susan said.

"Let's do *that*," Brian said. They sat together in silence for several minutes. Finally, Brian said, "Trust is hard."

"No shit," Susan said, looking away and wiping at her eyes. Her right leg bounced nervously.

"Do you want me to pray?" Brian asked.

Susan's face bunched up with emotion. She nodded, finally looking at him. Neither of them closed their eyes, but Brian looked toward the ceiling. "Adonai, you've had your hand on Dylan for as long as we've both known him. Neither of us believes that you're done with him. But we're scared for him—and we're also scared for us. Please help us now—give us courage, give us strength, and give us hope. Blessed are you, King of the Universe, for you have never abandoned your people."

"Amen," Susan said.

"Amen," Brian echoed.

"Susan Melanchthon?" a diminutive Asian woman called from the doorway.

Susan and Brian rose together and rushed over to where the woman stood. The woman looked down at her clipboard as they crossed the room. As they approached, she looked up and gave them a grim smile.

"I'm Susan. How's Dylan?" Susan asked.

"He's resting comfortably," the woman said. "He was assaulted earlier tonight." She rifled through some of the papers on her clipboard. "He was in the People's Park public lavatory when police found him. They called the paramedics immediately."

Susan's hands went to her mouth, and she nodded at everything the woman said. Brian stood behind her, his arms around her shoulders, holding her tightly. "Is he all right?" she asked.

"He's suffered severe blunt-force trauma to his nuchal region." She reached out and took Susan's arm. "But please don't worry. We did a CAT scan, and there's no discernible spine or nerve damage. My guess is that he'll make a full recovery, although there is the possibility that he'll experience some cervicalgia or occipital neuralgia— those are some pretty fancy words for severe or persistent neck pain. He may also experience some headaches." She withdrew her hand, but the worried look didn't leave her face. "There is...something else. Something we can't explain. Does Mr. Melanchthon have any drug allergies?"

Susan shook her head. "No, not that I know of. And we've been married ten years. Why?"

"We administered some non-steroidal anti-inflammatory medication soon after he arrived, and he had a massive reaction to it. So much so that we had to administer epinephrine to combat the reaction. Then...he had a reaction to the epinephrine." She looked chagrined and troubled.

"Oh my God, what does that mean?" Susan asked. "Is he all right?"

"We actually thought we might lose him, but he rallied. We've purposely avoided any medication beyond a simple saline drip. He's just starting to come around. He's likely to be very disoriented and might be frightened. I suggest only one of you go in for now."

"When can he go home?" Brian asked.

"We want to keep our eye on him tonight, but if the swelling goes down and he doesn't display any further signs of injury, you can take him home in the morning. Just...be careful with any medication you might give him. Even aspirin or acetaminophen might be life-threatening for him given his reaction to the ibuprofen we gave him earlier. I suggest you check in with his GP and get a referral to an allergy specialist as soon as possible. His drug reactions are...troubling. They're not normal."

Susan nodded, and Brian squeezed her shoulders. "This way, please," the doctor said and held the door for Susan.

"I'll be right here," Brian said.

Susan patted his hand and nodded, turning to enter the doorway. Once she did, the doctor rushed ahead of her and led her through the bustling ER, finally entering a room alive with electronic instruments and bisected with a teal-colored curtain. Sprawled spread-eagle in a bed was her Dylan, a nasal cannula resting on his upper lip.

She rushed to him and sat on the side of his bed, taking his hand. She was careful not to move it very much, not wanting to disturb the IV. Out of the corner of her eye she saw the doctor pull the curtain to give them some privacy. A tiny, out-of-the-way part of her brain registered gratitude for that.

She brushed his sandy brown hair away from his eyes and spoke. "Hey, Honey Pie. I'm here. How are you feeling?"

His eyes, which had been half-shut and unfocused, flitted in her direction. His brow furrowed as if he were searching for a connection. Then he brightened, apparently finding it. "Hey, Darlin'."

"How are you?" she repeated.

"Mah head hurts like a motherfucker."

She relaxed just a little. Her Dylan was still here. "You scared the shit out of me," she confessed.

"Am Ah in trouble?" he asked, raising his eyebrows.

"Oh my God. Yes, you are," she said, and finally dissolved into a cascade of sobs.

62

HIS HOST OUT COLD, it seemed an auspicious time to make a report. Duunel entered the in-between and waited for the haze to harden into perceptible shapes. The great, glowing eye of his master, Maaluchre, sharpened into focus above him, glowering and fierce. He bowed before it. "My master," he said, his ritual greeting.

"Rise and report," the prince commanded.

Duunel concisely recounted the previous day's misadventure, but he paused when he saw the great red eye shake with what appeared to be mirth.

"Is something...funny, my lord?"

"You don't think so?" The voice was amused, but it had an edge to it, too. He dare not contradict it.

"Well, perhaps if I was not so...caught up in the situation," he hedged, trying to internally gain some objective distance so that he could intelligently comment in a way that would make sense to his superior.

"I would think you'd be enjoying this," Maaluchre said.

"Huh. Well, you'd think so, I suppose..." Duunel didn't really know what to say. Did he like to see Richard suffer? Of course. Couldn't he, Duunel, just walk away anytime? No, actually. He would need a host, and neither of the options was very appealing. The cock-hungry nymphet was out. He shuddered at the notion of inhabiting her brain. And the giant moron was unthinkable. There was evil, and then there was batshit crazy. The moron was the latter. In such a brain, Duunel would be the prisoner, not the boss.

At least Richard was...sharable. He was intelligent, and he was funny. Duunel hadn't thought of *liking* a human in a very long time. He didn't dwell on it now, either. Instead, he spoke plainly to his master. "You need to get us out of here."

"Oh yes, our Father's greatest mobilization is underway, and I'm to reassign troops in order to lessen your discomfort?" The eye grew redder, brighter, angrier. "Oh, and in helping you I'd also be helping the leader of our enemies—who, I am pleased to inform you, are a pack of bumbling incompetents without him." The great dragon breathed fire, and Duunel, who knew his master well, understood this to be an indication of his contempt. "No, I think I'll keep him right where he is. The enemy's hand is upon him, so since we can't kill him—"

"These people might."

"Well, we can hope. Nevertheless, as far as what we are permitted to do, the best we can hope for is to detain him as long as possible. Grand things are underway, Duunel. I am trusting you to do your part. Don't kill him. Don't rescue him. Don't comfort him. Don't encourage him. Just keep him...otherwise occupied."

MONDAY

63

Larch awoke to blinding morning light seemingly concentrating in one hot point of pain directly behind his eyeballs. He grimaced and pulled the pillow over his eyes, willing the pain to go away. It didn't.

He threw the covers back and staggered to the bathroom down the hall, nearly tripping over Frater Turpelo just exiting after a shower. Larch grumbled a halfhearted "good morning" and shut the bathroom door. To his surprise, the steam from Turpelo's shower felt good, and he realized that at least some of his headache must be from tension. He tried to shake the stress from his limbs but quickly brought it under control when his movements caused his efforts at urination to venture out of bounds. Interior ablutions complete, he splashed water on his face and looked at himself in the mirror. His eyes were blood red. "Not good," he mumbled.

He showered without pleasure and threw on yesterday's clothes without thinking. He knew why he was tired—he had spent half the night researching the Hebrew letters on the Urim and Thummim. Like seriously compulsive researchers everywhere, he had not been able to quit until he had a working model down and ready for trial.

He grabbed his notes from his desk and ventured into the common room, where, he was pleased to see, Frater Khams had a pot of his typically thick-brewed coffee steaming on the table. He gratefully poured himself a mug and sucked at it like the salvation it was.

"Breakfast, Frater?" Khams asked, spinning out of the kitchen cheerily with a tray of blintzes between oven-mittened hands.

"Cream cheese?" asked Larch.

"Chèvre, with dark chocolate," Khams answered, placing the tray on the table and rushing back to the kitchen.

"And a side of Advil, please," Larch said staring at the blintzes. He started to drool but wiped his mouth on the back of his hand.

Khams reappeared a moment later and placed a tea saucer in front of Larch. Arranged on it were three Advil, a dollop of yogurt adorned with what appeared to be raspberry compote offset by a sprig of parsley. "Presentation is *everything*," Khams sang on his way back into the kitchen.

"You are exactly three and a half times too cheery this morning," Larch said, only half complaining.

The aroma of the coffee began to cut through the hazy fog of his perception. Better still, the point of pain behind his eyes was beginning to dissolve. Larch stretched his shoulders first one way, then the other, and carried his coffee into the common room. Walking over to a card table that must have been set up some time after he had retired, his mouth dropped open in disbelief. He nearly dropped his coffee cup.

There, on the card table, was a Parcheesi board, abandoned in mid-play. Instead of dice, the Urim and Thummim sat atop the game board.

Larch threw the coffee cup against the wall and roared with indignation. The cup shattered, and the coffee splattered the wall in a pleasing pattern. The fraters, panicked, scurried to the common room. Larch, headache forgotten now, possessed of a clarity born only of rage, turned on them. His eyes, still red, were now incandescent with ire. "What the Christ-napping fuck?" He pointed at the game board.

"What?" asked Purderabo. "We were playing Parcheesi. You like Parcheesi. It's been a while since we've had game night—"

"Have you No. Sense. Of. Propriety???" He barked at them. "What magnitude of idiocy compelled you to employ two of the most powerful relics in the Western world to play a *fucking* board game?" He grabbed a hat from a hook on the wall and began beating Purderabo's head with it. "What fucking lunacy possessed you? Did it occur to you that one of them might fall to the floor and be damaged?"

"Well, actually, I did drop one of them. Twice," Turpelo confessed. "Guess I don't know my own strength."

"Watch me pull a rabbit out of my hat," Khams interjected in his best Bullwinkle voice. "Nothin' up muh sleeve."

"But it *didn't* get hurt," Turpelo assured him. "Maybe a *little* scratch, just there..." He pointed at the underside of the Urim.

Larch snatched the sacred stones up from the table and replaced them in their velvet bag. "You are Never. To touch them. Again," he said and stormed past them, down the hallway, and into the temple where he did his private workings. He slammed the door and stood panting in the dim light peeking through the blackout curtains. He fought to master his rage before the headache returned. Too late, he realized.

"I'm surrounded by lunatics and fools," he said out loud. He needed guidance. Without pausing to think, he pulled the black velvet cloth from the Enochian table and fixed his gaze in the seer stone. The expected wisps appeared within just a few minutes of gazing, followed by the gauzy apparel of Pim waving in and out of view teasingly. Eventually, she danced into the center of the stone where he could see her. Petite and pixyish, her short-cropped hair and wide smile captivated him, as it always did.

He wasted no time on small talk. "We liberated the Urim and Thummim," he said, interjecting a note of pride into his voice.

"Nice work, big boy," she said, wiggling.

"Now that we have them, what should we ask them? What will do the most good?" he asked sincerely, almost desperately.

"Oh, poo on those baubles," Pim said, pouting. "The important thing is that you know that that army of yours will follow you. Consider your little bit of petty theft a test. Now that you know that you have real power, it's time to put your leadership to a more important use."

"Doing what?" Larch was genuinely surprised.

"Oh, I don't know." Pim tapped her finger on her chin. "How about...protecting the savior of the world?" She looked directly into his eyes and wiggled again.

It made him crazy, but he forced himself to focus. "The *savior* savior," he asked, "Or the savior *savior* savior?"

"Uh...the last one," she nodded in mock-seriousness. "And his prophet."

"Who's that?" he asked.

"I'll tell you when the time is right. Until then, you need to be a good general and care for your army." She pointed her finger at him and seemed truly serious for the first time. "Hell has been emptied. According to the law of demonic diffusion, they're pretty evenly scattered over the globe. But don't worry. They're stepping into...predisposed people and coming here. Even now, they're gathering in greater and greater numbers."

"Where? Where are they gathering?"

"Outside your house, silly," she giggled.

"Oh my God!" Larch grabbed at his remaining hair. Not pausing to properly end the session with Pim, he rushed to the window. Sure enough, about fifty people were outside, loitering on Haight Street.

Fortunately, lots of people loitered on Haight Street, and the newcomers had not been noticed. But if they began to gather in the numbers that had been visited upon the Blackfriars' place...He shuddered to think of it. The police were on the lookout for such a mob now. It wouldn't take long to clue into the fact that the new group of loiterers might be connected to the East Bay group. They would, in fact, lead the police directly to Larch's door.

He threw on a sweater with a hood and grabbed some sunglasses. He needed them for anonymity, certainly, but they wouldn't hurt as far as his headache was concerned, either. He nearly knocked Turpelo over on his way to the stairs.

"Frater, where are you—"

Larch didn't answer but pounded down the stairs and out onto the street. Marching into the thick of the loitering horde, he shouted, "Follow me!" He began walking toward the Upper Haight. He was relieved to see that the horde was indeed following him.

Tonight, no one would have to explain the new homeless people in Golden Gate Park. No one would notice.

64

WHEN RICHARD AWOKE, it was to a blinding pain in his forehead. *Good morning, sunshine,* Duunel said to him. Richard felt a rush of adrenaline as he remembered what had happened to him.

"You may never, ever call me that," Richard said. "Where are we?" He opened one eye just a slit, and saw that he appeared to be in a barn. It stank, for one thing, and slivers of light shone through the rough boards that made up the walls. "So, that was brilliant," Richard said. "You have demonic superpowers, and all you can do is bash me in the head?"

It's not like I had time to think about it, Duunel answered. *And yes, I can throw all kinds of objects through the air, not just religious snits.*

"Then why didn't you throw that guy who was built like Frankenstein's monster, what was his name? Gabe? Why didn't you throw fucking Gabe out of the way so we could get the fuck out of here?"

I just reacted. I'm practiced at throwing you around. It's my chief joy in life, these days.

"Oh gee, thanks."

It's not like you're providing me with a steady supply of sex kittens or anything.

"Sex kittens only exist in the fevered imaginations of Hugh Hefner and fourteen-year-old boys."

You've been a serious killjoy since the day I met you, Duunel pouted.

Richard tried to sit up, but the clanking of metal caught his attention. He looked down and saw a metal fetter around his leg. "Oh, sweet Christ," he swore.

That's not the worst of it, Duunel said. *Turn around. Slowly.*

Richard did. He froze.

The barn seemed to be arranged in a macabre tableau. At the far side a small wedding chapel had been arranged. An arch was set up on a riser, its whitewashed wood now fading into gray. It was covered in flowers, now long dead and dried, mere husks of their former glory. Propped up directly in the center of the arch was the body of a man, his face ancient, his skin taut and beginning to flake away. His mouth was open in the perpetual scream of death, and his eyes had been dust for years. Gold spectacles had been wired in place over his sockets.

Squinting in the dim light, Richard saw that the corpse was not standing up, really. A bucket of what looked like dried cement—or perhaps gravel, it was hard to tell from his distance—was on the floor directly between his legs, and a two-inch thick dowel—which might have been the handle of a shovel—disappeared into his torso. Richard winced as he realized where the handle had been stuck. No wonder the man looked like he was still screaming.

Richard was struck by the corpse's clothes. It was wearing a western hat, a black suit, and a bolo tie. Wired into its dusty hands was a black *Bible*. Richard realized that he had been a preacher of some kind, or at least was supposed to play the role of one in the tableau.

Just to the right of the archway was a dusty, stained mattress. Dried flower petals lay strewn across it. Richard glanced to the left. His breath caught in his throat as he saw that the tableau continued. Seated on two long benches—though Richard realized they were functioning as pews—were seven other corpses. They seemed to be arranged in the chronological order of their deaths. The one on the far right looked as old as the corpse of the reverend beneath the arch. The skin of the one next to him was not quite as dusty. Richard could see that the seventh corpse, the one nearest to him, was reasonably fresh. Maybe a couple of months old? He still had his eyes, for one thing, although they looked like deflated sacks of jelly sitting in his sockets.

The cause of their deaths was not hard to divine. Each of their heads was horribly misshapen as if struck by an object so massive and with such force that the skull had simply caved in upon itself.

Each of the seated corpses had been wired into place—they were not going anywhere, anytime soon. They were also wearing suits, Richard noted. Dried flowers hung off the buttonholes of a couple of them, and the last had a dried bouquet of flowers wired into his hand.

"It's a wedding chapel," Richard said in a horrified whisper. "That's the preacher." He pointed at the corpse under the arch. "And those are...the congregation? The groomsmen?..." he trailed off, uncertain.

The grooms? Duunel suggested.

A chill ran through Richard as he realized Duunel was right. A succession of grooms. Each of them felled by a massive blow to the head.

Richard began to panic. His breath came fast, and he felt faint. *Whoa, cowboy,* Duunel said. *We have to stay conscious if we want to get out of this...together. You need to calm down. Get a grip on yourself. We both need to think.*

Richard nodded and forced his breath to come more slowly. In a few moments, he felt the tightness in his shoulders relax, and his dizziness passed.

Phone? Duunel asked.

Richard felt through his cassock at his pockets. No wallet. No keys. No phone. His heart sank.

Just then, the door to the barn swung open, and Richard threw up a hand to shield his eyes from the glaring sunlight. Once his eyes started to adjust, he saw Sarah enter, followed by Gabe.

As repulsed as he was, he could not help noticing that Sarah was stunningly beautiful. She was adorned as a bride, in a white wedding dress, her hair piled on her head, wreathed in flowers. She held a bright bouquet in her hand.

Behind her, Gabe was in an ill-fitting but smart tuxedo, his greasy hair looking odd and out of place. He tugged at his cummerbund with one hand, and with the other tossed a black suit to Richard. "Put this on," he commanded.

"What for?" Richard asked.

"For your wedding day, silly," Gabe said, grinning a reprimand as if Richard should know better.

Not knowing what to do, Richard held up the suit. He quickly realized that he couldn't put on the trousers if his leg was chained. The inability to solve this simplest of problems paralyzed him.

Tell them you can't put on the pants unless they unlock you, Duunel commanded.

"I can't put on the pants with this on," Richard said dutifully, pointing to the shackle.

Sarah walked in a semicircle around him, smiling at him sadly. Richard imagined that this is how a cat must look before pouncing on her prey. "Sarah, what's this all about? What are we doing, here?" If he were going to fight this thing, he needed to understand it.

"We're getting married," she said. "After all, you were more than willing to fuck me last night. I mean, you would've. Right?"

Richard moved his head from side to side. If. If there had not been corpses on the couch. Sure. If her monster of a brother hadn't threatened him. Okay. If his Spidey-sense wasn't tingling so hard that he was almost going into convulsions. Yeah. If a demon hadn't almost crushed his skull against the ceiling. Granted. He probably would have fucked her.

"Well, where I come from, there ain't no free lunch." Richard struggled to make sense of this Zig Ziglar-esque bit of wisdom. "You want it; you got to pay for it," she clarified. "I ain't gonna just *give* it away. The way I see it, if you were willing to take it, you done committed yourself to me." She smiled, but there was no mirth in it. "So, we're gonna make it legal and shit."

She glanced over at the corpse beneath the archway. "I see you've met Reverend Sykes."

Richard nodded. "Pleased to meet you, Reverend," he said in all seriousness. But in his mind he clicked through what was likely to happen next. They would stand him up before the preacher, go through the motions of a farcical ceremony. Sarah would lead him to the mattress to finally consummate the union, then Gabe would cave his skull in, and wire him up next to the other grooms on the benches. *Hen-er-y the Eighth I am*, he thought. He gave himself twenty minutes, tops.

He didn't think. He just spoke. "Sarah, this isn't going to work. I think God brought us together not so I could be another one of your husbands, but in order to provide you with a real, live clergyperson."

"You think Pastor Sykes isn't a real pastor?"

"I think..." His brain worked furiously. "I think Raguel is a name that's only found in the Catholic Bible—in one of the deutero-canonical books. That means that your mama and daddy are Catholics, not Protestants. I'm sure Pastor Sykes is a fine pastor, but he's not Catholic. Maybe God is not blessing your...unions...because you're not being true to the Faith. Maybe if a Catholic priest were blessing your weddings, you'd have a baby by now."

Way to go, Ace, Duunel said. *That should buy us some time.*

Sarah lowered her bouquet and cocked her head, thinking. "Do you think that's really true?" She seemed to really see Richard for the first time.

Richard seized on that. "I'm a priest. I'm kind of an expert on such things."

"You're a priest who was ready to fuck me."

"I didn't say I was a *good* priest...just a knowledgeable one."

"Why would God bless my belly if you aren't a good priest?"

"Because Catholicism doesn't work that way," Richard said, adopting an intentionally pedantic tone. "Catholic sacraments function *ex opere operato*, which means that the sacraments are efficacious

—they work—regardless of the moral state of the priest performing them. As long as the priest is valid—and I am—then his sacraments are valid. It doesn't matter if I'm good or...not so good." He smiled weakly.

"Is that for real?" she asked.

"Swear to God and cross my heart," Richard said. He intentionally skipped "hope to die." He hoped she hadn't noticed. She didn't seem to. Her face was folded up in thought. Finally, she snapped into action. She walked swiftly toward the door, grabbing at Gabe's sleeve as she passed him.

"Where we goin'?" Gabe asked, perplexed.

"We're going to keep him," Sarah said.

"Like a puppy?" Gabe brightened.

"You killed the puppies, Gabe," she said sweetly.

"That was fun," he said.

"But you can't kill him. He's going to work for us. He's gonna be the new reverend."

"You mean I don't get to watch him get naked with you today?" His shoulders sagged.

She threw her arms around him and hugged him close. "Oh, my dear, I'm so sorry. Did you want to see him naked?" Gabe looked like he was about to cry. He nodded. Sarah reached up and touched his cheek tenderly. Then she turned and faced Richard. "Well, he was ready to fuck me. I don't see why you shouldn't fuck him."

She walked back to Richard and leaned down so that her face nearly touched his. "Since you're a priest, you won't mind bein' buggered, will you?"

Richard did not blink.

She straightened up and walked back to her brother. "You can do more than just see him naked, Gaby my darling. His butthole is yours anytime you want it."

65

IT TOOK Brian and Terry working together to get Dylan up the stairs. Finally getting him settled and comfortable, Brian returned to the kitchen to finish preparing breakfast. Susan sat on the bed next to her husband, and Terry hovered nervously, stooping occasionally to straighten something in the room or to make sure that objects were at right angles to each other.

Dylan's voice was thick but aware. "Dude, yer making me crazy. Can yah just sit down?"

Terry straightened up and stared at him. Then he straightened a picture.

"Guess not." Dylan turned to Susan. "Thanks for staying with me, Darlin'."

She squeezed his hand.

"Thing is, Ah'm in a lot of pain, here. Ah know, Ah know, me and Mary Jane are on the outs, but you gotta give me something."

"I'm sorry, Honey, but the doctor said you had a terrible allergic reaction to the pain medication they gave you. We're going to have to take this slow. You're going to have to ride it out for now."

"Thet's just cruel," he said, looking down. The mane of his red beard radiated from his face like a miniature sun. But it was a sad sun.

Terry finally lit next to Susan. He reached out and touched Dylan's knee. "Tell us what happened," he said.

Dylan shifted uncomfortably. "Waal, I wuz mad. I went out to score."

Susan looked away, but Terry just nodded. "We figured as much."

"But then I saw Larch."

Terry and Susan sat bolt upright as if Dylan had just pricked them with a pin. Dylan continued. "He was leadin' them possessed folks away from our house, so I followed 'em."

"Where did they go?" Terry asked.

"To the Jewish museum, down by the campus."

"The Maccabee?" Terry asked.

"Yup. Same one Brian speaks at."

"They just got robbed," Terry said.

"Right. I was there. Larch is behind it. Ah don't know how he's commandin' all them possessed folk, but he is."

Terry's eyebrows furrowed as he thought about this.

"And then?" Susan asked.

"Uh...and then Ah scored." Dylan looked down at his pudgy hands. "And then Ah had to pee. Thet's it, really."

Susan leaned in and kissed his forehead. "It's okay, Honey. You're okay. *We're* okay. Just...heal." She stood up. "I'll bring you some breakfast when it's ready."

He nodded and shot her a chagrined smile. Then he winced, and the smile faded quickly. Susan left the room, and Terry followed her out. Once they were out of the room, Dylan swung his legs from the bed and scowled. He knew Susan had some Vicodin left over from her root canal last month. Where had she put that?

MORNING PRAYER JUST ENDED, Kat put her prayer book on the shelf and turned toward the kitchen. The doorbell rang, so she dodged right instead of left. Looking through the peephole, she saw that it was Felicia Dunne, and a thrill of excitement stung her. She liked Felicia *a lot*. She opened the door with a cheery, "Welcome!"

Felicia's face, which had been drawn up in a worried scowl, brightened. "Am I in the right place?"

"I think anyplace *you are* is the right place to be," Kat said, grabbing her hand and pulling her in.

"Now that's an extravagant welcome." She laughed and drew off her jacket. Kat took it and hung it on a peg beside the door.

"I hope you haven't had breakfast yet," Kat said. "It'd be a shame to miss Brian's cooking."

"I *was* warned," Felicia reminded her. "So, I'm famished."

Kat gave her a bright smile and waved for her to follow, into the kitchen. "Felicia, you know Mikael, of course." Mikael raised his coffee cup in greeting from his place at the table. She gestured toward Brian, who was just placing a tray of home-baked muffins on the lazy Susan. "This is Brian, Terry's partner." She leaned in and whispered, "He's our Kabbalah guy."

"Kab*balah* guy!" repeated Mikael in a loud, television announcer voice. Brian struck a Superman pose then turned quickly back to the stove to turn the bacon.

Kat held her hands up to her mouth and said, "Okay, this is going to be a little weird." She gestured toward a mirror hanging near the back door, overlooking the end of the table. "This is my brother, Randy. He was an asshole magickian, until he got involved with the avocado thing...oh, it's complicated."

Felicia leaned in to look at the mirror and then bolted upright when she saw Randy waving at her. "Shit!" she exclaimed.

"Yeah, it's weird," Kat said again. "He's kind of trapped in there."

"I'm trying to embrace the reflective life," Randy's voice came from the guitar amplifier sitting on the bench just under the mirror. He smiled. Then he walked over to the reflected stove, dodged Brian's reflection, and grabbed a piece of bacon.

"Dude, that was reaching," Mikael said, but he smiled anyway.

"My bar is pretty low these days," Randy agreed.

"That's freaky," Felicia said, her eyes wide. "And you say *he* caused the whole avocado thing?"

"I'm ashamed to say it, but yes," Kat answered.

"And the dogs?" Felicia asked, referring to an experiment in which Randy's magickian friends had caused all the dogs to disappear simultaneously.

"His asshole friends," Kat said, nodding. "Not him directly, but definitely guilty by association."

Felicia nodded grimly, staring daggers at the mirror. Randy's shoulders slunk under her withering gaze. "Did you lose your dog?" Kat asked. "Didn't he come back?"

"It was my mama's dog. And yeah, she came back," Felicia said. "But not until my mama died of grief over her. I mean, like, *really* died."

Kat fumed in her brother's direction. "I'm so sorry," she said. "They were stupid. They had no idea what they were doing."

Just then, Susan walked in. Kat, relieved to change the subject, waved toward her. "This is Susan. She's completely kick-ass, *and* she's my hero."

Susan smiled weakly and shook Felicia's hand. Then she sat in her spot at the table. "My husband won't be joining us," she said, patting the bench next to her. "Why don't you take his seat?"

Felicia accepted gratefully and sat down. Terry walked in and gave Brian a kiss on the cheek. He greeted Felicia warmly and took his own place as Brian set a steaming platter of olive-and-Gruyère omelets on the lazy Susan. "Pray and eat," he commanded.

"I haven't got it in me to pray," Susan said, looking deflated.

"No problem," Terry said, taking Felicia's hand on one side and Kat's on the other. "Gentle Jesus, you alone know what we're up against. You alone know what we should do. You alone can give us the strength to do it. Help us to discern well and love better. Bless this food and everything we do today. Amen."

Amens all around, the lazy Susan was set to spinning, and everyone dug in. "How is he?" Kat asked, her mouth full of omelet.

"Agitated. Scared." Susan paused. "Ashamed...which makes two of us." She put her hand over her eyes and lowered her elbow to the table. Brian came up behind her and kissed the back of her head.

Kat gave Felicia a look that said, "I'll explain. Later." Felicia nodded, obviously respectful of Susan's grief.

They turned back to their breakfasts, and slowly the small talk returned to its normal, cheery level. Making sure everyone had seconds on coffee, Brian grabbed a mug himself and sat next to his husband. "What's the plan?" he asked.

"Well, as you know, Felicia is the rector of Saint James's, where the Spear of Destiny has been hidden for the last fifty years," Terry began.

"Amazing," Brian shook his head. "I mean, that it was so close to us, the whole time."

"Felicia was extorted by that creepy Preston guy, the bishop," added Kat, eyeing a last piece of bacon.

"I don't know if I would say 'extorted,'" Felicia said.

"I would. He threatened to out you to your Republo-fascist congregation, didn't he?" Mikael asked.

"They're not *that* bad," Felicia complained.

"I get it," Brian said. "No need to quibble over vocabulary."

"So, we know how Preston got himself elected—through the power of the Spear," Terry said.

"How does that work?" Susan asked. "I thought the Spear was just an unstoppable offensive weapon."

"That's a popular misconception," Brian said, warming his hands on his mug. "But the way it works is more complicated. According to my research, it only has power *against* power."

"Come again?" Kat asked, her eyebrows scrunching.

"Okay, let's say this salt shaker was the Spear," Brian said.

"Scariest damned salt shaker on the planet," Mikael added.

"Right," Brian smiled. "If I'm holding it, and you don't oppose me, then it's inert. It's just a salt shaker. No power, no nothing."

"Plenty of salt," Randy called from the mirror.

"Exactly," Brian affirmed. "It can only do what a normal salt shaker can do. But now let's say Susan tries to hit me—"

"It could happen," Mikael interjected. "She might be on a roll."

Susan scowled across the table at him.

"That's when the shaker's power leaps out. It meets the force coming at it with superior force and repels it. Susan might try to hit me, but the blow is turned back on her, only it's a little worse than what came at me," Brian said.

"So, in effect, the Spear functions as an amplified reciprocation talisman," Terry nodded, thinking hard.

"Only against opposition," Brian clarified. "If Susan were to shower me with kisses—"

"It *is* a hypothetical," Mikael added. Susan scowled harder.

"It wouldn't amplify the love," Brian said. "Motion toward, or affinity, or cooperation doesn't activate it. Only opposition."

"So, you're saying that Preston won election precisely because he was being opposed by the other candidates," Susan tapped at the table with her fingernails.

"Yes, the Spear exerted just enough power to beat them," Brian said. He turned to Felicia. "It wasn't a landslide, was it? The election, I mean."

Felicia shook her head. "No, it was close."

Brian nodded. "That's what I thought. That's how it works."

"So, you're saying the only way to beat Preston," Mikael said, "is not to oppose him?"

Brian nodded again. "That's the long and the short of it."

"That sounds like suicide," Kat said.

Felicia set down her coffee cup. "It's the Gospel." They all looked at her. "Well, it's what Jesus did, right?" She explained. "He met the forces of evil head on, but he didn't oppose them. He didn't meet power with power. He just walked into the midst of those powers and got steamrollered by them."

"*He could have called ten thousand angels, to destroy the world and set him free...*" Terry quoted the words of the old hymn.

"Right," Felicia said. "But he didn't. He let evil have its way."

"But why?" Kat complained. "What good does that do?"

"Because force is the way of empire," Felicia said. "Do this or we kill you. Coercion. Exploitation—"

"Extortion," Mikael added.

Felicia nodded her agreement. "Yes, even that. But none of that is the way of God. The Paschal mystery—"

"The *what* now?" called Randy from the mirror.

"The mystery of Jesus's death and resurrection," Felicia back-tracked, "is that evil can pull out the big guns and do its absolute worst, but in the end, it doesn't win. It can't. Love wins. That's the message; that's the promise of Easter. That's the Good News of Jesus in a nutshell. Force, coercion, evil, and hate might seem like they have the upper hand in the moment, but they won't have the last word. In the end, love will triumph."

Mikael sipped at his coffee. "So, the Spear was plunged into Jesus's side—it's kind of a negative sacrament of coercive power, isn't it?"

Terry sat up straighter. "That's a great way to think of it."

"I think you're all nuts," called Randy from the mirror. "Is this how you fight evil? You sit around and talk about it over crumb cake?"

"I don't see any crumb cake," Brian said.

Susan was staring hard at the table. "No, Randy's asking a very important question." She looked up and turned toward the mirror. "Short answer, Randy, yes, this is exactly how we do it. It's not shoot 'em up exciting, but that's partly why we're still in one piece—well, mostly in one piece. And it's not that evil can't be opposed. We oppose it plenty—we just don't meet it on its own terms. You can't fight evil with evil; you can't repel force with force. If you do, it wins. Instead, you have to dodge the blows—"

"Celestial aikido!" Mikael interjected.

"Kind of, yeah," Susan agreed. "The only effective way to meet hate is with love. That's what Jesus did. And if we're going to follow him, that's how we've got to do it, too."

"That's why we study magick, but don't practice it," Terry added.

"That's just crazy," Randy said.

"Lots of people have said so," Susan agreed. "But let's be careful about this. It's a temptation to see not fighting back as capitulation. But it isn't. It's a kind of fighting. It's not the same as being a doormat, or simply agreeing to be somebody's property or their punching bag. It takes amazing courage not to fight back in the face of evil."

"Right," said Terry. "Just look at the Civil Rights Movement, or Gandhi's philosophy."

"Both were philosophically rooted in the Gospel," Felicia noted. "Gandhi wasn't a Christian, but he was deeply influenced by the portrait of Jesus he found in the gospels."

"That sounds hard to do—not fighting back," Kat said. "I'm not sure I agree with that."

"It's counterintuitive, that's for sure," said Terry, draining his cup. "It requires a radical act of trust."

"Trust in what?" asked Kat.

"In God. In Love," Felicia answered. "That on the other side of the cross is the empty tomb. That if you walk straight into the mouth of evil—and don't give in to the temptation to return evil for evil—you'll come out the other side, scarred but victorious."

"That's a lot of trust," Kat said.

"That's a lot of trust," agreed Susan.

For a few moments, no one said anything. Finally, Randy's voice came from the guitar amplifier. "I think you've all got your heads up your asses."

"Thank you for your helpful input, Randy," Kat said, narrowing her eyes in her brother's direction.

"Okay, so Preston's got this Spear, which means that any form of opposition will be met with equal and greater force," Mikael reasoned. "And we've seen how that can work in a democratic situation. This week is the Republican National Convention, and we know he's pushing for Governor Ivory to be, basically, a write-in-candidate. If he can sway the Episcopal diocese, he can sway the Republican delegates."

"And we know what kind of man Ivory is," Susan continued. "He wiped out an entire American city because there were too many Muslims in it. He's the *real* face of evil."

"I got a text from Dicky yesterday," Brian added. "He pointed out that both Saint James and Prester John were known as the Moor Hammer."

"Add Ivory to that list," Terry said.

"What's a Moor Hammer?" asked Randy.

"Someone who hammers Moors," Brian said.

"Oh thanks. That explains everything," Randy returned.

"No, Brian's saying the simple truth of it," Terry said. "The Moors are Muslims, mostly. If you are known as someone who pounds on Muslims—"

"Okay, I get it," interrupted Randy. "Why didn't you say so?"

"I *did* say so," Brian objected.

"You know, Bishop Preston likes to bring up his ancestral connection to Prester John," Susan noted. "I think he might see his mission as continuing in his footsteps."

"Like a reincarnation?" asked Kat.

"Maybe, but not necessarily," Susan said. "You know how Bush Junior felt compelled to invade Iraq and defeat Saddam Hussein because Bush Senior hadn't finished the job? Maybe it's kind of like that."

"You're saying that Prester John pounded on the Muslims," Kat followed her reasoning, "but he didn't wipe them out. So, Bishop Preston wants to finish the job."

"Exactly," Susan said. "Perhaps it's part of some misguided desire to be faithful to his family heritage, to carry on the tradition, or to bring to completion a project that his supposed ancestor so fiercely desired."

"He may just consider it his Christian duty," Terry offered.

"Maybe," Susan conceded. "Either way, if he can get Ivory elected—"

"He'll have the might of the American military at his disposal to do it," Mikael finished.

Terry whistled.

"It's a good hypothesis," Brian noted, "but we don't have any *proof*.

We can't just act against such a wild notion, and besides, who would believe us?"

"That's never stopped us in the past," Terry smiled, and pinched Brian's leg.

"But we've never faced evil on this kind of...global scale, either," Susan said. "We're just a little group of...well, let's face it, religious..." she trailed off, searching for the word.

"Extremists?" suggested Randy. "Nut cases? Deviants? Fanatics? Cultists? Weirdos? How about 'unusualists'? That sounds kind."

Susan sighed, declining to finish the sentence. Randy had done that adequately.

"Look, this can't go anywhere," Kat said. "Even if Preston uses the Spear-magick-thingy, and the Republicans do elect Ivory as their presidential candidate, the Democrats are not going to just forgive and forget Dearborn. They're going to see Ivory as a dangerous person. There's no way he'll get elected."

"You're forgetting one thing," Felicia noted, running her finger around the rim of her coffee cup. "This nomination is not the only election Preston can control. If he prevails here, there's nothing stopping him from influencing the national election, too."

Kat's eyes widened.

"Wait, it goes beyond that," Mikael said. "The Spear is just a means to an end—getting into power. Once Ivory wins the presidency, he's still going to have access to the Spear." He paused to let them catch up with them. Eyes widened around the table.

"No one will be able to stop him," Brian breathed. "No one in the whole world. If he wants to wipe out Muslims..."

For a full minute, no one said anything. They stared into their cups or at the tabletop. Finally, Susan spoke. "So, we need evidence. We can't fight Preston and Ivory with force—we don't have any. The only way to win this is with information."

"I think you're all fucking delusional," Randy said. "Go to his office; put a spork through his chest. End of problem."

"Randy has a point," Susan said, looking sad.

"A spork is not what I would call an efficient weapon," Mikael complained.

"Dietrich Bonhoeffer was a Lutheran pastor during the Second World War who decided that the lesser evil was to assassinate Hitler," Susan said. "He wanted to stop the slaughter of the Jews. We're trying to stop the slaughter of another people. If we're right...Let's say we get evidence, and we're right. Isn't murder justified? One guilty life in exchange for millions of innocents?"

Brian brooded darkly as Terry's mouth dropped open. Terry shut it and shifted uncomfortably. "Abhorrent as that idea is, Susan, we can't not consider it."

"But wait," Mikael said. "Let's say we did try to kill him. How would we do that if the Spear repels all opposition?"

Brian, still looking grim, cleared his throat. "I can't say this absolutely, but the ancient sources say that its power has to be directed by intention."

"What do you mean, 'intention'?" Kat asked.

"I mean that the Spear probably doesn't have a will of its own," Brian explained. "I think it's a tool, like a hammer. A hammer is great at driving nails, but you have to pick it up and direct it to do that. Otherwise, the hammer just lies on the ground. The Spear is the same way. It isn't going to come to life and defend Preston from all comers. He has to pick it up and use it."

Kat nodded. Felicia looked at her hands. She shook her head. "Maybe it *is* justified, but I'm not prepared to go there. We have to remember love. We win with love."

"Are you fucking kidding me?" Randy said.

"Say more, Reverend," Terry asked.

"I think violence is the easy way out. If we sink to that level, then it isn't we who win, it's violence. Loving is harder. And I don't know how love can bring good out of this. I don't think the disciples had any idea, either, when Jesus went to the cross. I think the best we can do is trust that God can do it, and try to do everything with as much compassion as possible," Felicia explained.

"Well, we can try to have compassion on where Bishop Preston is coming from," Susan began in a tentative tone that said, *this is a thought experiment.* She continued, "I mean, what if he really is just doing what he thinks is right?"

"I don't think he's a good man," Felicia said. "In fact, I'm not sure that even *he* would say so. But I do think that, in his own mind at least, what he is doing makes sense—it's justified. He's trying to save the world—"

"By projecting the collective shadow of Western Civilization onto the Muslims?" Brian asked.

"Yes," Felicia said. "But the point is, we'll have a better chance of figuring out how he thinks if we sympathize with his driving motivations. We don't have to agree with him—I mean, none of us here thinks the problem is really Islam, right?" Heads shook all around the table—slowly, thoughtfully. "But if we understand why *he* thinks so, we'll be a step ahead."

"I agree," Terry said. "Jesus said that we should love our enemies, so if that doesn't start here, then we don't have any right calling ourselves Christians."

"Cult. My sister has fallen in with a fucking cult," Randy moaned.

Terry looked at Randy. Then he cocked his head. A smile began to spread across his elfin features.

"What's funny, Ter?" asked Mikael.

"I..." He looked around the table. "Yes. I have an idea." He turned to Felicia. "Can you get me in to see Bishop Preston? *Today*?"

"What are you thinking?" Mikael asked. "Preston's got to be crazy busy. He might have an opening sometime six months from now. What do you—"

Felicia held up her hand. Kat thought she looked small. "I'm ashamed to say that I nominated him for the job of bishop, from the floor, you know. He forced me to. He threatened me. But when I'd done it, he came up behind me and said, 'I owe you one.' I didn't think too much about that. But now...that's one favor I'll be glad to call in." She looked Terry in the eye. "You want in today? I'll get you in today. Now tell us your idea."

66

THE TRIP to the Islamic Cultural Center seemed long to Susan. She'd been there before, but only once. Intellectually, she knew that Oakland hadn't gotten any farther away than it was last week, but back then life had seemed a lot less complicated. Mikael seemed to be sleeping in the backseat. Brian drove grimly, silently. Susan touched his arm. "Worried about Terry?"

"Of course," he said.

"He'll be fine," she offered.

"He's walking into a dangerous situation alone," he said.

"No, he isn't," Susan said. "Jesus is as real to Terry as he is to me, or HaShem is to you. And Terry knows how to pray. This is a very good time to exercise our trust muscles."

"Trust muscles," Brian repeated, nodding. "So, speaking of Dylan, how are *your* trust muscles?"

"Jerk." Susan withdrew.

"I'm sorry," Brian said. "I'm half kidding. I didn't mean it...meanly." Coming to the end of Gilman Street, Brian took a left onto the I-80 on-ramp. "I know you looked in on him before we left. How is he?"

"Sleeping like a baby bear," she said, looking out the window as they got up to speed. "So, Brian, I have to tell you something. This allergy to medications that Dylan developed, well, overnight, it seems. He's not going to go down without a fight. He's an addict, and everyone knows it. He knows it. He's a long way from hitting bottom, and I'm scared for him. Before breakfast, I went through every pill bottle in the house and emptied them."

"You what?" Mikael called.

"Oh good, you need to know this because I emptied Kat's epilepsy medication, too," Susan said over her shoulder.

"Nice of you to tell us about it," Mikael said.

"I *am* telling you about it. Please tell Kat," Susan said, a little testily. "And nice of you to tell us that Kat is epileptic."

"Well...there's no reason to, really," Mikael said, a little defensively.

"Uh-huh. And when Kat and I are having tea and she begins flipping about on the floor like a landed trout, don't you think it would be good for me to have a clue as to what is going on?"

Mikael ignored the point. "So, what's Kat supposed to do about her meds?"

"There's a cookie jar shaped like a kangaroo in the high cupboard," Susan said.

"I hate that cookie jar," Brian scowled.

"Everything is in there, in snack baggies, labeled with a Sharpie."

"You *were* busy before breakfast," Brian said, merging over to Interstate 580.

"What? It only took ten minutes or so."

"Wait a minute," Mikael said, "I saw my pills in the bathroom just before we left."

"Nope," Susan said. "Those were white Good-N-Plenty's."

"Fucking brilliant," Brian smiled. "Let's hope Dylan isn't suddenly allergic to licorice."

"But Kat's pills are round," Mikael said.

"Altoids sprayed with antifungal foot powder," Susan said.

"Oh, that would do it," Mikael said, and laughed. He pulled out his cell phone. "Gotta text Kat about that."

Turning off at Fruitvale, Brian quickly navigated to the Islamic

Cultural Center. Street parking, however, proved difficult to find. "There's got to be a hundred people here," Susan said, taking in the scene. People were lined up out the door and down the sidewalk in front of the storefront meeting place.

"Yeah, pretty much as Nazim described it. He'll be grateful for the help," Brian said, scanning the block for parking. Three blocks down, he lucked out, spotting someone just pulling out of a parallel space. Soon they were walking back up to the cultural center.

"Uh, Susan, do you mind covering?" Brian asked.

"Of *course* I mind," Susan said, pulling a scarf out of her purse and winding it around her head.

"Thank you," Brian said, "and I'm sorry."

Needing to cover her head pissed her off momentarily, but as they drew near to the center, her anger morphed into shame. She wanted to avoid the eyes of the dark-haired women who watched them approach. She assumed they would be darting daggers at her, but when she met their eyes, no daggers were in evidence. Instead, she saw only grief. Worry and pain were there, too, and she instantly felt a mixture of rage and compassion.

Brian spoke briefly to the women at the front of the line, and they drew back, making room for them to pass. Inside, in a room that did triple duty as meeting hall, classroom, and mosque, Brian waved to his friend Nazim. Nazim waved back briefly and motioned them to a circle of chairs along one wall. Some of them were empty. Brian nodded and led Susan and Mikael to them.

Susan felt almost suffocated in the crowded room. The center had no windows, and the stark white walls and industrial carpeting gave her the distinct impression of being in a shipping container. *I feel like a can of Spam in here*, she thought.

A moment later, Nazim appeared, shaking his head and nodding in a way that must have meant something in his culture but didn't exactly translate for Americans. "My friends, I'm so glad you're here." He shook their hands, and Brian introduced them quickly. "It's been like this ever since the bombing," he said. "People just need to talk."

"What can we do for them?" Mikael asked, looking a little lost.

"Not a thing," Nazim, oddly, nodded. "I mean, materially or legally. All we can do is listen to them. And that is important. People are grieving, and they need someone to listen. If you want, you can pray with them. Here's a traditional Islamic prayer you can use." He pulled a few slips of paper out of his shirt pocket and handed them to them. "Or you can pray extemporaneously. Just don't pray in Jesus's name. We love Jesus, peace be upon him, but it's not a prayer form that we use. It will confuse people."

"Of course," Susan said.

Mikael stared dumbly. "So, we just…listen?" he managed finally.

"Yes, just listen," Nazim said. "Muslims are just like anyone else. If they are hurting, it is only Allah who can heal them. It is Allah who is doing the real work here. You and I can only create the space for a person and Allah to approach one another, to touch each other, to kiss. That's what heals. Not us." He smiled. "That's what all ministers do, yes?"

"Yes," said Brian, shooting Mikael a look that said, *snap out of it.*

"But…I need a *plan*…" Mikael protested. He looked like he was going to panic.

Mikael was having a very hard time, Susan could see. She placed her hand on his neck and pulled him down so that their heads were touching. "Trust. You don't need to be powerful here, Mikael. God is powerful. Just sit with them, and trust that God can do what needs to be done. Trust muscles."

"Trust muscles," he repeated. He seemed to relax, but Nazim looked concerned. "Mikael, why don't you watch Brian for the first couple of meetings? When you feel ready, you can move over to that corner over there." He indicated two chairs set up near a back door. "How does that sound?"

Mikael nodded, relieved to have a model. Brian clapped him on the arm, and Nazim led them to a small cluster of chairs and waved a man and his son over to them. Then Nazim led Susan to a dark-haired older woman just getting up from a meeting. "Raja, this is Susan. She's going to take the next shift."

"Oh, that is very good. Pleased to meet you, Susan," the older woman said. "Thank you for coming down."

"I'm just glad I can help," Susan said with a sad smile. The woman bowed slightly and headed toward the door, sunshine, fresh air, and a much-needed break.

Susan sat down and arranged her skirt so that it hung properly. Then she waved at the door, and a middle-aged woman wearing Western dress with a simple colorful hijab sat down next to her.

The woman had been crying. Susan moved a box of tissues within easy reach. "I'm Susan," she said. "Please tell me your name."

"I am Shifa," the woman said. "Are you Muslim?"

Susan shook her head. "I'm a Christian, but I believe that the God of Jesus and the God of Muhammad—peace be upon them—are the same God. I want to help. I'm so sorry about what happened in Michigan."

The woman met Susan's eyes and held them. *Is she deciding whether or not to trust me?* Susan wondered. She guessed that she was. Finally, the woman looked down and said, "My brother and his wife live near there."

"Were they hurt?" Susan asked.

The woman shook her head, but then she started to cry. "No, Allah be praised. But they have to drive into town almost every day. They might have—" she choked on her words. "If it was another time of day…if it were another day…" She didn't finish her sentence. She didn't have to.

Susan felt grateful that she didn't have the restrictions on touching that the men had. She reached out and took Shifa's hand and held it in both of her own. "Thank God," she breathed. "Have you been able to talk to them?"

The woman nodded. "Yes. Last night, I was able to get a call through. The cell phones are…overloaded, I think. But this morning, nothing. The phones ring, but no one answers." She looked up at Susan, panic beginning to tighten her face. "Is it true, what they are saying?"

Susan drew back a tiny bit, not comprehending. "Is what true? I don't *know* what they're saying."

"Is it true about the concentration camps?" Shifa said, her eyes like daggers.

Susan gasped and drew her hand up to her mouth. She didn't know, of course, and yet inside, she knew. A part of her knew that it was true. It had to be true. Oh sure, they wouldn't call them that. They would call them "relief encampments," or "detention facilities," or some other euphemistic nonsense. It would be "for their own protection," or "for the treatment of those physically or psychologically damaged by the blast," but only Muslims would be treated there.

She knew it was true. She knew it in her bones.

67

TERRY FIDGETED in his seat as he waited outside Bishop Preston's office. He'd been careful to put on a clean summer cassock. His stiff, wiry hair—the genetic gift of his Japanese father—required little attention. Yet his obsessive perfectionist streak made it difficult to relax. His mind raced through endless interior checklists. Was his nose clean? It was; he'd just checked in the bathroom mirror. Did he have to pee? He did not. Did he look fabulous? He did.

Nervously, he unconsciously fingered the frayed edge of the large art portfolio he carried with him. He checked his shoulder bag—a manila envelope containing the order's rule was there, freshly laser printed and up to date. He sighed deeply, willing himself to relax. His leg bounced.

Across from him was the desk of the bishop's secretary. She was in young middle age, with short-cropped hair and glasses that hung from straps—but the way she dressed, they were definitely in the sexy-retro-chic category. There was nothing school-marmy about her.

Terry remembered back to the last time he had been in this office. The previous Bishop of California had called the friars in to consult with them on a possession case. Terry counted back and realized that it was about three years ago, though that hardly seemed possible. In his mind's eye, he surveyed the bishop's office as he remembered it— the high ceiling, the spaciousness, the enormous oak desk in the middle of the room. He recalled the bookshelves lining the walls to the left of the desk, and the mirror hanging on the wall to the right next to two small oil paintings from the workshop of Cranach the Elder.

A phone buzzed on the secretary's desk. She picked it up, listened, and said, "Right away." She placed the phone back in the cradle and looked up at Terry with a tight, professional smile. "You can go right in," she said, waving toward the door. Terry stood, exhaled deeply, and picked up the portfolio. In a couple of strides, he was at the door. He turned the knob and swung it open.

A great wave of relief washed over him when he saw the room. Everything was exactly as he remembered. He was sure that the books on the shelves had changed, but that didn't matter. What mattered was the fact that the desk was where it was, a computer was on it, and the mirror hung right where it was supposed to be. A thrill of confidence arose in him, and in his head he said a short prayer. *Okay, Jesus. Help me lie like I've never lied before.*

The bishop looked up from his desk. He seemed unimpressed by what he saw and looked back down at his papers. "Please have a seat," he said, his Southern drawl immediately apparent. "You're a friend of Reverend Dunne's, I hear? She was quite insistent that I see you today."

"Yes, your grace," Terry said, making his way over to one of the low chairs positioned just in front of the desk. He set the art portfolio down so that it leaned against the chair.

"Well, sit down, sit down," the bishop said with a slightly irritated edge to his voice. "I don't have much time. I'm speaking at the Republican National Convention. Did you know that?" He looked up at Terry, his smile every bit like the cat that ate the canary.

Terry filed this away as useful information. The good bishop had a sizeable ego—that was clear. "No, I didn't know that," he said.

"Not surprised. It was just announced this morning," Preston said.

"So, I'm scrambling to get my speech together." He put his papers aside and sat back in his chair. "What can I do for you?"

"I don't know how much Felicia told you, but I'm with the Old Catholic Order of Saint Raphael. We're the exorcists."

"You say that as if I should have heard of you," the bishop scowled.

"Well...I'm sorry, I know you're new to the Diocese of California." Terry pulled out the manila folder, flipped past the Rule, and placed a stack of papers on the bishop's desk. "Those are invoices for the last fifty exorcisms that we've performed on behalf of the diocese. We've got another stack for the Roman Catholic Diocese of Oakland, the Roman Catholic Archdiocese of San Francisco, and in fact, every Roman and Episcopal diocese in California, Nevada, and Oregon."

The bishop picked up the invoices and flipped through them. "You've been busy," he said, sounding impressed.

Terry nodded. "The Enemy is busy, so we're busy."

"Hmph...that's not a popular position in the Episcopal Church these days," the bishop noted.

"No..." agreed Terry. "We don't get invited to Christmas parties much. But when one of your rectors has a parishioner on their hands that's levitating and throwing up pea soup, they don't usually hesitate to call us."

"I like your style..." Bishop Preston searched his memory.

"Father Milne. Terry," Terry supplied his name.

"Father Milne. I like your style." The bishop threw the stack of papers back within Terry's reach. "I still have no idea why you're here. *And* I have a speech to write."

"Of course," Terry said, scooting forward on his seat, his feet barely able to touch the floor. "About a week ago our bishop died. Car accident."

"I'm sorry, young man." Preston's eyebrows lowered sympathetically.

"I'm sure you can see where this is going. No bishop, no connection to the apostolic succession. No power over demons."

"Ah..." Preston leaned forward on his desk.

"I've come to request emergency oversight until we can find a new bishop. As you know, there's always been a history of fruitful collaboration between Anglicans and Old Catholics. I'm here to beg your grace to honor that long tradition of collaboration now, as a temporary measure until we can, well, sort things out."

Bishop Preston leaned back in his chair and tapped his sideburn with his index finger as he rocked back and forth. His face drew up in a scowl as he considered. But before he could speak, what sounded like a fire alarm painfully pierced the air.

Terry glanced at the clock—10:45 a.m., right on target. The slightest curl of a smile played on his lips as the bishop's secretary burst through the door. "Bishop, there's been a bomb threat. This way, quickly!"

Looking momentarily flustered, Preston snatched at the legal pads in front of him—the notes for his precious speech, Terry was sure—and raced toward the door. Suddenly, Terry was invisible, which was just fine with him. If Terry was right, the secretary would escort Preston down the stairs to the street where a limo would arrive in mere moments to whisk him off to safety.

Terry knew that soon a security guard would sweep through the building to make sure everyone was out, so as soon as the bishop and his secretary were out of sight, he sprang into action. As quick as a cat, Terry snatched open the art portfolio and pulled forth the ornamental mirror in which Kat's brother Randy was resident. Racing to the wall on the right side of the room, he removed the mirror hanging there and hung Randy's mirror in its place. He noted that the mirror itself was smaller than the one he removed, but the frame was larger, and it hung in felicitous relation to the Cranach paintings much as the other had done.

He quickly placed the bishop's mirror in the art portfolio, waved a quick goodbye to Randy, and, picking up the portfolio, strode confidently toward the waiting room, the stairs, and the street below.

68

RICHARD PASSED the morning in dread. The shackle attached to his ankle didn't allow him access to a chair, so the dusty floor of the barn was his only option. His bones creaked, and his spine was sore. Worse yet, the shackle had worn through the skin, and a crusty, swollen ring had formed around his ankle, oozing a sticky yellow pus.

He looked over to the workbench against the far wall where his wallet and his phone sat, far out of reach. He willed them to jump to his hands. They didn't. "Duunel, make them fly over here," he whispered.

You have far too high an opinion of my abilities. I can make them fly, all right, but aim is quite another matter, Duunel said, sounding bored. *I can try, but the great likelihood is that your phone will just end up smashed, in another corner of the room, but equally out of reach.*

Richard blinked back self-pity. He bit back on panic. And he nearly jumped through his skin when he heard the chain on the outside of the door rattle. Gabe ambled in, his eyes wide. He seemed to be drooling. He was also carrying a tire iron, which he swung from his primatial arm in a suggestive, menacing way.

Once inside, the giant closed the barn door and turned back to face Richard. "I wanna see you *naked*," he said. He was leering. He was also sporting a boner that was clearly visible through his overalls.

"I love Sarah, but she's not fair. She keeps all the fellers for herself. But today I am a lucky boy 'cause I always liked you best," Gabe said, coming closer, grinning in a weirdly obsessive way, unable to take his eyes off Richard.

"Duunel, throw him," Richard whispered. But there was no reply. "Duunel!" Silence. "Duunel, you asshole, don't you dare skip out on me!"

"Who's Dunnel?" Gabe asked, looking around. "Is there someone else here?"

"Apparently not," Richard said, seething and tipping over into despair.

"Good, 'cause I want you a-a-a-a-a-a-ll to myself. You gonna take your pants off, now. I wanna see your bottom," Gabe slipped one shoulder out from under an overall strap. Then he pulled the other strap off his shoulder and dropped his overalls altogether.

Richard stared, his eyes widening in disbelief. Gabe wore no underwear, and clad only in an extra-large T-shirt bearing the logo of Disney's Mighty Ducks, he advanced. Swaying like a giant bobble-head in painfully slow motion, Gabe's cock protruded a full fifteen inches beyond his drooping belly, thick as Richard's wrist, and twisted midway at what looked like a painful angle.

"Gabe, have you ever done this before?" Richard asked, clutching at any stray strand of thought that might help. "'Cause I have, and you can get diseases from people who do this a lot."

"Sarah said you'd try to talk me out of it," Gabe said. "Sarah is smart. How did she know you'd try to talk me out of it?" It was rhetorical. His face was shining with lust and anticipation. "Show me your bottom. Show me your bottom, *now*." It was a command that brooked no dissent.

The row of corpses on the bench seemed to be leering at him with their eye sockets, their skeletal grins vaguely mocking. Clearly, they were enjoying the show. Slowly, with hesitant, deliberate motions, Richard opened the flaps on his cassock and laid it aside.

Then he undid his belt, and dropped his black jeans around his ankles.

"Now do your unnerwear," Gabe said, unable to take his eyes off Richard's ass.

"Do you have any lube?" Richard asked. *If I have to bend over for this monstrosity, so be it*, he thought to himself. *But the best-case scenario here is an anal fissure, while the worst is a septic tear in my intestines. Minimize the damage.*

"What's loob?" Gabe asked. "Is this a trick?"

"No, it makes it feel better. For both of us." *Well, that was true*, he thought. "Your dick is way too big for my little hole. If you try to stick it in without any grease, you'll get hurt." *So will I, but I don't need to tell him that.*

"Is that for real?" Gabe asked, his massive boner still impossibly indicating true north.

"Look, I've done this before. Lots. You haven't. I'm trying to help you out. Really." And strangely, that was true. "Do you have any grease in this garage?"

Gabe looked around. "Yeah. Fer workin' on engines and such."

"That'll do just fine," Richard said. "Just grease up your pole good and thick before you stick it in."

Gabe shuffled over to a workbench against one wall, and looked under several piles of detritus. Finally, he turned away from the bench, a soiled can in one hand. His cock bobbed in slow motion as he walked back toward him.

"Goddammit, Duunel," Richard whispered through his teeth. "Now. Goddammit now!" But nothing happened. Gabe came near, raised the crowbar, and Richard lowered his briefs.

He watched with mounting panic as Gabe greased up his impossibly long cock with a brown, grainy engine grease. He raised the crowbar again, and Richard got on all fours, willing himself not to whimper at the thought of the pain that was about to hit him.

Through his legs, just below his own dangling junk, Richard saw Gabe's cock cut through the air like a cruel smile—no, a cruel smirk. A drop of pre-cum was already beading at its tip.

A frantic prayer to Duunel flashed through his mind, *My demon, my demon, why have you abandoned me?* Richard squeezed his eyes closed as he felt Gabe's rough hand paw at his butt. Gabe was shaking with excitement and anticipation as he fondled his testicles and grabbed at Richard's penis, limp as a salamander.

Richard gritted his teeth, waiting for the white-hot pain of penetration when he heard a groan behind him, and felt wet, hot spurts of cum lighting on his rump and running down his leg.

Richard laughed with relief and offered up a wordless prayer of grateful thanks. Rolling onto his side, he looked up at the panting giant still poised above him. "Don't worry about it, sport," Richard said, trying to sound comforting and casual; trying *not* to sound like he was about to break down into a sobbing, humiliated mass. "You just got too excited. You'll do better next time. It happens to the best of us."

69

KAT SAT BACK with a feeling of triumph. Terry had asked for an untraceable bomb threat, and she had delivered it right on time. But she had taken liberties. She assumed that Terry had meant "untraceable back to us." He didn't say anything about it being traceable to anyone else—like, for instance, a lodge of black magickians in San Francisco. She wondered how quickly the SFPD would decode her web of misdirection, and at what time they would be pounding on the door of the Lodge of the Hawk and Serpent. She couldn't stop the smile from spreading across her face. She didn't try.

She cracked her fingers and wheeled in a circle in her chair, looking out the tiny window that graced the office. She momentarily worried about Randy. He had impressed her with his willingness to cooperate with Terry's plan. She was proud of him. She thought back to their childhood together, how he had begun retreating into himself after their father had died. Her mother, working so hard that she nearly collapsed, didn't notice. And they had both turned to magick.

Her daydreaming was interrupted by the ding of an email alert. She swung around to the computer and clicked on the incoming message. It was from Randy.

"In like Flynn," he wrote tersely. "All according to plan. Nice office. Sucky computer."

Kat let out a huge sigh. She felt the tension drain out of her arms and took a few deep breaths. Good news. Very, very good news.

She grabbed her teacup and made her way back to the kitchen to heat the kettle. While waiting for it to boil, she stood in the doorway gazing into the Montague Summers Memorial Chapel. Looking at the spot where Terry had so recently taught her and Charlie, she felt a heaviness come over her that cancelled out her elation. That was the spot where Charlie had entered Hell.

She walked into the chapel and sat down in the choir, facing the patchwork Jesus icon. Made up of hundreds of photos clipped from magazines, it was a beautiful monstrosity. "Does he have to stay there?" she asked Jesus. "It doesn't seem fair."

The lips of the patchwork Jesus looked like they wanted to move. They also looked like they needed a good shave. *He looks like Chia Jesus*, she thought. But if she let her eyes go a little out of focus, he seemed to get clearer. *Very strange.*

"You scare the shit out of me," she said. "And partly it's because you aren't scary. And I don't really understand that. If you *were* scary, it would make sense, and in a way, you'd be *less* scary. But the fact that you *aren't* scary *is* scary. Does that make any sense?" She unfocused her eyes and moved her head up and down, so that it looked like Jesus was nodding.

"I know you didn't send Charlie to Hell," she continued. "In fact, I think it's really, really cool how you went there and ripped down the gates, and broke all the locks, and led all those people to freedom..." A feeling of deep love welled up in her, and she blinked back tears. "Wow. Okay, that was huge. That's why you let yourself be killed, isn't it? You didn't die to send anyone to Hell but to bust the place up, to break everyone out." She nodded through her tears. The patchwork Jesus became even blurrier, and paradoxically, more clear. "Charlie isn't there because of you. He's there because of *him*. Because he likes it there. Because he's...happy." Her chest filled up with—what? Pity?

Sadness? Remorse? She wasn't sure. "Why am I not okay with that?" she asked, but the patchwork Jesus didn't answer.

She sighed, not quite ready to give up on Charlie. To abandon him to Hell would feel an awful lot like failure. But something else was nagging at her, something on the very edge of her consciousness. What was it?

Charlie was a magickian, but she didn't feel a lot of shame about that. It was Charlie's shame, not hers. But Randy was her brother. He was a magickian, too, and she *did* feel shame about that. Somehow, his stupidity reflected poorly on her. On the other hand, she knew Randy thought she had turned into a religious lunatic. She knew that wasn't true, but she understood how it might seem so to him. There was the possibility that she understood him imperfectly, too. In fact, it was likely. Were they somehow even?

She wouldn't have thought that magickians were shameful before she joined the order. She hadn't seen them as being very different from witches. Since then, however, she had come face to face with the dark forces that magickians summon and presume to control—often to their own destruction. The magnitude of their stupidity simply baffled her. What they were doing seemed like kids playing with roadside bomb materials—they have no idea what they're doing, but they're playing nonetheless with powers of almost limitless destruction. She shuddered at the thought of it.

She felt responsible for Randy. She felt that it was somehow her duty to make his wrong right; to make up for his bad karma with good karma of her own—even though she knew that karma was not really a Christian thing. Just then, the connection that had been hovering just out of consciousness popped into view. She sat up straight as a rod.

Her connection to Randy was like Preston's connection to Prester John. She cocked her head and considered the two relationships. Prester John hadn't finished his job of destroying the Moors. He inspired Preston, but he had also failed. Just as it was her job to make good on Randy's failure, she saw that Bishop Preston felt compelled to make good on his relative's. For a moment, she felt a fleeting sense of kinship with the bishop. She understood him in a way that, mere moments before, had been mysterious to her.

A thought occurred to her, and she beat it back, but it was too late. As much as she wanted to unthink it, she couldn't. And now that it had been thought, she knew that she would do it. She knew she would worry about it, and agonize about it, and try to talk herself out of it, but in her gut she knew that, after all of that internal wrestling, she would do it.

And so, she dispensed with the agonizing and went straight to the doing of it. She looked the patchwork Jesus square in the eyes and repeated the words she had heard from Susan, "If you're going to sin, sin boldly." Quickly, she made her preparations. She took the kettle off the stove. She went to pee. She ate a couple of cubes of cheese. Then she locked the front door and returned to the chapel.

Settling down on a zafu, she relaxed, closed her eyes, and visualized the Void opening up before her. The cat's eye opening materialized quickly, shimmering brightly. With an agility and efficiency that surprised her, she stepped inside and onto the hot, dry desert plain.

As before, she noted the bundles of what looked like tumbleweeds, but which she now knew to be spirits, bound for unthinkable stretches of time. Were they conscious in their suspended animations? She certainly hoped not. She could think of few things more cruel.

After about fifteen minutes of walking, she felt a presence behind her. She looked over her shoulder and saw the arched, furry figure of a Sandalphon looming up behind her. Was this one of the same creatures they had encountered last time? It was impossible to tell. She suddenly flashed on what they reminded her of. "Aunt Beast," she said out loud, bowing to the approaching Sandalphon. "You remind me of Aunt Beast, from *A Wrinkle in Time*." The Sandalphon slowed as it drew near, weight shifting on its large, lumbering legs. It didn't seem to mind the comparison to the fictional creature. "I shall call *you* Aunt Beast," she said. The Sandalphon said nothing.

Kat felt a momentary flash of shame. She hadn't run this idea by any of the others. In fact, she wasn't entirely sure what she was hoping to accomplish. The Sandalphon had every right to stop her, yet it was not barring her way. It was just there, hovering, perhaps guarding.

So, she turned and resumed her march. "C'mon, Aunt Beast," she said over her shoulder. "We have miles to go."

After nearly an hour of walking, she saw Aunt Beast recede. She turned to see the great protective creature standing still. It bowed slightly to her, then turned and walked away. Kat was sad to see her go. But she knew what it meant. She had arrived.

Turning again, she marched on, and watched with awe as the Abyss came into view. She called for Abaddon and fought down the nervous butterflies in her stomach as the great hand lowered until it was level with the ground she stood on. She stepped off the cliff and into the soft safety of the floating palm.

"Abaddon," she spoke loudly, boldly, despite the quiver in her voice. "Take me to Prester John."

70

LARCH TRUDGED BACK to the Lower Haight under a considerable cloud. A homeless man approached him with hand outstretched but drew back reflexively after catching sight of his caustic glower. Larch dug his hands deep into the pockets of his coat, balled into little fists of frustration.

The city was noisy, alive, and foggy—so typically San Francisco. Larch passed boho kids, mothers pushing Humvee-style strollers, business people on their cell phones, and the occasional stray dog. He navigated them, but he didn't see them. He was lost in a confusing mixture of self-pity, panic, and uncertainty.

Getting his ersatz army away from the house had been a close call. He didn't really have that much respect for the gray matter of the men in blue, but it wouldn't take a genius to link a loitering horde in the East Bay to a loitering horde in the City. It had been a fire. He had put it out. The real question on his mind, though, was *what to do with them?*

Pim had suggested that he "protect the savior of the world"—of course he had no idea who that might be. He could ask her, but he knew better than to expect a straight answer from a spirit. He'd only get a couple of paragraphs of nonsense that would take days to decipher, if he ever did.

He sighed. Why couldn't the spirits just talk like normal people? They *weren't* normal people, of course. He suspected Pim was a demon, in fact, but he wasn't at all sure. If she were, she was the sexiest damned demon he had ever laid eyes on—all leg and bangs and turned-up nose, and blessedly free of tentacles or spines or beaks or other normally demonic ornamentation.

For all of her inscrutability, however, Larch still felt tremendously privileged. Out of the hundreds of greasy-haired, bodily odiferous, socially inept magickians in the world, she had chosen *him*. And she had placed him at the head of the largest army of the damned he had ever heard of—and growing larger by the minute. So yes, he felt special. He just didn't know what to *do* with the gift.

He had felt so elated to have liberated the Urim and Thummim from the glass-enclosed uselessness that was the fate of any artifact in a museum. At least in the hands of working magickians the stones would be active and useful. He recalled the indignity the stones had suffered just last night at the hands of his lodge mates, but he pushed the thought away. That was a result of his lack of diligence. It would not happen again. Thrusting his hand deeper into his coat pocket he felt at the velvet bag where they rested safely. The fact was, the stones would be "happier" if they were being used. He contemplated the relative happiness of inanimate objects for a moment.

As he did so, he almost ran into a police car. The lights were flashing, and as Larch looked up from the ground, where his eyes had been so firmly fastened, he saw that there were, in fact, several police cars. About twelve of them, in fact. And a SWAT van as well. All of them gathered around the decrepit Victorian that the lodge called its home.

Panic rising in his throat like bile, Larch began to back away. *Look natural, look natural!* he commanded himself, hands still in pockets. He chose another direction at random and began heading west toward Oak and Fell streets. His heart was pumping in his chest, so loudly that he was sure the cops could hear it.

He heard bullhorns commanding his lodge mates to surrender peacefully, to come out with their hands up. His hair stood on end as he heard the sound of a tear gas gun shatter the windows on the upper floors.

Oh shit, oh shit, oh shit, oh shit, he said to himself until he was able to put a full block of buildings between himself and the lodge. Once he had, he willed himself to relax. He nearly jumped out of his skin, however, when his cell phone buzzed to alert him to a new email.

Larch did not give out his email address liberally, and he scowled as he studied the address. He did not recognize it. Was this a trap? It had to be. But he couldn't help himself, either. He was curious. It might be important information about what was happening at the lodge. It might be a warning from one of his lodge mates who had recently changed his email address but neglected to inform him of it.

In other circumstances, he might have been able to think it through carefully. But he was off his guard, and he knew it. He punched at the new message and read it as an icy sensation crept down his back. It read,

To: Stanis Larch

From: Randall Webber

Subject: Have I got a surprise for you...

Larch, I'm alive and living in a mirror (don't ask). My sister has been brainwashed by a bunch of fanatics calling themselves the Berkeley Blackfriars.

But here's the crazy thing: They have located the Spear of Destiny. In my opinion, something this important should not be in the hands of religious freaks—and believe me, they are freaks. This is no hoax. This is the real Spear. And I can tell you exactly where it is...

71

GABE TOOK off his big straw hat, the one with the very wide brim. He looked up at the hot noon sun and wiped the sweat off his forehead with the back of his forearm. He surveyed his work. Sarah would be pleased. A couple of hours ago she had sent him out to repair one of the fences, and now he was nearly done.

It was a neat job—he could see that. *Even Daddy will be happy*, he thought. Replacing his big hat, he thought back to his exciting encounter with the new reverend. On the one hand, he felt a little ashamed that he had spurted out before he'd really gotten close to the reverend. He wanted *more*, but afterward he didn't seem to have more in him.

Yet he was not overwhelmed by the shame. It was more embarrassing than anything else. It had also been exciting. As he clipped wire, he remembered the pale white roundness of Richard's bottom, the way that the wisps of black hair peeked out from where his cheeks fit together. When he remembered the sight of Richard's dangling scrotum, he felt dizzy. He had to stop and catch his breath.

He heard a bark. He looked up but didn't see anything. He bent back down and, drawing a hammer from his tool belt, fastened a pin to keep the wire fence in place. At the sound of another bark, he held his breath, and his head snapped up.

"A dog..." he breathed. He *loved* dogs. There was almost nothing as much fun as dogs. He ambled out to the drive and in a few moments he saw a large, reddish-yellow dog trot up the road, pausing every few yards to sniff. When he saw Gabe, his tail wagged, and he rushed up eagerly.

The dog's nose worked furiously as he snorted at Gabe's clothing, his shoes, his hands. Gabe's heart leaped with excitement, even joy. "Hey, feller, what's your name?" Gabe asked. "I am Gabe." He stroked the fur on the dog's back, and took hold of his collar. He squinted at the collar, but it didn't make any difference. There was a tag there, but Gabe couldn't read. He would ask Sarah when they got back to the house—maybe it would tell them the dog's name.

Gabe reached into a little leather bag of materials and pulled out a thin spool of wire. He fashioned a makeshift leash from it and quickly finished fastening the last few feet of wire to the fence post. Then he gathered his tools and led the big reddish yellow dog back to the house.

As they were walking, Sarah passed them in her car, coming home from the store. She parked in her usual spot near the barn and clutching at one large grocery bag, walked briskly up to the house.

Gabe and the new dog were waiting for her on the porch. "I found me a dog, Sarah."

"I see that. What's his name?"

"I don't know. He has a tag, though."

"Okay, let's get inside, and I'll take a look. Hold this." She dumped the grocery bag in Gabe's free arm and unlocked the door. She swung it open, and Gabe and the dog followed her inside. The dog followed her movements as she hung her key ring on a hook beside the door.

"Put that in the kitchen, Gabe."

When he came back into the living room, Sarah was on one knee, studying the tags. "He's from Berkeley," she said. "He's a long way from home. His name is...Tobias. That's a strange name."

"Hey, Mama, Daddy," Gabe said to his parents, who leaned in toward each other on the couch, "I gots me a new dog."

They received the news stoically, but Sarah stood up and faced Gabe with her hands on her hips. "Is he going to last any longer than the last one?"

Gabe looked from side to side but said nothing.

"Just be sure to put down a tarp. Momma will bean you if you get blood on her Persian carpet again." Sarah yawned and put the back of her hand up to her mouth. "That sun was gettin' to me. I need to go lie down a bit."

"Okay, Sarah," Gabe said. "I'm gonna go get my toys." She nodded and headed toward the hallway to her bedroom. Gabe heard her bedroom door shut. "Now you stay right there, and don't you dare eat none of Mama or Daddy," Gabe scolded. The dog's ears lowered. "I'm gonna be right back. I'm gonna bring some toys, and we're gonna have us some fun."

He lumbered toward the hallway to his own room, wondering where he had left the tarp.

As soon as Gabe was out of sight, Tobias whirled about and faced the ring of keys. The angel knew it was too high for the dog to grasp cleanly, but he instructed Tobias to try. The dog leaped at the ring, snapping at it with his teeth. The keys rattled but did not fall free. Tobias leaped again—this time his lips pushed the key ring up and off the hook, but his upper lip got caught on the hook on the way down. The weight of the dog tore the hook through the flesh of his lip, and the angel stifled the dog's scream of pain.

Blood was gushing everywhere, but the angel asserted control with an iron hand. He instructed Tobias to pick up the keys in the very mouth that was raging pain. The dog whimpered but complied. Then rearing up on his hind legs, the angel used the dog's inefficient paws to turn the door handle. Having opened the door a crack,

Tobias forced his nose into it and burst from the house into the yard like a bullet.

He paused to sniff at the air, then at the ground. Despite the pain in his lip, Tobias's tail began to wag furiously as he picked up the scent. He followed it in a beeline to the barn.

"YOU'RE AN ASSHOLE," Richard said bitterly to Duunel now that the demon had deigned to reappear.

I've been called worse, Duunel said coolly.

Richard fought down the bright red rage that filled his brain and reminded himself that he was talking about a *demon*, here. *Of course* Duunel was an asshole. In demon terms, that was tantamount to saying that he was a stand-up guy.

"I hate your fucking guts," Richard said, arms crossed.

Someone is pouting.

"I would *never* have abandoned you like that," Richard spat bitterly.

That's because you are an idiot with no talent for self-preservation, Duunel replied. *You don't make it several thousand years like I have by cultivating sensitivity or loyalty or any of your other kumbaya virtues.*

"You're an asshole," Richard repeated. "And why are you even back? These seem like your kind of people. Why aren't you rushing out of me and into one of them? This little shop of horrors must seem like Disneyland to a demon."

Are you nuts? Duunel responded, finally taking the bait. *First of all, this is macabre, but it's small potatoes. You can only do so much harm to the Enemy on a little farm like this. It's self-indulgent. I'm a team player.*

"Could have fooled me," Richard said darkly.

Furthermore, who would I inhabit? Junior? He makes Lenny look like an intellectual giant. I'd tell him about the rabbits, but he'd need me to explain what rabbits even fucking are. And aside from my purely misanthropic mission, I'm in this for the quim. Do you think he ever gets any? He can't even manage to get his cock into your repulsive ass when it's handed to *him on a platter.* If disembodied voices could shudder, Duunel's did. *And what about the fucking black widow over there? Nothing doing. She* *likes cock even more than you do, and as you know, I do not swing that way.*

Richard picked at the crust surrounding his ankle. Its puffiness scared him. "I am not just going to sit here and wait to get my ass reamed out by fucking Igor."

I'm not stopping you, Duunel said testily. *Come up with a plan, and* *I'll support it.*

"Right. 'Cause you're a team player," Richard said.

Damn straight, said the demon in his head.

Just then, Richard heard a scratching at the barn door. A dog's whine pierced the quiet of the dim barn. "Oh great. Dogs now," he said, panic rising in him again. He began to cast around for anything he might use as a weapon. But there was nothing except for the metal shackle firmly attached to his own ankle. He imagined a ridiculous scenario where he stuck the iron band into the snapping jaws of an attacking dog with perfect aim. It broke the dog's teeth, and the dog retreated in pain.

"Like that would ever happen," Richard said, picturing the much more likely scenario of a large, slobbering Rottweiler trotting off with an assortment of Richard's torn-off limbs stuffed into its bulging cheeks like a chipmunk.

The dog had apparently given up on the door because the scratching stopped as quickly as it had begun. But Richard's head jerked to the right as he heard a mad scuffling at the side of the building. He squinted and saw a large dog squirming its way under a sizable gap between one of the boards and the dirt floor.

"Oh *Jesus,*" he said. It was a prayer.

A moment later, the dog was free, and it sprang like a tiger toward Richard. It was bleeding profusely, and its eyes were wild. As it came nearer, Richard could see the strawberry blond of the dog's fur, and caught an all too familiar scent of—

"Toby?" he called, his voice cracking in disbelief. The dog sprang on him, licking his entire face in great, slurping swaths of foam, spittle, and blood. Richard fell to the floor and hugged at the dog with both hands, bursting into relieved sobs at the sight of a friend.

As happy as Tobias seemed, he was also insistent. Greetings accomplished, the dog backed up and nosed something toward Richard in the dust. He sat up and snatched at whatever it was the dog was pushing at with his snout.

Keys.

Richard's eyes widened, and he clutched at Tobias's great red mane again, whispering, "Thank you, my friend." With shaking hands, Richard found the small key that fit the padlock on the iron shackle. It turned easily. Richard exhaled with extreme relief as the pressure around his swollen ankle was released and cool, healing air bathed the sopping wound.

Tobias sprang back toward the gap he had entered through, barking for Richard to follow. Richard started in that direction but reversed course, heading to the workbench where he snatched up his phone and wallet. He paused for just a moment, and his heart fell as he saw that his phone had been smashed. *Go! Go!* said the voice in his head. He turned and ran for the gap. "Go, Toby, I'm right behind you."

You'll never make it, Duunel said. The gaping jaws of the corpse grooms seemed poised for a scream of warning. The eyeless orbs of the reverend gazed on him with what could only be hopeless pity.

Richard forced himself to look away, and he consciously ignored the demon. Falling on his face, he wormed his way under the boards, scrabbling at the dirt until he was free in the blinding sun.

About five yards away was Sarah's Geo. Scrambling to his feet, Richard lunged for it, at the same time fumbling for the car key that would start it. The door, as he suspected in a rural area like this, was unlocked, and Toby leaped in as soon as he'd pulled it open. He jumped in after and had to make several attempts to fit the key into the ignition, his hands were shaking so.

The little engine roared to life, and Richard put the automatic into gear and gunned the engine. As he came around the corner of the barn, into full sight of the house, he slammed on the brakes. There, in the middle of the road, was Gabe, holding a shovel.

"Oh shit, oh shit, oh shit," Richard breathed.

Run him over, the demon said.

"Too late. I stopped." Richard cursed himself. Stopping was natural, after all. Every driving instinct he had was conditioned against running down pedestrians.

Do exactly as I say, Duunel commanded. *Get out of the car and lean against the door. Be cool.*

Richard was too panicked to have any ideas of his own. He obeyed. He unlatched the door and put one foot on the ground. He leaned against the open door frame.

Say, 'Hey, Gabe', Duunel ordered.

"Hey, Gabe," Richard said.

Smile, Duunel said.

Richard smiled.

"Whatcha doin' with my new dog, Reverend?" Gabe pointed at Tobias.

His lip is hurt real bad, Duunel said.

"His lip is hurt real bad," Richard said, cluing in to what Duunel was up to.

Sarah asked me to take him to the vet, Duunel prompted.

"Sarah asked me to take him to the vet," Richard parroted.

"I know the vet!" Gabe said. "His name is Doctor Duck. It's funny 'cause he's a animal doctor, and his name is Duck."

"Yeah, that's a riot," Richard agreed.

Don't ruin it with sarcasm, you idiot, Duunel warned. *You've got him in your pocket. Now just get him out of your way.*

"Hey, Gabe, you wanna go with me? After all, you know Doctor Duck and I don't."

"Yeah!" Gabe threw his shovel down and started to move toward the car. "I like Doctor Duck. A lot!"

"Great!" Richard said. He waved toward the other side of the car. "Hop in, and let's go."

Richard got back in the driver's seat. As soon as Gabe approached the passenger's side door, Richard pressed the accelerator to the floor and shot out of the drive in a pluming spray of dust and gravel.

72

As THEY GOT BACK in the car, Susan took shotgun. She sagged in her seat like a rag doll. Brian patted her knee. "Me, too, sister." She didn't have the energy to look behind her.

"Mikael, how are you doing?" she moaned.

Mikael didn't answer, so she mustered the energy to look over her shoulder. He looked like a dead spider, crumpled up in the backseat. He appeared to be already asleep. She turned back to face the front as Brian wheeled them about toward the freeway on-ramp.

"Did you hear the rumors?" Susan asked.

"About the concentration camps?" Brian said but then quickly added, "Oh, I'm sorry, you mean of course the *refugee* centers."

"Right."

"Only over and over and over again."

"Didn't that creep you out?" she asked.

"And made me so angry I couldn't see straight," he said. "Do you think that's real?"

She looked over at him but couldn't read anything except a driver's concentration. "Don't you?" she asked.

"I can't let myself believe it."

"That's how the Germans got through the Second World War, you know."

He nodded, and she saw his jaw tighten.

"I like Nazim," she said, deliberately choosing a lighter subject.

"I knew you would," Brian said. "We used to date, before I met Terry."

"I suspected as much," Susan smiled. "You have a...well, there's an energy between you."

"Yeah," Brian agreed. His smile was wistful and a little sad. "There's still a little bit of the old flame burning."

"Does Terry know?" she asked.

Brian shrugged. "It's never come up."

Susan nodded. "I know how that is. I sometimes wonder..." but she didn't finish the sentence.

"What?"

She shook her head. "Can you do me a huge favor?"

"Okay," he agreed.

"Can you swing by the house of that guy that I'm...well, trying to exorcise? It's time for his daily dose of whup-ass."

"Will that take long?"

"Five minutes," she promised.

"Really?" he looked at her with one eyebrow raised.

"Yeah. It's short," she said. "But if Luther's method is going to have any chance of working, it's got to be regular."

"You got it," he said, veering toward the Fifty-First Street off-ramp.

"Kat usually comes with me," Susan said, "but better to go without her than to miss a day."

Brian nodded. They traversed Berkeley in tired silence. A low but audible snore rose from the backseat. Susan felt the pressure of affection welling up in her for Mikael when she heard it, and she watched the cars and trees as they passed them with a detached interest.

She directed Brian to the house, and he quickly found a place to park a few houses away. "No need to get out, Honey," she said, opening the car door.

"You mean, 'Don't worry about me, I'm just going to face this demon by myself—be back in a minute'?" Brian reared back, giving her a withering eye. "Nothing doing. Sleeping Beauty here can guard the car, but *I'm* coming with you."

They heard a snort from behind them, and Mikael sat up. "Huh?" he said groggily.

"Thank you," Susan said, touching Brian's arm. "I know you're tired."

"Let's kick some demon ass."

"There's not much to it," she assured him.

"Good," he said. "Let's get it over with."

"Where are we?" asked Mikael.

"Mornin', beautiful. We're gonna do a quick exorcism," Brian said, looking at Mikael in the rearview mirror.

"I'm in," he said.

Together they walked to the house, and Susan knocked on the door. No one came. She knocked again, as Brian, hands behind his back, faced the street and waited patiently. Mikael rubbed at his eyes.

"Not home?" Brian asked.

"He's been home every day," she said, knocking a third time. "He knows I'm coming."

"Uh...Susan?" Brian said hesitantly.

"What?" she asked.

"Look," he said. She turned and followed the line of his finger. Small dark spots splashed the walkway up to the house.

Her brow furrowed as she walked over to the nearest splashes. She knelt down and examined them. "They're almost black."

Brian and Mikael joined her on their hands and knees. Brian spat on the sidewalk, and rubbed at one of the spots, resulting in a deep ochre smear.

"I think that's dried blood," he said.

73

WHEN DYLAN WOKE, his neck was throbbing. He downed another couple of pain pills from Susan's bottle and haltingly made his way downstairs. As he passed the chapel, he saw Kat sitting still, either in prayer or meditation. Respectfully, he tiptoed through and headed for the kitchen.

As he had hoped, a pot of coffee was still on the burner. It was, he realized, probably left over from breakfast. He swirled it around and gave it a sniff. Its viscosity was undeniable, its odor rank. He bobbed his head from side to side, equivocating—but he stopped such motions when his neck complained. "It'll do," he announced to no one in particular.

He reached for a mug and poured out the thick black sludge, topping it off with generous quantities of milk and sugar. He took a deep, satisfying quaff, savoring the rich beany stink of it, the acrid bite, the warm slimy coating moving down his throat. "Ain't nuthin' like coffee," he praised. He raised the cup for a second draft, then paused, wavering. With his other hand, he clutched at his gut, gasped, and fell over twitching.

74

THE HAND ASCENDED, so quickly that Kat lost balance and clung to the meat of the giant thumb for dear life. Panicked, she crawled toward the center of the palm for safety. Within moments, however, the ascent slowed and stopped. The hand brought itself level with a grassy field.

Cautiously, Kat stepped off onto the springy turf. She involuntarily grinned. The sun was bright, and a pleasant, fragrant breeze tugged at her hair. Wildflowers grew in patchy bursts of color over verdant, rolling hills. A copse of gnarled trees stood just ahead and to the left, but even these, rugged as they were, exploded in bright violet bloom.

For a timeless moment, Kat simply whirled in place, enchanted. She was sure that she'd seen places more beautiful sometime in her life, but she could not for the life of her remember *when*. She had no idea which direction to head, so she just headed *in*.

There was a spring chill in the air, a bit cooler than Berkeley's mild summers. Breathing in, Kat's nose tickled with the mingled scents of lilac, lavender, and rose, or something very like them.

Small animals scattered as she approached. Rabbits, she was sure, and birds, of course. It made her heart glad to see them. As she rounded the crest of a hill, she saw a deer in the distance pause with a mouthful of leaf. Then it turned away and resumed its meal.

After a while, she had to open the double breast of the cassock to let some air in. Her breathing was harder, and she realized she was more out of shape than she liked to think.

In her Wiccan training, she had been very good at visualization, but it was nothing like this. There was nothing imaginary about this. The grass beneath her feet was as real as any on Earth, and the sun shone with a brightness and clarity that rivaled any sunny day she could remember. Her body ached, too, as she walked. If she tripped on a rock, her feet hurt. "This is as real as Hell," she said out loud to herself.

After more than an hour of walking, she began looking around for a place to rest. One of the gnarled trees hovered above a smooth, grassy hill. She sat and stretched out her legs.

"*Assalamu 'alaykum*," said a voice.

Kat whirled her head about and saw a swarthy man about two yards away from her, leaning on a walking stick. He looked like he was about ten years older than her and was dressed like an extra in a performance of *The Arabian Nights* she'd seen at the Berkeley Rep.

Swallowing her surprise, Kat jumped to her feet and extended her hand. "I'm Kat," she said.

The man retreated, either offended or frightened by her gesture. She withdrew her hand and put it awkwardly behind her back. "Um...I'm still Kat," she informed him. Then it occurred to her that maybe the man didn't speak English. *Well, duh*, she said to herself. *He probably speaks Arabic.* The problem was, she didn't *know* any Arabic. *If only Brian were here*, she thought.

Realizing she was acting like something out of a cowboy and Indians movie, she put her hand on her chest and said, "Me Kat."

The man scowled at her uncertainly and took another step back.

Okay, striking out, here, she said to herself. "Can you take me to Prester John?" she asked.

"*Prest...*" the man repeated, puzzled. Then his eyes lit up. "Khan Jahn?"

She nodded, uncertain about that last phrase. But he clearly understood the name. A smile broke out over his face, and he nodded vigorously, gesturing with wild, looping movements that she didn't understand.

Continuing the circular arm motions, he turned and headed off in a straight line over the next hill.

"We're off to see the fucking wizard." Kat pursed her lips. Then she followed him.

The man didn't try to talk to her after that. He just walked. Every now and then he'd turn to make sure she was following. Then he'd smile and pick up the pace a bit. Kat thought her legs were tired *before*. But she still didn't mind. The countryside continued to be relentlessly beautiful.

As they passed through a copse of trees, she caught her first sight of buildings. As they drew nearer, she saw what appeared to be a medieval-style fortress built of sandy yellow stones. They were irregular and rough-hewn. The building was huge and at the same time squat and rambling.

As they approached a lovely carved archway, another man in Arabic dress stood solemnly by, holding a spear. He wasn't standing at attention, nor was he stiff like the guards outside Buckingham Palace. He was relaxed, but alert. As they approached, he shifted his spear from one hand to another and leaned against a pillar, watching.

Her guide began gesturing wildly again and speaking what sounded like Arabic. The man looked over her guide, for he was much taller, and gazed up and down. Kat had the distinct impression she was being checked out. She resisted the urge to glare. She heard the guide say the word "Khan," and the guard perked up. He nodded and waved the guide on.

The guide turned and bowed low to her with a bright smile. Then he walked past her, back to the road where they had come from. She realized he had gone out of his way to bring her here. Her heart filled with gratitude. The guard waved her toward him, and she followed.

This guy, too, had a dark complexion. *Not black but definitely well tanned*, she thought. His steps were confident, his strides long. Once again, Kat struggled to keep up. "No one walks slow here," she noted out loud. "Okay, got it."

The inside of the keep was made of the same rough yellow stone. A tall ceiling arched over a long hallway. Near the center of the walkway the stone was shiny and well worn. At the edges, where the stone floor met the crafted rock wall, it was dusty and dull.

They passed many dark wooden doors on either side, but the hallway was reasonably well lit from light pouring through long but narrow windows. She could see by looking out the windows that the walls were several feet thick, and also that they were not very far off the ground—in fact, the ground was *too* close. The hallway, she realized, must be cut into the ground, which made sense, as the rock and the surrounding air seemed unusually cool.

Soon they reached the end of the hall, which came to a dead end at a giant, bright aquamarine door. The guard held up his palm, which Kat took to be the universal symbol for "stay here" as he opened the door. She stayed.

A couple of moments later the great door swung inward, and the guard gestured to her again, this time to enter. Crossing the threshold, she discovered herself in a small antechamber, which seemed to be a waiting room. From a shadow, a short man, about Terry's height appeared.

"Are you Prester John?" Kat asked.

The man's dark eyes sparkled and he laughed. "No. I am his court magickian. I think you know something of this, yes?" He gave her a knowing look.

"Something of that...like that..." she agreed warily.

"I will bring you to the khan," he said. "But first some protocol—"

"How do you know English?" Kat asked, still wary.

"We have a lot of time here." The man's smile was large but not necessarily sincere. "Languages are a worthy pastime. And it's not as if your language is *hard*."

Kat had heard otherwise from non-native speakers, but she kept her peace.

"So, if you please, do not speak until the khan has spoken to you. When you enter his presence, you must curtsy."

"You must be joking," Kat said.

"Do ladies in your realm not show deference to their betters?" The man was curious.

"We have no betters," Kat said, trying to control her temper.

"Then you have no manners," he smiled again, but the mirth had gone from it.

"I think you're rude," she said.

"The feeling is entirely mutual," the man said. "Please come with me. Providing you promise to curtsy."

"Oh all right. I'll probably trip."

The man nodded and opened the door at the rear of the small chamber. Following him inside, Kat discovered a cheery blaze in a fireplace that was nearly as large as the room she and Mikael shared at the friary.

Staring into the fire was a giant of a man. He, too, was dark, but his eyes looked almost Asian, as if only one of his parents had been Asian, like Terry. His straight, stiff black hair was tinged with gray, and his cheeks bore more than one scar. His clothes, too, were Asian —a long golden robe hung to his feet, adorned with geometric designs embroidered in metallic green and purple threads.

"My khan," the magickian said. "I present to you...I'm sorry, I neglected to ask your name."

"Kat."

"That's it? Just Kat?"

"Oh all right. Kat Webber."

"May I present to you Kat Webber, who desires an audience with your highness." He whispered, "Curtsy."

Kat spread her cassock out and fumbled a one-footed bow. She knew it was pathetic, but the magickian seemed satisfied. He turned and walked toward a wall, where he seemed to disappear once again into shadow.

Ong Khan Toghrul turned to her and fixed her with fierce, cold eyes. When he spoke, his voice was that of a man who was used to being obeyed. "You may not *see* it. You may not *touch* it," he said, in heavily accented English. "You may not *hold* it. You may not *steal* it."

"Steal? What are you even talking about? Steal what?"

"The Graal."

Kat was taken aback. She had expected a polite if condescending, "Well, hello little girl, and what's your name?" which would have been irritating in its own right but a considerable cut above *this* opening volley. "What's a *grale*?" she asked.

"The Graal, the Graal!" he repeated testily. "The Holy Graal—pretend not that you are simple, woman, for it does not become you."

"Holy Grail? Like the Monty Python movie?" She was confused. She decided to roll with it and shrugged. "You know, I never clued in to what the big deal was about all that. I don't understand why saying 'ni' makes people giggle."

Prester John scowled at her, his fierce black eyebrows meeting and meshing in the center of his forehead. "Do you speak a riddle?"

"Nope. No riddles here." Kat fidgeted and pursed her lips, thinking to herself, *This is not off to a good start.*

"Your speech is coarse," the man pronounced, looking down on her. "Your attire is unbefitting—"

"What the hell is wrong with my *attire*?" Kat raised her voice.

"And your ends are obscure," he finished.

Kat cocked her head. "Come again? My ends are *fine*." She really had no idea what she meant by that, but since she was equally clueless what *he* had meant by it, she figured they were even.

But her response seemed to confuse the man. "You come from a rude country, and you know not how to *comport* yourself in the presence of royalty."

It was Kat's turn to furrow her brow. *What would Susan do?* she asked herself. And then she knew. "I know how to fucking comport myself just fine," she said. "And in the 'rude country' where I come from, guests are made to feel welcome. Where I come from, people are treated royally when they act royally. In the 'rude place' where I come from, women are given the same respect as *rude* men. In the 'rude place' where I live, people usually know a *friend* when they see one." She turned on her heel. "And you're an asshole," she said and strode toward the door she had just come through.

"Whither do you go?"

"Back to my *rude* fucking country." She waved her middle finger behind her and slammed the big aqua door with a booming thud that reverberated throughout the massive stone hall.

75

RICHARD GUNNED the engine whenever a straight patch of road appeared before him. He'd learned to slow down along the curves after Sarah's Geo nearly fishtailed into a stump, but his heart was still pounding and his adrenaline was still running high.

Tobias mostly kept to the wheel wells, apparently conscious of his center of gravity, and not keen to go careening to the floorboards. The thought flashed briefly through Richard's brain that this was the angel's caution, not Toby's, since the old Toby would be firmly in shotgun position with his tongue flapping in the breeze.

At last, Richard seemed to come to a major street, and he was able to really open it up. He felt himself relax as he was finally able to put some distance between himself and his captors.

He was just beginning to notice things again—like sunshine, beauty, trees, and wind—when a high-pitched whine intruded. Glancing in his rear-view mirror, he saw the flashing lights of a county sheriff blazing away, and all for him.

"Oh, freaking Christ-at-the-nipple!" he swore, resisting the urge to sink into sobs of despair. "Can you do something?" he asked Duunel.

What? You want me to throw him into the trees? Duunel responded.

"I don't know. I just want to get *away*," Richard said. "Can you scare him somehow?" But Duunel didn't reply. "Duunel! Duunel!!!" But the demon had apparently checked out. "Oh great," Richard said to himself out loud. "Abandoned. Again." He looked at Tobias. "What did I expect?"

A rap at the window made him jump. He rolled it down and attempted a smile. He failed. "What can I do for you, officer?"

"License and registration, please," the officer said. He wasn't wearing sunglasses, as Richard always expected cops to, but he *was* tall and portly. He had sandy hair and spotty red skin that still looked irritated from this morning's scrape with the razor.

Richard breathed a deep breath to steady himself as he fished for his wallet. Then he leaned over and opened the glove box. He wasn't sure if it was a good thing or not, but there was the registration, where normal, sane, non-parent-murdering folks also kept it.

He handed both to the officer, who took a couple of paces back to examine them. He stepped to the window again. "This is not your car, Mr. ...Kinney?"

"No," he said simply. What else could he say? Several scenarios raced through his brain, but the truth seemed like the path of least complication. Who knows, he might even help to catch a pair of serial-killing siblings.

"Do you have Miss Ecbatana's permission to be driving her car?" the officer asked.

"No, I don't," Richard said.

"Can you explain that?" the officer asked, looking sideways at him.

"Yes. I met Sarah at the truck stop, and she invited me to stay the night. When I got to her house, she showed me the corpses of her parents, which are posed in an upright position in her living room." He struggled to keep his voice tight, controlled, matter-of-fact. "There are eight other corpses in the barn. I believe that she and her little brother killed all of them. I was going to be the ninth, but I escaped. If you will allow me to open the door, I will show you the wound on my ankle from the shackle they used to restrain me. I escaped, and I stole Sarah's car."

The sheriff tapped Richard's driver's license a few times with his fingernails. "That's quite a story, mister," he said. "Can you prove any of that?"

"I mentioned the leg wound," Richard said. "It's hard to see how it could be caused by anything else."

"All right, open the door slowly, keep your hands where I can see them, and swing your legs to the pavement. Do it now," the officer said, drawing his weapon. Richard heard the click of the safety, and told himself to be calm, that the officer was just acting defensively.

Richard opened the door slowly, kept his hands up, and swung his feet out. Sitting sideways on the seat, he stuck his legs out in the air and slowly hiked up his cassock, revealing his ankles. His left ankle was purple, swollen, and crusty with yellow pus. The officer's face puckered with distaste.

"All right, you've proved your point. Stay there while I run your license," he said, and walked back to his car. Looking over his shoulder, Richard saw the sheriff speaking into a microphone and reading from his driver's license. He sighed. "Lord, you haven't let me down yet," he prayed. "Help me now."

Fuck the Lord, Duunel's voice said in his ear. *Here's the plan. I talk, you parrot. Got it?*

"Why should I trust *you*?" Richard said with mixed anger and desperation. "You keep skipping out on me—unlike the Lord."

Yes, but also unlike the Lord, I have actual, practical help, Duunel argued. *Just do what I say.*

"Where have you been?" Richard asked, not at all sure about Duunel's "plan."

Doing reconnaissance, Duunel answered. *Knowledge is power, and believe me, we have a lot of power in this situation.*

"Like what?" Richard wanted to know.

You'll just have to trust me. Say what I say.

"What if he doesn't like what I say?" Richard asked.

The way I see it, once we do this, one of two things will happen. If your badged friend over there has a conscience—always a liability, in my opinion—you'll soon be on your way.

"And if he doesn't have a conscience?" Richard wanted to know.

He'll probably kill you and stuff your body into his trunk.

"And I'm supposed to *like* this plan?" Richard asked, fighting back the hysteria. "I'm not going to do this."

I don't think you have a choice, Duunel said. *Let me tell you what's going to happen if you don't listen to me. He's going to ask you to get out of the car and cuff you. Then he's going to put you in the back of his car. Then you're going to sit here until animal control arrives.*

"Animal control?" Richard asked, eyes widening.

For Lassie here, Duunel said flatly. *What, did you think you'd share a cell? Are they gonna print him, take a mug shot? No, they're going to put him in the pound, and when no one comes for him in forty-eight hours, they're going to put a needle in his paw and put him down.*

"I don't think that's true," Richard said, not wanting to believe it.

Open your eyes, asshole. This is the Central Valley, where animal husbandry does not have sexual connotations. This place makes Tennessee look cultured. Here they don't see dogs as little furry people that go to spas and visit animal-intuitive therapists. Here they just chain 'em out back and put 'em down when they become a problem.

"Excuse me, Mr. Kinney. To whom are you talking?" The sheriff was at his door again.

"Sorry, officer. To my dog." Richard indicated Tobias, still lying low in the backseat footwell.

"Is that *your* dog?" the officer asked skeptically.

Richard sighed and lowered his head. "No. It's my best friend's dog."

"Stolen vehicle. Stolen dog. And an outstanding 5150 warrant in Berkeley. Mr. Kinney, I'm going to have to ask you to step outside your vehicle and put your hands behind your back." He clicked the little microphone hanging over his shoulder. "Dispatch, this is Unit 3, I'm going to need Animal Control at my GPS coordinates ASAP."

Richard was shaking. He had not moved despite the officer's command.

Say exactly what I say, Duunel ordered, and he began speaking Richard's "lines."

Richard obeyed. "Uh, Officer..."

Be confident, Duunel demanded.

"Get out of the car *now*, Mr. Kinney. Please don't make it worse for yourself."

"Officer, I want you to listen to me carefully. I'm investigating a serial murderer," Richard was repeating Duunel's words. "I know about Emily. I know where she is. Everyone in my organization knows."

Richard saw shock and non-comprehension register on the sheriff's blotchy red face. A rapid succession of emotions then passed over it: fear, anger, then resignation. He was obviously playing out the scenarios in his own head.

"We're not interested in your peccadilloes," Richard continued, repeating Duunel's words. "We're interested only in the Ecbatanas, and the larger web of terrorists that they inform. We don't want trouble. We don't need to drag your...indiscretions into this. But if you stop me now...my people won't have any choice."

"Who...who are your people?" the officer said, suspiciously.

"You don't need to know that. Just believe me when I say that we have much, much bigger fish to fry than you and your little...mistake."

The sheriff's hands dropped to his sides, and he stood with his head down. Was it shame? Richard couldn't be sure.

"Here's what you're going to do," Richard said. "You're going to tell me to drive on. Then you're going to assemble a team to raid the Ecbatana Ranch. Most of the bodies are in the barn."

"I thought you were interested in catching them yourself? I mean, your people," the sheriff said warily.

"We don't care who gets credit, and this will send a good message to the folks higher up, the ones we're *really* interested in." Richard smiled. "This is a big catch, Sheriff. But we don't mind you taking the credit for it. We have other priorities."

The sheriff nodded. He punched the button on his radio. "C1, C1, cancel that. Nothing to report here."

The sheriff just stood looking at the car. Richard shut the door and rolled down the window. "You do your part, and we'll bury the whole Emily thing. I promise," Richard said. "After all, everyone makes a bad call now and then. Doesn't have to ruin a man's life. Does it?"

The sheriff shook his head no.

"God bless, Sheriff. Careful of that Gabe—he's slow, but he's mean."

The sheriff nodded. Richard started the car and took off down the road once more. As they drove away, Richard said, "Do I want to know?"

Duunel replied, *If you knew, you'd have to do something about it.*

"That's true," Richard conceded.

Because you're an idiot, Duunel said. *And you have a conscience.*

"I think I peed myself," Richard noted.

76

TERRY GOT off the bus at Cedar Street and began to walk up the hill toward the friary. He was still elated from the success at Bishop Preston's office—but in the hours since, his mood had been tempered by sadness as he completed two pastoral visits. His first stop had been Children's Hospital in Oakland, just a short walk from the MacArthur BART station, where the child of one of the parishioners at Trinity North Church was undergoing chemotherapy. Terry had joked and clowned with the child, but she tired quickly. He had laid a hand on her and asked Jesus to heal her and protect her. There had been tears in his eyes when he left.

After that he had taken the bus north to El Cerrito, where he got off near a Safeway to pick up a few cans of soup, then walked several blocks to the house of a parishioner suffering from a raging head cold. He delivered the groceries—as the church secretary had asked him to—offered his sympathy after asking how the man was doing, but declined an offer to enter.

As he walked back to the bus stop he wrestled with his feelings of guilt over that. He knew that putting himself in the way of plague was a time-honored tradition among the clergy, and ordinarily he was not loath to do it. Indeed, ordinary visiting pastors put themselves in danger every day, every bit as much as the Blackfriars did. But, Terry reasoned, when the fate of the world was hanging in the balance, it was imprudent to take a risk with something as seemingly insignificant but potentially disastrous as a virus. He needed to be healthy, he argued. He felt depressed, and he knew that this day, at least, he had missed the mark as a pastor.

Finally, he stopped at Alta Bates to check in on Charlie. His vital signs were fine, but the tubes coming out of his mouth told a different story. Terry watched his chest rise and fall in a peaceful, regular pattern and comforted himself with the thought that Charlie was in no pain. He was, in fact...The word "happy" sprang to his mind, but he pushed it away as it wasn't right. "Content," he said out loud. That was it. Charlie was at home, and he was content. Terry shuddered.

During the bus ride home he sank deeper into a funk, and by the time he arrived, he was feeling sorry for himself and desperately craving a cookie. As he stepped into the foyer, he saw Kat sitting in the next room. She seemed to be at prayer, so he quietly hung up his jacket and fixed his look in the mirror. He moved his head from side to side, tweaked the little upturned brush stroke of his hair in front, then looked at himself in profile before announcing in a satisfied whisper, "I'd fuck you."

This bit of self-affirmation buoyed his spirits, and he tiptoed past Kat into the kitchen, where he promptly tripped over Dylan, sprawled like a beached manatee in the middle of the kitchen floor. Terry swore under his breath but collected himself quickly and knelt by his friend, a panic quickly rising in him. He felt under Dylan's jaw for a pulse—it was there, and strong. Terry let out a large, audible sigh of relief.

Dylan's head was to the side, and a pool of spittle had begun to collect on the floor. Terry opened Dylan's mouth to check his tongue, to make sure he hadn't been choking on anything. His mouth was clear. His breathing seemed to be fine.

Terry sat back on his heels and wondered at the scene. As far as he could tell, Dylan had decided to take a nap in the kitchen. But since that was highly unlikely—Dylan had never, to his knowledge, napped in the kitchen before—he wracked his brain for other explanations. Could Dylan have fainted? Could he have had a stroke?

He was still pondering this when he heard the front door open. He heard the distant voices of his husband, of Susan and Mikael, but they were not buoyant. They also hushed quickly when, he guessed, one of them had noticed Kat. Terry jumped up and went to the doorway. Catching Brian's eye, he motioned them to the kitchen.

All three rushed to join him. Wordlessly, he stopped them at the threshold and pointed at Dylan. Susan emitted a brief shriek of alarm and dropped to his side. Like Terry, she checked his pulse and his breathing.

"He seems fine," Terry said in a near whisper.

"He's *not* fine; he's unconscious," Susan retorted.

"I mean he's alive," Terry corrected.

Brian surveyed the room. "He was drinking coffee," he said, pointing out a shattered cup under the bench of the long dining table. Splashes of gooey brown liquid marred the linoleum in several places.

Susan looked up at Brian and met his eyes. "Are you thinking what I'm thinking?" she asked.

"That this is another allergic reaction?" he said. "Yeah. Are we going to have Dylan dropping like a sack of root vegetables every time we have a meal?"

Susan shook her head. "Maybe so, at least until we're able to sort out what he's allergic to and what he's not."

"This is going to be...challenging," Brian said, stepping over Dylan in order to get a dish rag. He began to scrub at the stains.

Susan slid from her knees onto her rump, close to Dylan's body. She held his hand. "I guess we wait."

"Unless he's had a stroke, in which case we should call the paramedics," Brian said.

Susan opened his eyelids one at a time. "His pupils are the same size, so it's probably not a stroke." She drew her mouth up in grim consideration. "I'm betting this is just an allergy thing. It's a strange one, but it's what was happening yesterday, so it's probably what's happing now."

Mikael was staring into the chapel. "What's up with Kat?"

"I thought she was praying. Or meditating," Terry said. "But come to think of it, if she were, she would have *noticed*..." Alarm punctuated the last word, and he leaped to his feet. Together, he and Mikael approached Kat cautiously.

Terry held up his hand. "No closer. She's not meditating or praying. She's in Vision."

"How can you tell?" Mikael asked.

"Rapid eye movements," Terry responded. "Look." He pointed at Kat's eyes, and indeed, beneath her closed lids there was a lot of activity. Her eyes darted back and forth, up and down. She was obviously elsewhere, interacting with an environment completely invisible to them.

"Where is she?" Mikael asked.

Terry shrugged. "Beats me. But we won't do her any favors trying to rouse her. She could get stranded in the Void if we do. Best to leave her alone, and she'll come home—"

"Wagging her tail behind her?" Mikael finished, but he wasn't smiling.

"I'll leave her tail to you, studly," Terry said. He slapped at Mikael's arm. "C'mon." He turned back into the kitchen.

"Well, while you're waiting for your respective spouses to gain consciousness," Brian started, picking up the shattered cup's pieces, "let's have something to eat."

"We need to pray," Terry said, looking at his watch.

"The Lord will understand if you eat first, then pray," Brian said. "Besides, by then you might have a chapel to do it in, and order mates to pray with."

"Point," Terry nodded. "And Jesus might be hyper-punctual, but he'll still show up even if we're not."

Mikael nodded at this, his arms crossed and his gaze fixed firmly on his girlfriend as he leaned in the doorway. Brian began setting out sandwich makings and brewing a fresh pot of decaf.

"How did it go, Terry?" Susan asked.

"All according to plan," Terry said. He swept his fingers through his hair and took his regular seat at the table. "That Bishop is one cool character, though."

"How do you mean?" asked Brian.

"Well, he's really in command," Terry said. "He *reeks* confidence. It's kind of intimidating."

"Well, wouldn't *you* be confident with the Spear of Destiny in your crozier?" Mikael asked.

"If I had a crozier, that is definitely how I'd want it stocked," Terry nodded.

"Really, though?" Susan asked. "If you had the Spear, right now, if any of us did, would we use it?"

They all looked at the floor. Finally, Terry spoke. "It's no different from any other form of magick, is it? It's against our Rule. Just because it's famous or Jesus-related doesn't make it *good* or exempt it from our vow."

"How about you, Brian?" Susan asked. "You and I haven't taken any vows."

"I think for me it would depend on the situation," he said thoughtfully, pausing over the laying out of Gouda. "And, with all due respect to the vows we take, it's going to be the same for any of us when it comes right down to it. I mean, just a few months ago, Richard used the Ring of Solomon when you were all under demonic attack, right? Was he wrong to do so? Did he break his vow?"

They paused to consider this. "Yes," Terry said finally. "He broke the vow. But you're right, I don't blame him—considering what was happening. And it turned the tide for us. Not in ways we could have foreseen...which is part of the problem."

Mikael leaned against the doorframe, scowling. "Okay, pardon me for playing Mr. Zeal of the Convert here, but isn't this the Gondor imperative? In Tolkien, the men of Gondor wanted to use the One Ring against the Dark Lord, but Gandalf wouldn't hear of it, and everyone thought he was crazy for wanting to destroy it."

"Yes, you're right," Terry said. "But Bilbo and Frodo both used it to get out of sticky situations. Was that wrong? They wouldn't have made it otherwise, would they? Besides, is it really as black and white in the real world as Tolkien paints it?"

"Isn't the point of this learning to depend on God's power instead of our own?" asked Susan.

"Sure, but at what point does 'I sent you a helicopter' kick in?" Mikael asked.

"I didn't vow not to ride in a helicopter," Terry answered. "I vowed not to use magick. And the Spear is magick."

"It's not demon magick," Brian pointed out.

"It's not *good* magick," Terry countered.

"So, what makes it bad magick," asked Mikael, "if not demons?"

"It's coercive," Terry said. "It's a byproduct of concentrated sin. Coercive power is corrupting, so it makes sense that a great concentration of corruption would result in a coercive talisman, doesn't it?"

"Is all coercive power evil?" asked Mikael.

"Luther says no, but he wouldn't say it was godly, either," Susan said. "It's part of his 'two kingdoms' theory—God approves of civil authority, which needs coercive power to keep peace—"

"Brigands must be dealt with," Brian agreed.

"But it's not the same as the Kingdom of God, in which coercive power has no place," Susan explained.

"Are those separate realms?" Mikael asked.

"Yes and no," Susan said. "They're overlapping jurisdictions, by necessity."

"That sounds paradoxical," Brian said.

"That's Luther for you," Susan agreed.

For a while none of them spoke. Then Dylan's eyelids fluttered. He opened his eyes, looked at Susan, then past his feet at Mikael. Mikael smiled and waved at him. "Welcome back, Sleeping Beauty," he said.

Susan caressed Dylan's face. "How are you feeling, Honey?"

Brian and Terry knelt where Dylan could see them, concerned but loving smiles on both of their faces. Terry reached for Brian's hand and squeezed it. Brian squeezed back. They'd been here—not

Dylan's exact situation, but dire enough. Terry's affection for his part-ner's steadfastness welled up in him, even as he expressed his concern for Dylan.

Dylan blinked. "Ah feel like someone just took a jackhammer to the back of mah eyeballs. What happened to meh?"

"Coffee happened," Brian said.

"Huh?" Dylan asked.

Susan spoke as if she were talking to a child, softly but firmly. "Something has changed, Honey, since you were attacked. You had terrible reactions to the medications the doctors gave you. Even Advil...well, it almost killed you. And now, we know that coffee is off limits, too."

"What are you tryin' to say?" Dylan asked suspiciously.

Susan's jaw quirked. "I'm not *trying* to say anything, Honey. I *am* saying what is happening to you. No subtext here."

"Ah think there is," he said.

"What do you think the subtext is, Dylan?" asked Brian.

"Ah think this is about weed," he said.

"I think that is a cause for concern," Susan said. "But none of us is *doing* this to you."

"God is," Dylan said.

"Okay, fine. God is." Susan rolled her eyes.

"Now Ah understand what Jaggy meant," Dylan's voice took on a faraway quality as he remembered his vision.

"What did he say?" Susan asked.

"He said the Powers was gonna help me," Dylan said. "Until I learned to help mahself."

"That sounds positive," Susan said.

"The Powers are vindictive sons-a-bitches," Dylan decided.

"I think someone is having *feelings*," Susan said, touching the tip of his nose with her forefinger.

"Damn right Ah'm havin' feelings," Dylan said. "This is about weed."

"How so?" Terry asked him.

"Weed is the wolf. Yer the little dog," Dylan said, looking up at his wife.

"Gee, thanks," Susan raised one eyebrow. "What the *fuck* are you talking about?"

"Y'all are the little dog. An' Ah *love* the little dog," Dylan sighed. "But Ah loved the wolf more." Tears welled up in his eyes. "Ah'm sorry, Darlin'." He tucked his nose in between Susan's breasts and started to weep.

Terry and Brian stood to give him some space. Terry went back to his place on the bench, and Brian finished setting out the cheese. Mikael looked on with concern and compassion. Susan rocked Dylan, making soft shushing noises until he quieted.

Brian set the platter on the table. "Make sandwiches whenever you're ready," he announced to no one and everyone. Mikael nodded but stayed at his post in the doorway.

"Am Ah in Hell?" Dylan asked, sniffling.

"I think you're in Heaven, Honey," Susan said. "Look, you're surrounded by the people who love you most. And there isn't anything any of us wouldn't do for you. I think it's just your addiction that's twisting your perception."

"You know, I heard an Orthodox priest talking one time," Terry said, spreading mayonnaise on a slice of rye. "He said that our ideas of Heaven and Hell are completely wrong. He said that when we die, we all go straight into the unmediated presence of God. The people who had opened themselves to God during their lives experienced his presence as bliss, but the people who had shut God out experienced his presence as overwhelming and painful."

"But they were both in the same place," Mikael nodded approvingly.

"Yup. It's just how they perceived it that was different." Terry placed a slice of cheese and fixed a final slice of rye on top. "Brian, are we out of pickles?"

"Oh damn. Sorry. We have pickles," he said, turning to the fridge.

"Brian, would you make me some tea?" Dylan asked, sitting up.

Brian stopped with the pickle jar in his hand and looked at Susan. "Do you think that's wise?" he asked.

"It'll be fine," Dylan said. "Arnault and Grandfather both gave me tea. Ah think it's mah consolation drug."

Susan sighed. "He's got to try it sometime. Might as well be now."

Brian shrugged and put the kettle on.

"Can someone tell me what's goin' on? Ah mean, like, fer work?" Dylan asked, wearily climbing into his seat at the table. He eyed Terry's sandwich like a begging hound.

Terry swallowed and gave Dylan a brief rundown on the events of the past few days. Susan sat next to her husband and reported the ominous gossip they'd heard at the Islamic Cultural Center, as well as the blood they'd found outside the house of the man she'd been exorcising. Through it all, Dylan scowled and nodded. When Susan stopped speaking, Dylan said, "So let me get this straight: Randy is in Hell—"

"No, Honey. I think you're still a bit disoriented," Susan patted his knee. "Charlie is in Hell; his body is at the hospital. Randy is in the mirror, hanging at Dio House, in the bishop's office. Kat is in Vision, but we don't know where she's gone to."

"And Richard?" Dylan asked. He seemed crestfallen. Richard was his best friend, after all.

Susan squeezed his leg. "We don't know. He's been incommunicado for more than a day. He doesn't answer his phone, or text messages, or email."

"Thet's not good," Dylan said. No one disagreed.

"We have a lot to pray for after dinner," Terry said through a mouth full of sandwich.

Brian set a steaming bowl of something that looked both white and mushy in front of Dylan, followed quickly by a mug of black tea.

"Grits?" Dylan sniffed.

"Let's start simple, then add things. That way, if you have another reaction, we'll know what you're allergic to," Brian reasoned. "If you do fine tonight, we'll know that you're A-OK for corn and tea."

"That sounds like a good plan," Susan said.

Dylan did not protest. He tucked into the grits with vengeance. Everyone held their breath. Dylan himself didn't hesitate. He finished bite after bite, stopping now and then to take a sip of tea.

"The man is still upright," Brian noted.

"That's a very good sign," Susan said, allowing herself to relax a bit.

"Now Ah want chocolate," Dylan announced, scraping the last of the grits from the bottom of the bowl.

"Don't push it," Brian scolded, swiping up his bowl and placing it in the sink.

77

KAT STORMED out of the keep, stomping over the lush green turf, cursing under her breath. This time, she did not see the brightness of the sun, or the brilliance of the flowers, or the delicate butterfly that she crushed beneath her Doc Martins. The flap of her cassock hung open, and her hands were balled into fists.

"This was a *stupid* fucking idea anyway," she said out loud. "What was I *thinking*?" Suddenly, she felt a sense of urgency, to get back to her computer, to see if there was a report from Randy. There he was, putting himself in danger, and she was doing what, here? Apparently, a lot of nothing.

"You're going the wrong way," a voice from out of nowhere said.

She stopped. She recognized the voice. It belonged to that slimy magickian. *Why are all magickians slimy?* she wondered. She realized that she was universalizing from particulars—only the magickians of her *experience* were slimy. Theoretically, she reasoned, it was possible that there were non-slimy magickians. Somewhere.

"Stop with the peekaboo," Kat said, hands on her lithe hips. The wind swept her black hair over her face. She spit a strand out of her mouth.

Obediently, the magickian stepped from a cluster of bamboo and bowed slightly. "That was an unfortunate meeting," he said.

"You're telling me," she said. "Do you know how far I had to come?"

"Oh yes," he said, tsking. "You must have been traveling ever since lunchtime."

She stared at him. "Are you making fun of me?"

He grinned, but it was a real grin. "Yes, Kat Webber. I am making fun of you. When the Khan ruled on Earth, men would travel for months to see him." He looked down and considered. "When he... withdrew, men spent their entire lifetimes searching for his kingdom. You, I believe, have not been greatly inconvenienced."

"You're saying I'm a spoiled brat," she huffed.

"I'm *thinking* it, but I'm not saying it." The man's head bobbed back and forth.

"You got here fast," she said.

"I've got two horses." He tossed his chin in the direction of the bamboo copse, "over there."

"Uh-huh," Kat said. "Why do you have *two* horses?"

"One for each of us."

"I'm going home," Kat said, and started walking again.

"You'll be walking a very long time in that direction," the man called. "As I said, you are headed the wrong way."

"Which is the right direction?" Kat asked.

"Come back to the castle with me, and meet with the khan. Then I'll give you a horse and send you with an escort to take you back to the Abyss. You'll waste no more time than you will if you continue on your present course. Less, I wager."

"*Why* should I go back?" Kat asked, a hurt look on her face. "Prester John is obviously more interested in accusing me of something than he is in hearing what I have to say."

"Prester John is...wounded," the magickian said. "In his mind. He has known great betrayal and much personal suffering. It has made him suspicious and inhospitable. Please accept my apology on his behalf." He spread his hands in a gesture of peace.

"I don't trust you," Kat said, crossing her arms.

"Then I see that you and my khan have much in common. You are both suspicious, and this has garnered you ungracious spirits."

"Hey, I'm *not* the same as him!" Kat snapped.

"Aren't you?" The magickian smiled a satisfied little smile that Kat was dying to rip off his face with her nails.

"All right, I'll go back," she said, her pouting face in full effect. "But I want an apology. From him, not from you."

"I can't promise that." The man shook his head. "He is a king. You are a commoner. He condescends to receive you. He will not condescend to apologize to you. You may as well ask the sky to be orange. It will do you no good to rail at it for being blue. Likewise, you cannot prosecute a king for being a king. And you may not require him to act like a slave in order to meet the whim of a common girl."

"Are you generally good at this persuasion thing?" Kat asked. "Because I'm thinking that you kind of suck at it."

"You must pardon me if I am not fluent in your most contemporary idioms." The magickian smiled again, this time obsequiously. "This way, please. The horses are just over here."

Despite the significant temper tantrum occurring in one room of her brain, Kat obeyed. Sure enough, on the other side of the bamboo grove, two horses were loitering, fully saddled and munching at the grass.

The man offered his hands to help Kat into the saddle, which she gratefully accepted. She had ridden horses a number of times in her life, usually on one-hour guided rides when her family drove through Arizona or Utah. She was awkward in the saddle, and in truth, she was scared of the great beast. Determined that it not show, however, she clutched at the reins, a little too roughly, since her horse gave out a scream of protest.

"No need to guide her," the magickian said. He had mounted himself, and he pulled up next to her. Taking the reins from Kat's hands, he dropped them onto the horse's neck. "She knows the way home."

Fair enough, Kat thought, but gave a little scream of her own as the horse started to trot after the magickian, and she grabbed at the saddle horn for a handhold.

The horses covered the ground much more quickly than she had done, of course, and in mere minutes they slowed as they approached the door of the keep. Dismounting quickly, the magickian helped Kat to the ground and bid her follow.

They entered by a different door this time, shortcutting through a lush garden so dense with foliage that it resembled a jungle. "Wait here," the man said, disappearing into a low door. He reappeared a moment later, his most gracious smile once again in place. "The khan will see you now."

But will the khan be a gentleman? Kat thought. An answering thought said, *Will you be a lady?* She knew the answer to that.

She stepped once more into the warm, romantic room with the giant fireplace. Tapestries hung on the walls. Huge, squat furniture—roughly fashioned from dark woods and cushioned with red and purple velvets—sat at a safe distance from the fire.

It took a moment for her eyes to adjust to the dim light, but as they did she located Prester John studying a map on a large oaken desk. His hair must have been long, for this time she noticed it had been gathered up in a topknot, fastened with a dark wooden clasp.

When Kat would later try to describe him, he sounded like a goofy crossdresser—a man in a yellow muumuu with his hair done up in a barrette. But in person, there was nothing effeminate or silly about him. It was obvious to her that this was a man of power, dressed in a way that communicated that power in his own culture. It was Kat who felt small and out of place.

She curtsied, and this time it was not forced, nor was it awkward. She averted her eyes, feeling quite properly chastened by his appearance this time. She stood nervously and waited to be spoken to.

"It seems you have more courage than sense," Prester John said, apparently to her. "I am sorry for the way I...I misspoke earlier. I hope you will pardon my offense."

She looked up and met his eyes. He was serious. She looked over at the magickian, who raised his eyebrows in surprise, shooting her a look that said, *You got your apology—unlikely as that was.*

"Of course," she said. "If you will pardon my"—she fished for an appropriate sounding word—"headstrong...ness." She mentally slapped herself on her forehead. *Fuck me,* she thought. *Really? "Head-strongness"? Is that even a word?*

Prester John, however, seemed to chalk it up to the ongoing mutability of language because he grunted and gave a stiff nod. "I assumed I knew what you had come for," he said, straightening up to his full, considerable height. "My magickian tells me I was wrong." Before she could answer, he continued. "I was inhospitable, but the mistake was honest. For hundreds of years men have visited me, and each of them has only been after one thing."

A painful look crossed Kat's face as she thought, *To get into your pants?* which was usually the end of a sentence like that, but she held her tongue. And her breath.

"The Graal," he said.

She let out her breath, relieved that the answer had nothing to do with pants. Despite the fact that Prester John wasn't wearing pants, she imagined that the king could fill some *formidable* pants. She shook her head briskly, trying not to think about what was in the king's pants, which was hopeless now that she had.

"I'm sorry, your highness," Kat said. "Where I come from, the only grail we know about is in a very silly movie."

"Movie?" The king looked puzzled.

"It's like a play," she reasoned. "I watched the whole movie, and never figured out what the grail even was. Is it a...cup? I remember something about a cup."

The king nodded, apparently measuring her sincerity.

"I find your ignorance of the Graal incredible," the king said. "But I will assume you tell me the truth."

"Yeah...we're not big on the grail thing," Kat said, not sure how to answer him and bristling a little at his use of the word "ignorance."

"The Holy Graal is the cup that our Lord Jesus Christ drank from at the Last Supper," Prester John said with an almost liturgical ring to his phrasing.

"Wow!" Kat said. "Well, *that's* a thing, isn't it?"

The king scowled, apparently mystified by her response. "I am the keeper of the Graal," he continued. "For centuries men have sought me out in search of its mystical powers."

"That's very, very...exciting." Kat nodded vigorously. "Can I speak to you about something kind of *important*?"

Prester John pierced her with his fierce black eyes. "Speak."

"I come from a time, like, a thousand years after you did your stuff. On Earth," she said, not certain of her words. "And there's this guy who says that he's your great-great-great—and lots and lots more greats—grandson. He's a bishop. And he's got the Spear of Destiny— I don't know what you call it, but the one that stabbed Jesus at his crucifixion."

"You speak of the Spear of Longinus." The Khan looked suddenly interested.

"Yeah, that's the one. I was using 'long johns' as a mnemonic device, but I still couldn't remember the damned thing. Anyway, he likes to talk about how you are his ancestor and all, and how you used to kill Muslims in battle—and he's real, real proud of that—and he's determined to finish what you started. His friend—I mean, I guess they're friends—the governor guy, Ivory, he already dropped a bomb on Dearborn—"

"Bomb? Dearborn?" the King shook his head. "These words are strange to me."

"A bomb is like...an explosion." She threw her hands up and made loud "kkkk-shhhh-ing" sounds with her mouth.

The king cocked his head in confusion. The magickian stepped forward. "If your majesty will excuse me, I believe the young woman speaks of something like Greek Fire. Only, perhaps in her time, more potent."

The king's eyebrows shot up.

"Sure, okay," Kat agreed, heartened that she was making progress. "And Dearborn is a city where a bunch of Muslims live—uh, lived."

"This man used Greek Fire on a whole city?" The king looked horrified. "And their women? And children?"

"KKKK—shhhhhhhh," Kat said again, moving her hands dramatically. "Everyone. Even people who were not Muslim got killed. But the governor did it—not the bishop. But the bishop *supports* him, you know, and is helping him get elect—you probably don't know what an election is. Into a position of even *more* power, so he can...you know...kill more...Muslims." She pursed her lips and scrunched up her nose. "Am I making *any* sense at all?"

"And he does this in *my name*..." Prester John looked like someone had punched him in the gut.

"Oh yeah. He mentions you every chance he gets." Kat nodded. "You're like his favorite subject, when he's not talking about killing Muslims. Except that he's usually talking about them together." Kat felt good that she'd finally blurted it out, but she felt flustered. She wasn't usually so ditzy. She wondered if there was something about the atmosphere of this strange world that was affecting her. On the other hand, it could just be the proximity of the enormous king and the thought of the correspondingly enormous contents of his pants. Kat realized she was incredibly horny. *Note to self*, she thought, *fuck Mikael blind at first opportunity.*

"Walk with me," the khan commanded. "Ismael, send wine." The magickian nodded and walked briskly from the room, in search of a servant, Kat reasoned. She followed the king as he stepped out into the cool brightness of the garden.

He walked slowly, with his hands behind his back. He seemed suddenly weary, older—definitely sadder. "Do you know why I'm here?" he asked her. "What do they say of me in your time?"

"Not much," Kat said. "I mean, no offense, but I'd never heard of you before Bishop Preston started talking about you. Everyone else in my order knew about you, though..." She thought about that for a moment, feeling a bit sheepish. *Boy, do I have a lot to learn*, she thought.

"I have had fewer and fewer visitors, which I now understand."

He nodded approvingly. "It is good that I am little known. I want no one to suffer what I have suffered."

"It looks like you've got it pretty good," Kat said.

"Let me tell you my tale, and then you can tell me how felicitous my reign seems to you," the king said.

Kat worried briefly about her brother but was now too interested to hurry off. "Please," she said. "I'd love to hear about it."

"I arrived that day at Damietta to find the European armies scattered. I gathered them and used them like a fist to break down the walls of the castle. Without mercy, I murdered the Saracens—you call them Muslims. I killed their comrades until one of them talked, then I killed the rest of them anyway. I hunted down their king, who was making strikes at us from the desert, and I killed him, too, along with all his men. I killed his camp women. I killed their children. Then I went from city to city, and we killed every Child of the Prophet we met. We waylaid caravans, we cut them down, we stole their goods, we slew their livestock. And we did this all in the precious name of Christ, our Lord." A cloud had descended over the khan's countenance, dark as a thunderhead. "That is how I spent my life. That is how I made my fame: Khan Jahn, the Moor Hammer. That is how I became a saint, beatified by Pope Honorius even if I was only a Nestorian heretic." A pained smile flitted over his mouth at the thought of this, but it only lasted a minute.

"And when I died, I discovered myself here." He waved at the garden. "In my old castle, still king of my own lands. Only...my people are gone."

Kat was puzzled. "But I've *seen* people. There are people here."

"Yes, but they aren't *my* people." He looked down and caught her eye. "Have you not guessed, Lady Kat, who my subjects are now?"

Kat was lost. She saw the grieved mirth in his eyes, but she shook her head.

"My subjects are all Moors...Muslims. In fact, they are, every one of them, the very people I killed."

Kat gasped. Yes, she realized now, every one of them looked Middle Eastern.

They had come to a small clearing in the jumbled tangle of plant life. In the open space was a stone table with two stone blocks for benches on either side. Atop the table were a pitcher and two goblets.

The king bade her sit and filled both goblets with wine. He sat with a heavy sigh and continued, "At first, I was outraged. I was filled with fury, with horror, with revulsion. That such heathens, such savages, such animals should be my subjects? It was unthinkable. I believed God had either made a mistake or that he was mad.

"In time, I understood that God was not mad, but wise. For in time I discovered...not Saracens...but *people*. I have found them to be witty, intelligent, and clever. I have discovered that they are loyal, generous, and kind. They are clean, industrious, ingenious, and learned. I have also found them to be devout—their devotion to God puts me to shame." He sighed, and his sigh carried the weight of the world. "I discovered that I was no saint—despite what I had told myself, despite what some Roman bishop might have declared. I discovered the depth of my sin...and it is deep indeed."

He looked like he might cry. Kat felt sorry for him, but she didn't know what to say. She took a sip of the wine. It was hearty, but sweet. She liked it so much that she involuntarily licked her lips.

The king looked into the sad distance, and when he spoke again his voice was weary. "I expected to be granted a place amidst the glory of God. Instead, I must suffer the devotion of the very people I have wronged. Their kindness wounds me. Their care, their obedience stings. Every day I curse the day I was born. Every day I strive to be worthy of them, to be a better king than any earthly ruler has ever attempted. They give me all I could ever hope for. And I give them everything I have. And thereby, I pray someday, if I am a good enough king, that God will grant an end to this Purgatory."

Kat asked the thing that kept bugging her. "So, don't the people you killed...resent having to serve you? I know I would, if you'd killed me, that is."

The king shook his head, gravely, slowly. "They remember nothing. Oh, they remember their lives, their families, their labor. But nothing of the battle. It is Allah's kindness." He leaned over and whispered, "They think they are in *Heaven*."

"Maybe they are," Kat said.

"How could it be?" Prester John asked, but it was rhetorical. It was clear he thought it impossible. "So, you see," he continued, "your news makes me sad. I have come to love this people. The thought that they are still being killed in your time, and by my sons yet...it is a grievous thing to me."

He downed his wine in a single gulp and then slammed his cup down onto the table. Kat jumped. Not seeming to notice, the khan poured himself another cup. This he also dispatched quickly. Again, he brought the cup down on the table with a bang. Kat felt the urge to chant, "Chug! Chug! Chug!" but she restrained herself. Prester John wiped his beard with the back of his hand and looked at Kat with what seemed like sincere affection.

"My daughter, I am saddened by your news, but I am glad to have met you. We will meet again." And with that, he rose, bowed to her almost imperceptibly, and walked off through the garden.

"Huh," Kat said out loud. She took another sip of the wine, wondering. In a moment, she saw movement out of the corner of her eye. It was the magickian, making his way through the brambles toward her.

"Your horse is ready," he said, "if you would like to return home."

She would, she realized. And yet she had been seduced by this place. Maybe it wasn't Heaven, but it was *heavenly*. It was no wonder the Muslims thought they had entered paradise. If she had woken from death here and had been told this was Heaven, she would believe it. She wasn't sure that she didn't believe it now. She drained the wine, wiped her mouth on the back of her own hand, and stood.

"I'm good, Ismael," she declared. "Let's go."

78

RICHARD'S HANDS were still shaking as he drove into town. Images of cooperating law enforcement agencies taking down the Ecbatana Ranch danced in his brain, and he felt a thrill of vengeful satisfaction as he watched them play out. He had no way of knowing, of course, whether that was happening, or would happen, or if, in fact, someone was looking for the stolen car he was driving. There was so much he didn't know. *I know this*, he thought, *I am not out of the frying pan yet.*

Just as twilight was beginning to fall, he saw a rental car agency to his right and a block later pulled into a grocery store parking lot. "C'mon, big boy," he said to Tobias, holding open the door for the dog. "Time for us to get a new car. Maybe one that no one's looking for. And then let's find a vet and get that lip looked at."

79

BISHOP PRESTON LIT a cigar and leaned back in his chair. Governor Ivory raised a glass to his friend. "Here's to your speech tomorrow, John. You ready?"

The Dio House was so quiet it was creaky. It was the way Preston liked his office best—and always had, as long as he had been a bishop. The staff had gone home, night had fallen, and the peace that the church had always promised its people seemed to descend on him in a way that was real and present to the senses. Metaphorical peace was all right, he supposed. But this peace, this night peace, *this* passed understanding. He craved it during the day, and he reveled in it now.

"I am as ready as I'm going to be." Preston poured himself another scotch. "Here's the way I've always looked at it: Whenever I've had to deliver a *big* sermon, I'm just making myself available to preach the Good News. It's God's job to make it shine."

"You think God's going to help us out?" Ivory looked skeptical.

"We are doing God's work," Preston said. "I believe that. Don't you believe that?"

"I do."

"Well, God ain't gonna leave us swingin' in the wind, David. He's atramplin' out the vintage where the grapes of wrath are stored. You wait and see."

Ivory chuckled. "I trust you know your business better than I do." He took a swig and made a face. "Isn't that a Yankee hymn?"

"Best damned lyric a Yankee ever wrote," Preston grinned. "Besides, I did all right against them liberal wonks on Block Jamison's show, didn't I? I trust you got some good responses?"

"Well, there's no shortage of hate mail, of course, but those seem to be coming almost exclusively from the left." Ivory moved his head from side to side. "But among the GOP faithful, the support has been o-ver-whelming. I can't thank you enough for that, John. You put it into a context that I couldn't have done, speaking for myself. It would have sounded too defensive."

"I think you're right about that." Preston ran his finger around the rim of his glass. "But I'm not surprised by the response. Tomorrow I'll make my speech, and Wednesday I'll take the case to the floor. I'll be damned if we don't blow the walls off that place."

"The speeches tonight were good. Ridgeway's pretty confident." Ivory looked worried.

"Let him. That's what we want. They know we're making noise, but they just think I'm being a cranky old man. They don't know the lightning that's going to strike tomorrow night when I make my address."

"You sound pretty confident."

"I am."

Ivory looked skeptical, but he nodded and sipped from his tumbler. "There are lots of people in the party who don't like me."

Preston leaned forward on his great oaken desk. "Here's what we've got to keep in mind, David: This is not *about* you. Any one of those flag-wavin' clowns you're goin' up against would make a decent president, in my opinion—"

"Except for Chesterton."

"Ain't no way Chesterton is going to get the nomination, and you know it. But if any of the rest of them got it, I'd vote for them, and that's a fact." He drew on his cigar. "But this isn't about minor policy differences. This is about the war on Western civilization. And you, Governor Ivory, are the only man I trust to take decisive action. You ready to get down to business?"

"I'm having my people go through the Magog Protocol with a fine-tooth comb now, tweaking it and updating."

"We put that thing together five years ago. Might be wise to start from scratch," Preston scowled.

"I thought of that, but all the key players are there. It just needs updating. The basic plan is the same. Besides, we'd lose time starting over. A lot of good work went into that, and 95 percent of it is still accurate. By the time I get the nod...if I get the nod...we'll be able to start circulating it to the party chiefs."

Preston laughed. "Ha! Won't they be surprised!"

"They'll be blown away by the detail. And the rationale is impeccable. We've got a small window of time to act. If they read it, they'll see it—"

"And if they see it, they'll act," Preston finished.

"Exactly." Ivory nodded in large, looping movements, indicating that he'd perhaps had one scotch too many.

A smashing sound obliterated Preston's sacred silence. A rock landed on his desk, accompanied by a cascade of broken stained glass. Preston jerked back from the desk and held his arm up over his eyes to shield them.

"Holy shit, what was that?" Ivory barked.

"Get away from the windows," Preston ordered him, and he sprang to one of the bookshelves for cover. He waited as Ivory rushed to one of the walls. When it was quiet again, he strained to listen. Outside, he heard the faint sound of...growling? It sounded human, but strange, as if someone were making a deep "grrrrr" sound in his throat—or rather, a group of people were. It sounded vaguely like the buzzing of deep-throated bees.

"Stay there," Preston ordered Ivory and ran from the room. He flew down the stairs to the basement, where the security monitors were. Blue light filled the room, and it hummed with the sound of hard drives recording the closed circuit feed. He blinked, not sure what he was seeing. Just outside the Dio House, a large crowd had gathered. But the people weren't doing anything. Most of them were just standing there, arms hanging limply by their sides. One of them was shaking all over as if he was having an epileptic seizure but didn't have the good sense to lie down.

"What in the world?" he breathed. It was the strangest sight Preston had ever seen. Then a man came forth from the crowd, striding with resolution. He was the only one who seemed to have any initiative. The man was tall and thin, looking vaguely bohemian in his attire. He was gesturing toward the Dio House—in fact, he seemed to be making a speech. Preston desperately wished he could hear what the man was saying. Whatever it was, it didn't look good. Had *he* thrown the stone?

Preston didn't have time to consider it because with a flourish from the bohemian man, the crowd surged forward as one. They rushed toward the back door, the one nearest Preston's office, which was on the same level as the cathedral complex. He watched as they threw their bodies against the large wooden door. Even here in the basement, he heard the great groaning thud of it, and the sound sent shivers all the way to his rectum.

For the first time, he realized he was scared and not merely alarmed or curious. The crowd surged again, and again the door groaned. Preston had only one thought in his head: Get the Spear. It was the only thing that might save them. Any moment now, that door was going to give. Preston prayed he could make it back to his office before it shattered under the assault of the mob.

He launched himself up the stairs, taking them two at a time. The idea flashed through his mind that, in that moment, he did not feel like an old man. It felt good.

The door thudded again, its deep boom accompanied now by the high-pitched sound of splintering wood. Preston dashed past the besieged door and into his office, throwing his office door closed behind him and locking it. Of course, he knew that such a move wouldn't deter them, but it would frustrate them for another few seconds—seconds he knew he might need.

"Did you call the police?" he barked at Ivory.

"No, I—"

"Well, call them, you idiot. We're being attacked! What have you been doing up here?" It appeared that the intended candidate had simply been standing there shaking in his trousers.

"Who do you think it is?" Ivory asked, fumbling at his cell phone.

"I have no idea," admitted the bishop, snatching his crozier from where it was leaning in the corner. "It's San Francisco, so it could be militant homosexuals, it could be the local Democrats, it could be the Muslims—" although that was unlikely, he realized; the people he saw on the security monitors didn't look Middle Eastern "—it could be the fucking Irish Republican Army. Who cares? The only thing that matters is that they're about to come through that door, and we have no security detail."

Ivory finished dialing just as the outer door gave way with an earth-shuddering crash. "Here they come!" Preston shouted, standing facing his office door with the crook of his crozier poised and ready. In a splintering shower of wood, metal, and sheetrock, the office door exploded inward.

80

WHEN KAT STEPPED BACK through the Void, she emerged into the comforting sound of prayer. Opening her eyes, she discovered herself still seated on her zafu—but instead of the bright, empty chapel in which she had first begun her journey, it was now filled with her order mates, and except for the golden glow of the candles, it was dark and peaceful.

Yet she did not feel at peace. She was in pain, and she realized that she needed to micturate like a racehorse. Wordlessly she slipped out of her seat and padded to the bathroom where she was able to relieve her screaming bladder. She sighed deeply as peace returned to her guts, and she returned to the prayer of her community a happier woman. This time, she sat next to Mikael, who greeted her with a raised eyebrow which she took to mean, *Where the fuck have you been?* She squeezed his hand in answer.

She found she had a lot to pray for: Randy, Charlie, Dylan, Richard, Doug, and the fate of the Muslim world—indeed, the whole world. All of these things would have overwhelmed her, but she was practicing what Terry had been teaching her. "It's Jesus's job to carry stuff," he'd told her. "He can carry as much as you can let go of." She remembered his lavender T-shirt that said Jesus is my Sherpa and smiled.

In her mind's eye, she watched herself handing a huge bundle over to Jesus. She watched herself letting it go. As she did, she felt a wave of peace flow over her. She felt her muscles relax. She took a deep breath and let it out slowly. *Holy crap, this stuff really works*, she thought. *Thank you, Jesus. Thank you for holding all my gnarly shit because it's too much for me to carry.*

Dylan's lovely and tired voice intruded on her private prayer, but it was not unwelcome. Kat smiled, hoping he would be all right.

"Visit this place, O Lord, and drive far from it all snares of the Enemy," Dylan prayed. "Let your holy angels dwell with us to preserve us in peace, and let your blessing be upon us always, through Jesus Christ our Lord."

"Amen," she said, along with Terry and Mikael. She saw that even Susan joined them tonight.

"May the almighty and merciful God—Father, Son, and Holy Spirit—bless us and keep us, now and forever. Amen," Dylan finished.

"Amen," they all said again, crossing themselves.

As everyone rose, they gathered around Kat in curiosity. Brian waved at her from the door of the kitchen. "Come make yourself a sandwich," he said.

She nodded. "I'm famished."

"Not so fast," Mikael said. "We were worried about you. Where were you?"

Kat saw the same question on every face. "Uh...I went to see Prester John."

Terry's jaw dropped. Eyes widened all around. "How did you find him?" Terry asked.

"I went to the Abyss and asked Abaddon to take me to him," Kat said.

Terry straightened. "Wow. That was easy. Why didn't I think of that?" He looked concerned. "What did he say?"

Kat moved her head from side to side. "Eh...he was sad. He might have been angry, I guess, but he seemed more depressed, really."

"What did he look like?" Susan asked.

"Kind of like Terry," Kat smiled. "Only twice as big." She moved toward the kitchen. "I'm not sure what I expected him to do. Maybe I just thought he should know—about Preston, I mean. *I'd* want to know."

She looked at the platter of cold cuts and began salivating. She grabbed a slice of wheat bread and started to spread mayonnaise on it. "How did it go at the Islamic Center?" she asked.

Mikael shrugged. "I think we helped some. It was hard. I wish there was something we could actually *do*."

"I think we did a lot," Brian said, putting on the kettle.

Putting the final touches on her sandwich, Kat motioned to Mikael with her head to join her in the office. Wordlessly they slipped into the other room. Kat was relieved that no one else seemed to notice since their lively conversation continued in the kitchen.

"What's up?" Mikael whispered.

She grabbed the collar of his cassock and pulled him down until their lips met. Her tongue entered his mouth, and he reached around her and pulled her close to him. After a kiss that left them both breathless, she broke free of his mouth and panted. "I was hoping Nobzilla was on the rampage," she said. "I know about a little patch of Tokyo that *desperately* needs stomping."

A flash of lust came into his eyes, and he kissed her again. When they surfaced, Mikael looked sheepish. "I have to take a rain check on that particular apocalypse," he said.

"Why?" Kat asked, smiling playfully. "All the kids love the monster."

"The monster isn't going anywhere," Mikael assured her. "I just have...another engagement." He told her briefly about what they had found at the house of the possessed person she and Susan had been visiting.

"That doesn't sound good." She looked horrified.

"Right. The roommate isn't talking. To us, anyway."

"But you're thinking he might talk to...*The Confessor*?" Kat curled one side of her lip.

"It's worth a try," Mikael nodded.

"All right, man of mystery." Kat kissed him again. "But you've been warned: Tokyo is going to need more than a simple stomping."

"The monster is insatiable for destruction," Mikael promised.

"He'd better be." Kat let go of his collar. "Tokyo is built on a swamp."

"I don't think Tokyo *is* built on a swamp," Mikael argued.

"Don't you have someone to intimidate?" Kat asked. "Why are you still here?"

"I'm going, I'm going," Mikael said, holding up his hands and moving from the room.

Glancing over at Susan's big computer, Kat felt a stab of panic for her brother. She sat down in the big comfy office chair and opened a web browser. Logging into her own account, her eyes went wide when she saw a message from Randy. She read quickly, forgetting to breathe.

"Uh, guys!" she called.

Susan was the first one through the door, followed quickly by Dylan, Terry, and Brian. Crowding around the computer in the tiny room, they leaned in over her shoulder. "What's up?" Susan asked in her ear.

She punched up the point size on Randy's email and sat back so they could all see. "Preston and Ivory," Terry read. "No surprise there."

"What's the Magog Protocol?" Kat asked.

"Gotta be a reference to the thirty-eighth and thirty-ninth chapters of Ezekiel," Brian said.

"Or the twentieth chapter of the Book of Revelation," Terry added.

Dylan nodded. "In both cases, they refer to an army risin' up against God."

"I'll get on it," Susan said, snagging her laptop from the shelf and firing it up.

"It's a heathen army," Brian reasoned, crossing his arms. "Like the way Prester John would have thought of the Moors."

"He doesn't think that now," Kat asserted.

"Ah *definitely* want to hear more about that," Dylan said.

Distantly, Kat heard the front door shut.

"Who is that?" Susan asked without looking up from her screen.

"Mikael," Kat said. "He's...checking something out. Wait, another message from Randy just came in," Kat said, opening it.

Brian stood bolt upright as he scanned the page, and Kat covered her mouth with her hand. "Oh my God."

"Read it to me," commanded Susan, typing furiously. "And what is Mikael 'checking out'? Intentional vagueness makes me nervous."

Kat gathered herself and read. "Sis, send help. I can't see what's happening, but it sounds like there's a huge mob outside. They're trying to break down the door. Preston has whipped out the Spear. I think I did this. I'm so sorry. I didn't know Larch would do it this way. Call police. Randy."

"Oh, freaking shit," Terry swore.

"I'm on it," Brian said, whipping out his iPhone and dialing 911.

"Maybe we should just let whatever is happening happen," Terry said. "I mean, maybe Larch is doing us a favor. Maybe he's doing what we *can't* do."

"That's a terrible thought," Susan said, eyes still glued to her laptop.

"Yeah, but maybe he'll do what needs to be done, and our hands will be clean," Terry said. "It's selfish, but that doesn't mean it isn't true."

"Ah think yer forgettin' two things," Dylan said, straightening up. "First thing, Larch is attemptin' to take that Spear by force. Ah think it's Larch that needs the police, not the Bishop."

"That's right, Dyl," Brian nodded. "What's the second thing?"

"If he succeeds, the most powerful man on earth will be Stanis Larch."

No one moved. Everyone just looked at Dylan, paralyzed by the very thought of it.

Even Susan looked up. "Oh my God," she said. "That is exactly right."

"Don't get me wrong, Ah kind of like Larch," Dylan said. "Ah mean, as a dinner guest, he's kinda near the top of my list. He's funny, he's smart, he has very cool ideas."

"But he's one seriously misguided motherfucker," Terry breathed.

"Word," Dylan agreed.

"I've got something," Susan said. Kat whirled around to face her, and everyone turned. "There's an entry on the Dataleaks website on the Magog Protocol. It's a PDF file, and it's taking its time downloading. Which means it's probably pretty big."

"More information is good," Brian noted.

"Okay, it's done," Susan said. She pursed her lips as her eyes flashed over her screen. "It looks like a study of a hypothetical military scenario."

"What's the scenario?" Terry asked, almost in a whisper.

For several minutes, Susan didn't answer. Then her shoulders sagged. "It's a projected strategy plan for a coordinated response..."

"Response to what?" Brian asked.

"An Iranian nuclear strike on Israel," she said.

Terry whistled. "We've got to get that Spear," he said. It was a fact. No one disputed it.

"Ideas on how to do that?" Susan asked.

"I got close to Preston once," Terry said. "Maybe I can do it again."

"And do what?" Dylan asked. "Are ya gonna say, 'Hey, look at the squirrel,' and snag it when he looks away?"

"It's not the worst plan I've ever heard," Terry said. "Given the right squirrel."

"So, let's break it down," Susan said. "We need two things: proximity and the right squirrel."

"Wait," Kat said. "Just to clarify. We're not talking about an *actual* squirrel, right?"

"No," Terry reassured her. "We're talking about a metaphorical squirrel."

"Okay, just checking. You never know around here."

"Point," said Terry.

"I mean, Dylan might keep squirrels in his room, for all I know," Kat explained.

"Thet thar is an anti-hillbilly, bigoted statement," Dylan pointed his finger at Kat, raising one bushy, menacing eyebrow.

"Calm down, Hatfield and McCoy," Susan said. "We're getting off topic. Proximity and squir—diversion. Chop chop."

"Thet thar is an anti-Chinaman, bigoted statement." Dylan pointed his finger at his wife. She scowled at him. He dropped his finger and sighed.

"How do we get Terry—or one of us—close enough to Bishop Preston to snag the Spear?" Brian asked.

"How can we snag it if he has it?" Kat asked. "I mean, there's no crossing him as long as he's holding it, right?"

"That's just it," Terry said, almost bouncing up and down. "It's only effective if he's holding it, and focusing it with intention. If he sets it down to piss for a second, and we snag it, then *we've* got it, and no one can cross *us*."

"Except that we can't *use* it," Dylan pointed out.

"But nobody there knows that," Terry said.

"You're planning to bluff your way out of there?" Dylan said. He seemed surprised and a little pleased by the sheer audacity of it.

"Wait, where's 'there'?" asked Kat. "I'm confused."

"Wherever it is we can get close to him," Terry said. Susan was cruising various web pages rapidly. "He's speaking at the Republican Convention tomorrow night," she said. "He said he was going to nominate Ivory from the floor—that would be the next day. Tomorrow he's going to make his case."

"How do you know all that?" Dylan asked.

"Logic," his wife winked. "You should try it sometime."

"It's one o' the many things Ah'm allergic to," he said, winking back.

"C'mon, guys," Terry said. "Ideas. We need ideas. Brainstorm. No idea is too crazy right now."

Just then they heard a succession of deep thuds. Kat jerked up. "What the fuck was that?"

"It sounded like it was coming from outside," Brian said. Then he cocked his head. "Did I just hear a horse whinny?"

"A horse? In Berkeley?" Susan scowled, but she stopped when she looked at Kat. "Kat, what's up? Your eyes are huge."

In answer, Kat walked to the back door and threw it open. A giant of a man dismounted from an obviously agitated horse. The man was clothed in mail that clanked as he moved. A tunic bearing the Crusader's cross covered a hauberk. A cervelliere was fixed to his head, and bushy pepper-colored hair stuck out from every side around it. As he stepped into the light, she saw the scars on his Mongolian face. "My lady," he said, and bowed slightly.

"Uh, guys," Kat called over her shoulder, "we have company."

81

"DAVID, GET BEHIND ME!" Bishop Preston called to his friend as the first wave of attackers poured through the door. They immediately fell over, apparently dead. In a flash, it occurred to Preston that the force needed to bust down the door had been so great, that these first few had been crushed by those coming up behind them.

It seemed that hundreds of snarling, savage monsters were on their heels. Yet, Preston knew, they were not monsters. But something was seriously off. He could see that. They were normal-looking people—businessmen and baristas and boho chicks and homeless guys and everyone in between—but their actions were strange. It was as if they were being driven by some intelligence that did not know how to work the bodies. Their movements were birdlike and stiff. Their eyes were glaring and glazed. A couple of them were jerking about in periodic spasms. Several were drooling. No one looked happy. And all of them were advancing toward him.

Preston glanced over his shoulder to make sure Ivory was there. The governor was climbing up into a window loft, crouching like a cat. The bishop brandished his crozier and concentrated his thought on the Spear contained within a compartment on its handle. As he did so, a golden ball of fire collected in the crozier's crook, spitting energy like lightning.

The first of the attackers to come within reach lunged at him, and Preston felt the crozier kick, much like the recoil of a rifle, as it punched back at the advancing man, sending him flying backward with the same force as his forward lunge. As more of the attackers came near, he struggled to maintain a grip on the crozier as it bucked to and fro, sending the frenzied, monstrous horde flying one by one. As the attackers were kicked back, they landed on several of their fellows, crushing heads, injuring limbs, and pinning some where they lay under the dead weight of their broken bodies.

"John, how are you doing that?" Ivory called, his voice quavering but straining to be heard over the din of the snarling mob.

"Did you call the police?" Preston asked.

"No...I..."

"Call the fucking police, damn you! If you're waiting for the apocalypse, it's here!"

Ivory fumbled for his cell phone again but dropped it. From the height of the inset window, it hit the polished wood floor in a splash of electronic parts. All Ivory could do was stare at the scattered pieces of what used to be his phone. "It broke!" he called to Preston.

"No shit, it broke!" Preston called over his shoulder in between jerking blasts from his crozier. His arms and shoulders hurt like a motherfucker. *Fighting monsters*, he thought, *is a younger man's sport.* For just a moment he flashed on the image of that tiny, vaguely Jap-looking friar who had visited him earlier that day. What was his name? But he remembered the name of the order—*Saint Raphael.*

Just then, Preston heard the wail of sirens and saw the blazing red strobe lights of the police cars flashing through the stained glass of the office. Sweat poured down his face as he turned quickly from one side to the other, repelling the attackers with reactive thrusts that threatened at any moment to rip the crozier from his now raw and aching hands. Turning quickly to meet the rush of one frenzied, jerking man in a Hawaiian shirt, another stepped in as his back was turned.

Suddenly, the crozier took on a life of its own. It shot the man in the Hawaiian shirt back against the wall, so hard that Preston heard his spine crack. Then he barely kept hold on the crozier as it whirled overhead and met the oncoming swipe of a fierce-looking matron in trendy cat-glasses. The thrust of her attempted clawing was met, matched, and bettered as she spun away, knocking down more of the snarling crowd.

Preston heard gunshots, and heard the tinkling of broken glass. Smoke began to fill the room, and—one by one—he saw his attackers succumb to the effects of an unknown gas. He stayed upright as long as he could, continuing to brandish his crozier until it became too heavy and he was overtaken by darkness.

82

ARRIVING in front of the house where Susan had been attempting her exorcism, Mikael took a couple of deep breaths. "Maiden voyage of the *SS Confessor*," he said out loud. He pulled on his mask and settled the cowl over this cassock. It all felt right. He opened the door of the car and got out.

Catlike, he moved with speed and grace to the house. It wouldn't do for The Confessor to simply knock on the door, he decided. He saw light in the windows, so someone was home. But the lights were farther back in the house. Accordingly, he snuck around the side, looking for the source of the light. The window of a back bedroom shone out against the moonlight, even though the shades were drawn.

Mikael continued around the back and tried the door. It was open and, willing his heart not to beat quite so furiously, he slipped inside. He flattened himself against the wall in the little anteroom by the back door where there was plenty of shadow. Folded paper bags stuck out on either side of his head, and boxes blocked a firm placement for his feet. He leaned out and peered into the hallway.

It looked like someone was in the bathroom. The light was on, and Mikael could hear a fan. The door was ajar about three inches, but he didn't see anyone. Quietly, he stepped into the bedroom where the light was, and crouched in the open closet. It afforded him a clear view of the room, but he would not be immediately noticeable.

He willed his pulse to slow and his breathing to quiet as he sat. A part of his brain was railing against every bit of this. *That's the Mikael part*, he told himself. *I have a new identity now. The Confessor does what has to be done.*

The Mikael part of his brain told him that sounded ridiculous. The Confessor part of his brain told him to shut up. The Mikael part of his brain screamed that they were going to get into big trouble. The Confessor part of his brain insisted that there were things worth risking trouble for.

Before the argument could escalate into a civil fistfight, someone entered the bedroom. It was a man in his early thirties, dressed in flannel pants and a T-shirt. The man picked up a bottle of beer and took a long pull. As he turned toward the bed, Mikael could see that he had a black eye. His nose looked swollen as well.

"Get into a fight?" Mikael asked, intentionally deepening his voice.

The man jerked around, his eyes wide. He stumbled, nearly losing his balance, but he sat on the bed and steadied himself. His eyes darted from one side of the room to the other, looking for the source of the voice.

Mikael rose to his full six feet five inches and spread his shoulders as wide as he could manage before stepping out of the dim closet into the room. The effect was every bit as dramatic as he'd hoped. The man's jaw dropped, and he cowered on his bed.

Mikael placed his hands on his hips and stared at the man for several moments in silence. He suddenly realized he didn't know the name of the man who was possessed. His shoulders sagged momentarily as a wave of guilt washed through him over this fact. He caught himself, though, just in time. *Appearance is everything*, he thought, and he drew himself up again to his full, broad-shouldered height.

The man did not seem to have noticed his brief diminishment—because he was visibly shaking. "Look, I've already been beat up once today," he said. "Just tell me what you want."

Mikael took an intimidating step toward the man. "I'm not here to hurt you. And I'm not here to steal from you. I only want information."

"What? What kind of information? I don't know anything!" the man almost whined. "I work at the fucking DMV!"

Mikael thought of commenting on how there might be lots of pissed off people wanting to get even with the DMV, but he let it go. "I'm interested in your roommate," Mikael said.

"Doug?" the man said. "Or Vincent?"

"The one who's been acting *strange* of late," Mikael said, lowering his head menacingly, a motion that said, *Don't trifle with me.* He also liked the slightly archaic phrasing. *Very nice. The Confessor will have to do more of that*, he thought.

"Oh...Doug," the man looked down. "Yeah. He beat me up."

"Your roommate did this to you? Your black eye?"

"Yeah. He promised to take me to work. I lost my license. DUI. If I don't get to work, I lose my job. I was coming back from the store, and we were supposed to go in, like, five minutes."

"Go on," Mikael said, still hovering over the man and concentrating on keeping his voice low.

"He was walking out of the house. He had...that look."

"What do you mean?" Mikael asked.

"That look he's been getting lately, like he's somewhere else and no one else matters. It's creepy. It's like it's not even him."

"How long have you known Doug?"

"I don't know...about five years," the man said. "So, you're not going to beat me up?"

"No," Mikael said.

"Or rob me?"

"No," Mikael said. "I just want to talk to you."

"You could have just knocked on the fucking door," the man said.

"Are you supposed to be some kind of superhero or something? You scared the shit out of me."

Mikael didn't know what to say. He deflated a bit. "You're right," he said, "I could have just knocked on the door." He motioned toward the bed. "May I?"

The man scooted back a bit and nodded warily. Mikael sat. He sighed. "I'm sorry for scaring you. But the truth is, I didn't know what I was going to encounter here. We found blood on the walk outside. We thought your roommate had been kidnapped or taken into hiding. You do know he's possessed, right?"

"Possessed? What does that mean? Like *The Exorcist* possessed?" The man looked at Mikael like he was out of his mind.

"Exactly like that," Mikael said. He waited a moment for it to sink in.

The man shook his head slowly. "Oh man, that makes so much fucking sense. It's crazy, but it makes so much sense."

"We were afraid that maybe one of you—his roommates—was also possessed. Demons sometimes gather in nests. We thought maybe you were trying to keep him from...well, from getting the help he needs."

The man relaxed a bit. "No, I like Doug. I'd do anything to help him. Especially since he's been...getting weird. It's just not *Doug*. I know that Vince feels the same—we've talked about it. He's at work now, but he gets home about 1 a.m. You can ask him yourself."

Mikael nodded. "I don't think that will be necessary. I take it the blood outside was yours?"

"Yeah, that's my blood. I told Doug I had to leave now...*then*...to get to work on time. He ignored me. He just up and left the house. I kind of panicked, and I rushed out to stop him. I yelled at him, but he just pretended I wasn't here. Finally, I stood in his way."

"And he hit you?"

"Yeah, fucking flattened my nose," the man said. "It was gushing blood. Didn't stop for about a half hour. Hit me in the eye, too."

"I can see that," Mikael said, a note of sympathy in his voice. "What happened then?"

"I don't know. I was on the ground."

"Do you have any idea where he was going?"

"Oh yeah. That was the one thing he did say. He was headed for San Francisco."

83

When Bishop Preston opened his eyes, two things intruded on his awareness. One was a powerful headache so profound that it made the sky he was looking up into start spinning. The other was the fact that what was left of his dinner was coming up quickly. He turned on his side and vomited.

He squeezed his eyes shut and gritted his teeth, choking back on the acrid taste. He was surrounded by people—firemen and police. He could see red and blue strobe lights through his eyelids.

Someone bathed his face with a wet cloth. He opened his eyes and saw a plainclothes detective with the cool wet cloth in his hand —his other hand was on his shoulder. The man was African-American, in a dark blue suit that had seen better days. Preston blinked. "Thank you," he said. "Ivory?" He waited.

The man nodded. "Governor Ivory is fine. Sick, like you, but unhurt. It's the gas. It'll pass. You'll both be fine. That headache you feel should clear in about an hour."

"That seems like an eternity," Preston managed.

"I can ask someone to give you some morphine," the detective offered. "One dose should do you until it passes."

Preston shook his head. He had too much to think about, and too much to handle. He couldn't afford any degree of brain fog. "I'll manage," he said. He pointed with his chin toward the smoking building that was his office—the energy required for using his finger to point was simply beyond him. "Who did this?"

The detective cocked his head. "I was hoping you could tell me. Several of them are dead, and we have several in custody." He bit his lip. "Trouble is, we can't find anything relating these people. Other than the fact that a lot of them were also involved in a break-in at the Jewish Museum in Berkeley yesterday, we got nothing."

"I've never seen any of them before—not that I know of," Preston said.

"Do you have any idea why someone might want to attack you?" the detective asked. It seemed his legs were getting tired of crouching, so he just sat down on the ground.

Preston thought hard. "I have plenty of enemies, Detective..."

"Tanner."

"But none of them rises above the level of simple spite. I represent a kind of Christianity that's out of style right now. People are annoyed at me. Some clergy feel alienated when I have to hold a boundary or discipline them. But that's what bishops do. I can't think of anyone who might engineer something this—"

"Ambitious?" Detective Tanner suggested.

"Exactly. But David, on the other hand..."

"Do you mean Governor Ivory?"

"Yes. He has real enemies."

"You're referring to the Dearborn thing?"

"Yes...and given his policies on Muslim issues, a *lot* of people are... upset." Preston's mouth quirked, a suggested but brief smile. "You know...I'll be putting him forward as a presidential candidate. That's going to ruffle some feathers, even among his friends."

"The Secret Service is already on the scene," Tanner nodded. "They're tending to the governor now." He patted the bishop on the arm. "You rest. If you remember anything, please tell me. I'll check back in with you in a few minutes."

Bishop Preston nodded. He closed his eyes and struggled into a sitting position, leaning against the tire of a police car. All possibility of thought seemed obliterated by the staggering block of pain that filled his head. He probed it in his mind for some way around or through, but it seemed impenetrable. The only thing he could do was endure it.

So he entered into it. He chose not to resist it. This reminded him that nothing could resist him. Not with the Spear—

His eyes snapped open. Panic filled him. Where was the Spear? He felt around on the gravel. It was nowhere to be found. His eyes scanned the paving stones that made up the cathedral close—nothing. He staggered to his feet and began to lurch toward the open door of his office.

Light was blazing inside. Wisps of smoke still trailed out of it. Through the windows he could see firemen with gas masks poking around and talking to one another. His right knee gave out under his weight, and he went down, striking his kneecap on the stone. A red flash of pain cut through his entire body, and even slashed through the pain already resident in his brain—pain on pain.

He struggled to rise again and stumbled. Suddenly, though, hands caught at his elbow and buoyed him up. Turning his head, he saw his secretary, Ms. Finn. He smiled at her. "Thank you, Patricia," he said.

She tried to pull him away from the Dio House. "You can't go in there, Bishop. It's a crime scene."

"I need my crozier," he said matter of factly.

"If it's in there, it will be fine."

"You don't understand. I *need* it." He met her eyes.

Her eyebrows lowered, and he could tell she was judging his mental state. "Would you please ask the detective...Detective Tanner if he would ask one of the firemen to bring it out for me?"

"If I do, sir, will you sit down?"

"*And* I'll behave," Preston promised.

"You sit. I'll ask the detective. Deal?"

"That's a deal," he said, knowing when he was beaten. In all honesty, he could not have walked to his office under his own power anyway. He sat gratefully.

He watched Ms. Finn as she wove her way through the mob of emergency responders. She disappeared from his view quickly, but in about five minutes she came back with Detective Tanner in tow.

When they reached him, Ms. Finn sat down next to him. Detective Tanner squatted again. "How are you feeling, Bishop?"

"I'm clearer. Head still hurts. But I don't need to throw up again."

"Thank God for the small favors," Tanner smiled. Preston could tell that he was observing him closely. He could not guess what the man was looking for, however.

Whatever it was, he seemed to have found it because he stood and put his hands on his hips. "I'm going to go talk to the site chief." He pointed over to where the fire trucks were congregated, down the hill on Taylor Street. "I understand this...crozzy-thing is pretty important."

"A crozier...it's a ceremonial shepherd's crook. It's priceless. If anyone stole it...it would be the worst tragedy of the evening."

"Okay, okay. I'll see what I can do." He kicked at a protruding edge of one of the paving stones and set off toward the stairs.

"Can I get you anything, Bishop Preston?" Ms. Finn asked him. "Some water?"

He hadn't been thinking of water, but the moment she mentioned it, he realized how desperately thirsty he was. He nodded vigorously for a moment but stopped that when it made his head hurt worse. He grimaced and waited as she got up and went in search of a water bottle.

In a few minutes she was back, putting a plastic bottle into his hands. She guided it to his lips, and he drank greedily. He drained the bottle. "More," he said. But before she could rise, a fireman approached with what appeared to be a large stick. As he got closer, Preston could see that it was his crozier. He sighed deeply, every muscle in his body relaxing.

He reached out his hand and snatched the crozier as the man offered it to him. No sooner did he have it than the pain in his head was forced back and out. At least that was what it felt like. The pain, after all, was a form of opposition. The Spear met it with equal and greater force. Preston shook his head. It was pain free.

He stood, and his legs were steady. The dizziness was gone. He straightened his suit coat and dusted himself off. He turned to Ms. Finn and saw the fear on her face as he did so. It occurred to him that he should have gone slower, that his recovery had been too quick, too miraculous. She was frightened. He didn't care.

"I have a big day tomorrow, Patricia," he said to her, beginning to walk toward the street. He leaned on the crozier like a walking stick, although there was little need for that now. "This kind of thing...can't happen again. There is too much at stake here. Don't you agree?"

He looked over at her, and his eyes narrowed. She was so terrified that she looked about to cry. "Ms. Finn, we are not in ordinary times here. Miracles happen. We are about God's business. I need you to pull it together. Can you do that, or do I need to find another assistant?"

He saw her swallow. She looked from side to side uncertainly. Finally, she found the courage to meet his eyes. "I don't understand what's happening. But I'm here to help you."

"Good," the bishop said, continuing toward the street. "First, get me a cab. Second, I need you to get those exorcist friars on the phone."

84

PRESTER JOHN STEPPED into the kitchen with a loud stomp of boots. Kat felt the floor shake under his step and noted with alarm how close his head was to the ceiling. He was taller than Mikael, she noted. Why hadn't she noticed that in the khan's own world?

She turned toward her friends. Brian's eyes were wide. Terry's mouth was open as was Dylan's. Susan clutched at her husband's shoulder protectively, her maternal instincts obviously in high gear. Kat didn't know if they knew who their visitor was, but his militant attire alone made him an object of wonder. *Well, better get it over with,* she thought. "Guys, this is Prester John."

The khan nodded curtly to Kat. He then turned to consider the others. He looked unimpressed. He sniffed. "Fetch a boy for my horse, and bring wine. It has been centuries since I have journeyed forth from my kingdom. This air is strange. It tires me."

Kat wasn't sure how to respond to this. "Yes, tired. I know how you feel," she laughed nervously, looking back and forth between the king and her friends. They looked at her. They looked at the khan. She turned to Prester John. "Um...we don't have a boy," she said. "We don't have horses here."

"You are peasants?" the khan scowled, his piercing black eyes incredulous. "Who is your lord? Take me to him."

Brian stepped forward. "Your majesty, please allow me to welcome you. This house is a friary dedicated to the use of the Order of Saint Raphael. Father Dylan is our acting prior—"

Dylan wiggled his fingers at the khan.

"And Kat, whom you seem to know, is an oblate."

"There are no women friars," the khan looked suspicious.

"Much has changed since you ruled on Earth, your majesty," Brian explained. "Women are now friars, priests, and bishops in many Christian communions. Also, in our part of the world, horses are no longer the primary means of conveyance. We do not use them, so we do not have facilities to house them."

"You are a child of Abraham," Prester John stated.

"I am," Brian returned.

"How come you to be in a Christian friary? Is someone ill?"

"No," Brian smiled. "I am not a doctor. I am a scholar. And a cook. The friars are...not celibate. Many are espoused. This is Father Dylan's wife, Susan. And this is Father Terry, my husband," Brian said, indicating his beloved. He held his breath.

Prester John looked at Terry. He looked at Brian. He looked back at Terry. Then he turned to Kat. "This is a strange country," he said.

"This is Berkeley," Kat said. "You have *no idea*."

"Does your strange country have wine?" he asked.

"Yes," Kat said with a nod.

"Then it will be tolerable," the khan said.

"I'll get wine," Brian said, heading to one of the cupboards. "Terry," he called over his shoulder, "can you back the clunker out of the garage and make a space for Prester John's horse?"

Terry nodded and headed for the front door. Kat heard the jingle of keys as the screen door slammed behind him.

"I'm afraid we have no hay," Brian said. "But I can manage some oats in the morning." He leaned over to Dylan and whispered, "Good thing I just made a Costco run."

"Word," Dylan whispered back.

Brian poured a large glass of wine and invited the Khan to sit. The normally large kitchen seemed small and crowded as Prester John attempted to fold himself and all of his plate armor onto one of the benches. Once seated, however, he seemed less imposing, and more weary.

He lifted the large wine glass and examined it, obviously curious. "I have never seen craftsmanship like this," he said, a note of wonder in his voice. "It is very fine."

"IKEA," Kat nodded.

The khan cocked his head at her.

"It's Swedish," she said.

"Your words are strange," he said. He sniffed at the wine and jerked back in surprise. He took a sip, and Kat saw a succession of emotions play over his face. He took a large swig. Then he knocked back the whole glass in a gulp. He burped loudly and slammed the glass down on the table. It shattered into several delicate shards.

For a moment, everyone just stared at the broken glass. "Uh...we don't have that tradition, here," Kat said. "The whole goblet-slamming thing, I mean."

Brian quickly moved to sweep up the shards. As he tipped the dustpan into the trash can he said, "Dyl, can you grab one of the brass Eucharistic chalices from the chapel?"

Dylan rose and tottered into the chapel. A moment later he returned with a gold-plated brass chalice. Brian took it from him with a nod of thanks and filled it with wine. He set this before the khan with a smile. "This one will not break as easily," he said.

Prester John admired the cup. "How do poor friars merit vessels of such finery, or wine of such vintage as this?" He chugged the second cup of wine and slammed the chalice to the table.

"We're not poor," Susan said. "We're pretty solidly middle-class."

The king's eyebrows moved together. He looked at Brian. "What does this one mean? What is middle-class?"

"She means we are neither poor nor wealthy. We are like merchants, in between," Brian said. "For friars, we make a good living." He looked at Kat. "Does he know we're exorcists?"

Kat shook her head.

"Exorcists?" Prester John's eyes grew large. "Then you are brave souls. I will speak to your leader. Alone."

Dylan looked from side to side. "He means you, Honey," Susan said, patting his knee.

Kat's heart fell. She realized that, as much affection as she felt for Dylan, she had no confidence in him as a leader. *If only Richard were here*, she thought.

"Ah," Brian interrupted her thoughts. "Here is another custom you will be unfamiliar with, your majesty. The Order of Saint Raphael is a *consensus* order. The prior may issue orders in the heat of battle against evil forces, but until battle is enjoined all share in the process of making decisions."

Prester John turned to Dylan. "Does this not dishonor you?"

"Nope," Dylan said. He smiled a big, goofy smile.

Prester John frowned. "I do not understand how this..." He fished for a word.

"Works?" Brian offered.

"Yes, that will do," the khan said.

"Waal, mostly we just sit around and talk about shit," Dylan said, "and what we need to do becomes clear. Usually around time for dessert."

"I do not understand this...*shit*," Prester John said.

"Yeah, that's pretty clear," Brian laughed. "Don't worry, your majesty. All we're saying is that it is not the order's way for the leader to make the decisions by himself. The counsel of all is sought and honored."

Prester John nodded slowly. "I predict that you exchange many words and rarely act in haste."

"You are most astute, your majesty," Brian bowed slightly. "That is a very accurate assessment."

"Why are none drinking with me?" the khan asked.

"Thet thar is a fine question," Dylan seconded. "Let's put some wine in some coffee mugs, and we can all pound the fuckin' table."

Brian shrugged and started setting out coffee mugs. When he set one down in front of Dylan, however, it was already full.

"Is this tea?" Dylan sniffed at it.

"Yes," Brian said, pouring a decent Sonoma merlot into the rest of the mugs.

"God hates me," Dylan said.

"Now you sound just like Richard," Susan said.

"Heavy is the head that wears the fuckin' crown," Dylan took a sip and wrinkled his nose. "Ah'll get used to it. But Ah won't be happy about it."

Brian raised his cup toward the khan. "To our guest. May your mission be blessed." He clinked glasses all around. Prester John watched the strange ritual with detached curiosity.

"Uh, thet reminds meh," Dylan said, setting his cup down. "Jus' what is yore mission, anyway?"

The khan drained another round of wine and once again slammed the chalice down on the rough wooden table. "Can you not guess?" He looked at each of them in turn, but he held Kat's eyes as he spoke. "Children are often in need of admonishment."

Just then the disco strains of Abba's "Fernando" rang out, and Terry fished in his pocket for his cell phone.

"It's awfully late for a call," Brian frowned.

"It might be one of the parishioners from Trinity North Church," Terry said. "A couple of them are in the hospital, after all." He frowned at the screen. "I don't recognize the number." He punched at the On button and held it to his ear.

"Father Terry, here," he said cheerily.

"I guess I'll get Char—the spare room ready for our guest," Brian said. He smiled at Prester John. "Your majesty, I regret that your feet will hang a bit off the edge of the bed, but I hope you'll be comfortable."

"Terry, what's wrong?" Susan asked. Everyone looked at him. He had grown white as a sheet, and his mouth hung open as if he were about to speak but couldn't quite manage it. He held up one finger, listening intently.

"Was anyone hurt?" he asked. "Well, that's something."

Susan raised her eyebrow. "It might be time for cocoa," she whispered to Brian.

"It's definitely time for cocoa," he agreed and moved to the stove, looking back over his shoulder at his partner.

"When do you want us?" Terry asked. He signed for pen and paper. Dylan scrambled to the office and rushed back with a yellow legal pad and a Sharpie. He thrust them in front of Terry, who started writing. "I understand. We should probably arrive around 10 a.m., then," Terry said. "Where?" he paused, listening. "Are you sure you won't need an escort?" He wrote an address. Kat noted it was in San Francisco. "Service entrance. Got it. How many of us?" His eyes darted back and forth. "Just a minute," he covered the microphone and said to Dylan. "Are you in play?"

Dylan didn't hesitate. "You bet yore sweet ass Ah am." Terry looked at Susan for a confirmation. She shrugged. "I'd say no, but I can't keep him prisoner."

Terry nodded. "We'll have four friars on site, and two support personnel—one for research and one for tech. They work remotely, usually."

Kat sat up straighter. "Sounds like a job," she said.

"Uh-huh," Terry said. "Of course," he said. Then he listened for a long stretch. Finally, he nodded and seemed to be interrupting. "There's just one thing—that episcopal oversight we discussed? Our power is severely limited..." He trailed off, listening. "That's fine, then. We'll see you tomorrow." Terry lowered the cell phone and put it on the table.

"Okay, then," he said. He pursed his lips and stared straight ahead.

"He looks a little dissociated," Susan said, mostly to Brian.

Brian set a cup of cocoa in front of his partner. "This should do it." He tapped Terry on the shoulder. "Okay, Honey cakes. Time to brief us."

Prester John scowled, his head moving back and forth, obviously trying to assess what was happening and not entirely sure he understood. He turned to Kat. "There were voices coming from the little box?"

Kat nodded. "To talk to people at long distances. It seems magickal, but it isn't. Not really. It's just a machine."

"You use them like pigeons?" Prester John asked.

"Kind of," Kat nodded. "Less poop, though."

"That was...the child in need of admonishment," Terry said, sipping at his cocoa.

"My son?" Prester John asked. "My son was speaking in the little box?"

Terry nodded. "Yes. He was attacked tonight, at the Dio House."

Everyone sat up straighter. Susan said, "I don't know whether to say 'that's terrible' or 'that's wonderful.' I'm conflicted."

"Who attacked him?" Dylan asked. "Do Ah get one of those?" he asked Brian. Brian set a mug in front of Dylan. He sniffed at it. "Goddam fucking tea," he said.

"He didn't know. He only knew that there were hundreds of them. He said they were acting like zombies. But some of them were floppers. He guessed that they were possessed. I think our neighborhood horde moved on to San Francisco after the heist at the Maccabean Museum."

"Which means that Larch is probably behind this," Brian said.

"That's what I'm thinking," Terry nodded. "So, the bishop has hired us to provide security for him tomorrow at the Republican National Convention."

Dylan whistled through his teeth. "Thet's at the Moscone Center, right?"

"Yup. The Secret Service will meet us at the service entrance to process us and provide us with security badges and such." His eyes were large as if he could not believe what he was saying. "So, anyone have any outstanding warrants?"

They looked at each other. Dylan raised his hand. "Ah got an overdue parking ticket," he said.

"I think we're safe on that score," Terry answered. "We'll be in San

Francisco, after all, far out of the jurisdiction of the Berkeley Parking Nazis."

"Goddamned BPN," Dylan seethed.

"I've got a question." Kat raised her hand. "We still don't have a bishop."

"We do now," Terry said. "The Order of Saint Raphael is now under the episcopal oversight of the Bishop of California—Bishop Preston."

"The well of irony jus' never runs dry, does it?" Dylan sipped at his tea. He stuck out his pinkie finger as he did so.

"It's the perfect opportunity," Susan said. "We couldn't ask for better. It won't ever be this easy to get close to Preston."

Terry nodded. "The problem is that the place is going to be thick with security. We'll be close, all right, but getting away with anything is going to be tough. Plus, there's one more little snag the bishop mentioned."

"What's that?" asked Susan.

"The Republican organizing committee isn't letting any of their people through the door unless they're carrying," Terry said.

"Carrying what?" Dylan frowned.

"Packing," Terry clarified.

"Yer shittin' me," Dylan said.

"Nope. Every single Republican delegate will be carrying a firearm." Terry set down his cup. "Yippie-kai-yay."

85

LARCH TOUCHED the skin dangling from his beaked nose and flinched as he tore it off. He applied some triple antibiotic ointment and repeated the process for the rest of the injuries to his face. Leading his very own army of the damned was not turning out like he'd hoped.

The last of his bandages in place, he turned off the lights in the motel bathroom and lit a single candle, which he placed behind him. He ran hot water in the shower until the room steamed up. Then he leaned against the door, unfocused his eyes, and waited for *her* to appear.

It didn't take long. But this time, she didn't spin playfully into view. There were no gauzy dresses or fetching glances. Instead, she just materialized and looked at him with a caustic gaze that could remove wallpaper. "What have you done?" she asked.

"I did...wait, what do you mean?" Larch asked defensively. She'd never appeared like this, and he was taken aback. Sure, the raid on the bishop's office had been a disaster, but he expected her to be sympathetic and encouraging, not cross. Indeed, that's why he was summoning her. It was time for a pep talk. And she was a spirit with plenty of pep.

Not now, though. "We...*I*...specifically told you to *protect* the savior, not attack him."

"I don't understand. First, who is the savior? I was never clear on that." Had she ever said? He wracked his brain but couldn't think of it. "Second, any job I have to do will be easier if I have the power to do it. One step at a time, right? Once I have the Spear of Destiny, nothing will be able to stop us. I'll do whatever you want."

"You're an idiot," she almost spat through the mirror.

His shoulders fell, and he felt at a complete loss. He felt a panic rise up within him, mortified at having displeased her. *His* Pim. "I-I-I hope—" he stammered, but he couldn't finish the sentence. "I don't understand," he said finally.

"Governor Ivory is the one my Masters have set their hopes upon. All our plans at this point depend on him. And you, you fucking imbecile, almost got him killed."

"I did? When?"

"He was in the bishop's office when you and the army we *graciously* gave you attacked it."

Larch deflated even further. "He was? Oh shit." His head was swimming. "I had no idea. I thought..." But he didn't know what he thought. He just stood there feeling like a naughty schoolboy. It was a very old feeling, and not one that he liked—not at all.

He had to redeem himself. He couldn't bear the look of anger and spite on Pim's face. He wanted her so badly, he would do anything to win back her winsome smile.

"Give me one reason why we shouldn't choose someone else to lead our army?" Pim crossed her arms. Although her feet were out of frame, he could see by the motions of her leg that she was tapping one foot, too.

"I-I'm sorry. I didn't know. I was trying to...do the right thing." He was sincere, but the words landed wrong as soon as he'd said them—like the dissonant clunk of lead pipe on concrete. "Please tell me what to do. I have every intention of being your obedient servant." He bowed slightly to her. He also felt ridiculous, but he didn't let that stop him.

She narrowed her eyes at him, apparently thinking. "Just a minute," she said and walked out of frame. He heard faint voices—arguing. Five minutes passed, and he turned off the shower, as the steam was so great now that it was beginning to impair his vision rather than facilitating it. He also took a leak. He leaned against the bathroom door again and waited some more. Eventually, Pim walked back into frame.

"You're a very lucky man," she said. "Some people have more...*invested*...in you than I do."

His heart fell. He felt the awful stab of the wounded lover. He wanted to cry, but he blinked it back instead. He said nothing but merely waited for her to continue.

She crossed her arms and looked out of frame. She moved her head from side to side. "Give me a fucking minute; I'm getting to it," she said to someone in the nether-wings.

"Okay, here's the deal. We'll let you keep the army—for now." She scowled at him. It was a bad scowl. "The savior will be at the Republican National Convention tomorrow. You need to protect him. Especially from the Blackfriars."

"The Blackfriars?" Larch was surprised. Then he remembered that the friary was the place the army had congregated first. It suddenly dawned on him that the Blackfriars were the only people that Pim and her masters were really afraid of. He pursed his lips in curiosity, thinking this odd. As much as he respected Richard, he'd always thought the others to be kind of buffoonish. He flashed on his own lodge fraters and winced. *The pot calling the kettle black*, he thought.

"But be warned, magickian. One more fuckup and—"

"And what?" he asked, a wet chill running down his spine.

"Let's just say that's how people get eaten," she said. For the first time in their conversation, she smiled

TUESDAY

86

Susan watched her husband sleep. With her eye, she traced the broad length of his nose. The red in his beard caught the morning light just starting to peek through their bedroom window.

Dylan stirred. He opened one eye. He saw her looking at him. He jerked up. "What's wrong?" he asked.

"Nothing's wrong, silly," she said, touching his nose with her finger. "I'm just looking at you."

"Why?"

"Because you're beautiful. And I love you," she said. She smiled. "And I'm proud of you."

"Keep talking," he said, scooting over to nuzzle her.

She wrapped her arms around his bulky chest and squeezed. "You were an addict when I married you," she said.

"O God, here it comes…" he moaned.

"Stop it." She slapped at his balding pate. "And you still are; we both know that. I'm so grateful to Grandfather and Jaguar and the Powers. I can see a big difference in you already."

"I have no idea what yore talkin' about," he said. "And they're all sons-a-bitches."

"They love you and they saved you," she said.

"From what?"

"From you," she said. "From that compulsion to constantly numb yourself out."

"Sons-a-bitches," he repeated. He lowered his nose and pressed it between her breasts. "Mah favorite spot."

She stroked the back of his head. "I wish I knew what you were afraid of."

"I ain't afraid of nothing," he said in a mammary-muffled voice.

"You're brave, all right," she said. "I've seen you and Richard go up against things that would make Schwarzenegger run for cover. But there's something even scarier than demons in your head. Something that makes you hide out from your own feelings, over and over and over."

"Yer soundin' like a psychologist," he said, coming up for air. He nestled his head in the crook of her neck.

"I think you should see a psychologist," she said.

"Fuck that," he said. "Too expensive."

"I'll bet the others wouldn't bat an eye at paying for your therapy from the common fund. I bet they'd pony right up."

Dylan said nothing.

"You're embarrassed," Susan realized, and said it out loud. "I don't think you need to be. If we could do it all ourselves, we wouldn't need Jesus."

"Ah'm feelin' distinctly Pelagian this mornin'," he said. "Ah'll thank you to keep yer Augustine to yerself."

"Augustine was judged right," Susan countered.

He pulled away briefly and squinted at her. "How is it that you manage to win an argument fifteen hundred years before y'ore even born?"

"Behold my power, and despair!" she teased, pinching him.

He yelped. "Do that again."

"Nope. Intermittent reinforcement is the most effective means of operant conditioning."

"If yer quotin' Skinner, thet means y'ore tryin' to get me hot," Dylan said. "Are you tryin' to get me hot?" He moved one hand down her belly, coming to rest in the warm pressure between her thighs.

"I'm not saying no," she said and rolled on top of him. She straddled him and pressed her vulva against his hardness.

He grabbed at the fleshiness of her hips and pressed up into her. She shivered and lowered her face down to kiss him, wetly and deep. Breaking off the kiss, she sat up and rode him, swaying back and forth and delighting in his moans.

He rolled her off him before he came and kissed his way down to her belly. It was her turn to moan.

When they were both satisfied, they snuggled again. Susan looked at the clock. "Brian will have breakfast ready soon," she said. "You'd better go pray, or Terry will start without you."

"Ah'm prayin' for bacon," Dylan said, and smacked his lips.

"How are you feeling?"

"Ah'm feeling fiiiiiiiiine," he said. "Ah am now, anyways."

She slapped at his shoulder. "Aches? Pains?"

He smiled at her. "Ah'm fine, Darlin'. Honest to God."

"Good. 'Cause we've got a big day ahead of us," Susan said.

"Uh-huh."

"Are you ready for it?" she asked.

"As ready as Ah'm gonna be, Ah reckon," he said, unconcerned.

"The others are going to be looking to you to lead them," she reminded him.

He grunted.

She continued. "Richard's gone...somewhere. Terry can't do it. He's too abrasive, and Mikael won't listen to him. Mikael and Kat are too green. That leaves you."

He grunted.

"I mean it, Honey. You've got to find your power here. If you don't step up and lead today, we're not going to see tomorrow. You know that's true."

He grunted.

"You can't hide anymore." She put her head on his chest. "The Powers have taken that away from you..."

"Sons-a-fucking-bitches," he breathed, looking at the ceiling.

"So, what are you going to do?" She played with the hair on his chest.

"Y'know, someday y'er gonna wake up and realize yore *not* Katie von Bora," he complained.

"What are you going to do?" she repeated.

He said nothing. She stroked his chin. "I know you're scared," she said softly. "So am I. I don't want you to do this alone. I want you to go downstairs and pray for help. I want you to lean on Jesus like you've never leaned before. I want you to call the smart shots and put our people in the places they can do the most good, keeping in mind their talents and their limitations. I want you to trust God and do the thing that scares you most."

"You want me to man-fucking-up and play drill sergeant, is that it?"

"If you want to live to hump another day," she said, "then yes."

87

MORNING PRAYER WAS PARTICULARLY POIGNANT. Kat always enjoyed the ritual of it—the meditative stillness, the synchronistic, scarily applicable symbolic messages that the appointed scripture readings for the day always seemed to hold, the vulnerability of her brothers in the order as they laid their fears and hopes before God. She loved them terribly. And she felt loved. She fought to keep the tears bottled up as they named their intercessions.

She knew that every one of them was aware that they may not be alive to pray in this room tomorrow. And they poured all of that anxiety into their prayer. She felt it charged with power. Even the picture of the patchwork Jesus that covered the chapel wall seemed worried. *That* must *be my imagination*, she thought. But it didn't change what she saw.

The incense of their prayers was soon displaced by the delicious odor of bacon, and as they said their final amens, they drifted greedily to the kitchen. The lazy Susan in the center of the table was overloaded with the fruit of Brian's labor—sausage and cheddar omelets, and molasses-caraway buns—both were steaming, both fresh and hot. The fried potatoes with sun dried tomatoes were beginning to cool. Brian was just filling coffee mugs as they streamed in.

Susan was already in place, and she handed a cup of tea to her husband. Dylan sniffed at it but otherwise accepted it without any derisive comment. As Kat sat down, she worried about her brother. She thought back to what they'd heard about the attack on the bishop's office. Of course, Terry couldn't have asked Bishop Preston, "Oh, and how did that mirror on your wall fare?" But it's what she most *wanted* to ask. Directly after breakfast, she would email him and hope against hope for a reply.

"Did anyone rouse the khan?" Brian asked.

Terry perked up and leaped to his feet. "Jesus! I didn't even think —" But just then they heard the sound of hard boots on the stairs, and in moments Prester John was ducking to clear the door frame. He stepped into the kitchen, his eyes severe.

"How did you sleep, your majesty?" Brian asked.

"Your magick is not wasted on bedding," the khan announced.

"Um…is thet a good thing?" Dylan asked uncertainly.

"Never in my life have I slept so well," the khan clarified.

"We are glad to hear it," Brian said. "But in truth, there's no magick to it. Most people in our land sleep as well."

"Then your nation is blessed of God," Prester John said and worked himself into a space at the table.

"There's really no need for armor at the table, your majesty," Brian said, smiling.

"We are joining battle this very morning, are we not?" The khan looked confused.

"Waal, that's definitely somethin' we gotta talk about," Dylan said. "Can someone say grace so we can dig into this loveliness?"

Susan obliged. "Fortify us with this food, Blessed One. Because we need your help and strength. Amen."

"Amen," they all agreed, and the lazy Susan began to spin.

Kat noted that Prester John ate with undisguised gusto. He also ate without any hint of Western table manners, and she fought to keep from staring at him as he lowered his face into his plate and shoveled in his eggs, using his spoon as a trowel. She noted that others were struggling not to watch him as well, and then it was hard not to simply laugh. Again, she felt a pain of poignancy, recognizing in that moment of glee everything she loved about her life, about these people. The precariousness of their continued life together struck at her heart like a lance.

As soon as their first helpings were nearing completion, Dylan wiped his beard and threw his napkin on the table. "All raaaght, friends-n-neighbors, we gots us a hell of a day before us. Time to make a plan."

Mouths froze in mid-mastication as they stared at him. Terry cocked one eyebrow suspiciously. Dylan ignored them and continued. "I suggest we head over to the City by BART; thet way we can all stay together since we only gots the one car. We got us a bishop, so make sure you got yore kit bags with you—God knows what we'll encounter once we get there. But use yore small kits—just the essentials—we don't need to be slowed down by a bunch of luggage."

Mikael put down his fork. "Who are you, and what have you done with Dylan?"

Dylan ignored him. "Terry, you've got a relationship with Preston. Ah wants you to stick to him like glue. You're our best chance at snatchin' that crozier when he ain't lookin'. And once you've got it..."

Everyone held their breaths.

"Don't think. Just act. Am Ah clear?"

Terry nodded curtly. "The rest of us will be decoys. We'll let them deploy us however they want, but let's keep track of where Terry is at all times 'cause as soon as he's got it, we gotta be there to close ranks and keep him safe."

"You do realize we'll be the only people in the building who aren't carrying guns, right?" Terry asked.

"Which will be a moot point once you've got yore mitts on that Spear," Dylan said. "An' in case Terry gets taken out, whoever's closest to Preston has got to take his place."

"That's the whole plan?" Mikael asked, a note of uncertainty in his voice.

"There's too many variables to go into more detail," Dylan nodded. "The more we define it, the more flustered we'll be when things don't go as planned. So, the plan is simple: We do whatever they tell us to do—within the bounds of our Rule, o' course—and try to keep Terry clear to stay as close to Preston as possible."

Dylan watched as one by one his order mates nodded their agreement. "Thet means that if someone tries to call Terry away, one of us leaps in and does whatever is bein' asked. Keep Terry free. First chance he gets to snatch the Spear, he does, and we get outta there. That's it."

More nods.

Dylan turned to his wife. "Darlin', Ah wants you on the computer. Monitor the convention, as well as any incoming messages from Randy. Group text us anything you think is relevant."

"Aye-aye," she said. Kat saw tears brimming in her eyes.

"Brian, Ah want you at the library in case we need research support. Never know what the fuck we're gonna run into, and if it's anything like what we usually run into, Ah'm gonna need information fast and reliable-like."

Brian nodded. "You got it, Boss. Which library, do you think? Berkeley Public, GTU?"

"Ah'm gonna suggest the Bancroft," Dylan said. "Thet way if you need to rush over ta the GTU, you can do it in five minutes. We can cover the most bases that way."

"The Bancroft will probably give us everything we need anyway," Brian nodded. "Good plan."

"All agreed?" Dylan asked.

"Dylan, if you don't mind me asking," Terry said cautiously. "I don't...I mean, I've never seen you...like this. Why couldn't you do this last week? I mean, you're *good* at this."

Dylan puffed up his chest, staring at Terry. Kat thought he looked angry. Then he deflated, and he looked down at his hands. "Ah been wonderin' the same thing, Ter. An' here's what Ah think. Ah think Ah told mahself that the pot was helpin' my anxiety. An' it kinda was. It relaxed me as soon as Ah smoked it. But Ah ignored the fact that it made me *more* anxious, too."

"It often has a paradoxical effect on people," Brian agreed. "I noticed the same effects in myself."

"So, Ah think I wuz usin' it to treat mah insecurity, an' all the while it wuz makin' me *more* insecure," Dylan said, a sad wistfulness in his voice. "Ah sure do miss it, though. It's like losin' a limb. Or a fambly member."

"You're losing a large part of your identity," Susan said, taking his hand. "If you're not the pothead friar, who are you? You're proud of that identity, I know. It says something powerful and true about the goodness of creation and the liberty of the Gospel. But it's a flag someone else will have to carry now. You have to figure out who Dylan is *without* pot."

"Ah feel like I jus' died." Dylan continued staring at his hands.

"A part of you has." Susan leaned over and kissed him. "I'll mourn him, too. After all, it was the pothead friar I fell in love with. But I made a vow to you, the true Dylan, no matter how you change, or what you'll face. Including this weird allergy illness. And to be honest, Honey, the pothead was eclipsing the friar. Something had to give."

Dylan closed his eyes. It was shame, Kat realized. Her heart went out to him.

Prester John leaned over and spoke in Kat's ear. "What in the name of heaven are you all talking about?"

Brian overheard and laughed. "Hashish madness, your majesty. Dylan has had hashish madness for years."

Prester John burst out laughing. It was a large, booming laugh that filled the room and shook it. It was also infectious. Soon, they were all smiling, if a little uncertainly. Dylan looked like he wasn't sure if the mirth was directed at him or not. In the end, it didn't seem to matter. Prester John pounded the tabletop, and when his guffaws subsided he looked at Dylan with renewed respect. "This explains much," he said.

When he stopped laughing, he drew himself up and directed a question directly at Dylan. "But what of me?"

Dylan met his eyes. "What do yuh mean?"

"I have come to chasten my son," he said. "Surely, I must accompany you."

Dylan blew air out of his cheeks. "Waal, yer majesty, thet's gonna be a problem. See, uh, no one is gonna let you through the door like that, and it's gonna be hard fer you to pass as one of us, an'..."

He looked at Brian for help. It occurred to Kat that if they gave Prester John a cassock and allowed him to tag along, much of their energy would be spent babysitting him, keeping him out of trouble, maybe keeping him from getting shot when he challenged some clueless Republican flunky to a swordfight.

"Your majesty," Brian said, "surely when you commanded armies, you had a small number of trusted men that you sent into the most dangerous situations. We call them 'special forces.' What was your name for them?"

The khan's eyebrows knit together as he thought. "I did indeed have such men. I called them *itegekü*."

"The...trusted?" Brian guessed.

"Yes, that is very close," the khan nodded.

"Your majesty, the Blackfriars are your *itegekü* here," Brian said calmly, without a hint of condescension. "You must trust them, just as you trusted your own special forces, to go into the most dangerous situations and act on your behalf. If they are successful, there will be nothing to stop you from confronting your descendant, Bishop Preston. But you must first let them infiltrate the enemy, and draw them out."

Prester John nodded. "This is fair counsel," he judged.

Dylan nodded. "We got one shot at this, y'all," he said. "We got one day to get that Spear, or there will be nothin' to stop Governor Ivory gettin' to the White House. An' that means that ain't nuthin' gonna stop World War III. The only thing standin' between this world and Armageddon is us, so Ah'm gonna say this an' Ah want you all to hear it: Lean hard on Jesus, and don't fuck it up."

"Amen," said Terry.

"Amen," said the rest.

88

RICHARD LOOKED down to double check the map. When he looked back up, he realized that he was out of road. He spun the wheel and slammed on the brakes, skidding to a stop within mere inches of a drainage ditch. "Goddamn," he breathed, and got out of his car to survey the road. He had, apparently, looked down at just the wrong moment. For no apparent reason, the road did a fishback, heading off in a direction that Richard did not want to go. *That's dangerous*, he thought.

To his right he could see the campus of Pacific Christian College. A row of enormous palm trees adorned the massive lawn, trailing off into the horizon. To his left, about a hundred yards from the fishback, was a small coffee shop—or diner, he couldn't be sure. He looked back at his directions. He looked at the diner. "Could that be it?" he wondered aloud.

Richard got back into the car and cautiously made as tight a turn as he could, coming to a full stop just outside the diner. Its yard was untended. The tiny parking lot sported more mud than gravel. The only identifying marker on the place was a piece of plywood with the words NO EXIT painted on it in blood-red splashes.

Yet for all its unkempt façade, the place seemed to be hopping.

Richard looked at his watch—9 a.m. It *was* time for coffee. He leaned in the window of his rental car. "Stay here, Toby. If you see anything strange, bark like a motherfucker."

The dog barked exactly once, which Richard took to mean "message received." He slapped the hood of the car, straightened his cassock, and went inside.

The screen door slammed behind him, and he waited for his eyes to adjust. To his right were dusty bookcases filled with secondhand books. Atop the middle book case was a foot-high statue of Nataraj, the dancing Shiva. Looking to his left, he saw a bar with a cash register at one end and behind it a mirror reminiscent of saloons in cowboy movies. Obscuring the mirror at one end was an espresso machine.

Richard continued to scan the room, counterclockwise. On the wall was a mural of what seemed to be Jesus wearing a cowboy hat and chaps. Surrounding him were a cadre of boho-looking disciples, frozen in place, some of them sipping espresso and others playing liar's dice. At one table, a German shepherd sat upright, tipping back a Dos Equis, apparently charming a poodle bitch. Beneath the picture, in the same rough script as the sign above the door outside, were the words, The Great Omission.

Scattered around the room were the very same sorts of tables depicted in the mural, many of them occupied. There were no wooing canines, but otherwise, the mural seemed to have gotten it mostly right. About half of the clientele were people in their thirties and forties, sipping from enormous mugs and definitely running through a good supply of croissants. He guessed the other half were students at the Christian college as they were both younger and louder.

The place was filled with an energetic conviviality that touched Richard deeply.

"Is that your dog?"

Richard registered the question but didn't see the asker, nor did he know whether the question was being put to him. A wave caught his attention. Behind the bar, a sandy-haired man smiled at him. "I said," he raised his voice, "is that your dog?" He pointed out the window at Richard's car.

Richard walked over to him and nodded. "Yeah, that's Toby."

"Why don't you bring him in?" The man's eyes twinkled at him. His smile was genuine and warm. Was he...flirting?

Richard pushed the thought away. "Is that allowed? I mean, health codes and all."

"I see that you are debilitated and require your companion animal," the barista said with a mock-curt nod.

Richard laughed out loud. "Sure, I'll bring him in." In a few moments, Toby burst through the door, and Richard made sure it didn't slam behind them. A mild cheer rose up in the room as Toby rushed to sniff out the first table he came to, to the apparent delight of the diners.

"Welcome," the barista said.

"That's one dangerous curve in the road out there," Richard complained.

"Tell me about it." The barista visibly bristled. "I can't tell you how many times I've complained. There's usually an altar of some kind set up there."

"It's not hard to see why," Richard admitted.

"What can I get for you?" The barista pounded a hand on the bar.

"What's the favorite, here?" Richard leaned against the bar. The barista's hair was beginning to thin, a tragedy Richard knew well. He was younger than Richard by about ten years; shorter, too. He was thickly built, but not overweight. *Solid*, Richard decided.

"Well, we got a full morning menu," he said. "I recommend the honeydew-green matcha latte, but if you're a meat-and-potatoes guy, the fair trade Italian roast is probably the way to go. It's the default morning drink around here."

"And the default evening drink? Just out of curiosity?"

"That would be either the house red or the Riverside Firehouse IPA, on tap. 'Course we got the holy trinity of Guinness, Bass, and Harp, too, if you're not feeling adventurous." He smiled. "But that's all academic—we don't pour anything harder than a triple espresso until 4 p.m."

"As it should be," Richard slapped the bar. "I'll take a mug of that Italian roast, please."

The man nodded and grabbed a mug from a precarious pile against the wall to his left. "What's your name, stranger?" The twinkle in his eye revealed that the man knew he was using a *Gunsmoke-* worthy cliché.

"Richard Kinney," Richard said, his tummy burbling under the assault of the delicious aromas filling the room.

"Then I've been expecting you." The man put a steaming cup in front of him. "On the house. Welcome."

"That's very kind," Richard said. "So, I'm guessing you're Bishop?"

"The one and only," the barista said. "I hope. Because if not, a complicated science fiction scenario would ensue, and I like a quiet life."

Richard laughed. He liked this man. A *lot*. He felt his libido rise.

Don't you fucking go there, Duunel's voice said in his head. *We have a deal.*

In answer, Richard simply sipped at the coffee and smiled into Bishop's eyes. *Okay, I'm now officially flirting*, Richard thought. *Well, when it's right, it's right.* Out loud, however, he said. "And are you?"

"Am I what?"

"A bishop."

"Yeah, but I don't trumpet it. It's how I got the nickname, though, of course."

"So, *not* your given name, then?" Richard wasn't sure his grin could get any wider, but he risked his facial integrity to manage it.

"Terrence," he said, moving his head from side to side. "I prefer Bishop. Oh, excuse me a minute, please," Bishop said. "Gotta make the rounds." He grabbed a coffee pot and headed into the room, topping off mugs and chatting playfully with the clientele. He stopped for several minutes at a table where a very tall, bearded man in a Western-style shirt seemed to be in the midst of an animated discussion with a short, stocky man who was waxing blustery. A very amused younger woman was also at the table and seemed to be teasing the stocky man. Bishop looked like he was arbitrating a dispute. In a few minutes, he detached himself and walked back behind the bar. He set the coffee pot on the burner and turned back to Richard. "I'm thinking you need a croissant. Or a bear claw," he said.

"A bear claw would be great," Richard said.

"Peanut and allspice marzipan," Bishop said, placing one in front of him.

"Good God," Richard exclaimed. He realized he was ravenous. As he tucked in, Bishop filled a bowl of water and placed it on the floor. "Thank you," Richard said. "Toby will find that soon enough."

"No problem. I can probably scare up some leftovers for him later, too."

Richard took another long pull and waved at the patrons. "Tell me about them."

Bishop nodded. "Okay, so the table I was just at? The tall guy is Stockton, and the shorter guy is Paulo. They're graduates of the college. I am, too. We all went to school together, back in the early '90s. The young woman is a current student. Her name is Tilly. You'll like her. She's bubbly."

"What are they arguing about?" Richard asked.

"The exact meaning of *homoousian*," Bishop said. "Stockton is maintaining that it means 'identical,' while Paulo insists it means 'of common origin.' Tilly is a Unitarian, and she thinks they're both splitting hairs."

"Oh my God," Richard said. "This is exactly the kind of shit my order mates argue about."

"Okay, see that larger table, over there?" Bishop pointed toward the far corner.

"Yeah," Richard said. About six people were gathered around it, all of them looking down intently at their books. "Study group?"

"In a way," Bishop said. "It's a weekly working group, half Christians, half Thelemites. They're mapping Paul's Epistle to the Galatians to—"

"To *The Book of the Law*," Richard breathed. "Fucking brilliant. How far are they?"

"About halfway through," he said. "They're using Paul as their organizing structure, and hopscotching around *Liber Al vel Legis*, but you'd be surprised at the number of parallels."

"No, no, I wouldn't," Richard laughed. He took another sip and sighed deeply. "I feel like I'm...home."

"I'm glad," Bishop said.

"You've got your own little corner of the Kingdom going here."

Bishop nodded, with obvious satisfaction. "It's imperfect, but Jesus shows up." He leaned on the bar and looked Richard in the eye. Richard felt chills run up his spine. He also felt the fern leaf of his penis begin to unfurl. He ignored Duunel's profanity-laced complaints. He stared back into those eyes.

"So, I gather you need a bishop," Bishop said.

"Oh. Desperately," Richard answered.

89

PRESTER JOHN STOOD outside and watched the Blackfriars walk down the street toward the "BART station," whatever *that* was. They waved back at him as they neared the end of the block. He raised his hand in farewell. Then they turned the corner and were gone from his sight. He sighed. "'Special forces,' my hairy bollocks," he said out loud to himself. He turned and went to tend to his horse.

90

A SILENCE FELL over the Blackfriars as they boarded at the central Berkeley BART station. People stared at the strange gaggle in their Anglican cassocks. Kat smiled at them patiently. It had taken a while to get used to wearing the long black robe, but she was beginning to grow fond of it. It was roomy, smart looking, and one didn't have to waste precious time wondering what to wear for the day.

She pulled out her phone and emailed Randy. In a couple of minutes, a reply came back: "Can't hover near the computer for long. Lots of activity here today. I hear you're providing security—good, he'll need it. I know you guys think he's the Antichrist or something, but I kind of like him. And I think you're nuts anyway. BTW, I'm not sure how clear he was with that gay Asian guy of yours, but when Bishop Preston said he'd meet you at the service entrance, he meant the southwest service entrance. Don't be at the wrong place! Ciao, Sis."

Kat felt relief wash over her. He was okay. More than okay, he was on mission. She leaned over and handed the phone to Dylan. He read it slowly and carefully, and his eyebrows shot up near the end of it. "Good stuff!" he said. "Ah know Moscone Center has two halves to it,

East Center and West Center, but it never occurred to meh to ask which one."

He passed the phone to Terry, who nodded. "Good catch, *Randy*," he said. "But I have to object to being reduced to 'the gay Asian guy.' There's so much more bloom to my flower than that."

"After all, *you're* an artist," Mikael added, accepting the phone from Terry. "And a chef renowned for your bean pâté, *and* you're an international man of mystery—"

"Just stop," Terry commanded. "Although my bean pâté is no slouch."

Mikael grinned a mean grin as he read the message. He handed the phone back to Kat, who pocketed it.

The rest of the ride passed quickly, and as the doors opened on the Montgomery Street BART station, Kat acquiesced to the current of the stream of people passing from the train up the stairs to the surface.

Once there, the walk was brisk, as was the weather. Although Berkeley was comfortably warm, all bets were off in San Francisco, a mere fifteen miles away.

Kat loved watching the teeming crowds as they rushed to and fro in San Francisco's business district. As they crossed Market Street, she saw the garish façade of the Museum of Modern Art to her left, while straight ahead a mob of protesters was corralled behind waist-high metal fences bearing the SFPD insignia. Bullhorns raged, but the sound was so distorted that Kat couldn't make out the words. The signs were easy enough to read, though. One read, GREAT LAKES GENOCIDE, and another read, MOSQUES NOT BOMBS. Kat breathed deeply and kept walking.

To her right, the massive Moscone Center edged unobtrusively out of the ground. Kat had been inside several times—most recently, the Blackfriars had attended a science fiction convention there together. It was mostly underground, split like a butterfly into equally spacious centers east of Howard Street and west of it.

Turning right on Howard, Dylan strode ahead of them. To the left Kat saw the stairs leading down to the half-mile-long row of doors that served as the entrance to the East Center. A parallel string of doors stretched out to her right for the West Center. Both sides were teeming with life, with black-suited men hurrying up and down the stairs, talking in rapid-fire bursts with smart-looking women in pantsuits and power dresses.

Dylan went past the westside doors and turned right again on Fourth Street, where another barricade kept protesters at a respectful distance from the center. These were singing, "Jesus loves the little children…" One huge sign had a picture of a vaguely Middle Eastern little girl. Kat's heart leaped into her throat. These people probably thought they were going to the convention. She wished she could let them know somehow that she was on their side, that she felt like them—that she, too, was so angry that she could hardly see straight.

But of course, there was no time. They turned right into the first alley leading to the southside rear entrances of the West Center. It was a typical San Francisco alley, and nothing particularly stood out to Kat. Debris littered the ground. A bicycle was chained to a No Parking sign, and dumpsters were scattered in an asymmetrical pattern.

The alley dead-ended at a black metal wall of doors that must, Kat supposed, be their destination. Dylan seemed to think so, too, as he strode resolutely toward the doors and pounded on one of them with his thick, hammy fist. He bounced on the balls of his feet until the rest of them caught up to him.

"Just as I imagined," Mikael said.

"I was expecting more of a welcoming party," Terry said. "You know, Secret Service agents waving their handheld electronic probes—"

"*That* was your wet dream last night," Mikael teased.

"Fair enough," Terry smiled. "A girl can hope, after all."

"Where the devil are they?" Dylan asked again.

"Hey, Kat, check that message again," Mikael said. "Maybe we misunderstood Randy's message. I read it pretty fast."

Kat pulled out her phone and repeated Randy's instructions. Dylan shook his head. "Nah, thet's exactly where we're at, mah friends." He checked his watch. "Waal, we *are* a couple minutes early."

"Yeah, but with all that's going on here today, I'd expect every one of these entrances to be teeming," Terry countered.

"Remember, this is Republicans we're talkin' about," Dylan counseled. "Don't pay to impose sense on the situation."

"Sad but true," Terry agreed.

"Uh...guys. Turn around. Slowly," Kat instructed. As they did, they saw what she saw: a swarm of people moving in a single, lurching mass had followed them into the alley. They now blocked the only exit, sealing it up tight with their assembled bodies like a cork in a bottle of wine. They were beginning to look the worse for wear—suit pockets hung torn, ties were loose or missing, many were wearing what looked like rags, and a couple seemed to be naked.

Their movements were unnatural. Although a few of them moved swiftly and easily, most stumbled forward uncertainly, stiffly. One or two jerked spasmodically as if it were only proper for such a disheveled army to be ornamented by break dancers undergoing intermittent electric shocks.

As they advanced, more and more followed them into the alley. Kat could see no end to the lines of people flowing toward them. Dylan pounded harder and louder at the wall of metal doors, but they remained sealed, a solid and impenetrable wall behind them. Before them, another wall—this one composed of lurching, drooling flesh—advanced.

And the gap was closing.

91

THE MORNING RUSH HAVING FINISHED, Bishop could finally relax and enjoy a cup of coffee of his own. He came out from behind the bar and invited Richard to join him at one of the tables. Toby followed and found a spot underneath the table, cuddled at Richard's feet. Stockton and Paulo were now playing liar's dice, and the working group was still going at it, chatting excitedly, but most of the other patrons had filtered out to their jobs, their errands, their lives.

"What time *do* you roll out of bed?" Richard asked.

"Oh, usually about four," Bishop smiled. "You get used to it. There's lots to do, of course. On a good day, everything's wrapped up by closing time, but sometimes there's still a dish or two to wash in the morning."

"What time *do* you close?" Richard asked.

Bishop moved his head from side to side. "*Close* is a very definite term. Officially, we stop serving at 10 p.m., but that doesn't mean that people leave."

"When does your shift end?" Richard asked.

"Shift?" Bishop asked. "I'm afraid that I'm all there is. Officially."

"I'm getting the idea that 'officially' doesn't have a lot of meaning around here," Richard smiled.

"The Law was made for people, not people for the Law," Bishop nodded.

"I'm going to pretend that wasn't half as cryptic as it actually sounded."

"You're a kind man." Bishop winked at him.

Richard fought down a fluttery feeling of lust. *Don't you dare fucking go there*, Duunel said in his head. Richard ignored him.

"So, if you're the only employee, and you close at 10 p.m. and get up at four, when do you sleep?" Richard asked, a little concerned.

"Well, I try to get a siesta in about midday," Bishop said, playing with a napkin. "And I pretty much wander off to bed whenever I get tired." He motioned to the back room. "Folks quiet down. They leave money on the counter for whatever they drink. And they lock the door when they go."

"Are you kidding me?"

"It's the Kingdom, remember? If someone fails to pay for a beer, so what? I assume they just don't have the money."

"You *live* here?" Richard asked.

Bishop looked a bit sheepish. He nodded. "I've got a room in back. Want to see it?"

It was an odd question. One that Richard expected a friend to say when they were twelve—he didn't expect to hear it from an adult. It occurred to him that it might be a come-on. He hoped it was. "Maybe later. So, you're open at 6 a.m., you close at 10 p.m., and you're the only employee," Richard said. Bishop nodded. "When do you get out?"

"I don't," Bishop said.

"Really," Richard pressed him, "when do you get some Bishop time?"

"I get plenty of that right here," he said. "I'm in the place I love best. My place. And my friends come to me. I don't leave. I'm serious. I don't leave. Ever."

"Ever?" Richard asked, cocking his head in disbelief. "When was the last time you left this building?"

"Hmm..." Bishop thought hard. "What year is it?"

"Are you fucking kidding me?"

Bishop ignored him and counted on his fingers. "Twelve. Thirteen—no, twelve years." Bishop's shoulders slouched, and Richard saw a look in his eye that absolutely melted him. A look that said, *I know that's fucked up, but please don't reject me.*

"Bishop, I find that...incredible. You haven't been to the doctor—"

"Strong as an ox," he said.

"Or a dentist—"

"Haven't had a cavity. My people aren't English, thank God. Great teeth." He flashed Richard an exaggerated grin, exposing more of his pearly whites than Richard was really comfortable seeing. On the other hand, it was hard not to imagine a mouth with such impressive plasticity going down—

Don't you fucking even think it, Duunel almost screamed.

"Can't help what I think," Richard said under his breath.

You fucking well can, and you will. Of all people, I would think you would understand discipline.

"That's a fine thing coming from a demon," Richard whispered.

Just don't forget: we have a deal.

"That's a very odd conversation you're having with yourself," Bishop had leaned back, eyeing Richard curiously.

"Well, since we're playing true confessions, there's something I'm a bit hesitant to tell you about myself, too."

"Let me guess, you eat all the crème middles from Oreos but throw the cookies away."

"Worse," Richard grinned.

"You actually watch *American Idol*?"

"Uh...I *have* done that," Richard confessed, "but that's not it."

"Okay, I give up," Bishop said. "What could possibly be worse?"

"I'm possessed by a demon. Named Duunel." Richard forced a pained smile.

"Oh. Yeah. That's worse," said Bishop. Then he tilted his head to one side. "Can he cook?"

92

TERRY WATCHED the lurching horde advance toward them. Some sneered, sporting gleeful, hateful grins, but most of the faces were slack as if the inhabitants of those bodies had their hands full just operating the legs and couldn't be bothered with minutiae like facial muscles. "It's Larch's fucking army," he said.

"That'd be mah guess," Dylan agreed, "Republicans usually shower." He doubled his efforts at trying to get someone's attention inside Moscone Center. He pounded with desperation, but no doors opened.

"Prepare for impact," Terry said.

Dylan turned and judged their distance and the time they had before their inevitable engagement. "Terry, set wards," he said. "Mikael, front and center—you keep as many of them motherfuckers busy as you can. Kat, you get on your phone, and get help here, fast."

"What are you going to do?" asked Terry, sprinting off to find wardable objects.

Dylan tore a ragged board off a pallet leaning against the wall of the nearest building. "Ah'm gonna bust me a few heads before Ah go down!" he answered and gave the board a test swing as if he were a batter stepping up to the plate.

Kat punched at her phone, then held it to her ear as she watched Terry scramble, snatching up palm-size chunks of concrete, empty soda cans, and any other portable, distinguishable objects which might, at least for a while, bear the burden of warding.

The 911 operator picked up the phone. "Uh, hello?" Kat said, "Please send help! We're outside the Moscone Center—"

"The Bret Harte Alley," Dylan called to her, "at Fourth Street!"

Kat repeated this information breathlessly. "Please remain calm, and tell me what is happening," the operator instructed.

Kat wanted to shout, "It's the Zombie Apocalypse, you clueless bitch!" But she mastered herself. "We're being attacked. By a large group of people. They're going to kill us!"

"Units are responding now," the woman said calmly. "Are the attackers armed?"

"They *have* arms—most of them," Kat replied, "but no guns that I can see."

Apparently having gained enough of the objects, Terry ran toward the advancing horde. He stopped several yards shy of them and dropped to his knees, placing a soda can on the ground and holding his hands over it as he invoked what Kat assumed to be an archangel or other spiritual forces.

"How many people are attacking you?" The woman's voice was eerily sedate.

"Uh...I'd say about 250," Kat estimated. "With more on the way." The line of people turning into the alley from Fourth Street had not abated, she was distressed to see. They continued to flow in, a steady current of the damned.

Leaping up, Terry crossed to the other side of the alley and knelt again. Just then, one of the faster-moving of the possessed ran directly toward him. Kat had never seen Dylan move so quickly. In three strides he met the attacker. Kat saw his beefy arms grow taut beneath the fabric of his cassock as he swung the jagged board and caught the possessed man square on the jaw, sending him spinning off into the advancing wall of his fellows. This slowed the advance of the east flank momentarily, but others were hard upon them. Kat began barking hysterically into the phone as Mikael sprang forward, determined to buy her more time.

She watched in horror as he faced a wall of the horde alone and unarmed. As one of the damned lurched toward him, Mikael went into full *randori* mode. He dodged, grabbed the man's arm, and pulled him off balance. Allowing his momentum to swing him around, Mikael ducked and shot his foot out, tripping another attacker. Another reached down to where Mikael now lay on his back. Mikael used this to his advantage by grabbing both shoulders and pulling down quickly as he rolled to his right. The man's head hit the pavement, and Mikael swung to his feet, hands up, ready to ward off any blows. They were not long in coming.

Kat was so terrified, she no longer heard the operator's voice, now escalating in its assertiveness. She dropped the phone and screamed as the body of the one of the damned struck the wall mere inches from where she was crouching, thrown there by one of Mikael's rapid aikido strikes. The man groaned, and Kat gasped in recognition.

"I know you," she said. The man's head was bleeding, and his eyes blinked, confused. Just then, she saw the real person—the *human* person—emerge in his eyes. They grew large as he recognized her, but then he jerked in terror at the violence erupting all around him. "You're Doug!!" Kat shouted. "Dylan, I *know* him!"

Dylan was swinging his board wildly, connecting again and again with the heads, shoulders, and torsos of the damned, but Kat could see that he was losing ground. "Uh...thet's great, Kat. Give 'im mah regards!" He began to swing even more wildly, and Kat saw bits of hair and skin flying from the jagged board only to be trampled underfoot by those who followed after.

One of the damned had thrown himself on Mikael's back, and Kat gasped as she saw Mikael stumble. Another threw himself on top of the first, and Mikael went down. "Mikael!" Kat shouted and leaped up, rushing now into the fray.

Kat was small, she knew that, but she was also catching many of them off guard. She pulled those leaning over Mikael backward and leaped out of the way as they stumbled. She instinctively resorted to fighting tactics she hadn't used since elementary school, grabbing at a woman's hair and yanking her off balance, then quickly stepping into her vacated place, trying to get closer to her beloved.

"What's happening?" Doug cried. "Who are these people? What do they want?"

Kat didn't pause to answer him. Instead, she kicked, spat, yanked, slapped, and punched her way into the knot of people piled on top of Mikael. In her peripheral vision, Terry leaped up and shouted, "Warded!" at the top of his lungs. She barely heard him, and it hardly mattered. A giant of a man roared, and she saw his shadow descending upon her before the weight of him hit. She crouched and screamed, holding her hands above her head in a useless gesture of protection when she heard an ear-splitting "thunk" and saw the man stagger aside, deterred from his deadly course by one well-aimed blow from Dylan's makeshift bat.

Without pause, Kat dove back into the dogpile that covered her boyfriend, punching and clawing and dragging the bodies off him by sheer force of hysterical will. Moments later, she realized the work was going faster, and looked up to see the confused but determined face of Doug working beside her.

As she pulled them off, she saw Terry standing behind her and slightly to her right, pushing the damned back the way they had come. It occurred to her that the horde was thinning. She permitted herself a quick look around and realized that Terry's wards must have succeeded. There seemed to be an imaginary line bisecting the alley —a line that the possessed could not cross, like an invisible force field from some old science fiction film. At one point, the damned simply could go no farther. As their fellows continued to rush in behind them, Kat could see the massed crowd's crushing effects on those unfortunate enough to be in the front line.

That left a finite number of the damned on *their* side of the warded line, which seemed manageable until it registered that, not counting those they had wounded, it still left them outnumbered by about ten to one. *Not the best odds,* Kat thought, *but I'll take it over the hundred to one on the other side of that line.*

"Who did you call?" Dylan shouted over his shoulder at her.

"What?" she asked, still yanking crushed bodies out of her way.

"On the phone! Who did you call?"

"I called 911!" she called back. "For what good it did!"

She hadn't been paying attention to anything except the pile immediately in front of her. But now she understood why Dylan had asked. The piercing wail of sirens echoed off the alley's walls, and a glance over her shoulder revealed the red strobe lights reflecting off the glass of the building's windows next to them. For a moment, her hopes raised. But then she realized that the police were on the other side of the bottleneck of the possessed still pouring into the alley from Fourth Street. The police could no more get to the Blackfriars than the Blackfriars could get to the police. She set her teeth and attacked the pile in front of her with renewed vengeance.

"Call Susan," Dylan ordered.

"Now?" Kat asked, incredulous.

"No, ten minutes *after* we provide supper fer the damned here," Dylan managed a one-two slice that took down three of the damned at once. But Kat could see his strength flagging. His cassock hung crazily on his out-of-shape frame, and sweat was streaming down his face.

"Go," Doug reassured her. "I'll get this."

She gave a curt nod and leaped free of the dogpile, snatching her phone from her pocket. It only took a few seconds to relay their situation to Susan, and she leaped back in, dodging, striking, and screaming like a banshee.

"Got him!" Doug shouted and Kat leaped to him, seeing Mikael's wild mane of jet-black hair. She knelt and felt at his pulse. It was strong. But he wasn't conscious.

"Let's drag him clear," Kat called, and she and Doug each took an arm while Dylan covered them. As soon as Mikael was safe, both Kat and Doug turned and faced the remaining horde.

"Kat!" a voice called. She looked around and saw Terry by the pallet. He tore off a board and tossed it to her. He nodded at Doug and tossed him one, too. Then taking one up himself, they rushed in to relieve Dylan, who was beginning to stagger.

As they stepped up, she saw Dylan withdraw, drop the board, and steady himself, doubled over with his hands on his knees. Out of the corner of her eye, he saw him looking up as if at the rooftops. "Fuck me," he said.

"What?" she called to him, beginning to get the rhythm of the whole found-wood warfare thing: swing-parry-reset, repeat.

"Two o'clock, aim high," Dylan said through his teeth. She could hear him still panting, fighting to regain his breath. After her next blow connected, she risked a look up. It took her a moment to see it, but then she did. On top of the building at the Northwest corner of Fourth and Bret Harte, a lone figure surveyed the melee in the alley.

"Larch!" Dylan bellowed. "What the fuck do you want?!"

"The same thing we do!" Terry called over his shoulder, swinging wildly but largely ineffectually. Kat could see that he was keeping the damned at bay, but he wasn't exacting much damage.

"So why attack *us*?" Dylan asked.

"Maybe because he knows we're the only people on Earth who can stand in his way," Terry reasoned.

"Damn *straight*!" Dylan spat. Then he picked up his board again and came forth swinging. Kat watched with wonder as he sliced at the horde without mercy. While she was content to be a delaying annoyance, she saw the demons quail when Dylan held forth. His baritone voice rang out and echoed resoundingly throughout the alley. "In the fuckin'" WHAM! "name o' Jesus," THUCK! "Ah repel thee," FOCK! "all y'all evil," BAM! "motherfuckin'," CRASH! "sons-a-fuckin'-bitches!" CRACK!

Heartened by Dylan's display of strength, Kat doubled her own ferocity. A man nearly twice her own weight in a military uniform lunged at her, and her swing sent a spray of blood cascading across the frosted windows of the building to her left. No sooner had he staggered, clutching at his neck, than a woman who looked to be about the age of Kat's mother threw herself to the street and rolled into Kat's feet, striking up into her cassock with a hard, balled fist, catching her in the lower abdomen.

Kat was winded at first, and caught off balance since the woman had cleverly contrived to get too close for striking. Not so much thinking quickly as reacting to the crazed, wildly jerking man about to thrash her, Kat jumped with both feet onto the woman's torso. She gasped and curled onto her side like a potato bug curling up into its shell.

Just then, Kat heard the crack of a rifle, and she ducked reflexively. "Thet's gonna be the police!" Dylan called over the din. He didn't miss a beat but continued to swing the battered, blood-spattered board. "Don't get too afeared of 'em," he continued. "Them'd be riot guns, prob'ly with rubber bullets."

"*Probably* with rubber bullets?" Terry called. "Did you say *probably*?"

"Ah'm gonna operate on that assumption, yeah," Dylan said. He swung up this time, catching a man in black-checked cook's trousers under the jaw and sending him flying three feet off the ground.

Kat heard the loud click of metal on metal behind her, and out of the corner of her eye she saw the steel doors of the service entrance opening. "Finally!" she cried. "Thank you, Susan!"

"*Now* y'all duck!" shouted Dylan. Kat watched him dive for the dirt, and without another thought she did the same. She was just in time. Behind her, she heard the blazing of guns, so numerous and so loud that any other sound was indistinguishable.

93

"WHAT'S it like to be possessed by a demon?" Bishop leaned forward, looking in Richard's eyes as if he expected to see a little devil lounging in his iris. The close heat of his body and the musty smell of him made Richard light-headed—and in fact, a little crazy. His cock started expanding, seemingly of its own volition, and he began to sweat. He shifted in his chair.

"Uh...it's like being handcuffed to your college roommate at all times," Richard said. "And not your bookish roommate, either. I mean the boorish asshole who thinks that women are just jizz sponges—who has no manners, no boundaries, and no self-control."

I love you, too, Duunel said spitefully.

"Oh, and he never shuts up," Richard said. "Unless, of course, you're about to be raped by a hulking Neanderthal, in which case he's nowhere to be found."

"Sounds like there's a story there." Bishop narrowed his eyes and squirmed uncomfortably.

"*Sounds* like it," Richard agreed. "Let me process the trauma of it a little more, and I'll tell you about it. Right now...I don't care to relive it."

"It sounds like you've had a hell of a time," Bishop said. He reached out and touched Richard's hand. Richard squeezed it and looked in Bishop's eyes. He could lean over. He could kiss him.

You do that and I'll short-circuit something in your brain. That's a promise, Duunel said. *Now back the fuck off, homo-Romeo.*

Richard blinked. He smiled. The moment had passed. Bishop withdrew his hand, but not the subject. "Are you partnered?"

Richard shook his head. "No. I had a boyfriend, but he broke up with me a few months ago. Still...adjusting. I had a girlfriend before that." His eyes darkened. "She died."

"I'm so sorry," Bishop said. "What ha...how? I mean, if you're okay..."

Richard held up a hand. "I'm okay. She...was in the wrong place at the wrong time. Frenzy demon. Massive head trauma. They kept her alive for a few days, but then..." Richard's heart felt like lead. He tried not to think of Emma, and on a good day he succeeded. "One of the risks of our business. Partners are also sometimes in the line of fire."

"Are your brothers in the order partnered, then?"

"And sisters. Yeah, all of them, now," Richard said. "Except me. And I can't. Right now, anyway."

"What do you mean?" Bishop asked.

"Well, if I met a wonderful woman, there wouldn't be a problem," he said.

"Oh..." Bishop leaned back, nodding slowly. "I get it. You can play for either team, but the demon—"

"He's strictly a straight shooter," Richard nodded. "And he's pretty vocal about it."

"That's a bitch," Bishop said, giving Richard an odd, forlorn look.

"Tell me about it," Richard agreed.

"Is this a...permanent arrangement?" Bishop asked.

"No, it's...let's just say it's a marriage of convenience," Richard said.

"How long does he plan to stay?"

Richard blew air out of his cheeks. "Until we can find a suitable host."

"You mean, someone for him to *possess*?" It was Bishop's turn to look aghast.

Richard drained the last of his coffee. It was his fifth cup, and he was beginning to feel distinctly buzzy. "Well, right. I talked him out of inhabiting a little girl. We're just waiting for the right...person to come along."

"And you feel comfortable...damning someone like that? Isn't that a little...I don't know, God-like?"

"Tell me about it," Richard said, playing with the ring of wet coffee on the table. "That's why he's still here. I have no idea how to make this decision, or whether he'll even go along with it when I do. It has to be by mutual consent, of course."

"And until then you can't..." He presented the most obvious bedroom eyes Richard had ever seen.

"No," Richard said. "I can't take the Eucharist, either. Nothing he'd find offensive."

"That's burdensome," Bishop scowled.

"Yes," Richard said. "But we have an agreement. If I want him to keep his side of the bargain, I have to keep my side."

"What's his side of the bargain?" Bishop asked.

"Not taking over my consciousness and going on a killing and raping spree," Richard said, matter of factly.

"Oh. That would be bad," Bishop said.

"It would," Richard agreed.

94

KAT PRESSED her hands to her ears to shut out the pain, but the deafening noise continued. She rolled to face the doors, felt the wind of a passing bullet, and tried not to flinch. She forced open her eyes and saw a front line of Secret Service men, complete with their trademark sunglasses and midnight-black suits. Two of them held shotguns, and Kat flinched as fire erupted from their muzzles. Four more of them were emptying the clips on their handguns. Spreading out behind them was a motley assembly of what looked like ordinary people—ten of them, now twenty, now fifty of them pouring out of the conference center, all of them with guns blazing.

She rolled again and watched with fascinated horror the destruction the assault wreaked upon the army of the damned. Plumes of blood erupted as the buckshot tore open arteries and sent brain matter spraying over the roiling horde. Faster than she could count, she saw their attackers fall, and yet others—the demons more adept at working the human bodies, she guessed—seemed undeterred, despite the fact that they sported two, three, five blooms of blood where the bullets had entered them. These continued to advance, and Kat saw a shotgun blast to the head finally fell one of them. The agents must have picked up on this because the heads of the other, more determined attackers were not far behind. Kat flinched as she saw the top half of a woman's head disappear before her eyes. The neatly dressed woman pitched forward as a broken string of pearls scattered and rolled toward Kat over the concrete of the entrance landing.

Motion atop a far building caught her eye. The figure that must have been Larch was waving his hands wildly. She couldn't hear him, but as the horde on their side of the warding line ceased their advance, she guessed that he had called a retreat. *But how could they hear him?* she wondered. She didn't know, but she couldn't bother to ponder it now, either.

There were more people behind her firing guns than there were possessed on their side of the warding line. These few fell quickly, or pressed back into the wall of their fellows. Kat watched, fascinated, as the great mass of the damned turned to shuffle out of the alley toward Fourth Street. Meanwhile, those who had faced them at the very edge of the warding line dropped like stones as the pressure from their rear was removed. Kat realized that those who had not been shot had been crushed by those pressing from behind.

A great cheer rose up behind her, and Kat turned again to see cowboy hats tossed into the air and agents dispassionately speaking into walkie-talkies. Struggling wearily to her feet, she stumbled over to where Mikael lay crumpled in a heap. "Call an ambulance!" she called to no one in particular. But she saw several of the convention-goers reach for cell phones, and she wordlessly blessed them.

Looking up, she saw Doug crouched beside her. "Thank you," she said, but before he could reply she saw a flash of red in his eyes, and his face became slack. "Oh no, you fuckin' don't," she said, and without thinking she grabbed for one of the dropped planks and clocked him across the jaw. She saw a tangle of teeth and blood fly in a red arc. As the man tottered before her, she tossed the plank, seized him by his hair and raised her voice in a defiant prayer.

"Okay, Jesus, you and me haven't done this before, but this sorry guy has suffered enough. I can't drive out this demon, but you can, and if you don't mind me saying so, it's about fucking time. So, if you got it, you'd better bring it 'cause this guy fuckin' needs it."

Nothing happened. Kat felt angry. She remembered Susan talking about holding God accountable for his promises. Something in her snapped, and she raised her head to the sky and screamed, "Are you fuckin' deaf? You've got responsibilities here, asshole! *Do it!*"

She stamped her foot to punctuate her command, and as she did, Doug began to jerk uncontrollably. His eyes rolled back in his head, and a presence rose up in him—his eyes glowed bright red, and a smile spread across his face in a display of naked, proud wickedness. Kat realized that she was staring into the face of pure evil, and it made her spine feel like ice. She was riveted to the spot, unable to flee, unable to speak.

Before anyone else could move, the possessed man's face shook, and the smile faded, replaced by confusion and dismay. The being howled, and the sound ripped at Kat's soul. But she stood her ground as the howl ended and the man collapsed to the concrete like a sack of rags.

The onlookers holstered their guns, wide-eyed, and began to applaud. Terry rushed to Kat and caught her as she began to topple. He steadied her, hugging her to him, and speaking reassuringly. "You did it, Kat. You hung in there and brought the message. You did great. Just relax. The demon is gone. Your friend, there, is delivered."

"He's delivered of his *teeth*," said one of the Republicans, leaning against the wall with his arms folded, chewing tobacco. He spat.

"What in God's name..." Kat heard a familiar voice and turned to see Governor Ivory emerge from the doorway, his face growing white as he surveyed the damage. A shorter figure walked up beside him, taking his arm to support him. Kat rocked back on her heels to get a better look at him. It was Bishop Preston.

"This is exactly what I was afraid of, David," Preston said. "That's why I hired these good people."

"Holy God..." Ivory looked like he was about to fall over.

With a jerk of his head, Terry motioned for Dylan to go over. Dylan scowled momentarily at Terry but then obeyed. He walked up to the governor and the bishop, transferred the ragged board thick with blood and hair to his left hand, and offered his right to shake. Governor Ivory stared down at it in horror. Kat saw that it, too, was covered with blood. "Uh...sorry 'bout that," Dylan said, and wiped his hand on his cassock. He offered it again, but it was little better.

Nevertheless, Preston took the hand and shook it warmly. "Your courage is heroic," the bishop said. "I'm so grateful that you're here."

"Holy shit..." Ivory continued to marvel.

Terry walked up beside Dylan and offered his own hand to the bishop. "Good to see you again, Bishop Preston. Sorry to be so...unpresentable."

"Please come in, and avail yourselves of my dressing room," the bishop said, with real compassion in his eyes. "You can clean up and get some refreshment. Our Secret Service folks will want to speak to you—I'll have them meet you there."

"One of our order mates is wounded," Dylan said. "We need to make sure he gets taken care of."

Kat stood. "I'll stay with him and wait for the ambulance," she said. "And Dylan, I'd like to go to the hospital with him."

Dylan looked uncertain. He looked at Mikael, then up at Kat. "We need you here," he said. "But Ah understand. If'n it was Susan lyin' there, ain't nuthin' would keep meh from her. Okay, but if ya can come back, do it. If ya can't...Ah understand." He turned back to Preston and placed his hand on Terry's shoulder. "Let's go."

95

"Well, can I show you around?" Bishop asked.

"I was about to ask about the restroom," Richard said. "You only rent coffee, after all."

Bishop nodded and stood up. "This way," he said.

"Toby, stay," Richard commanded. The dog, reclining completely on the floor with all four paws in the air, only blinked at him.

Bishop led Richard around the bar, where an open door led to a short hallway. "Here's my room," he pointed into a door on his right. "It's my office, too," he said. Richard glanced in and saw about what he had been expecting—a desk was in one corner, adorned with piles of papers. A window directly above it illuminated it brilliantly. On the other side of the room, a twin mattress lay on the floor, covered by a single fitted sheet. A wad of bedclothes lay coiled upon it like a snail.

"The restroom is here," Bishop said, pointing into a room on the left. He pointed to a final door down the hall. "That last room is storage—not much of interest there unless you really want to stare at sacks of coffee beans or beer kegs."

Richard nodded, still mildly horrified at Bishop's anchoritic existence. He closed the door of the bathroom and leaned against the sink, feeling a disquieting tangle of emotions. One the one hand, he found Bishop's warmth, his intellect, and his bookish good looks to be an almost irresistible mix. On the other hand, he was repelled by the magnitude of neurosis that had effectively rendered him a prisoner of his own fear. Richard simply could not imagine that sort of life.

His imagination leaped to the logical consequences of getting involved with such a man. Richard had tried long-distance relationships before. Actually, *endured* was the word that came to his mind when he thought about such attempts. If he got involved with Bishop, it would mean a lot of travel—and it would all be on him. Bishop, after all, would not travel to Berkeley, would he? Richard sincerely doubted it.

Richard sighed and lifted the lid on the toilet. As he emptied his bladder, he thought about the advantages. He'd finally have a partner who would not resent the time he spent pursuing his vocation. Despite all of Richard's quirks, Bishop would be grateful to have him. *Whoa, boy*, Richard warned himself. *Just put the brakes on here. You don't even know if he's a bottom.*

Okay, did not *need that image*, Duunel complained. *Your faggoty obsession with this guy borders on cruelty for the rest of us stuck in your head.*

"If I only had a dollar for each of the times I've heard that sentence," Richard noted aloud.

I'm just sayin', Duunel almost whined.

"I'm keeping my promises," Richard assured him. "But it's not like you filter your thoughts before you so generously share them."

You don't think so, huh? Duunel countered.

That caught Richard off guard. Did Duunel have the ability to filter his thoughts? Richard had assumed that Duunel's limitations were similar to his own. Now he wondered about that. If that were true, what was Duunel *not* sharing? Richard shuddered at the thought of it.

Richard washed his hands and splashed some water on his face.

He dried both quickly and rejoined Bishop on the floor of the coffee shop. The working group was breaking up, and Bishop was exchanging hugs with several of the patrons. Richard watched them as they left. As the screen door slammed, Bishop turned to face him. "Just you and me," he said.

"Don't forget the dog and the demon in my head," Richard said.

"You say the sexiest things," Bishop noted.

Richard smiled broadly—a little too broadly, he decided, and tempered himself.

Bishop checked his watch. "Hey, I've got a lunch rush coming in about an hour. Care to help me make sandwiches?"

"I'd love to," Richard said. He followed Bishop back behind the bar. Bishop pulled several bags containing different kinds of breads from the refrigerator and set them on the workspace below the giant mirror.

"We're going to prep these for fillings—lunchmeat, cukes, and sprouts. Let's put ham here, turkey here, and sliced beef here, like this," Bishop said, preparing one sliced beef sandwich as an example.

"No condiments?" Richard asked.

"We'll add condiments and the kind of cheese the customer wants when it's ordered. In the meantime, the bulk of the work is done," Bishop smiled.

"Sounds good," Richard said, nodding.

"If you'll do that, I'll get the soup ready to go," Bishop said. For a while they worked together in contented silence. Then Bishop asked, "So, your order is in need of a bishop. What happened to your old bishop?"

Richard felt a heaviness descend on him. After all, it had only been a few days since he'd heard the news about Bishop Tom. Richard missed his friend terribly. Briefly, he recounted what he knew of Tom's motorcycle accident.

"That's terrible," Bishop said. "You see? That's exactly why I don't go out. The world is not a safe place for mitred Americans."

Richard smiled, but it was a thin smile. He appreciated Bishop's attempt to cheer him, but he needed to grieve Tom. And with all that had been going on in the last week, he hadn't really had much time to do that. He thought about sharing these thoughts with Bishop, but he felt too tired all of a sudden to try.

"Hey, I'm sorry," Bishop touched his arm, apparently noticing Richard slide into himself. "I didn't mean to make light of your bishop's death. I take it, it was more than just a professional relationship?"

Richard nodded. "He was a very close friend. There aren't many people who understand what we're doing—not really. And he...well, he really put his neck out for us." Richard remembered back to how Bishop Tom had stood up to the other bishops of the Old Catholic Synod of the Americas. He had quit rather than allow the Blackfriars to be cut loose without a bishop. He knew how important what they were doing really was. Richard made an attempt to be more lively.

"So, when he died, we lost our connection to the apostolic succession," Richard said.

"Along with your ability to perform the sacraments," Bishop nodded.

"Worse than that, we lost our ability to command demons," Richard said gravely.

Tragic, said Duunel in his head. *Cue the violins*. Richard ignored him.

"Which leaves you..." Bishop began.

"In a very vulnerable position," Richard finished. "Before I left the friary, we had an army of several hundred possessed people loitering just across the street. If it weren't for the wards that Terry set years ago..." he trailed off, staring off into space.

"I totally get it," Bishop said. "Now I understand your desperation. But there are lots of bishops in the Independent Sacramental Movement, especially in the Bay Area. Why did you need to come all the way down here?"

"Have you ever *met* half of the bishops in our movement?" Richard asked, one eyebrow dangerously raised.

"Riiiight," Bishop said, nodding. "Half of them are good, dedicated, earnest pastors—"

"The other half are self-aggrandizing, delusional, and more often than not, abusive lunatics," Richard finished.

"Well, people do often come into the movement because they've been rejected by the 'big boy' denominations," Bishop said with a tone of commiseration.

"And often, rightly so," Richard said. "You know the joke about how to get ordained an Independent Catholic priest, right?"

"Get the bishop drunk enough, you mean?" Bishop cracked a wry smile. "Yeah, I know that one. It's only funny because it's true."

"Sadly," Richard agreed. "So, let's just say that among the bishops in our area that we *know*, we're experiencing a serious shortage on sanity."

"I'm not sure I'm much better." Bishop stirred a large pot of stew on an electric burner. "Some people might consider my...isolation...a form of mental illness."

Make that most people, Duunel commented.

"Do you?" Richard asked.

"Well..." Bishop paused for a long time. Just as the silence was becoming uncomfortable, he said, "Yes, I guess I do. It's certainly not normal. And it *is* a form of fear. I like to tell myself that I'm an anchorite for spiritual purposes, but it isn't true." Bishop paused in his stirring. "On the other hand, there's crazy, and—"

"And there's *crazy*," Richard finished. He came up behind Bishop and pressed against him, laying his head on his shoulder. He felt Bishop relax, and felt his hand on his own.

Warning! Duunel screamed in his head. *Inappropriate touching! Put your hands up, and back away from the faggot! Do it now!*

Richard once again let Duunel go unheeded and squeezed Bishop hard. "I don't think you're crazy," he said softly in his ear. "I think you're wounded. Just like the rest of us."

Bishop turned to face him, and Richard saw tears welling in his eyes. Richard ran his hands along Bishop's shoulders, kneading them, and stared into his eyes. He felt the hot breath of his mouth and was close enough now to smell the spicy musk of his sweat. Bishop raised his mouth to him and despite the temper tantrum the demon was throwing in his thoughts, Richard felt drawn to touch them to his own, pulled by an irresistible, primal force.

Just as Richard brushed Bishop's upper lip with the tip of his tongue the moment was shattered by the squeal of tires, the blaze of horns, and the deafening crash of metal on metal.

96

WITH DISPASSIONATE EFFICIENCY, Homeland Security agents ushered Dylan and Terry to Bishop Preston's dressing room. As they waited in the hall, two agents entered and quickly searched the room, then one of them wordlessly held the door for them. Definitely feeling a little over his head, Terry ducked in first, followed by Dylan. The door snapped shut behind them.

"We've had ourselves a lot of weird days, mah friend..." Dylan started, setting down his kit bag.

"This is definitely right up there," Terry agreed.

"Just you and me," Dylan held his fist out.

Terry bumped it. "We'd better be careful with that around here," Terry noted. "Could have Democratic associations."

"Word," agreed Dylan.

"You okay?" asked Terry.

"Ah'm gonna be sore as a mutherfucker tomorrow," Dylan admitted. "But Ah still got the use of mah limbs. So, Ah'm good."

"Why don't you go first, though?" Terry suggested, gesturing toward the bathroom. "I think you got it a bit worse than I did."

"Much obliged, and Ah will not say no," Dylan said and made for the bathroom door. "Uh...Ah never thought Ah'd be utterin' these words, but if there's any way to get a cup o' tea around here..."

"I'm on it," Terry said, giving a nod with exaggerated military briskness.

Dylan flashed a grateful but pained smile and shut the door behind him. Terry heard the sound of water in the sink and for the first time allowed himself to take in their surroundings.

The room was spartan, but there had definitely been some thought to it. There was a makeup table that Terry supposed could double as a desk, but set upon it was a plastic hospitality basket and a bright, overlarge arrangement of flowers.

Turning, Terry saw a couple of padded folding chairs, a cot, and a freestanding wardrobe that looked like a cross between a queen-size high school locker and an industrial cabinet. Except for the flowers, there was nothing even remotely homey about the place. No artwork adorned the walls—it was all about efficiency. Despite the fact that the temperature was on the warm side, the room made Terry feel distinctly chilled.

He wondered if that was all due to the room, or might he chalk some of that up to their mission? It was hard to say. He was certainly nervous. He wished they had more of a plan. *Still*, he thought, *except for Mikael getting hurt, so far, so good.*

The phrase "inevitable casualties" crossed his mind, but it was too painful to consider, and he forced it back. He flashed on the scores of people they had just killed or mutilated outside. *We had no choice*, he thought. *It truly was them or us.* Their only crime, he knew, was having the rotten luck to be possessed by demons.

His rationalization kicked in, and he considered that demons were much more likely to enter someone who had, to some degree, already surrendered to them—those habitually engaged in some egregious sin, for instance. *So, in the end*, he wondered, *did they deserve what they got?* No. He couldn't even think it.

Terry shook his head and realized that if he kept going down that road, he'd be paralyzed by guilt or shame or by the simple enormity of the task before them. *Stay present*, he told himself. *What needs doing right now?*

"Tea," he said out loud and began looking. He opened the wardrobe and saw a few hanging shirts and a freshly pressed and dry-cleaned suit still in its plastic bag. *For Preston's speech tonight*, Terry thought. He stooped, and on a low shelf he saw what he was looking for: a single-cup coffee maker. He pulled this out and checked the plastic hospitality basket on the makeup table—two bags of English Breakfast tea were plainly visible on top. He started heating the water. Then he paced.

Terry realized he was pacing, so he forced himself to sit and willed himself to relax. He'd just started to pray when Dylan opened the door, definitely looking fresher. *He certainly looks wetter*, Terry mused.

"Uh, dude, Ah ripped mah cassock, here," Dylan pointed to a jagged seam under his arm.

"No problem," Terry pointed to the hospitality basket. "There's a needle and thread in there. I don't think Preston will mind. Tea, coming up."

"You are a true friend," Dylan said, reaching for the tiny sewing kit.

Terry turned toward the bathroom and closed the door behind him.

A few minutes later, he emerged. He'd dusted the grime from his cassock, tended to his personal toiletries, and even managed to get his hair to stand up in just the cute way he liked, even without a fresh dose of gel. Like Dylan, he knew he was going to be sore, but for now he felt ready to meet the world.

"Lookin' good, dude," Dylan said, sipping at his tea. He put the cup down and faced his friend. "Are you wonderin' how Larch knew we'd be at that service entrance?"

"Nope," Terry replied. "I'm not wondering at all." Terry put his hands on his hips. "I'm pretty sure I know exactly what happened."

"Yer thinkin' Randy?" Dylan asked.

"Aren't you?"

"Waal, Ah don't *want* to think it, fer Kat's sake. But Ah reckon it's the truth."

"If it wasn't Randy, I'll eat my fairy slippers." Terry narrowed his eyes. "How's the tea?"

"Ah never did give tea its due," Dylan confessed.

"Any minute now, Preston is going to be here for us," Terry started.

"Ah know it."

"I'm going to stick to him like glue," Terry continued.

"Thet's just what Ah was gonna suggest," Dylan said. "And Ah'll stick to you. You see any opportunity to snag that crozier, you do it. Ah'll run interference fer ya."

"Uh, Dylan," Terry took a deep breath. "What if we *don't* get that chance?"

"Ah don't want to think about that," Dylan said. "But if'n it comes to that...Ah guess we'll have to just confront 'im."

"What good would that do?" Terry said. "Any opposition would be moot."

"Waal, what if we don't oppose 'im?"

"What?" Terry shook his head. "I don't get it."

"Like Mikael's aikido, or Jesus goin' to the cross, or Gandhi's nonviolent resistance," Dylan said. "What if we confront 'im but don't oppose 'im?"

"What good would that do?" Terry still couldn't fathom it.

"Isn't that what they were askin' Gandhi?" Dylan wondered.

"But how would that force Preston to surrender the Spear?" Terry asked.

"Mebbe by not forcin'," Dylan suggested. "As we all know, coercion is not God's way."

"I don't see it, Dyl," Terry said. "And let's hope it doesn't come to that. If it does...I guess I'll just have to trust."

"Thet's all God ever asks of us, dude," Dylan clapped him on the shoulder. "'Course, thet's easier at some times than at others."

There was a knock on the door, and the handle turned. Into the room stepped Bishop Preston. Outside, Terry could see a gaggle of

Secret Service agents. He was surprised to see Governor Ivory there, too, looking nervous, pulling at his shirtsleeves.

"How are you doing?" Preston asked, placing a paternal hand on Terry's shoulder. "That was some nasty business. Will you be all right for the rest of the day?"

"Put us in, coach," Dylan affirmed. "We're good to go."

Preston cocked his head and faced Dylan. "Kentucky?"

"Nah, suh, Tennessee."

"I pride myself on being able to place accents. You just took me down a notch," he smiled. Terry thought it was the most lizard-like smile he'd ever seen.

"Well, come on, then," Preston said. "We've got to head over to makeup. I'm on in less than an hour. I notice that neither of you are armed. I'm sure we could find a couple of sidearms for you, if—"

"No thank you, sir," Terry said. "And we *are* armed"—he picked up his kit bag and slung it over his shoulder—"with precisely the weapons that are most effective against the kind of enemies you hired us to protect you from."

Preston nodded. "Good enough, then. Shall we?" He opened the door for them. Terry went first, then Dylan slung his kit bag over his shoulder and followed.

As soon as they hit the hallway, the group started to move. Terry motioned Dylan to take point with one of the Secret Service agents. Dylan nodded and double stepped until he was in position. As they walked, Terry took up the rear, staying close enough to hear Preston and Ivory's conversation.

"You can't hit this too hard, John," Ivory said, looking down at the bishop. "You have to go out there and win hearts and minds. If you just play to the base, it'll get us nowhere."

"You forget that a preacher's first job is to persuade," Preston said coolly. "Don't worry, David, it's going to go fine."

"The Democrats are ready to clap me in irons, and our own moderates are wavering on Dearborn. You've got to convince them it was the right course of action. That's the goal today."

"That's where you're wrong," Preston said. "The goal today isn't just to convince them that you did the right thing—which you *did*—but to likewise convince them that the kind of leader that had the courage to take such decisive action is exactly what this country needs right now."

"You don't think you're biting off more than you can chew?" Ivory asked.

"Did your people vet my speech or not?"

Ivory said nothing for a few seconds. "It's the press I'm worried about. If all they're interested in is questioning my motives and painting me as some kind of monster..."

They rounded a corner, and Preston placed a warning hand on Ivory's shoulder. "Well, here's your chance to find out."

Down the hall, Terry could see the blinding lights of camera crews. As soon as they saw who was coming, they rushed over, yelling questions over one another in an impossible cacophony. They were mostly shouting for Ivory, so the governor stepped forward and held his hands up. "One at a time, please," he insisted.

"Governor, what can you tell us about the firefight outside about a half hour ago?" Terry saw that the speaker was a reporter he recognized from the local CBS affiliate.

"Homeland Security and the Secret Service are investigating. The only thing we can say right now is that it appears that one group of protestors turned violent and began to attack innocent people, necessitating the use of appropriate force. Any further questions will have to be directed to Homeland Security."

A balding man from MSNBC yelled out the next question. "Governor, what do you say to your critics regarding the Dearborn action? Did you overreact? Did you overstep your constitutional authority?"

"Son, I have seen the intelligence. You have not. I am not at liberty to reveal classified information, but I will say one thing—there would not be a San Francisco to stand in today had I not taken the action I did. And that is in no way an exaggeration. It is the simple, God's honest truth."

A tall, strikingly handsome man from ABC news shouted out, "Governor, will Lansing become the next Guantánamo?"

Ivory stiffened, "I am not at liberty to discuss classified national security matters. Next question."

A short blonde woman from FOX pushed to the front. "Governor, Bishop Preston has promised to nominate you from the floor to be the Republican presidential candidate. If he does, will you accept?"

Ivory stood taller and took on a distinctly presidential air. "I am dedicated to serving my country in whatever capacity the people think best. If the delegates decide that I'm the man for the job, I will not hesitate to do my duty."

Looking pleased with this answer, the woman asked a follow-up question. "Governor, what do you consider to be the finer things in life?"

A chill ran down Terry's spine. Rarely had such an innocent question held so much portent. *If the press are already beginning to ask him human-interest questions*, Terry thought, *that means that not only is all forgiven but that they're beginning to invest in him as a person, as a candidate.*

Ivory seemed pleased by the question but stumped as well. Terry wavered. On the one hand, he wanted Ivory to fail, to come off as a bumbling boob. On the other hand, it was not Terry's way to simply stand back and watch someone flail. After a split second of hesitation, Terry stepped forward, and tugged on the governor's shirt sleeve.

"Uh, excuse me, please," the governor said, and leaned down to receive Terry's whisper. "Thank you, Son," he said. He straightened back up and faced the cameras again, this time with a confident smile. "The finer things in life? Well, ma'am, I only know of two: cowboy coffee and Wisconsin cheese."

97

"OH GOD, NOT AGAIN," Bishop's face screwed up into a mask of pain.

"What the fuck was that?" Richard asked, whipping his head around.

Tobias began barking urgently, his nose already at the door. Rearing up on his hind legs, he fumbled at the catch with his paws, and after a moment of effort, the door swung outward and Toby bounded out, quickly followed by Richard.

Running out into the blinding light of midday, Richard squinted and put a hand over his eyes to shade them as he looked around. He saw a yellow blur that he took to be Toby and followed after at a dead run.

Out of the corner of his eye, he saw Bishop hovering in the doorway, and barely heard his thin voice over the wind, "Tell me what you need!"

"Call 911!" Richard called over his shoulder. Toby barked incessantly, and Richard struggled to keep up with him. Rounding a corner, he saw precisely what he feared: two cars lay side by side as if in a lover's tangle, the metal of their bodies twisted like bedclothes. Steam erupted from one of the radiators.

Richard saw immediately what must have happened. A compact

had hit the same switchback that had almost done him in earlier, but before the driver could correct, a sedan coming too fast in the other direction had swept the little car off the road, and both of them had ended up at the bottom of the viaduct.

Toby was already skittering down the steep slope of the viaduct, his claws scratching loudly as he slid. The dog flailed to regain his footing, but in the end he surrendered to gravity and slid down the cement wall. Richard launched himself after the dog. In a few moments, both of them were sliding to a stop at the bottom.

Richard threw himself up onto the car's side and into the window of the sedan. There he found the driver, a thirty-something business-woman lying on her side against the driver's side door—which was the lowest part of the car now that it was on its side.

Richard climbed down to her, careful not to step on any of her flailed limbs. Her eyes were open but as far as Richard could tell, unseeing. He felt at her neck for a pulse, but there was none.

"Shit!" Richard swore, but he lost no time. With an agility that surprised even him, he climbed out of the sedan and jumped to the ground. Toby was fixed to a spot just outside the windshield of the compact—a Cooper MINI—barking without rest.

Richard tried the handle of the door that was free and skyward, but it was locked. He stooped and looked through the windshield for the driver. A middle-aged man was crumpled against his own driver's door, motionless. Terrified that he, too, might be dead, Richard cast about for a stone. Finding one, he leaped up onto the topmost part of the car and swung the jagged corner of the stone against the passenger's side window. The window shattered, and Richard thought, *Must have caught that just right*. The car was too small for him to climb down into it, but heedless of the glass, he lay down prone on the side of the car and lowered part of his torso through the broken window, clutching at the wheel for purchase.

Richard's right hand found a good grip on the steering column. His left hand felt at the man's neck. The pulse was faint, but it was there. Outside, Richard heard Toby continue to bark. He tried to shut it out and think. The driver's limbs were at odd angles. His neck was twisted, tilting his head in a way that looked—at best—uncomfortable. Through his baby-blue T-shirt, blood was beginning to seep.

Richard knew that he dare not move him—if the man had a spinal injury, he might do more harm than good. But he also knew in his gut that this man would not survive long. Indeed, Richard despaired of the man living to see the inside of a hospital.

Toby barked and began to scrape at the windshield. Richard looked up through the glass at him, annoyed. *Why is he trying to get in here? What good could he possibly do?* Richard wondered.

He felt at the pulse again. It was weaker. The man was slipping. Richard's heart began to race. He bit back on his panic. What could he do? He couldn't keep that man alive—

Then it hit him. "I can't keep him alive, but Toby can—the angel in Toby can," Richard said aloud. His mind raced on the logistics of trying to get the dog close enough to make the exchange. Feeling the man's life slipping away beneath his very fingers, however, Richard knew there was no time for that. But there *was* time for another exchange.

"Duunel, this is the moment. This is your new host," Richard said. "But you've got to go now."

Now? Duunel asked. *I was so enjoying watching you play the clueless paramedic.*

"Watch me fuck up from another perspective, then," Richard demanded. "Just go, and keep this man alive. You keep him alive, and he's yours. I can't promise that he won't be delivered—but I promise that I won't exorcise you."

Or your order mates? Duunel inquired, hesitating.

"No. I won't let them, either. Just go! Quickly!"

Richard shuddered as the demonic presence passed out of him. Once the last of it was gone, Richard felt sick to his stomach. He also wanted a shower, badly. Yet he did not move. Instead, he stayed exactly where he was, his fingers probing at the man's neck for signs of life.

The man's eyes snapped open. Richard jerked back in fright, but he forced himself to breathe deeply, realizing it was just Duunel taking possession of the man's body. The eyes looked back and forth, and a slow, sly grin spread over the man's face. "Oh yes," Duunel said. "Yes, this will do very nicely." He met Richard's gaze. "Oh, you have *no idea* what this man was into..."

Richard shook his head. "Of course not. I've never met him before."

"Oh, this is going to be *fun*," Duunel said.

"If it's all the same to you, I'd rather not know," Richard said.

"That's because you're a killjoy and a prude," Duunel said, using the injured man's mouth.

"Yes," Richard agreed. "That's me, all the way. Mr. Ascetic." Under his fingers, Richard felt the man's pulse surge, then fall into a strong, steady rhythm. He felt at the prominent beat of it beneath his fingers with pride, with relief, with gratitude. "Thanks be to God," he breathed.

"God has almost *nothing* to do with this guy," Duunel said.

"Just do your job," Richard said. He heard the sound of sirens and leaped up, climbing out of the car. He jumped down and landed on the dusty concrete. "C'mon, boy," he said to Tobias, "let's get out of here before anybody starts asking questions."

98

TERRY WATCHED Bishop Preston like a hawk. Amid the swirl of TV cameras, blinding lights, Secret Service and Homeland Security agents, and all the glitz and pomp of the national convention, Preston remained calm, detached, even regal. Terry struggled not to feel overwhelmed by the sensory overload, and his admiration for the bishop increased exponentially as he saw the man gain greater mastery as the craziness around him exploded.

Terry modeled his affect on the federal agents around him, cultivating a stony, impassive stare, a military precision to his movements, and a cock-heavy parade rest position as he waited on the bishop. Once, he stuck his hip out but realized that the pose exuded runway-model cool, not agent cool, so he withdrew his hip and pursed his lips fetchingly at a good old boy in a flannel shirt who shot him a curious look.

As Terry stayed within arm's reach of the bishop, Dylan roamed the crowd. He never went farther than fifty feet, but it was clear he was being watchful. Terry was sure that Dylan had no idea what he was looking for, but like him, Dylan was trying to look cool and official. Terry had never felt more out of his element in his entire life.

As they arrived at the makeup room, Terry hoped that this would be his opportunity. He expected Preston to lean his crozier against a wall before he sat down in the makeup chair but watched incredulously as the bishop walked to the chair with his shepherd's crook firmly in hand. Sitting down, he slung the crook over his shoulder, indicating to the makeup artist that she should spread her protective bib over his shoulders as usual—meaning over the crozier as well.

Terry tried not to let his disappointment show. The last thing they needed was for Preston to clue into what they were really up to. He glanced at Dylan, whose eyes were wide in an *Awww shit* expression. Terry sighed. They would simply have to wait for another opportunity.

The makeup artist worked quickly. Terry was impressed by how she had taken years off the bishop's appearance. He vowed to himself to get more serious about makeup as he followed the bishop's double-time steps out of the room.

Terry heard the roar of the crowd. Every now and then, he would catch wind of something going on in the massive east wing of the Moscone Center where the delegates held forth around a center stage. But the west wing, where the catering, offices, dressing rooms, television control centers, and press offices were contained, was filled with the scattershot sounds of thousands of people doing their jobs, and scurrying as they did so.

Dylan came up beside him. "Thet was our best shot, Ah thought," he said.

"Me, too, dammit."

"Do yuh think he suspects somethin'?"

"I don't think he suspects *us*," Terry answered. "But I don't think he trusts people in general."

"Ah wouldn't."

"No, neither would I," Terry agreed.

"So, if we think like him," Dylan started, "under what circumstances would we set the thing down?"

"None," Terry said. "Under no circumstances. For God's sake, he had Larch's army of the damned come down on him and he didn't let go of the damned thing."

Dylan nodded. "We're kinda screwed."

"It isn't *us* that's screwed," Terry said. "This isn't about you or me, or even whether we get out of this alive. Dearborn was just the down payment on bombing the whole fucking Middle East back to the Stone Age. It's half a billion people we're trying to save here. We're not trying to seize the Spear, not really. We're trying to stop Preston and Ivory from blowing up half the world."

"Waal, when you put it like thet," Dylan started. "Ah guess you and me don't really matter thet much, do we?"

"We're just two people. They're...hundreds of millions. And every one of them loved by God."

"An' they all got mothers, and daddies, and children and dogs..." Dylan nodded.

"They don't have dogs," Terry said.

"Huh?" Dylan asked, his eyebrows bunching in confusion.

"Muslims don't usually have dogs," Terry repeated. "I think the Prophet was a cat person."

"I've heard tell that cat people are good folk, too."

"Theoretically," Terry agreed.

"We're runnin' out of opportunities here, mah friend," Dylan said.

"I am well aware."

"Ah'd trade mah left nut fer a doobie about now," Dylan said. Then he squared his shoulders and made his way to the front of the entourage.

In a few moments, they were passing through the connecting hallway between the two wings of the center. Terry could hear the previous speaker wrapping up. Preston and Ivory were huddled, obviously consulting on last-minute details of the bishop's speech. His eyes were inevitably drawn to the death grip the bishop kept on his crozier. Everyone was lined up at the doors, agents spoke into the microphones in their sleeves. Inside, delegates raised signs, jumped up in the air, and cheered.

Terry hadn't heard this much noise since he'd accompanied Mikael to the Nine Inch Nails concert a couple of years ago. He didn't like it. He tried to ignore it. He caught movement out of the corner of his eye and saw Preston walking toward a restroom. Momentarily skipping to catch up, Terry fell into step behind him. *Surely*, he thought, *the bishop will lean the crozier against the wall when he goes to the urinal.*

Inside the bathroom, Terry's heart sank as he saw Preston head into one of the stalls—carrying his crozier in, too, of course. Terry breathed deep and willed himself to relax. He prayed for courage, that God would keep him from despair. *Open my eyes, Lord, to see the opportunity*, he finished.

His eyes snapped open. *When the bishop washes his hands!* Terry thought. Quickly, he moved to the urinal, pushing aside the folds of his cassock, and mimed taking a pee. Out of the corner of his eye he watched for the bishop. As soon as the door to Preston's stall opened, Terry moved toward the sink.

To his horror, though, he found himself and Preston moving in different directions. Preston wasn't moving to the sink; he was going straight out of the door. *Ewww*, Terry thought. *How does a man get to be so powerful if he doesn't even wash his hands after going poop?* Truly, it occurred to him, there was no justice in the world.

Terry corrected his own trajectory to match Preston's. *And I shook that hand!* he thought, horrified. *Those are the hands he distributes communion with! Ewwww...*

Terry tried not to panic. Instead, he struggled to stay close to the bishop in spite of the density of the crowd. Over the loudspeaker, he heard the announcer say, "Ladies and gentlemen, I am privileged to introduce to you the Episcopal Bishop of California and an indefatigable champion of traditional Christian values—please welcome the Right Reverend John W. Preston!"

A cheer erupted from the crowd, and Preston moved from the doorway into a stream of people, guided toward the stage by black-suited federal agents. Terry fell into step directly behind them, attempting to look like he belonged there. *Who are you fooling?* asked a voice in his head. *You're a queer hardcore liberal and a socialist at heart.* He couldn't argue with the voice. The best he could do was to be an actor, and play his part to the hilt.

As Bishop Preston stepped out onto the floor of the convention center, a booming cheer rose up. Terry stayed just a step behind him, unnerved by the magnitude of energy roaring at them from the crowd. He saw images of the bishop and himself on enormous Jumbotron screens in every corner of the hall, and he fought against a rising feeling of vertigo. Glancing at Dylan, he saw his friend give him a thumbs-up as their entourage made its way to the stage.

Once there, most of the agents surrounding them fanned off one way or the other, leaving the bishop to climb the stairs onto the stage by himself. Preston looked back at Terry and winked, motioning for him to follow. Blinking, Terry obeyed.

The vertigo asserted itself aggressively once he cleared the stairs —the lights and the noise were almost more than he could process. Looking at Preston, however, he saw that the bishop was clearly in his element. He waved and smiled, and seemed to be making a very personal connection with everyone in the room. Terry marveled at the man's sheer charismatic force.

Terry moved to a place behind the podium and a little to the left, amid a wall of other dignitaries and aides. Now still, he found it easier to assimilate what he was seeing.

The convention hall was massive. When Terry had been there before, it had been a warren of booths and displays. Now it was open, cavernous, almost cathedral-like. Thousands—no, tens of thousands —of people stood in clearly marked sections. Down the center of the massive hall was a runway similar to a fashion show or a rock concert where the singer could come out into the crowd.

That was exactly what Preston was doing now—walking out onto the runway, his crozier in hand, pointing to people he knew, waving at the rest. The cameras threw his avuncular face—miming surprise, joy, concern, elation in quick succession—onto the enormous television screens.

Terry eyed the podium, wondering if he would speak from it or the runway. The teleprompters were clearly aimed toward the podium. Terry relaxed; he would be coming back. And he would lean his crozier against...what? *Perhaps I should offer to hold it for him?* Terry wondered. *No, it can't be that easy.* He decided to step forward when the bishop returned to the podium to make it clear that he was at his service should he choose to hand it to him.

Soon, Preston began walking back toward the front. As he neared the podium, Terry stepped forward and gave a subtle bow. He held his hands out, but Preston held his free hand up and shook his head, smiling gratefully. Terry dutifully stepped back in line with the others, fighting back his panic.

Preston stepped up to the podium but kept his crozier firmly in his grip as if it were the very symbol of his legitimacy. It occurred to Terry that it was, indeed, his only claim to it. *No wonder he's holding to it for dear life*, he thought.

Preston held his free hand up until the crowd noise subsided. "Greetings and peace in the name of our Lord and Savior, Jesus Christ," the bishop began, sounding as if he were reading the prologue to a Pauline epistle. The crowd roared again.

"I do not stand here today as a concerned citizen," Preston said. "I do not even stand here as a Republican. I stand here as a Christian, as a man who believes he has a mission to a lost and hurting world. I stand here because God is in the business of saving lives and curing souls."

He had to stop when the crowd roared again. He smiled patiently and held up his hand. When the crowd quieted, he continued. "I come from a long line of people who have fought manfully against the world and the devil. My ancestor was Prester John, the Crusader king who rescued the European forces from the Mohammedan sword and ensured that Europe remained a place where Christ is king."

The crowd roared. "Let me set that scene for you. When Prester John rode up to the castle at Damietta in the Year of our Lord 1220, the Fifth Crusade was nearly lost. The European army had been decimated by the Muslims. The Islamic terrorists of the thirteenth century were winning the day. The European forces were leaderless. They were tired. They had begun to despair.

"But then Prester John rode over the hill onto that Egyptian plain. He rode on a war horse bred in Mongolia. He wore the red Crusader's cross over his chain mail, and was crowned with a helm of iron. He rode with his head high and his shoulders square. He was kingly. He was resolute. He rode with the confidence of a man who knew that he fought for Almighty God!"

The crowd went wild, enraptured by the romantic vision Preston was spinning. Terry realized that he himself was captivated by the performance. He shook his head and breathed deeply in an effort to stay present and aware, to not get taken in.

Preston continued. "My friends, we are in the midst of a new Crusade today." A cheer rose up, but there were a few boos, too, Terry could hear. Preston held up his hand and nodded gravely. "I know, I know, that is a loaded word. But the Crusades were our best efforts to save our lands from certain destruction. A crusade is a sacred conflict. So, I use the word cautiously and intentionally. We are in the midst of a new Crusade—a conflict for the destiny of the free world, a conflict for the salvation of our nation."

He paused and waited for the cheers to subside. Then he continued. "Our forces have been every bit as decimated as the Crusaders at Damietta. Decades of conflict in the Middle East have left our forces beaten down. We have been demoralized. We are on the brink of giving up and slinking back to our strongholds, leaving the defenseless and the embattled to the mercy of cruel and godless men. This is not our calling as Christians! This is not our calling as Americans!"

The crowd stamped and cheered its agreement. A couple of celebratory shots rang out, echoing explosively through the hall. Terry's eyes grew wide as he saw hundreds of pistols raised in the air like a salute.

"The Islamic terrorists are winning because we are losing heart. We are floundering without leadership. We are losing the war against terror, against godless heathenism, against violence and despair."

More guns went off to punctuate his words. The bishop held his hands up, looking both patient and pleased with the response. "We need another man like Prester John. We need another leader who will rise fearless before our common foe, who can unite our scattered and despairing forces. We need someone presidential, someone resolute. We need someone with the confidence that he is fighting for Almighty God!"

A cheer rose up, so loud that Terry wondered if perhaps the Hayward Fault had finally given way. The crowd hooted and stamped for a full three minutes as cameras and handguns flashed. Bishop Preston looked grave as he waited. When the noise level fell, he continued.

"I'm not going to lie to you, my friends. My job as a minister of the Good News is to tell you the truth—even when that truth is hard. None of the people put forward by the nominating committee have that kind of resolution. And I can say that with confidence because deep in your hearts, you know it's true."

A murmuring filled the hall, and Terry could see heads nodding all around him. "But you know something else, too. You know that there is in your midst one man who has already proved that he has the courage, the resolve, the innate sovereignty to stand up to the forces of evil; one man who can unite the scattered Christian armies; one man who can carry the cross into battle and emerge victorious.

"We know he has the courage because he has already acted. We know he will be victorious because he has already saved this nation from unparalleled destruction. We know he is the man because the Muslim forces in Dearborn, Michigan, never knew what hit them."

The cheer that erupted was so thunderous that Terry put his hands to his ears to block out the noise. His head swam. He watched the bishop closely, looking for an opportunity to step up and snatch the crozier, but there was none. Terry began to hyperventilate. He began to panic.

Then he noticed a disturbance out in the crowd. Straining to see, he watched as a lone figure climbed up onto the runway from the floor. It was an undignified scramble. The figure almost fell, but finally he got his leg up and pulled himself onto the boards. Then he stood. Terry's heart fell into his stomach as he recognized Dylan, standing alone in the spotlights, facing the stage. His thinning hair was mussed, and his cassock was dusty. Terry could even see that the ragged edge of his hastily sewn rip had come undone.

Dylan swayed back and forth, and Terry was terrified that he would simply topple over. But he caught his balance and simply stared directly at Preston. Terry held his breath. *What in the world is Dylan up to?* he wondered.

But Dylan didn't do anything. He just stood there. Bishop Preston seemed stymied. He stared at Dylan. He opened his mouth, but nothing came out. He closed it and cocked his head. On the enormous monitors, Terry could see a close-up of Dylan's terrified face, beads of sweat dripping down his wide Melungeon nose.

Preston looked behind him, directly at Terry. His eyes were furious and pleading. Terry gave an exaggerated shrug, and he mouthed the words, "I don't know." He really didn't. Was this what Dylan had meant by "confronting but not opposing"? Terry thought it was crazy. And yet...

And yet it had stopped Preston cold. It had shattered the momentum that was beginning to verge on collective delusional hysteria. Everything had simply...stopped. The crowd fell silent.

On the Jumbotron, Terry could see Dylan's hands shaking. His heart went out to his friend. He wished there was something he could do. But Dylan was doing it all, simply by standing up and *not doing.* Not opposing, not forcing, not fighting—just being. It was madness. It was brilliant. It was, Terry realized, prophetic in the grand tradition of the Hebrew prophets who stood before power armed with no power of their own, who had the courage to say, "This goes no further."

Then, behind Dylan, Terry saw the telltale shimmer of an opening in the Void. At the far end of the runway, he saw a ripple in the veil that separates the worlds, and out of that ripple a Presence emerged.

A Mongolian stallion twenty hands high stepped out of the Void and onto the runway, blowing and snorting its protest. A firm hand on the reins, however, kept the distressed beast calm and under control. The hand belonged to a Crusader king, who sat erect and tall in the saddle, his royal carriage obvious to all. His mail shone like silver in the bright lights, and his blinding white cappa bore the jagged slash of a bright red cross.

He reined to a stop and removed his helm, hanging it on his saddle. Jerking the reins to the right, he turned the stallion clockwise as he cast his eyes around the room, taking in his surroundings. Once again facing the main stage, he halted, and his dark brows lowered as he took in the speaker.

He urged his mount forward, and with slow, deliberate steps, the stallion advanced toward the stage. Dylan scrambled to get out of the way, more or less throwing himself clear of the runway and into the relative safety of the Republican throng.

Terry's muscles froze as he recognized the Mongolian khan. It was as if time were standing still. The Jumbotron appeared frozen on Bishop Preston's face, his mouth gaping open in stunned disbelief. There was no sound—only the echoing of plodding hooves on planks and a screaming whinny so alien and fierce it sounded like the howling of a demon.

And then, like a booming crack of thunder, a cascade of applause erupted into the air. The crowd hooted, stomped, and shrieked their excitement and joy as they watched the Crusader king advance. They waved their arms, and a few random shots were heard. When the guns went off, Terry saw the horse start, but the Khan's hand was sure and the beast bucked but did not bolt.

The crowd, however, would not be controlled. Here was political theater at its most surreal, its most bombastic, and they were loving every moment of it. Never had they seen such a pageant, never had a speaker's words been so dramatically enacted in their midst. A hundred thousand voices raised at once to cheer their assent, their wild approval, their glad participation in this unexpected stagecraft.

Only Bishop Preston seemed immune to the infectious carnivality of the moment. His visage, still plastered on the Jumbotrons, was confused, dazed, and scared. Moved to compassion for him, Terry stepped forward and placed a comforting hand in the middle of the Bishop's back. "You invoked Prester John," he said in the direction of the bishop's ear. "And now he is here."

Bishop Preston looked over at Terry with stunned disbelief. "Is this a stunt?" he mouthed.

Terry shook his head gravely. "It's him. It's *really* him. I know because I've met him."

"You've *met*...?" The bishop seemed to shrink three inches before his very eyes, and Terry could see the fear tearing at the lines on Preston's face as control of the situation was wrested from his grasp. "How...?" he began.

"Did you think you were just playing with *ideas*, Bishop?" Terry asked him. "Prester John isn't a *story*. He's a *person*."

Preston's eyes registered fear and despair, in equal measure. "But he's supposed to be a *dead* person."

"Either we share in the Resurrection, or we don't," Terry said.

Preston looked at him like he was out of his mind, but Terry could see the wheels spinning in his head. The bishop looked back at the khan, who was now nearly upon them. Oblivious to the cheering crowd, Preston quailed, and his knees buckled. Terry's hand, however, was fast around his waist, and he steadied the bishop. Preston struggled to regain his footing. He clutched at the podium, glanced around, and seeming to remember where he was and what he was doing, he regained his poise.

The Ong Khan Toghrul dismounted his horse. Terry felt the boards beneath him dip and buck under the weight of the horse's hooves and the great mailed feet of the khan. The crowd's ecstasy reached riotous proportions as the Crusader king approached his descendant. Preston's hands shook, but he looked at his ancestor with both wonder and terror in his eyes.

In that moment, Terry realized that, misguided as the bishop might be, he believed his rhetoric. If this truly *was* Prester John, then the bishop had every right to expect his blessing and it seemed to Terry that he stood before his ancestor in exactly the same way as he would one day stand before his Lord—with hope and fear.

Terry stepped back as the khan approached the bishop, and held his breath as the great mailed arms rose—and then closed around the bishop in a tender embrace. Preston's hands falteringly reached up, clutching at the khan's back, as he returned the bear hug uncertainly.

Prester John broke the embrace and held the bishop by the shoulders, looking into his eyes. It seemed to Terry that he was searching Preston's soul, yet so impassive was the khan's expression that Terry could not divine what he read there.

Terry held his breath as the khan threw a mailed arm around the bishop's shoulders and turned to face the cheering crowd. "This is my son!" His voice boomed out with royal authority, clearly audible above the cheering of the crowd. "This day I have rendered my judgment upon him!"

Terry saw a flash of silver in the khan's free hand. After a blur of motion, an arc of blood sprayed high into the air, and Prester John cast the bishop's body into a crumpled heap at his feet.

The roar of the crowd plummeted into dead, stunned silence. Looking directly into Terry's eyes, the khan gave a curt nod. "Today, Hell will feast," he said. The hall echoed with his words.

Then, with a swift, elegant motion born of years of mastery, the khan swung himself into the saddle, and the massive stallion neighed, reared, and plunged forward, disappearing into a ripple in the air.

It seemed to Terry an eternity before anyone moved—then chaos erupted. Women screamed, men shouted, guns fired, and black-suited agents swept in from all sides and flocked around the bishop.

Terry watched the scene with a surreal sense of detachment. Everything seemed to be moving in slow motion, and Terry felt a dread calm descend over his mind and body. Dodging the agents flying across his path, he walked serenely past the cluster gathered around Preston. Distantly, he heard one of them shouting for a doctor. Terry walked directly to where the crozier had fallen, calmly picked it up, and with an unhurried gait turned and strode offstage, disappearing into the roiling crowd.

99

RICHARD STARED at the streams of late afternoon sun coming through the shades. He was sitting in Bishop's room on the mattress, nursing a beer and waiting for his sense of calm to return. Toby lay on the floor beside him, all four paws in the air, snoring loudly. The room was messier than he liked. It made him uncomfortable, and he resisted the urge to stand up and start sorting Bishop's laundry.

Down the hall he could hear the sleepy bustle of the coffee shop. It sounded like there were only a couple of customers, but every now and then he heard a sharp laugh—Bishop's laugh. *For all of the guy's problems, he seems happy*, Richard thought.

A few moments later, Bishop appeared in the door with a cruet in his hand. "Stockton's going to mind the store for a while. So, we have some time together." He shut the door and sat next to Richard on the mattress. A cowlick was acting up, and the goofiness of it made Richard's heart melt. His urge was overwhelming.

Before he could act on it, though, Bishop leaned over and kissed him. Tentative at first, but then crushing. Richard opened his mouth to receive his tongue, and his passion roared to life. Panting, Bishop sat back and laid his hand on Richard's chest.

"You know, I've been thinking," he said.

Richard didn't want to hear about thinking. He wanted to hear about fucking. But he smiled patiently and said, "Oh?"

"About your problem," he said.

"Which problem?" Richard asked. "I have a deluxe assortment."

"I'm thinking about your bishop problem," he said, moving his hand playfully across Richard's chest, slowly making its way down to his belly, then threatening to move lower.

Richard grabbed Bishop's hand before it made him so crazy he couldn't carry on a conversation. He kissed it and let it go. Then he rubbed at Bishop's arm encouragingly. "Do tell," he said.

Bishop smiled, taking the minor rebuff in exactly the right way. "I don't think I should be your bishop," he said.

Richard sat up straighter, tensing. "Why not?"

"Well, two reasons." Bishop tried to soothe him by grabbing his hand and squeezing. "First, dual relationships. I like you. I want to see you again. If I were your bishop, it wouldn't be...appropriate."

Richard hadn't thought of this, but of course he was correct. Richard wasn't at all sure about an ongoing relationship, mostly because of the distance, but it occurred to him that Bishop would be an ideal fuck buddy. He didn't bring it up—there was plenty of time to negotiate the specifics later. *Best to keep to the point*, Richard thought. "Okay, I can see your point," Richard said. "But that puts me back at square one as far as the order is concerned."

"Not necessarily," Bishop said, the light in his eyes dancing play-fully. "It's not appropriate to have a relationship where there's a power disparity, but there's *nothing* wrong with a relationship between equals."

"What do you mean?" Richard asked, turning to face Bishop squarely.

"It seems to me that a lot of your trouble has come from superiors who just don't understand you."

"Very true. Tom did, but no one else ever has. That's why we've had so much trouble with the synod."

"Right. So why not cut out the superiors?" Bishop asked.

"Meaning?"

"You are prior now, right?" Bishop asked.

"Yes," Richard said.

"Why shouldn't you be bishop?" he smiled.

"I...I never thought about it."

"Think fast—because, you know, in extraordinary circumstances, it only takes one bishop to make another."

"Are these extraordinary circumstances?" Richard asked.

"Feels extraordinary to me," Bishop said and kissed him again. When he came up for air, Bishop extended the cruet he'd been carrying.

"What's this?" Richard asked, although in truth he didn't care. His cock was about to burst through his jeans, and he was becoming impatient with all the talk. He shifted uncomfortably, trying to find a position in which his groin wasn't screaming.

"I spent the day mixing spices for this oil. Musky, *manly* spices," Bishop said and nibbled at Richard's ear.

"There are *manly* spices?"

"Well, they're *strong*."

Richard laughed. He pulled the cork off the cruet and sniffed. He smelled frankincense, myrrh, lavender—cardamom? He couldn't be sure. Whatever it was, it was pungent and rich. But his concentration broke as he felt Bishop's hand reach under his cassock and light on the blood-thick bulge of his cock, straining manfully against the containment of his jeans.

"So, are you suggesting that we use this for lube, or the chrism of consecration?" Richard asked, referring to the oil used in the ceremony for the ordination of bishops.

"Well," Bishop said, squeezing at the bulge in his jeans, and leaning down to nuzzle Richard's cheek. "Why choose?"

"I'll read the Gospel," Richard volunteered.

"I'll smear the oil," Bishop whispered.

"Let's pray," Richard said, arching his hips up against Bishop's hand and pressing his lips hard against his.

A QUARTET OF EPILOGUES

EPILOGUE 1

HOLY APOCRYPHA FRIARY, BERKELEY

TERRY SAT IN THE KITCHEN at his regular place, hoping that coffee would magickally appear in front of him. It did. Brian leaned down and kissed his cheek. "Good morning, sunshine," he said. "You missed morning prayer."

Terry gulped at the coffee. It burned his tongue, but he ignored it.

"Sorry," he said.

"It's okay with me, Honey Pants," Brian said, laughing. "The others are just wrapping up."

Terry nodded. He faintly heard Dylan's sonorous voice chanting the final benediction. Reflexively, he crossed himself. Today, that would have to do.

He felt catatonic. No, that was hyperbole. He felt exhausted. "Is it okay if I do nothing today?"

"Honey, it's okay if you do nothing this *week*," Brian said, putting a large platter of waffles on the lazy Susan. A platter of sausage followed. "I think you've earned a vacation. Where should we go?"

"You mean, if we had the money?" he asked.

"Uh...right. If we had the money, where should we go?" Brian asked again.

"Some place without magick," Terry said flatly.

"Ah, but you know what?" Brian placed a bowl of yogurt and fruit on the table. "You'd be miserable there."

Terry said nothing. Susan came out of the office, waving an empty coffee cup. "They done yet?"

Dylan shot through the door and caught her around the middle. "We're finished, but we'll never be *done*, Darlin'."

Susan laughed. "I don't even know what that *means*." She planted a kiss on his bulbous nose. "And neither do you."

As soon as Dylan cleared the doorway, Mikael followed with Kat right behind him. Mikael's head was bandaged—Terry noted the blood seeping through the gauze that had been a brilliant white the night before. No doubt Kat would change the dressing after breakfast.

Looking at Kat, Terry noted that she had just about the worst case of bed hair he had ever seen. He had never thought of her hair as angular, but here it was, a tangle of black vectors pointing in every conceivable direction. He realized that it was not dissimilar to Mikael's normally shocking mane when it wasn't buried under bandages.

"Well, ain't we a sight?" Dylan pronounced as Mikael and Kat took their places.

"Just bless the food so we can eat," Terry said wearily.

"Fine. Let us pray," Dylan put his hands up in the orans position and prayed with his eyes looking toward Heaven. "We bless you, O God, our redeemer and deliverer, 'cause you don't abandon your friends—"

"Much," Terry added.

Dylan ignored him. "Ya been faithful ta us, and ya saved us and you're lovin' on us *all* the damned time. Thank you fer stickin' by us yesterday. Do yer healin' thing on Mikael's head if'n you don't mind. Bless, and save Dicky and Toby, too, wherever they are. Bless this food, too, if yer willin' 'cause we need healin' and restoration. Ah'm asking this 'cause Ah'm a teeeeeny little bit o' yer son, and you *know* you gotta listen ta him. Amen."

"Amen," they all said, and the lazy Susan started spinning.

"Did you really need to twist God's arm like that at the end?" Mikael asked.

"Sometimes ya gotta get the old man's attention," Dylan said.

"That is so offensive, I don't even know where to begin." Susan shook her head.

"More coffee?" Brian asked her. She nodded and held out her cup to him.

"Fine, next time, *you* pray," Dylan said a bit sulkily.

"Well, aside from recoiling from the image of God as an actual old man, I'm just suggesting that the whole 'you catch more flies with honey than with vinegar' thing might be true of God as well," Susan said, putting her cup back on the table.

Terry ate slowly, deliberately. Strangely, waffles had never tasted so good. For several minutes, all were silent, intent on their food. Brian leaned back on the stove and crossed his arms, a satisfied look on his face. Terry winked at him. Brian winked back.

A bark punctuated the early morning air. Dylan froze with his fork halfway to his mouth. "Toby?" he asked. He looked like he didn't dare believe it. But then someone was scratching at the screen door, fumbling at the catch, and before any of them could get up, the big yellow dog burst through the back door and bounded straight for Dylan.

Dylan turned and extended his arms to him, and when Tobias leaped up, the two of them fell in a heap on the kitchen floor. Dylan hugged Toby around the neck, and the dog slurped at his face with his enormous tongue and they rolled about in the bliss of reunion.

Susan knelt beside them and buried her face in Toby's fur. "Welcome home, old friend," she said. "I'm so relieved you're well."

Toby leaped up and made the rounds, then, sniffing at everyone and receiving their warm salutations. Dylan sat up in place on the floor. "Uh, if Toby's back..."

"Richard," Brian said, and turned to look out the kitchen window. "Dicky!"

They all leaped to their feet and stared out the window. Sure enough, Terry saw Richard standing just on the other side of the ward line across the street, looking at the house, his home—a place he had not been able to set foot in for months.

"We have to go to him," Susan said. "Let's get shoes on."

"No, wait," Brian said. "Just watch."

Indeed, Richard had started walking. He took a step toward them, then another. Then he crossed the ward line.

"Oh my," Susan said. Terry looked over and saw tears welling in her eyes. His own were a little moist as Richard got closer to the house. He stopped within a few yards of the kitchen window, flashed them a huge, goofy grin, and waved. Kat sprang for the front door, throwing it open. Terry and the rest of them were not far behind her.

In a few moments, Richard stepped over the threshold and caught Kat up in a hug. "Welcome home, Dicky," she said and kissed his cheek.

"Thank you," he said. His voice was thick, and Terry saw tears streaming down his cheeks. Tobias barked and ran in between them excitedly as they all took their turns embracing him, slapping him on the back, teasing him for God knows what. The words weren't important. Their friend, who was dead, was alive again. He was lost, and now was found.

"I'm betting some coffee would sound good about now," Brian said.

"Actually, I've had more than enough—I've been driving most of the night," Richard said.

"Where's the car?" Brian pointed out the window.

"Uh...*long* story," Richard said.

"We've got nothing else on the calendar today," Brian said. "Waffles?"

"I could eat the entire International House of Pancakes franchise," Richard said, shaking his head.

"C'mon, then," Brian said and led the way into the kitchen.

It was nearly noon when they had finished telling their stories to one another. Brian kept the coffee flowing and had begun to lay out sandwich makings before Richard had finished.

"So, Duunel actually saved thet guy's life," Dylan said, shaking his head. "Ah'm surprised he agreed."

"Well, to tell you the truth, I think he was getting as tired of the cohabitation as I was. Our ideas of fun diverged at several definite places."

"Ah can imagine," Dylan said. "Brian, could Ah bother you for another pot o' tea?"

Richard scowled. "Tea? I thought Mikael was the one that got bonked on the head."

"Uh...thet's *another* story," Dylan said. "Ah'll tell ya later. Let's jus' say it's now mah drug o' choice—not that Ah had any *choice* in the matter, really."

"Okay, I look forward to *that* one," Richard said, raising one eyebrow.

The doorbell rang. Tobias barked and raced out of the kitchen toward the door. "I'll get it," Susan said, throwing one leg over the bench and standing up.

For a few moments, silence reigned in the kitchen. It seemed to Terry to be a blessed time, filled with gratitude and relief, warmth and family and plenty. A sharp cackle filled the air coming from the foyer—a glad sound, and Terry saw Richard's mouth turn up in a wide smile.

"Maggie!" he shouted as Mother Maggie waddled through the door, her crooked and gnarled fingers extended toward them all in greeting. Richard caught her up in a bear hug, rocking her back and forth as she slapped at his arm.

"Stop that, you'll crush me!" she complained. "The Lord delivered me from Leviathan, but from Richard there is no reprieve!"

Dylan laughed and gave her a hug of his own.

"Brilliant, boys and girls!" she declared. "I've been watching the whole thing on YouTube all morning."

"It's on YouTube?" Terry asked.

"Everything's on YouTube," Mikael confirmed.

"I couldn't be more pleased—*we* couldn't be more pleased," she said. "I mean, the throat-cutting was a nasty bit of business, and I don't know how you managed the whole Prester John masquerade thingy, but it was expertly done, and the Episcopal Diocese of California is forever in your debt."

"How *much* in our debt exactly?" Susan asked, pursing her lips sideways.

Maggie fished in her handbag and pulled out a rumpled bit of paper. "I faxed this check request to the diocesan comptroller this morning," she said. "Don't worry; no one is going to balk."

Susan's eyes grew wide, and she passed the paper to Dylan, who coughed when he saw it. Brian took it from him and looked at Terry slyly. "Anyone know a place without magick?"

"There's something that keeps buggin' me," Richard said. "If no one could oppose Bishop Preston when he had the Spear, how was it that someone could kill him?"

"The Spear requires intention, so Preston could stop anything he knew was happening," Terry said. The fog had begun to lift about an hour ago, and he was almost feeling human by this time—although still far from his normally perky self.

"Ah..." Richard said, nodding. "So, he couldn't bring the Spear to bear upon something if he didn't know it was coming."

"Exactly," Terry said.

"If only we'd known thet," Dylan said with remorse.

"Well, we knew intention had something to do with it," Brian reasoned, "but we didn't know its limits, that's true."

"Even if we had, would we have done anything about it?" Richard asked. "If we knew we could kill Bishop Preston by surprising him, would we have done that?"

"We discussed that beforehand," Brian said, "but we didn't really come to consensus."

"T'save so many lives, Ah think it would be the right thing to do," Dylan nodded.

"Really?" Terry asked, incredulous. "Would you, Dylan Melanchthon, have killed Bishop Preston given the chance?"

"Dietrich Bonhoeffer would have," Susan said.

"I knew Dietrich Bonhoeffer, and you, sir, are no Dietrich Bonhoeffer," Mikael said, feigning a Boston accent.

"Thanks a lot," Dylan scowled. "Truth is...Ah...Ah don't know if Ah would or not."

"Thank God you didn't have to find out," Susan said, squeezing his arm.

"Do you think that Prester John knew that the bishop could be taken by surprise like that?" Richard asked.

"Wait a minute," Maggie said, sitting down on the bench beside Dylan. "Are you telling me that that wasn't an actor? That that really *was*—"

"Prester John," Terry nodded. "The very one. In the flesh. No deodorant." He wrinkled his nose. "Very stinky. Terrible table manners."

"Oh my God," she said, bringing her hands to her mouth. "The Guardian of the Graal."

"Yeah—he's kind of sensitive about that, I've found," Kat said. "I wouldn't mention it to him if I were you."

"I didn't expect him to be Chinese," she said. "I thought that was just an odd casting choice."

"He's not Chinese; he's Mongolian," Brian said. "His people are Nestorian Christians."

"Oh yes, they evangelized China in the seventh century," she said, raising one gnarled finger, remembering. "Amazing. Oh! I almost forgot. I have a surprise for you all." She leaped off the bench and waddled back to the foyer, returning in a moment with a large package wrapped in a bright hunter's-orange blanket.

"I volunteered to be part of the cleanup crew at Dio House after the bishop was attacked. I was able to sneak this out without raising any eyebrows. A little bird told me you might be wanting this back."

Richard peeled away the blanket, revealing the mirror that had been hanging in the bishop's office.

"Randy!" Kat shouted, almost launching herself across the table to get a closer look at the mirror.

Terry squinted. Sure enough, there he was, looking sheepish over by the reflection of the stove. "We're gonna fucking *talk*," Terry said to him. Randy's shoulders fell even farther, looking exactly like the kid waiting outside the principal's office.

"Damn straight," Dylan agreed. Mikael's bandaged head nodded his assent.

"So now we have to elect ourselves another bishop," Maggie said.

"Oh, uh...speaking of that, there's one thing I neglected to tell you all," Richard said. "We have a bishop—if you want him. There's just one thing: if you elect him, I'll have to step down as prior."

Terry looked at Richard quizzically. "Stop being cryptic," he said. "You'd have to step down because..."

"Because according to our rule, a bishop cannot occupy the office of prior," Richard said.

Dylan shook his head. "Ah still don't get it."

Brian's eyebrows shot up. "Richard, are you saying you've been consecrated a bishop?"

"I have. But of course, I'm not *your* bishop—unless you want me in that role and elect me."

"That bishop guy did it?" Kat asked.

"Yes," Richard said.

"When?"

"Uh...sometime between the fellatio and the analinguis." Richard gave an exaggerated cringe.

"Okay, TMI," Mikael declared, setting down his coffee cup with a bang.

"Why are straight people so fucking squeamish?" Terry asked Brian. "It's like they run screaming if they see a little poop." Terry slapped the table and lowered his finger at his order mates. "Lighten up, breeders, it's just poop!"

For a moment, no one said anything. Then Kat snorted. She slapped Mikael's arm. "He called us 'breeders.' Ha!"

"Was this a *real* consecration?" Dylan asked, "Because it's kind of important what with the demons and all."

"Well, I'd say the setting was unusual, and it was part of a larger 'prayer service' that lasted...most of the evening," he coughed, "but everything was done word for word from the Roman Rite. It was as valid as any other Independent Catholic extraordinary consecration. And Bishop is a duly consecrated bishop, from Spruit's lineage."

"That's as solid as it gets in our movement," Terry nodded. "I say we vote."

Dylan nodded. "Uh...Richard, would you mind leavin' the room?"

Richard nodded, "Of course." He rose and trotted off in the direction of the chapel.

As soon as he was out of sight, Dylan said, "All right, by show of hands, all in favah of acceptin' Richard as our bishop?"

"Wait, don't you technically mean 'abbot' since we're an order and he's a member?" Terry asked.

"All right, fine. All in favah of acceptin' Richard as our abbot *and* bishop, just to cover our bases?"

All the order members raised their hands. "Thet's unanimous then. Okay, Richard, c'mon back. Welcome to yer new see, yer grace."

Richard appeared at the doorway. He was blushing. "Okay, but who's going to be prior, now?"

"I don't think there's any question about that," Terry said, smiling at Dylan.

"What?" asked Dylan, looking around.

EPILOGUE 2

SAN FRANCISCO

LARCH FORMULATED A QUESTION in his mind, then he spoke it into the room. "Lord God Sabaoth," he said through gritted teeth. He hated praying to this deity—this deity that he considered the Enemy. But now and then a magickian had to do distasteful things. It was just the way it was. "Reveal to me thy will. Should I abandon magick? Should I just go and get a job? Should I hook up with a different lodge?" He scowled, realizing that he was asking too many questions, and probably the wrong kind, as well. Best to ask one at a time, and to keep them simple—yes and no questions, maybe. He tried again. "Lord God Saboath, should I abandon magick?"

He rolled the Urim and Thummim and waited breathlessly until they came to rest. The six-sided Urim revealed the letter *reish*, while the seven-sided Thummim revealed the letter *tav*. His brow furrowed as he thought about this. As near as he could figure, *reish* stood for "ra," to do evil. And *tav*, to the best of his interpretive skills, stood for "torah," instruction or Law.

So, regarding magick, he reasoned, *if Saboath's permissive will declares it evil, but his perfect will declares it Law...*He was stumped. He simply did not understand how the higher good insisted that he practice magick while the lesser good implied that he should run the other way as fast as he could.

He grabbed the notepad with his hotel's insignia on it and jotted down the result of the roll. Then he rolled the sacred dice again. This time, the Urim registered *lamed*, meaning "no." The Thummim came to rest on *samekh*, which probably stood for siyum, "completion." Larch drummed his fingers. The reading seemed to be saying precisely the same thing—the Enemy's permissive will said no to magick, while the Enemy's highest will declared it "perfect."

Larch sighed. He went to the window and looked out upon the cloudy San Francisco summer. How many bicycles could he count? He smiled, remembering the game he and his mother used to play. He did not count the bicycles now. The memory triggered in him a sadness that seemed so strong it was almost crippling. How much had he lost? His family, his closest friends, any chance for a real career with some kind of financial security? And what had it gotten him? Had he acquired the secrets of the universe?

A month ago, he would have said yes, but now...he wasn't so sure. Was he simply a dupe of greater powers? Had he been manipulated by—By whom? Surely, even if Pim were a demon (and he strongly suspected she was), didn't that mean that they were on the same side? Didn't they stand together against the Tyrant?

He thought of the many years he'd spent trying to lead his lodge mates. Did he truly respect any of them? Maybe Purderabo. Did he *like* Purderabo? His heart fell as he realized that he didn't. He might have led them, but he didn't *like* them. He certainly didn't love them. Did he feel loved *by* them? The question, he realized, was absurd. His true motivation, he knew, was to master them.

That really is the key, he thought, and he felt a swelling of pride in his chest. *It's about mastery. To master others, to master oneself, to master the secrets of the universe. To master and to be master.* That was his calling, he knew—his goal, his purpose, his pearl of great price.

And that was why he hated the Tyrant so. He remembered squirming in the pew in church every Sunday, hearing about the Tyrant's demands. His mastery over all the earth, over all the nations, over Larch's own tender soul. And he had the nerve to call it love.

"No," Larch said. He had said it then, and he said it now. No man, no god, would be his master. He would be his own master, and the master of others. It was, he knew deep in his bones, his destiny.

Which is why Pim's fickleness disturbed him so. *Whose side is she on, anyway?* he wondered. They should be united against the Enemy, the Tyrant, that monster god Sabaoth. They should be fighting shoulder to shoulder to bring down the shadow hegemony that held the world in its unthinking, yes-man thrall.

He should ask her. *Why not?* he wondered. He'd been afraid she'd rip him a new one for failing, for not stopping the Blackfriars, for not protecting the savior or his prophet. But maybe she should be the one on the defensive. Maybe he should hold *her* accountable. *It might be*, he reasoned, *that this is where true mastery can still be shown. I will not quail before her. I will be the master. She will quail before me.*

It occurred to him that this was ridiculous, but he shook it off. Everything about being a magickian was ridiculous. The robes, the secrecy, the horror-show aesthetics, the anal meticulousness. But he had never let that stop him. The urge to mastery, the will to power, was simply too great. It trumped everything, including dignity, including self-consciousness.

He went into the bathroom and turned the hot water spigot. Then he lit a candle and shut the door behind him. He leaned against the wall and allowed his eyes to unfocus. In a few moments, he saw the mists swirl in the mirror, and Pim swarmed into view, her gauzy dress torn, her ponytail askew. She appeared to have several claw marks on her shoulders and a painful-looking black eye.

"Pim," he said in greeting, grinning at her. "*You've* had better days."

"No thanks to you," she said. "I'm lucky I haven't been devoured."

"The day is still young," Larch said, but the humor in his voice was cold.

"Why are you so smug, you fecal worm?" She spat. "You can be eaten, too."

"Are *you* going to eat me, Pim?" Larch asked. In truth, he didn't know what had gotten into him. Pim used to have such power over him...He stopped and considered this. Yes, she had. And now she didn't. Why hadn't he seen that before?

"I'd love to."

"Eat me, Pim." It was a taunt and a sexual putdown. It also felt really, really good. He watched the bunching of her eyebrows in anger. Her pouty mouth drew up into a tight sphincter of rage.

Larch was enjoying this. He breathed deep, and as he did so all of the doubt and uncertainty and the feelings of failure drained right out of him. In that moment, he realized that he wasn't fighting for either side. He was fighting for freedom—for the freedom of the soul, for the freedom of every man to seek his own level of mastery.

And he knew who was master here. *He* was. "Goodbye, Pim. I won't be seeing you again. Feel free to torment some other lost soul. Enlist him in your cause—if you can. I won't be your slave anymore."

"You commanded *armies*." She was shaking with rage.

"I was middle management, at best," he smiled. "But not anymore."

He blew out the candle. He opened the door. He was, he realized, hungry. His spirit longed for fresh air, for recreation, for trees, even. Perhaps he'd go up to Muir Woods? *I deserve a break*, he thought. *And then I'll get back to work. But this time, I'll work alone. This time, I won't be a dupe for the other team. I, even I, will face the Tyrant and bring him down, and usher in a new age of freedom.*

That sounded grand. *Too grand?* he wondered, but then he shrugged. "Why not aim high?" He was, after all, intent upon *mastery*.

EPILOGUE 3

ONE WEEK LATER, HOLY APOCRYPHA FRIARY

The doorbell rang for what seemed to Kat like the hundredth time. She sprang for the door, dodging guests. She'd never seen so many people at the friary. She opened the door to see the Reverend Felicia Dunne and her partner, Jan. Felicia was in full clerics and had a garment bag over one arm—vestments, Kat assumed. Her partner, shorter and much rounder, with a warm, jovial face, held up a box covered with brightly colored paper.

"Where do you want gifts?" she asked.

Kat held the screen door open and awkwardly hugged Felicia. She shook Jan's hand and answered, "In the office, please—we're just stacking them on Susan's desk for now. Please help yourself to some *hors d'oeuvres*; they're in the living room. I'll be there in just a minute —I hope!"

"Not to worry," Felicia said. "I remember my own ordination to the diaconate—it was pretty crazy, too. At least, the reception was."

Kat paused to catch her breath, saw some paper plates left on the stairs, and scooped them up to take them to the trash can in the kitchen. Passing through the chapel, she saw Richard and Dylan discussing something that seemed to be about the liturgy. Terry was lighting candles.

Reaching the kitchen, she dropped the plates into the trash under the sink. Brian was setting a plate of petits fours on the table. "You know, we ought to set a trash can out in the living room," she said.

"I hadn't thought of that," he said. "Can you snag Susan's from the office?"

"Sure." She turned and ran right into Mikael. He'd just come down the stairs and had on a brand-new clerical shirt, but the collar was sticking out of his pocket. "I bet you're just itching to fix that on your shirt," she said, grabbing him around the waist.

"It's a rite of passage," he said. "But, yeah, it'll feel good."

"I'm proud of you," she said.

"You're well on your way," he said.

"Hey, I want to be an exorcist, and I like being a friar. But I'm not sure I want to be ordained."

"Really? I thought...Well, why not?"

"I don't know why not," she said, resting her head on his chest. They rocked back and forth. "I guess I just haven't thought that far ahead, or dreamed that far ahead—"

"Or *discerned* that far ahead?" Mikael asked.

"Yeah. That's a good word." She smiled up at him. "I love the party, but I can't wait to have you all to myself."

"Do you have an ordination present for me?"

"Oh, you can bet on it," she pulled him down and kissed him. "Mmmmm..." she moaned. "Deacon sex." She kissed him again. "Definitely wear the collar."

"To bed?"

"Who said anything about bed? I was thinking the Chapel of the Chimes."

"That enormous maze of a mausoleum in Oakland?" He jerked up, surprised. "Oh. Wow. Okay. Can't wait for that present, then."

She pushed him away playfully and heard the whinny of a horse.

"Prester!" she said, springing for the back door. Tobias barked and rushed into the kitchen, his tail wagging furiously.

The khan stooped to enter and grinned. He was dressed in the same golden robe of office that he had been wearing when Kat first met him, with a leather bag slung over his shoulder. It was clear that his hair had been cut and oiled, and his mustache looked as if it had been waxed or something, making him look vaguely like some kind of Chinese cowboy mob boss. Kat giggled at the thought.

"My lady," he said, bowing to Kat.

"Hot pot, coming through!" Brian announced, coming between them with a steaming cauldron of mulled wine. He set it down with an audible "oaf" on a hot plate set near the back of the kitchen table. "Good to see you, your majesty," he said, turning back toward the stove.

"Brian," said the khan. He then gave Mikael a curt bow. "Deacon Mikael, this is a most auspicious day. This day you enter into the lineage of power reaching all the way back to Our Lord and his apostles."

"Okay, now that's the kind of talk that makes a fellow nervous," Mikael said, stiffening.

The khan turned to Kat. "I have a gift to bestow. But I would like to do so...away from the crowd."

"No problem," Kat said. "Come with me." She bounded up the back stairs and heard the heavy footsteps of the khan behind her, followed by Mikael's lighter step. Once inside their room, Mikael closed the door. Kat noted with dismay that Prester John had to stoop in order to stand.

"We don't have much time," she warned.

"I will need little," said the khan. He turned to Mikael. "You have been blessed with a good and godly woman."

Kat almost choked. "Godly? You got another woman on the side there, sweetheart?"

Prester John ignored her. "She loves you and has visited me concerning you."

"She did?" Mikael looked at Kat. She shrugged.

"She has told me of your calling. She has spoken of how you lack...How did you put it, Kat?"

"Leverage?"

"Yes. An apt metaphor. I think this should help." From the leather bag over his shoulder he took a small medal hanging from a leather thong. "This is the Talisman of Amitiel. It is my gift to you."

"Wow. Okay. What does it do?" Mikael took the medal. It felt warm in his hand.

"The next time you...hear 'confessions,' bear it with you, and hold it," Prester John smiled. "It ensures verity."

"Verity is a good thing," Mikael nodded. "Thank you, your majesty."

"Verily, verity is a very...good thing," Kat said, trailing off.

"She is also silly," Prester John said to Mikael.

"You just noticed that?" Mikael asked.

"Likewise, I have something for your bishop—but it is only a... what is the word? Not to keep."

"A loan?" Kat offered.

"Yes. Just for today's worship. There will be a Divine Liturgy, I trust?"

"Of course," Mikael said.

"Then he will perhaps like to use this." Prester John pulled another prize from his leather bag, this one in a brilliant purple velvet pouch with a drawstring.

"What is it?" Kat asked.

"It is the cup our Lord drank from on the night before he died," the khan said, and he was deadly serious.

"The Holy Graal?" Mikael's eyes were wide.

"There is no other," the khan agreed.

KAT WATCHED as Richard rose from his seat in the west choir and looked around the room. The chapel was packed. Not only was every seat in both choirs filled but people were standing in the foyer and kitchen, looking on as well. In addition to the friars, Kat saw Mother Maggie, the Reverend Oberlin, Prester John, Davy Shannon, Astrid, the guys from Mikael's band, almost everyone from the Christo-Pagan coven she and Mikael belonged to, and lots of people she didn't know. She glanced up at the large mirror, which had been hung next to the mural of the patchwork Jesus just for the day, and she gave a tiny wave. She couldn't see if Randy waved back.

Richard stood before the altar and gave a nod. At this, Mikael and Terry rose as well, and standing shoulder to shoulder, they faced him. Terry gave a wide smile and in a booming voice, announced, "Richard Kinney, bishop in the Church of God, on behalf of the clergy of this order and the congregation here assembled, we present to you Mikael Bloomink to be ordained a deacon in Christ's holy catholic church."

Kat didn't hear much after that. Her eyes teared up as she watched Mikael standing proudly. Her mind raced, thinking of the short time they'd had together and yet all that they'd been through. She admired him, standing before God and his friends, taking these vows, promising his very life. It made her want to do the same.

Richard turned to either side, addressing the congregation. "Is it your will that Mikael be ordained a deacon?"

"Yes!" they all shouted.

"Will you uphold him in this ministry?"

"Yes!" they all shouted.

"In peace, let us pray to the Holy One..."

After the prayers, the scriptures were read. Then Reverend Dunne moved to the lectern that faced the altar between the choirs and unfolded her text. Setting it down calmly, she smoothed out the pages and smiled warmly.

"I feel privileged to have been asked to preach today. I only met Mikael Bloomink a little over a week ago, when he and a couple of the other Blackfriars burgled my church." That got a huge laugh. "I can tell that everyone here knows them well enough that you believe that, you are not surprised, and you probably even approve. I'm not sure I'm quite there yet." She made a face. "But I will say how much I admire these folks and how grateful I am that they have the courage to do what they do.

"Mikael, today you enter into a sacred covenant—between yourself and God, and between yourself and God's people. You are about to be ordained into the historic succession that, legend tells us, began with Jesus and proceeds in an unbroken line to your own bishop. That might be so, and it might not—it is, as I said, legend. I don't believe it or disbelieve it. Instead, I rest in the mystery of it, as I do so many things in the life of faith.

"One thing I am clear about is that this succession is not about power. I don't believe that some kind of spiritual mumbo-jumbo is being handed on. I don't think this ordination makes you more powerful than anyone else—"

"Ah do," Kat heard Dylan mumble under his breath. Susan elbowed him in the ribs, hard. Kat stifled a giggle.

"Instead, what it confers upon you is responsibility. Not authority, not power-over, not magick—but responsibility. A responsibility to the people around you, to strangers, to all those in need—to serve and not to be served, to help with no thought of reward, to heal and not to harm.

"In our epistle for today, Saint Paul says that Jesus 'emptied himself of power, and took the form of a servant.' Just so, today you are charged with the very ministry of Jesus himself: to empty yourself of all authority, privilege, prestige, or power, just as he did, and to stand side by side with those who have none of those things, to share in their lot, to minister to them, to speak for them where they cannot even if it means losing your life to do it. That's what Jesus means when he says to 'take up your cross and follow me.'

"Today, you stand before God and all those you love and vow to make this your path. Yet isn't this, in fact, the duty of all Christians? After all, our real ordination is baptism—it is baptism that joins us to Jesus's life and ministry. It is baptism that makes us a priestly people —which is to say, it makes us into servants and charges us with Jesus's own mission. All of this is true.

"So why the sacrament of Ordination? Ordination not only

affirms this vow but also affirms that you will make Jesus's mission your profession, your life's work. While all Christians are charged with the responsibility to carry on Jesus's mission, those of us who are ordained do so with a heightened degree of accountability—to the church, to our neighbors, and to God. Today, this responsibility will be conferred upon you.

"Shaking in your boots? You should be. Because this responsibility is heavy. Jesus asked God to 'let this cup pass from me' because it was too bitter to drink. You will pray this prayer, too. From what I have seen, you have probably done this already a time or two. And yet here you are. This assures me of one thing: your vocation is a true one.

"But heed my warning well. The temptation to power is great. Others will try to put you on a pedestal—but you must climb down. Administration of your church or order might give you a big head—deflate it. You might begin to think you are infallible or invincible—you are not. If this mission comes with any power whatsoever, it is none of yours. The power is God's, and God's alone. Let us not lean on our own understanding. Let us not proceed under our own steam. Let us not think that we can do any of this by ourselves—because we can't.

"The mission is God's."

A cheer of "Amen!" rose up from the congregation.

"The healing is God's!"

"Amen!" More joined in.

"The plan is God's!"

"Amen!" By now everyone was shouting.

"The power is God's!"

"Amen!" Kat yelled along with everyone else.

"The world is God's!"

"Amen!"

At this, Felicia looked straight into Mikael's eyes, and Kat held her breath. "Your life, Mikael. *It. Is. God's!*"

"Amen!" they all shouted, and Reverend Dunne picked up her notes and sat down.

Richard stood before the altar again and led them all in the Nicene Creed. Then Mikael stood before him once again, this time alone. Terry moved a *prie-dieu* out into the aisle between the choirs. Mikael knelt on it, facing Richard.

"My brother," Richard began, "do you believe that you are truly called by God and his Church to the life and work of a deacon?"

"I'd better be," Mikael replied. Richard scowled. "Uh, yes."

"Do you now, in the presence of God's people, commit yourself to this trust and responsibility?"

"I do."

"Will you be faithful in prayer, and in the reading and study of the scriptures?"

"Oh yeah. Good stuff there."

"Will you look for Christ in all others, being ready to help and serve those in need?"

"I will."

"Will you do your best to live your life according to the example of Jesus, to be a good example for all people?"

"A good example?" Mikael screwed his face up. "Me?"

"Just say 'I will,'" said Terry. "The promise is to 'do your best.'"

"I will," Mikael obeyed.

"Will you in all things seek not your glory but the glory of the Lord Christ?"

"I'm not sure what *glory* really means, but I will seek it."

"Good enough," said Richard. "May God's grace uphold you in the work that is before you." Then Richard said a prayer—a little too long for Kat's comfort. Then he put his hands on Mikael's head and prayed, "Therefore, O God, through Jesus Christ, give your Holy Spirit to Mikael; fill him with your grace, fill him with your power, and make him a deacon—a servant for the world."

EPILOGUE 4

TWO DAYS LATER, IN HELL

TERRY JERKED BACK ONTO the curb, narrowly avoiding a hurtling taxi. "That was close," he said. "It's good to see things are getting back to normal here."

Hell was buzzing. The streets were congested with cars, and the sidewalks were packed with humans and demons of all dimensions and dispositions, all of them seeming to be in a very great hurry to get somewhere.

"It's like a totally different place than it was last time," Kat agreed. Mikael squeezed her hand. Dylan, Susan, and Richard seemed almost bored with their surroundings, and it was obvious to Kat that they had been here many times before.

Brian stepped out into the road again, shifting the large picnic basket to his other hand. "Okay, it's clear. Let's cross."

"I'm relieved to see all the demons back at their regular jobs," Terry added. "At least I'm not wondering what they're up to."

As they stepped up onto the curb at the far side of the street they were instantly caught up in the flow of foot traffic. No one fought it, and before long they were turning left and heading away from the bustle toward the Dis gates.

Once through the battered, ancient archway, Kat felt instantly relieved. The roar of the city faded quickly, and the desert landscape soothed her spirit. The rolling hills, the scraggly trees, the brown brush underfoot thrilled her. Once again, it reminded her of being in Arizona or New Mexico, or even of pictures she'd seen of Israel or Turkey. It was lovely. "Is it weird to say that I love it here?"

"That's just fine," Mikael said, "as long as you don't get any ideas about staying."

"No," she answered. "It's not home, but..."

"It's a nice place to visit?" Mikael winked at her sideways as they walked. "Yeah, I know just what you mean. I love it, too."

In about ten minutes they arrived at the hill dotted with cells. Just as before, most of them were empty, and none of them were locked.

"This is the place!" Terry said, turning around with a flourish.

Brian set the basket down with a *thump*. "Good! That was getting heavy." He pulled a blanket from its straps along the top and gestured at Richard with his head. Richard grabbed an end, and together they spread the blanket out on the sand. Dylan lost no time getting comfortable on it, and Susan sat beside him, cuddling into him. Brian started setting out lunch items.

"Charlie!" Kat called.

"Over there," Terry pointed, "remember?" Kat nodded and hesitantly approached the cell that Charlie had called "home." Grabbing the bars that made up the door, she leaned on them and looked in.

He was there. Sitting cross-legged on the floor, he was weaving what looked like a placemat out of strands of scrub. He looked up and saw her. "Oh hi," he said. Then he looked back down at his work.

Kat swung the door open and stepped inside. "Uh, Kat—" Mikael began to protest, but Terry touched his arm.

"It's okay," he said. "She's not going anywhere."

Kat laid her hand on Charlie's shoulder and kissed the top of his head. He took no notice. She sat next to him. "Whatcha making?"

"I'm not sure," he said. "A beach ball, maybe?"

Kat laughed. "Yeah, that's a great start on a beach ball. You keep going with that."

Charlie smiled but didn't stop working.

"We thought we'd come see how you're doing. Bring a picnic. Is that okay?"

"Sure, why not?" he said, not looking up from his weaving.

"Will you come out and have some lunch?" she asked.

At this, he faltered. He looked up at the door, then he looked back down. He didn't look at her, nor did he answer.

"Or...we can bring some food in here for you," she said.

"Okay, that's good," he said, nodding. "What do you have?"

"I don't know. But it's Brian, so you know it's going to be good."

"Yeah, that's true, huh?" he nodded, almost eagerly.

Kat stood up and touched him on the shoulder. Then she went back out. She must have looked troubled because Mikael nearly pounced on her. "Are you okay?"

"I'm fine," she said. "Just...it's disturbing to see him like that."

Terry overheard and stepped over to them. "It's like he's autistic or something, right?" he asked.

"Yeah, exactly," she nodded.

"It's always the same. They just go deeper and deeper into themselves until...well, until they're not there anymore."

"Figuratively or literally?" Mikael asked.

"Both," he said flatly.

Brian stood and dusted off his hands. He took one more item from the large basket and walked up to where Kat and Mikael were talking to Terry. Richard started toward them as well.

"How is he?" Richard asked.

"About like you'd expect," Terry answered.

Brian entered the cell and spoke jovially. "Hey, Charlie. I've got a little something to spruce up your place, here." He pulled a rolled-up poster from a cardboard tube and unrolled it, setting rocks on the corners to hold it flat. It showed a colorful Kabbalistic Tree of Life peppered with cards from the Rider-Waite tarot deck.

"It's the Builders of the Adytum poster," Brian said. "It's always been a favorite of mine. I thought you'd like it." From his jeans he pulled a plastic bag, from which he took a ball of putty. Tearing off bits from the ball, he hung the poster on the wall of the cell.

Charlie scowled at the poster and cocked his head as if he didn't like it there but wanted to give it a fair shake before he said anything disparaging. But instead of speaking, he rose to his feet and walked over to the poster. He took it down—and tossed it outside.

Brian followed it and watched as the wind picked it up. It finally came to rest, stopped by a rock about thirty feet away. "Yeah, it definitely looks better over there," Brian said. "For sure."

Kat looked like she was about to cry. "There's enough of us," she said. "We can bring him back; we can *make* him come back."

Terry turned to face her with his hands on his hips. "Haven't you been paying attention? We can't coerce him."

"*Can't*, or *won't*?" Kat asked. There was bitterness in her voice.

"It's okay," Mikael said, putting his arm around her.

She buried her face in his shoulder. "No, it's not."

"You're right," he said. "It's not okay, and I don't know how to fix it."

"There are lots of things we just can't fix," Richard said, shaking his head sympathetically. "That's why we need faith."

"So, is God going to fix it?" Kat asked. "When?"

"God's going to fix everything," Richard said. "That's the Christian hope. Clinging to that...it's how we carry on every day, doing what we're doing."

Terry nodded gravely, looking at Charlie's cell. "Everything is broken. And God's going to *fix* everything broken. Someday."

"Sounds like a fairy story that you tell yourself," Kat said, crossing her arms.

"I prefer to think of it as the cause that I've dedicated my life to," Richard answered.

"So, while we're waiting for this miraculous...healing—what?" Kat cried. "We grieve?"

"And we work," Richard said. "And we pray. And we hope."

"It's not enough," Kat said.

"It's enough," Richard countered.

"I feel so helpless," Kat said.

"Yeah," Richard agreed.

"There's talk," Charlie's voice wafted to them from the cell. Richard stepped up and ducked into the cell, with the others close behind, listening from the door.

"What do you mean, 'there's talk'?" Richard asked. "Who do you talk to here?"

"Guys. They come by. They talk." Charlie had returned to working on the woven mat.

"What do they say?" Richard asked.

Charlie didn't answer. He just kept folding grasses.

Richard tried again. "These guys, what do they talk about?"

"You."

"What do they say?" Richard asked again.

Again, Charlie didn't answer. He held the mat up and considered it. Then he started sorting the grasses in a little pile beside him.

"Charlie," Richard prodded him.

Charlie raised his head then, and looked Richard square in the eye. Richard blinked. "I hope you're up on your sigils," he said.

"What's that supposed to mean?" Terry asked.

"I'm not sure I want to know," Richard said.

Brian called to them and waved them over. "Let's eat!" Terry scampered over and joined Susan and Dylan already digging in.

"C'mon, I'm famished," said Mikael. He touched Kat's elbow.

Kat stood her ground, her fists clenched, staring back at Charlie's cell.

"People have to make their own choices," Mikael said. "Charlie can come back anytime he wants to."

"No, he can't. He's...It's like he's psychologically damaged."

"But he's not," Mikael said. "You've got to let him make his own choices. You can't control everything. You can't control *him*. You've got to let it go." He paused and watched her for a moment. "Think of it as a spiritual practice..."

Summoning all her effort, she gritted her teeth and balled her fists. Then she turned away and willingly but resentfully relinquished her power.

CLAIM YOUR FREE BOOK

To find out more about the Berkeley Blackfriar's universe, download your free copy of *The Berkeley Blackfriar's Companion*. Includes photos of main characters, a complete glossary, a walking tour of the Blackfriar's Berkeley, recipes from Brian's kitchen, a short history of Old Catholicism, a Q & A session with author J.R. Mabry, links to music and videos associated with the books and more!

Click on <u>BookHip.com/DXDCAS</u> to get your free copy!

REVIEWS

If you enjoy the Blackfriars books, please help other people find them by leaving a review. Please consider leaving an honest review on amazon or kobo or wherever you buy books. Thank you!

Keep reading!
Turn the page to start the next book now...

THE GLORY
Berkeley Blackfriars • Book III

PRELUDE 1

PALASTINE, 1878 BCE

"IF WE TELL him Joseph is alive, it will kill him." Rueben sighed.

It was after breakfast, and Serah the daughter of Asher was cleaning up after her uncles. They barely noticed her as she gathered their plates and carried them to the kitchen, but she took notice of them. Not a word escaped her.

"I agree. He won't survive it. The strain on his heart will be too great," Dan added.

"Then we will have the death of both our brother *and* our father on our souls," Naphtali said, flicking a walnut shell across the room.

Serah dropped the plate she had just picked up. Her uncles looked up at her, their knotty eyebrows raised at her error.

"My Uncle Joseph is...alive?" Her eyes were wide.

The brothers glanced at each other, then looked down. None of them were giving her reproachful looks now.

"How could you have kept this from us? How could you have kept this from grandfather?"

"You don't understand," her father said, with more edge in his voice than usual. She understood his meaning. That edge in his voice meant, *It is not for you to know, and it is not for you to question us.*

"Then perhaps you should explain it," she demanded, putting her hands on her hips. Cool evening air wafted in from the windows, stirring a hanging cluster of bells.

"Asher, control your daughter," Reuben commanded.

Serah ignored him.

"Serah," her father's tone softened. "I will explain it to you...later."

"You will explain it to me *now*."

Her uncles gasped at her impertinence. Wives spoke to their husbands like this in private, but never in public. A daughter never spoke in such a way—not ever. The brothers looked at Asher, expecting him to discipline her. He looked at the rug below his chair. "Serah, I must speak to your uncles in private. Then I shall come and speak to you. Do not shame me in front of my brothers."

Serah looked at her father, then at her ten uncles. Without a word she snatched up the last of the plates and turned, slamming the door to the kitchen behind her with her heel. She handed the plates gently to her mother and put her forefinger to her lips. "Shhhhh." She leaned her head against the kitchen door and listened.

"—is shameful." She couldn't tell who the speaker was.

"Maybe," her father said. "But no daughter could be more precious to me than her. She always tells the truth."

"That is not always a good thing," her Uncle Levi noted.

"It is when she does it."

This made some of them laugh.

"No, I am serious. She's normally a quiet girl, so you may not have noticed. But when she does speak, she says what is true—and when she tells the truth, it somehow...makes things better."

"Is she touched by God, then?" Uncle Simeon asked.

"I believe she is," her father affirmed.

Serah felt her chest swell. Her father had never complimented her that way before, certainly not in front of her. *He's not doing it in front of me now*, she reminded herself. Serah watched her mother tiptoe to the basin, trying to carry on her work without making any noise.

"Asher, are you saying that whenever your daughter speaks what is true, good comes of it rather than evil?"

"That is exactly what I am saying." There was a long silence.

Serah held her breath. She backed off the door a bit, worried that one of her uncles might burst through it and find her eavesdropping. She glanced at her mother and she smiled, unconcerned. It didn't bother her mother one bit that Serah was listening—her mother did it all the time.

When no one opened the door, she leaned closer to it. *Is what father said true?* she wondered. She had always considered telling the truth to simply be a good idea. And in her experience, good always resulted when she did. *But is that not true for everyone?* She had never thought of herself as special in any way.

"This is news indeed," Uncle Reuben finally spoke.

"Asher, your daughter might just prove to be our salvation," her Uncle Zebulun said. He rarely spoke, but when he did, people tended to listen.

"What do you mean?" Uncle Reuben asked.

"When we threw Joseph into that well and left him for dead, we created a deep pool of evil that each one of us drinks from every day. And it is poisonous to us. I fear it will be poisonous to Jacob our father as well."

Sarah's breath caught in her throat. Her uncles had always told her that their brother Joseph had been killed by mountain lions. *Is even my father guilty of this?* It seemed he was. Her mother continued to smile. She was oblivious. Serah longed to tell her mother this awful truth. But...later—she didn't want to miss anything. She kept her ear pressed to the door.

Uncle Zebulun continued: "Every day you send Serah to the well to draw water. This day let her draw healing forth from our poisoned well. Let *her* tell our father Jacob the truth about his son. Let her tell him, so that good and not evil will come of it."

THE SUN WAS SETTING when she slipped into her grandfather's bedchamber. He was standing at prayer, bobbing toward the window, his hands palms up before him, as if to catch the last rays of the sun. It was not unusual for one of his daughters or granddaughters to enter, tidy his room, or remove his soiled clothes from the pile in the corner. Serah gathered up his laundry and set it by the door. She hummed as she worked, as she often did. Her grandfather continued his bobbing, not disturbed by her presence or her song. When she finished humming a verse, she added lyrics.

> *"Joseph is in Egypt*
> *And dangling on his knees*
> *are two of Jacob's grandsons*
> *whom he has never seen.*
>
> *Joseph is in Egypt,*
> *living like a king.*
> *His heart breaks for his father,*
> *whom he would like to bring*
>
> *to Egypt,*
> *to Egypt land,*
> *to Egypt,*
> *to Egypt land."*

When she finished singing, she leaned against the wall and looked at her grandfather. He had stopped bobbing, his eyes were open, and tears streamed down his cheeks. "I cannot tell," he said, his eyes still fixed on the darkening sky, "if you are the messenger of God or if you are simply a cruel, cruel child."

"Grandfather, you know that I love you. Have you ever known me to be cruel?"

"No."

"Have you ever known me to lie to you?"

"Not once."

"Then believe me now, and be glad. Your son, my Uncle Joseph, is alive in Egypt. My father and his brothers met him when they went there for food last month. They were afraid to tell you."

"But he is dead."

She shook her head. "No. They lied to you."

"Wicked children." He turned his face away so she could not see it.

"Yes. They were wicked children. But as men they are contrite."

His face was still turned away, but his fingers reached for her, trembling. "My son, the son of my heart, he is...alive?"

"He is alive."

"He is well?"

"Yes. He is all but king, I hear."

"Glory be to the God of my father, Isaac. Glory be to the God of my grandfather, Abraham. Glory..."

He sank to his knees and clutched at his heart. She rushed to him and held him up. His eyes traveled to the window again. "What is all the noise? What is happening?" he asked her.

"They are readying the wagons. They are going back to Egypt. They are going back to tell Joseph that you...that you *know*."

Jacob staggered to his feet and clutched at the window for support. "I will go to Egypt."

"Go and speak to your sons," Serah told him. "Let them tell you with their own lips about their sin. Let them receive from your own hand their pardon. They have carried the weight of this for twenty years, and it has been heavy indeed."

"They have?" He shook his head in disbelief. "I have carried this grief for twenty years. Has it not been heavy?"

"I know it has, grandfather. I am so sorry."

He looked at her then. He held his arms out to her and she went to him. He embraced her and rocked her as as his tears trickled down his face. "The mouth that sang this wonderful news will never taste death."

Serah felt something catch in her chest. She hugged her grandfather close to her and wondered at his words.

PRELUDE 2

SAN FRANCISCO, PRESENT DAY

CONSUELA WOULD NEVER FORGET the look on her father's face. "She's a witch," he'd said, and there was fear in his eyes. Consuela could never remember seeing fear in his eyes. Never. He was always the one in control, the one who held the power. The one who beat her. But when Mama's mother had come to visit, Consuela saw so many things she'd never seen before—someone who stood up to her father, who gave as good as she got, who made him afraid.

It was a revelation. For the next twenty-four hours she felt like her world had turned upside down. Her Abuelita became her hero. She showed her what was possible in the world. She gave her hope.

And if Abuelita was a witch, then that was what Consuela wanted to be, too. She started by searching the web and was amazed at the wealth of information she found. She wondered if the nuns at school knew about the overwhelming abundance of witchery happening just out of sight, beneath their noses, and around, it seemed, every corner.

Obviously there was much to learn, but where to start? She thought about ordering *Witchcraft for Dummies*, but the truth was, she hated reading, especially in English. No, she needed a tutor, a mentor, a teacher.

She had so many questions, after all. What is *Wicca*? Is it just another word for witch? Did witches go to hell? That was important, because she definitely did not want to go to hell. It was in the middle of her third night of web-surfing about witchery that her laptop pinged at her, signifying she had a message. She did not recognize the person contacting her. Babylon1961? Who in the world was that? She clicked on the message to open it.

Babylon1961: Hey, it looks like you're interested in witchcraft.

Her breath caught in her throat. She brought her hand to her chest and looked around to see if she was being watched. Her stuffed animals stared back placidly, but no one else seemed to be around. She took a deep breath and tried to will herself to be calm.

ConnieQT: Yes. I want to be a witch.

Babylon1961: Do you know why? It is not an easy path. It requires great commitment.

Consuela's thoughts raced. *I want to punish my father. I want to be as powerful as my Abuelita.* That was all too personal. She didn't know this person, after all. *I want to be in control of my own life.* "That's it," she said out loud.

ConnieQT: I want to be in control of my own life.

Babylon1961: There are many answers you could have given. But that is the right one. That is the secret password.

Consuela felt a rush of pride flow through her. She got the right answer! Maybe she could be good at this. Maybe she, too, could make her father afraid.

ConnieQT: I want to learn how to be a witch. I need a teacher. Do you know a good teacher?

Babylon1961: I know several. But I think that I might be a good fit for you. Why don't we meet someplace for coffee? Someplace public, safe for both of us?

This person seemed to know how she thought and what she

needed. She or he knew that she might feel unsafe meeting for the first time. A public place, for coffee? That seemed perfect. She began to feel that she could trust this person.

ConnieQT: That sounds good. Where shall we meet?

Babylon1961: There's only one place where witches and other people in the occult community in San Francisco go. It's called The Cloven Hoof.

PRELUDE 3

BERKELEY, PRESENT DAY

TERRY GLANCED AT HIS SMARTPHONE. The blinking car on the screen indicated that his Ryde driver would arrive in under a minute. He'd never used this app before, but the first all-gay taxi service application had been all the rage in the media in the last few days. *Why not?* he'd thought and downloaded it. After all, he needed to go a bit off the beaten track that day.

He reveled for a moment in the cool breeze, lifting the arms of his cassock to catch the wind. It felt good to just be. He and Brian had fought that morning and he'd had a shitty day after that. *I'm still angry about it,* he realized. Sex was the problem—and sex had never been a problem for them before. Brian seemed to need less of it, which just made Terry want it all the more. He was so horny he was afraid his erection could be seen through his cassock. Terry sighed.

When he opened his eyes, a dark maroon SUV pulled up just in front of him.

The passenger window lowered. "You Terry?" a voice called from inside.

"That's me," he said, snapping out of his reverie and pulling on the door handle. He swung into the passenger seat, turned to face his driver, and melted into his seat.

"Well, aren't you a cutie?" the driver said, offering his hand. "I'm Ben. I'm here to give you a Ryde."

"I...uh...I'm Terry," Terry said, completely lost in the driver's unruly shock of bright red hair, athletic build, and most disarmingly, the dimple square in the middle of his chin.

"I know that, silly," he said. "It's on the app. This your first time?"

"Uh...yeah."

"I love virgins," he said, wiggling his eyebrows. "What are you, some kind of priest?"

"Yes, I am," Terry said as they sped away from the curb.

"So, there's that whole pesky celibacy thing to deal with. How is that?" Ben asked.

"Uh...our Order isn't celibate."

"You don't say?" Ben smiled. His dimple seemed to take up half of his face. "Are you—let me guess—Japanese?"

"Nice guess. Half Japanese. On my father's side."

"Oooh. So you know what that means, right?"

"Uh, no. What does that mean?" Terry asked, relaxing enough to flirt back a little.

"It means that you, Mr. Terry, are just my type."

PRELUDE 4

OAKLAND, PRESENT DAY

WITH A CRACK OF SPLINTERED WOOD, the front door smashed inward, leaving T-Ray and Darnell framed in the doorway, two black silhouettes against the orange curtain of urban twilight. T-Ray glanced behind them to see if anyone had witnessed their crime and saw only a bag lady minding her own business, shuffling away from them toward the 580 freeway overpass. T-Ray gestured for Darnell to enter quickly, and throwing a last glance over his shoulder, Darnell followed. Inside he blinked, waiting for his eyes to adjust.

The foyer was really a hallway, with stairs to the left. T-Ray snapped open the bag he'd brought, and began to cast about for "stealables" as his cousin used to call them, but there was nothing in the hallway except a bunch of old pictures on the wall. T-Ray squinted at them. They were pictures of...nuns? He blinked in confusion, then turned to watch Darnell turn the corner and freeze.

"What?" he whispered. Darnell didn't answer. The hallway doglegged to the left, and T-Ray poked his head around the corner and froze himself. He was looking at a dining room, that was clear. Stretched nearly the length of the room was a dining table, each place set with care. About a dozen old women sat stock still in front of their empty plates.

"There you are!" a cheerful voice called out.

T-Ray and Darnell both jumped.

An old woman spun through the butler door, a large steaming bowl between two potholders in her hands. Her wrinkled face broke into a broad, warm smile at the sight of them. "You, my dears, are just in time for dinner."

Every instinct in T-Ray's body told him to abandon the caper and sprint, but he seemed strangely rooted in place. He licked his lips and nearly vibrated in place from nerves.

"Did you—" the old woman started, ducking past them and peering around the corner at the front door. "Oh, *sugar*! You didn't have to break the door down, sillies. It was open! Tsk..." She waved away her objection. "It's never locked, not here." Walking back toward the dining room, she shooed them inward.

Darnell looked over his shoulder directly into T-Ray's eyes. He'd never seen his homey this scared. Not even when they were being shot at. Then he realized why. None of the old ladies seated around the table were moving, or perhaps *could* move. Then one of them succumbed to gravity and her head pitched face forward into her plate.

Their host tsk-tsked again, and pulled the woman upright again. "Please, have a seat," she said. "We always have a couple of extra seats." T-Ray and Darnell stood as still as the ladies around the table. "Sit!" the old woman commanded. Glancing at one another, they obeyed, each taking a seat between two of the frozen women.

"Everything is hot, so dig in. There's roast beef—it's leftover from last night, but that's when it's best, I think. Mashed potatoes are here," she said, pointing to a covered bowl. T-Ray could see the steam rising off of it. "And carrots, steamed with rosemary, here." She smiled at them with a look of satisfaction. "Please, help yourselves." She grabbed the potatoes and began to serve herself. "So, please tell me your names, young men."

T-Ray blinked and looked at Darnell. He wanted to think of an alias, but he couldn't. Before he could answer, though, the old woman continued. "I'm *fascinated* with the life of crime. You probably wouldn't guess this about me, but I'm a member of the Ellery Queen fan club!"

"Who?" asked Darnell.

"Shut up, fool!" T-Ray whispered.

"Are you gentlemen in the habit of stealing from nuns, then?"

T-Ray looked at the old women. It was only then that they noticed that each of them seemed...well, a little butch. They also had crosses dangling from chains around their necks and were staring, sightless and unblinking, at the feast before them.

"Ya'll are nuns?" T-Ray asked.

"Yes, what did you think? We run the Oakland Food Pantry down the street. Perhaps you know about it? Anyone can get food there, no matter who they are or what time of day it is. Or night." She smiled warmly. "So tell me about yourselves—are your parents living? Do you have siblings? Oh, you haven't touched the roast beef yet! What's wrong with you?"

Darnell reached hesitantly for the platter of meat and looked up into T-Ray's eyes briefly. His hands were shaking as he lifted a slice of roast to his plate.

"You are not going to find much of interest in this house, I can tell you that. We might have some old silver, but we don't wear jewelry. We have a television, but it's the same one we've had for fifteen years —it's not one of those fancy flat screens. How do those work, anyway?" She shook her head and nibbled at a forkful of mashed potatoes. "In any case, you are welcome to anything you find here. And take your time! I won't be calling the police—not that they'd come anyway. This is Oakland, after all! I only have one request, and I ask you to take this very seriously. Please take only what you truly need. And next time, my dears," she flashed them a conspiratorial smile, "just knock."

T-Ray nodded, but his eyes widened as he watched the old lady's head roll back on her neck. Her jaw opened, then opened wider, as if her jawbone had moved out of joint to allow her mouth to stretch and widen unnaturally. Her tongue darted toward the ceiling, then withdrew. A moment later, a thousand ravens erupted out of the old woman's throat and spilled into the air, filling the room with pounding wings, oily feathers, and the hungry screams of scavenger birds.

Keep reading! Buy *The Glory* today!
http://apocryphilepress.com/book/glory/

www.ingramcontent.com/pod-product-compliance
Lightning Source LLC
Chambersburg PA
CBHW020605040726
47498CB00003B/637